Daylight

DAVID BALDACCI

Daylight

MACMILLAN

First published 2020 by Grand Central Publishing, USA

First published in the UK 2020 by Macmillan
an imprint of Pan Macmillan
The Smithson, 6 Briset Street, London EC1M 5NR
Associated companies throughout the world
www.panmacmillan.com

ISBN 978-1-5098-7457-6

1 3 5 7 9 8 6 4 2

A CIP catalogue record for this book is available from the British Library.

Printed and bound by CPI Group (UK) Ltd, Croydon, CR0 4YY

Visit **www.panmacmillan.com** to read more about all our books
and to buy them. You will also find features, author interviews and
news of any author events, and you can sign up for e-newsletters
so that you're always first to hear about our new releases.

To Ron Kunihiro,
who has the heart of a lion and is loved and
respected by all who know him

Daylight

CHAPTER

I

Now is the moment of reckoning.

FBI Special Agent Atlee Pine was sitting in her rental car outside of Andersonville, Georgia, with her assistant, Carol Blum, next to her.

She hit the name on her contact list and listened to the phone ringing.

"Pine, how nice of you to call," the dripping-with-sarcasm voice said into her ear.

The man speaking was the FBI's top dog in Arizona, Clint Dobbs. He was the one who had given Pine permission to take a "sabbatical" in order to find out what had happened to her twin sister, Mercy, who had been abducted from their home in Andersonville thirty years before. Six-year-old Pine had nearly died in the process.

"Sorry, sir, it's just been a little busy."

"I understand that you *have* been extremely busy. You solved a series of murders down there, prevented other killings, nearly got blown up in the process, and discovered something truly remarkable about your past. Hell, the Bureau might owe you a bonus."

"I take it you've been kept informed through other channels."

"You could say that, yes, since *you* have been remarkably uncommunicative."

"Would that source of info be Eddie Laredo?"

Laredo was an FBI special agent who had been sent down to Georgia to help in a murder investigation. He and Pine had a history, a complicated one, but she believed they had resolved things.

"I have multiple sources keeping me informed. What did you find out about your sister's disappearance?"

"When my mother was a teenager she was a mole in a sting operation involving the mob back in the eighties. One of the guys that went down as a result was a man named Bruno Vincenzo, who was murdered after he went to prison. Bruno had a brother in Jersey named Ito. Apparently, Ito found out what happened and blamed my mother for his brother's death. Somehow he discovered where we were, came down to Georgia, and kidnapped my sister."

"Do you have a line on this Ito Vincenzo? Is he even still alive?"

"I checked the state's official online database. There's no record of his death, but he might not have died in New Jersey. I found out that he lived in Trenton. I've got the house address. It's in the name of a Teddy Vincenzo—that's his son."

"Sounds like he might have inherited it, so maybe his old man *did* die. Maybe he was a snowbird and breathed his last in Florida. If so, he might be beyond your reach, Pine."

"I can still talk to his family. They might know something helpful."

"Okay, *if* they'll talk to you. And where is this Teddy Vincenzo?"

Pine let out a long sigh. "In prison at Fort Dix."

"Ah, well, crime indeed runs in the family. At least he's in Jersey. So you want to go to Trenton now? Is that why you finally called me?" There was an edge to Dobbs's voice that Pine did not care for.

"I don't see any other way."

"Oh, you don't, do you? Maybe you and I have a different idea about that, Pine."

"I just need a little more time. I got sidetracked by the murders down here. But for that I could have made a lot more progress."

"So what you're saying is that while you've been on leave, you've actually still been working as an agent."

"That's exactly what I'm saying."

"I agree with you, Pine," said Dobbs, surprising her. "You did great work down there, as I already pointed out. If it were up to me, I'd tell you to take as much time as you need, but while I'm the top agent in Arizona, I do have people above me, Pine, a lot of them. And there have been grumblings around the Bureau."

"I didn't think I was that important," said Pine sharply. "And who's complaining?"

"Let me point it out then. I've got *two* agents on rotation covering for you in Shattered Rock, even though they've got their own assignments. They're not happy about that because they've got no backup, which you apparently enjoy but they don't. And I've also had to redirect admin resources there because Carol's with you. And while I know this is the twenty-first century, the fact that you are, well, you know…"

"You mean the fact that I'm a *woman*, that the guys don't think I'm carrying my weight?"

"They think you're getting special treatment—and, in fact, you are. I've had more than a few complaining that they've all got problems but they still have to get up and go to work every day, so what's the deal with you?"

Pine barked, "You were the one to tell me to work out this issue if I wanted to keep working at the Bureau. And the only way I can do that is to find my damn sister."

Blum put a calming hand on Pine's arm.

Dobbs said, "I will take into account your natural anger, but just keep in mind who the hell you're talking to, Pine."

Pine took a long breath. "I just need a little more time, sir. A few more days."

Dobbs didn't say anything for so long that Pine was afraid the man had hung up.

"Trenton, New Jersey, huh?"

"Yes," said Pine quietly.

"Funny thing, Pine. I started out in Trenton more years ago than I can remember. It was going through some challenging times back then. It's going through more challenging times right now." He paused. "Okay, a few more days. If you need any backup or info, dial up the guys there and tell them Clint Dobbs said it's okay. They won't believe you, but they'll believe it when I tell them it's true."

Pine glanced at Blum with wide eyes. "Um, I was not expecting that."

"I wasn't expecting to say it, Pine. The offer just popped into my head. But I need to make this point as clear as I can: You have to finish this and come home. You got that? The Bureau pays your salary to work for them. I know I told you to go after this to get your head straight, but at the end of the day that's your problem, not mine. And you're not the only agent I have to deal with, okay? I got hundreds of them, and they all got problems. You got that?"

"Yes, sir. Got it. And I'm so grateful. Thank you for—"

But Dobbs had already clicked off.

Pine slowly put the phone down. "New Jersey, here we come."

CHAPTER

2

Two DAYS LATER, Pine was driving in her rental car through a working-class neighborhood on the outskirts of Trenton. She was thinking about what she would say to Anthony "Tony" Vincenzo, who sometimes stayed at the home his father, Teddy, had apparently inherited from *his* father, Ito Vincenzo. She didn't want to deal with the inevitable red tape of visiting Teddy Vincenzo in prison if she didn't have to; Tony was low-hanging fruit. But with her current frame of mind, if Tony chose not to help her, she might just shoot him.

As the grandson of Ito Vincenzo, Tony could possibly tell her something about Ito—hopefully where he currently was, if he was still alive.

And that might lead to Mercy, which was why she was here, after all. The road to Mercy had been long and tortuous, and some days the destination seemed as unreachable as the summit of Mt. Everest. But now that Pine finally had a breakthrough in the case, she was going for it. And if it took her longer than a few days, so be it. Pine had been compelled to hunt for her sister after a disastrous encounter with a pedophile who had kidnapped a little girl in Colorado. Her rage, fueled by the memory of her own sister's abduction, had resulted in Pine's almost beating the man to death and breaking every rule the Bureau had. Clint Dobbs had given her an ultimatum: Resolve her personal issues about her sister or find another line of work. But now she didn't need any motivation from Dobbs or anyone else. Now she would willingly chuck her FBI career in exchange for finding her sister.

It's not just my job that I won't be able to do if I don't find out what happened to my sister. It's my life *that I won't be able to do.*

Being able to admit this to herself had been both frightening and liberating.

With a Glock as her main weapon and a Beretta Nano stuck in an ankle holster in case everything else went to hell—which it often did in her line of work—Pine pulled to a stop three cookie-cutter houses down from Vincenzo's humble abode.

All the homes here were salt boxes with asphalt shingles, about 1,200 square feet set over a story and a half of unremarkable architecture. The area was all post–World War II housing, constituting a grid of homes that had surrounded virtually every city across the country within a decade after the "boys" had come home from fighting Hitler, Mussolini, and Hirohito. Nine or so months thereafter, Baby Boomers by the millions were born in neighborhoods just like this. Those Boomers were now taking their rightful place as grandparents to the Millennials and the Z generations. What was left was an old, tired group of dwellings inhabited both by the elderly and also those just starting out.

Though they looked alike, the properties did differ. Some yards were neat and organized. Siding and trim were freshly painted. Mailboxes rested on stout metal posts, and washed cars were parked in driveways that had been kept up.

Other homes had none of these attributes. The cars in the driveways or parked in the yards were more often resting on cinder blocks than on tires. The sounds of air-powered tools popping and generators rumbling foretold that some of these places had businesses operating out of them, either legal or not. Siding peeled away from these structures, and front doors were missing panes of glass. Mailboxes were leaning or entirely gone. Driveways were more weeds than concrete or gravel.

She counted three dwellings with bullet holes in the façade, and one that still had police crime scene tape swirling in the tricky wind.

Tony Vincenzo's place fell into the houses-that-hadn't-been-kept-up category. But she didn't care what his home looked like. She only wanted everything he held in his memory or in hard evidence about his grandfather Ito and any others who might have played a role in her childhood nightmare.

She eased out of her car and stared at the front of the house. Ito Vincenzo had once owned this place and had raised his family here with his wife. Pine had no idea what sort of a father and husband he was. But if he had it in him to nearly kill one little girl and kidnap another, she would rate his parental skills suspect, at the very least.

Tony Vincenzo worked at Fort Dix, the nearby army installation. The prison where his father was behind bars was part of that complex. Maybe the son wanted to be close to the father. If so, maybe Tony visited Teddy regularly and thus might have information to share about Ito that he'd learned from his old man.

Pine headed up the sidewalk where the concrete had lurched upward, corrupted by decades of freezing and thawing and no maintenance. She imagined Ito Vincenzo, her sister's abductor and the man who almost killed her, walking this very same path decades before. The thought left her nearly breathless. She stopped, composed herself, and kept going.

Pine reached the front door and peered in one of the side glass panels. She could see no activity going on in there. If the guy had followed in his daddy's footsteps, the criminal element would not be out in the open. They usually did their dirty deeds in the basement and away from prying eyes. Yet the guy *was* gainfully employed at Fort Dix, so maybe he was completely law-abiding.

She knocked and got no answer. She knocked again as a courtesy and got the same result. She looked to her left at the house next door, where an old woman was rocking in a chair on her front porch, some needlework in hand. It was sunny, though cool, and she had on a bright orange shawl. Her gray hair looked freshly permed, with patches of shiny pink scalp peeking through here and there like sunlight through clouds. She took no note of Pine;

her bespectacled eyes were focused on stitch one, purl two. Her yard was neatly kept, and colorful flowerpots with winter mums in them were arrayed around the porch, adding needed color to what was otherwise drab and cold.

"Tony's in there," the woman said quietly.

Pine walked over to the far end of Vincenzo's front porch and put her hand on the wooden railing. "You know him?"

The woman, keeping her eyes on her needlework, nodded imperceptibly. "But I don't know you."

"Name's Atlee."

"Funny name for a girl."

"Yeah, I've heard that. So, he's here?"

"Saw him go in an hour ago and he hasn't come out."

"Just him?"

"That I don't know. But I haven't seen anyone else." The whole time the woman spoke quietly and kept her eyes on the knitting. Anyone not standing as close as Pine would not even be able to tell she was speaking to her.

"Okay, thanks for the heads-up."

"You here to arrest him? You a cop?"

"No, and yes, I am," said Pine.

"Then why are you knocking on his door?"

"Just want to ask him some questions."

"He works at Fort Dix."

"Yeah, I've heard."

"He probably won't like your questions."

"Probably not. Does he live here full-time? I couldn't find that out."

"He's in and out. He's not nice to me. He calls me bad names and he pisses on my flowers. And I don't like the look of his friends. This used to be a nice neighborhood. But not anymore. Now I just want to make it out alive."

"Well, thanks."

"Don't thank me. Boy's bad news. You watch yourself."

"I will." Pine walked back over to the front door and knocked again.

"Anthony Vincenzo?" she called out.

Nothing. For one, two, three seconds. Then something. A lot of something.

A noise exploded from the back of the house. Pine had heard that sound many times.

A back door being kicked open. Then another familiar noise: feet running away. People were always running away from her. And with good reason. And with equally good reason, she wasn't going to let that happen.

She leapt over the porch railing as the woman looked up from her yarn and needles.

"Go get the little prick," she said, a smile creasing her heavily wrinkled face.

Pine's boots hit the pavement. She was at full speed in five strides.

Inhale through the nose, out through the mouth. Motor the arms and the legs will follow.

A blur of blue shirt and lighter jeans and clunky white sneakers was up ahead and pulling away.

She redoubled her speed but wasn't making up any ground. Tony Vincenzo was over a decade younger, and undoubtedly faster, even with Pine's longer legs. And he had the added fuel of fear. Fear could make the slow fast and the weak strong.

And turn a coward into the bravest of the brave, if only because there's no way out.

"Tony, I just want to talk to you, that's all," she shouted out as she sucked in one quick breath after another.

Vincenzo merely increased his speed. Asshole was an Olympian now. She'd need a car to catch him.

Shit.

Pine looked around, eyeing any way she could take a shortcut and catch up to him. She briefly contemplated pulling her weapon and firing a warning shot just to scare the shit out of him, maybe making him run crazy, hit something, and fall over. That would be all she'd need.

She saw it at the last possible second: movement to her right. Then she was blindsided. She tumbled heels over ass, kept rolling on purpose, and popped to her feet in a controlled squat, her Glock out and pointed at the man who'd nailed her.

Only thing was his weapon was out and pointed at her.

"FBI!" she barked, mad with fury. "Drop the gun. Do it!"

"Army CID!" the man barked right back. "Put your weapon down. Now!"

The two were frozen, staring at each other for the longest time.

The man was over six three, ramrod straight, about two hundred extremely fit pounds, and also instantly familiar to Pine. She blinked rapidly, as though hoping it would not turn out to be who she thought it was. It didn't work.

She lowered her weapon. "Puller?"

John Puller holstered his regulation M11 pistol. He looked equally stunned and was shaking his head. "Pine?"

Tony Vincenzo was long gone.

"What the hell are you doing here?" she asked.

He looked past her, in the direction of where Vincenzo was headed. "I was here to make an arrest."

She blanched and looked over her shoulder as the truth hit her. "Crap! Tony Vincenzo?"

He nodded, frowning. "Long in the works, Atlee. And you, unfortunately, walked right into the middle of it."

3

THE COFFEE SHOP, the sign outside said, had been in business since 1954. It held cracked red vinyl seats, pasty linoleum flooring, and scarred wooden-backed booths. The kitchen, glimpsed through the pass window, had pots and pans and grease that looked about as old as the restaurant. What it lacked in ambience and cleanliness, it didn't really make up for with anything else, but maybe that was the point of a beloved local hangout. A few elderly customers were dawdling over their meals and looking at their smartphones.

Pine and Puller sat facing each other in one of the booths, both cradling cups of coffee.

Next to Puller was a man in his early thirties, and who had been introduced to her as CID Special Agent Ed McElroy. He was working on Puller's team in the Vincenzo case and had been there to help take the man into custody.

"So you two go way back, I guess," said McElroy.

Puller nodded and glanced at Pine. "You want to tell him?"

Pine took a sip of her coffee. "Puller wasn't a chief warrant officer yet. And I'd only been with the Bureau about four years. I was still on the east coast back then. I'm assigned out near the Grand Canyon now. Anyway, I was appointed to serve on a joint task force with the Army. A businessman the Bureau was investigating for bribing public officials managed to get his hooks into a couple of senior Army officers."

Puller took up the story when Pine paused and glanced at him.

He said, "The 'former' generals were court-martialed and spent some time reflecting on their sins in the custody of the military branch they once served." He paused and shot Pine a look. "It got dicey a couple of times."

"How so?" asked McElroy.

Pine said, "Well, turns out the businessman had ties to a group of mercenaries from overseas. Really bad dudes with no problem killing anybody they were paid to. How many times did they try to kill us, Puller?"

"Three. Four if you count the car bomb that we found before it went off."

"Damn," said McElroy. "And what happened to this 'businessman'?"

Puller said, "He's having a wonderful time in a federal lockup and will be for pretty much the rest of his life."

Pine glanced at Puller. "I'm really sorry for blowing your bust."

"You had no way of knowing. Just bad luck all around."

"So, you were chasing Vincenzo for crimes committed at Fort Dix?"

"Among other things," replied Puller, setting his coffee cup down. "Ed and I have been on this sucker for about a month and Tony Vincenzo is right in the middle of it."

"How long have you been in the Army?" she asked McElroy.

"Going on fifteen years, the last five with CID. Been working with Chief Puller for about nine months now."

"You have a family?"

"Back in Detroit. Wife and two kids. She's used to deployments but they were hard. This job is a little more flexible."

Pine turned to Puller. "So you were about to bring the hammer down on Tony? How come?"

"He's part of a drug ring operating out of Fort Dix. He works in the motor pool. A good mechanic by all accounts, but apparently his pay wasn't enough to support his lifestyle. He got hooked up with some really bad guys on the outside."

"He's not military then?"

"No. But he was committing crimes on a military installation, which is why I'm involved. Dix is technically under the jurisdiction of the Air Force Air Mobility Command. Base operations are performed by the Eighty-Seventh Air Base Wing, and it provides management as well."

"But if the Air Force oversees it, where do you come in?" asked Pine.

"It's a *joint* base installation, so there are Army and Navy elements there as well. Each branch retains complete control of their commands there. Vincenzo was employed by the Army, so the problem fell to me. He also recruited some stupid Army grunts as part of his plot, so that falls to me, too. The Air Force is in the background only. Army carries the load on this one."

"Boy, and I thought the Bureau's structure was unwieldy."

"The Army out-complicates everybody," noted Puller matter-of-factly. "And is very proud of that."

"Was he selling into the military, then, from these outside sources?"

Puller nodded. "We believe so at least. And the readiness of our military isn't helped by soldiers who happen to be druggies or who can be blackmailed by enemies of this country into doing stuff they should never do."

"I can see that."

"And why did you want to see Vincenzo? You working a case involving him? We might want to team up then."

"No." She glanced at McElroy for a moment. "It's personal, John. It…it has to do with my sister."

"Vincenzo did something to your sister?" said Puller.

"No. This goes way back to his grandfather."

It was a long story, but Pine managed it in a string of succinct sentences chock-full of information, including what she had recently discovered in Georgia about Ito Vincenzo having taken her sister. She didn't want to burden Puller with her problems, but she had great respect for him as both a person and an investigator. And it just felt good to get it off her chest.

"Damn," said Puller when she'd finished.

"Roger that," said McElroy. "Really sorry that all happened to your family, ma'am. That's just awful. Nobody should have to go through that."

"Thanks."

Puller said, "Well, Tony Vincenzo's old man is a bad egg, too. He's in federal prison at Fort Dix."

"Yeah, I knew that. But all I wanted to ask Tony was where his grandfather Ito was. If he's even still alive. Since the house is in Teddy's name, he may not be."

"New Jersey has an online database for death records," said Puller.

"I checked there—nothing. But he might have died in another state, and not all of them have online databases you can search."

"I see your dilemma. But surely Tony or Teddy will know if he's alive or not."

"That's what I'm hoping."

"Sounds like your mother had quite the unique experience working undercover like that and bringing down the mob. And you have no idea where she is now?"

Pine shook her head. "If she's still alive, she's beyond even the Bureau's ability to find her, because I've tried." She glanced at Puller. "Look, I blew your collar. What can I do to make this good?"

"I'm not sure. We were going to make the arrest because we needed to lean on Vincenzo to get him to rat further up the chain. He's small fry. CID wants the big boys, and none of the grunts we busted are really privy to their identities. I was deploying a team around the property when you walked into the circle. Ed was heading up the rear flank, but they weren't in position yet. That's how he was able to escape out the back."

"Can I bring any Bureau assets to bear on this?"

He shook his head. "Thanks for the offer, but we're well stocked with manpower and resources. And we'll find him. He doesn't have many places to hide."

"Will you let me know when you do?"

"I'll definitely do what I can."

"I appreciate whatever you can do."

"We better get going. Got paperwork to file on this."

Puller rose and so did McElroy.

"A lot more paperwork, because of me," said Pine.

"If I had a buck for every wrong move I made, intentionally or not? So, kick it out of your head. Just one of those things."

After they left, Pine stared down at her unfinished meal and muttered, "Shit."

CHAPTER

4

"YOU HAD NO WAY OF KNOWING," said Carol Blum.

Pine had returned to her room at the hotel where she was staying with her assistant, Carol Blum, who was in her sixties and had been in admin at the Bureau for nearly four decades. A mother of six grown children, Blum was rarely surprised or intimidated. She was traveling with Pine to help her on this case. Normally, Pine and Blum worked out of a single-agent office in Shattered Rock, Arizona. Known in Bureau parlance as an "RA," or resident agency, as opposed to the far larger FBI field offices that were located in metro areas.

"I know, but I still feel bad. Puller is a good guy. Knowing him, he'd planned this down to the last detail, only he had no way of realizing I'd walk right into the middle of it and blow the whole thing."

"But Tony Vincenzo *was* there? He definitely was the one running away?"

"Yes. John thinks he can track Vincenzo down pretty quickly, but I'm not so sure."

"Is there any other way to get to Ito's whereabouts, other than his grandson?"

"Tony was Plan A. But Plan B is I can talk to Ito's son, Teddy. He's in the prison at Fort Dix right here in Trenton."

"Is Fort Dix a military prison?"

"No. It's just on the military installation's land. It's run by the federal Bureau of Prisons. Minimum to medium security, though they've got some crime bosses doing time there, along with politicians and businessmen gone bad."

"Okay. By the way, have you heard from Jack Lineberry?"

"He was supposed to leave the hospital yesterday. He can afford the best home care around."

"Yes, I'm sure. But I was talking about—"

"I know, Carol," Pine said sharply. In a calmer tone she added, "I haven't come to grips with it, if you want to know the truth. I thought he might be able to help me find my mother, but right now he needs to concentrate on healing."

"Understood."

"But I will check in and keep him in the loop. And he might have some information for me that could help."

Pine pulled out her phone. "I was going to try to schedule a meeting with Teddy Vincenzo. But an idea just occurred to me."

"What?"

"I'm going to have Puller make the request to the prison. He may very well want to talk to Teddy Vincenzo, too, about Tony. Teddy might have some clue about where his son has gone to ground. And while it's a federal prison, it *is* located on a military installation, so Puller can help cut through the red tape. We can get in faster that way."

"Sounds like a plan," said Blum.

Pine made the call and Puller answered on the second ring. She told him what she wanted, and he said he would make it happen, with one condition.

"I want to go with you when you talk to Teddy."

"I was going to insist that you do," said Pine.

"I'll try for zero nine hundred tomorrow, okay?"

"Works for me. I'll meet you there."

"See you then." Pine clicked off and looked at Blum.

Blum said, "Well, this might be a silver lining. I imagine Teddy might know more about his father than Tony would about his grandfather."

"I was thinking the same thing. Now the only question is, will he talk?"

"With prisoners, it's always about the quid pro quo."

"I know, Carol. But we'll come up with something to dangle in front of him."

"So what now? We wait until you meet with him?"

"No. I have another plan."

"What's that?"

"After Tony got away we searched for other people in the house, but I didn't really search the *house*. I think I need to correct that oversight."

"Do you have a warrant?"

"No, but Puller did. I can piggyback off that."

"He won't have a problem with that?" asked Blum, looking skeptical.

"I don't see why he would. We're on the same side."

"Well, he's looking to nail Vincenzo for a crime and use him to get bigger fish. You're looking to find out about Ito and solve what happened to your sister."

"And you think they're mutually exclusive?"

"Not necessarily. But I'm not sure they're wholly compatible, either."

"Well, I'm willing to risk it."

"That's what I thought you'd say."

"And you disapprove?"

"If I did, I would have said so. But just keep what I said in mind, that's all."

"I keep everything you say in mind, Carol."

CHAPTER

5

"You didn't get him, did you?"

Pine looked over at the front porch of the house next to the Vincenzos', where the old woman was still in the rocking chair, though her yarn and needles were nowhere in sight. It had grown chillier and she had on a heavier coat. Pine saw the orange glow of a rusted standup outdoor heater next to her.

"No, I didn't."

"He's fast. But I thought you might have a shot. You've got long legs."

"Not long enough, apparently. Hopefully, I'll get another chance. You stay outside all day? It's pretty raw."

"There's nothing in the house to keep me occupied. I like to know what's going on around me. People passing by, punks running from the cops. Speaking of which, they're inside the house."

"*Military* cops, yeah, I know. I saw their cars parked out front. You have any idea where Tony might've gone?"

"They already asked me. I'll tell you what I told them: no. I don't make conversation with that man if I can help it. I know what he is, and he knows I know. Anybody pisses on flowers, well..."

"Okay. Anything else you can tell me that might be helpful?"

"I have to live here, you know."

"I know, Ms....?"

The woman shook her head. "Sure you can find out if you want to but..."

"I'm going to leave my card in your mailbox. You think of anything and you want to tell me confidentially?"

The woman looked away, made the sign of the cross, mumbled what sounded like a prayer, pulled out a book from her coat, and started to read it in the fading light. Pine saw that it was a small Bible.

Pine watched her for a few more seconds and then knocked on the front door.

Her creds and mentioning John Puller's name got her inside, where she spoke with a CID agent named Bill Crocker, a buzz-cut young man with a trim, runner's build and a serious expression. She explained her interest and he said, "We've looked where we needed to look and bagged what we needed to bag. Chief Puller wants us to stay here until he says otherwise, and he told us about you. So look around. But if you find something we missed...?"

"You'll be the first to know, I promise."

"Yes, ma'am."

She started on the top floor and worked her way down. The place was a mess. There was a hole in one wall of a bedroom that allowed one to see outside. The faucets were all rusted, the sinks stained, and the carpet and padding was so threadbare she could see the subfloor in numerous places. Tony's bed was a sleeping bag laid out in one room. His clothes were not hung in the closet; they were rolled into a massive ball on the floor. Empty fast-food containers littered the floor. A flat-screen TV hung on one wall. An Xbox controller lay under it.

Well, at least he has his priorities right.

The kitchen had far more ants and roaches than pots and dishes. And the few that were in the sink had food crusted on them so deeply that she wasn't sure in which year they had been placed there. It was so filthy here, the very air seemed permeated with grime, germs, and a burgeoning plague.

She finally arrived in the basement. The dust patterns in the floor told her that CID had taken several large items from down here. The walls were paneled in cheap plywood, and someone had attempted to paint them the ugliest brown she had ever seen. The carpet was ripped and ratty and pulled up in several places to reveal the concrete slab just below. The air was musty enough down here to make Pine's nose wrinkle and lungs twitch.

She leaned against a wall and peered around the space. She would bet that the white residue on the carpet was coke dust or shavings from a pill mill machine. And the dust patterns were probably the outline of the base of said pill machine. Vincenzo obviously did his criminal manufacturing work down here where prying eyes could not reach. Normally she would be interested in that, but nothing about her current situation qualified as normal. Yet what she might be interested in was possibly staring her right in the face.

The wall of old framed pictures. They were all hanging off-kilter, and Vincenzo had apparently never bothered to set them right. She doubted he ever looked at them while he was down here doing his drug alchemy. It was probably just his family, after all.

She strode over there and flicked on the overhead light right above this section of the space. The fluorescent tubes popped, flickered, and then came to life, turning murky to milky. She started from the top left with an eye to working her way to the bottom right.

Halfway through Pine stopped and stared at the image of a younger Ito Vincenzo, the man she believed had taken her sister, Mercy. And then he had tried to blame all of that on her poor father. She thought his features, surprisingly enough, were kind. She knew him to be anything but, at least when it had come to herself and Mercy.

Her gaze continued to travel along the rows of pictures. She spent a little time with Bruno Vincenzo, Ito's mobster older brother, whom she recognized from another photo of the man she had seen in a newspaper. He had been coming out of a federal courthouse and trying to shield his face with a paperback book. Pine believed that Bruno was the reason Ito had done what he had. It was retribution against her mother for having helped send Bruno to prison, where he had ended up getting a shiv in his carotid for turning snitch on his fellow mobsters.

Next to Ito's picture was the framed image of a woman. The

photo was old; she could tell by the clothes, hairstyle, and picture quality. It looked like one of those instant Polaroids. The woman looked to be about the same age as Ito. Was it his wife, Tony Vincenzo's grandmother? Possibly another source of information, if Pine could only find her.

And maybe I might have someone to ask about that who is very close by. And why the hell didn't I think of it before? Come on, Pine, start bringing your A game.

She hustled upstairs and out the front door and over to the edge of the front porch where the old woman still sat in her rocker, still reading her Bible.

"How long have you lived here?" asked Pine.

"My husband and I bought this place a year after we were married. Got a good deal. We raised our kids here."

"So a long time, then?"

"Over fifty years."

"So you knew Ito Vincenzo? He lived here back then with his family."

"Yes, I knew him."

"What can you tell me about him?"

"What do you want to know?"

"Anything."

"Why?"

Pine walked over to the woman's porch and perched on the rail in front of her. She wanted to be on the lady's home turf when she said what she was about to say; it might make all the difference.

"I think he might have abducted my twin sister thirty years ago and nearly killed me."

For the first time Pine thought she had the woman's full attention.

"And Ito came back the next morning and got into a fight with my father, trying to blame him for what had happened. For a crime *he* had committed."

The woman sized her up. "Thirty years ago. You must've been just a child."

"I was six."

"Why would Ito have done that? That wouldn't be like him at all. He was a good, God-fearing man."

"Maybe something else came along that he was even more afraid of: He had a brother, Bruno Vincenzo."

The woman visibly shuddered.

"So you knew Bruno too, I take it?"

"Night and day, those two. Ito was nothing like Bruno. We all knew what Bruno was."

"You mean the mob?"

"I mean a lot of things and all of them bad. It got so that Evie wouldn't allow him to come over."

"Evie is Ito's wife?"

"Yes."

"And Ito was okay with that?"

"To tell the truth, Ito couldn't stand his brother."

"That's interesting and informative."

"So I can't believe Ito would have done something like that. He was a nice guy, raised his kids right. Helped me and my husband out when we needed it. Fixed our furnace, helped reroof our house. Folks did back then. Now? Nobody knows nobody."

"Teddy's in prison. And we both know about Tony. So how good could Ito have really been as a father?" She looked at the woman questioningly.

"Well, Ito had a business. He worked long hours. And Teddy took after Bruno, I think. Always a bad one. Nothing you can do about that when it's in the blood. Always in trouble. Looking for the quick buck."

"What happened to Teddy's wife? I assume he was married?"

"Yes. She left him. About ten years ago. She'd had enough. I would've never lasted that long. They used to live here. Fights all the time. The thugs Teddy had over, and they *were* thugs. They threatened us. Would've gotten bad, but I do have to say that Teddy wouldn't let them hurt us. Maybe because we were friends with his parents. Only kind thing I ever knew him to do. So Tony grew up around all that. No wonder he turned out the way he did."

"Do you know where Teddy's ex is?" asked Pine.

"Jane? No. I haven't heard from her in years. I hope she found happiness somewhere. That woman deserved it if anybody ever did."

"And Ito Vincenzo's wife, Evie?" said Pine. "I assume you knew her well."

"Yes. Evie was very sweet. We were good friends. And my husband enjoyed Ito's company. And that man could cook. The meals we had over there! Everything made fresh. I thought Italians just ate pasta, but Ito made a lot of fish. It was always delicious."

"Do you know where she is now? Is she still alive?"

The woman nodded slowly. "Evie lives in a nursing home. Kensington Manor. It's about five miles from here. The name sounds a lot nicer than it is. They always do, I guess."

"Her family didn't help her out?"

"Teddy and Tony are the only ones still nearby and they're useless. About five years ago Evie went to the nursing home when she couldn't take care of herself anymore. I've visited her there. It's…it's not a nice place. But it's probably where I'm going to end up, too, sooner rather than later. My kids are very good to me, but they have their own problems. And the nicer places cost way too much, far more than they could afford."

"You could sell your house."

"I don't own it. I did one of those reverse mortgages. I needed the money to pay the bills. As soon as I'm gone they'll take the house."

Pine gazed around at the other homes. "I guess a lot of people are in that situation."

"The government tells you to spend your money to help the economy, create jobs. And then when you do spend pretty much all of it, they turn around and tell you to save money because you'll need it to retire on. So which is it?"

"I'm afraid I don't have the answer. I'm just sorry you have to be in this position."

"At least I know I'll end up with a roof over my head and three meals a day. I'll just sit there in my own drool," she added bitterly. "So much for the golden years."

"You don't know it's *that* bad."

"Most of my friends are in state-run nursing homes paid for by Medicaid and whatever dollars they have left. I visit them. It *is* that bad."

"I'll take your word for it. Look, do you know if Ito is still alive?"

"I don't know that for sure. He just up and vanished one day. Long time ago."

"Was it in the late eighties?" asked Pine sharply. "That's when my sister was taken."

"No, it wasn't that far back" was her surprising reply. She mulled over this. "If I had to guess it was sometime around 9/11, or maybe the year after, but that's all I can remember."

"What did Evie think had happened to him?"

"I don't know. Any time I brought it up, she changed the subject."

"So she doesn't know if he's dead or alive?"

"Not that she ever told me. But him disappearing like that? It left a hole in her heart as big as the Lincoln Tunnel. I could never understand it. Sometimes I think Bruno came back from the grave and killed him because that's just who Bruno was."

Pine thanked the woman and walked back to her car. She called Blum and asked her to take an Uber and meet Pine at the nursing home.

"Her old neighbor said five years ago Evie could no longer take care of herself. She might have deteriorated a lot since then."

"Well, we can only try," replied Blum.

Story of my life, thought Pine as she walked to her car.

6

As Pine met Blum outside of the nursing home, she said, "There's one thing that has bugged the crap out of me."

"What is that?" asked Blum.

"How could Ito have possibly found out that my mother was a mole for the government? She never testified in court. Her identity was kept secret."

"And we learned that before you and your sister moved to Andersonville, attempts were made on your lives while you were in WITSEC," said Blum, referring to the Witness Protection Program run by the U.S. Marshals Service. "So how did *those* people find out?"

"Do you think whoever was behind that might have leaked the information to Ito or his brother, Bruno? He was still alive at that time, albeit in prison."

"It certainly could be that the two things are connected."

The nursing home looked like it had been built in the sixties with lots of poured cement and now-dated architecture. The roof-line was flat, and they could see rusty rooftop AC units perched up there in a linear formation.

They walked into the facility. The place had a musty odor, and the furnishings and wall coverings were old and frayed. Pine saw some elderly people moving slowly down the halls in either wheelchairs or walkers. Though old, the place looked relatively clean and uncluttered, but it certainly didn't seem "cheery."

Pine showed her creds and badge to the receptionist and they were directed to a supervisor's office.

"What is this about?" asked the woman, who was in her thirties and dressed in a white smock. The remains of her lunch were sitting on her desk, in an office that was small and messy.

"We just want to ask Mrs. Vincenzo some questions in connection with an inquiry," Pine began.

"Don't you need a search warrant or something?" said the woman, who had not identified herself, but whose name tag read SALLY.

"Not for just talking to someone voluntarily, *Sally*," replied Pine. "We're not *searching* anything. Just asking questions. It's about Mrs. Vincenzo's husband."

"I didn't even know she had a husband. No one ever comes to visit except an old neighbor of hers."

"She was the one who told me Mrs. Vincenzo was here, that she couldn't care for herself any longer."

Sally shook her head. "The poor folks forget to take medication, fall down, break a hip, try to drive, leave the cooktop on all night. It's the old story."

"So can we talk to her?"

"I'm not sure how much good it will do. She's in our memory care unit."

"'Memory care unit'?"

"She's been diagnosed with dementia."

"I'm sorry to hear that, but so long as we're here? Can we at least give it a try? It's important."

"Well, I guess it can't hurt. It might be good for her to have some visitors, poor thing."

She led them down the hall to a set of double doors where a stenciled sign read MEMORY CARE UNIT.

Sally slid a card through a reader and the door clicked open.

She led them to one room along the hall and knocked on the door. In a singsong voice she said, "Mrs. Vincenzo? Evie? You have visitors."

She opened the door and they entered the room.

Evie Vincenzo was sitting up in bed and gazing placidly at them. She had on pink pajamas and there was a pink scarf over her curly hair. Many of the items in the room were also pink.

"She likes pink," noted Sally. "It soothes her."

"I'm fond of pink myself," said Blum.

"I'll check back in a bit," said Sally. "Any issues, just hit that red button over the bed."

She left, and Pine and Blum drew closer to the woman. Pine sat in a chair while Blum stood next to her.

Vincenzo gazed up at Pine. "Do I know you, young lady?" she asked in a pleasant voice.

"No, but I know your neighbor. She likes to knit. She called you Evie."

Evie said nothing and her eyes started to close.

"She lived in the house to the left of yours?" Pine said helpfully.

The woman opened her eyes, but again didn't respond.

Blum said, "Do you enjoy visitors? I think I would. It's nice to talk to people."

"I…I don't know you, do I?"

Pine glanced at Blum. "No, but we wanted to visit you today."

"My…I…not many visitors."

"Your neighbor told us you were here."

Evie shook her head, clearly frustrated. "Old woman."

Pine drew closer. "Yes, I, uh, I was talking to her about your husband?"

"My…husband?"

"Yes, Ito? Do you remember him? She said he was a wonderful cook."

Evie looked down at her lap. "I…used to…cook." She glanced at a wall. "They took my…stove."

Blum reached over and put a gentle hand on the woman's shoulder. "I like to cook, too. I'm so sorry that you can't."

"Evie, do you think you could answer some questions about It—your husband?"

"My husband?" she said again. "I…no husband." She shook her head. "I…so miss cooking."

"Yes, I'm sure you do. Now, you have a son named Teddy and a grandson named Anthony."

In response to this Evie took off her scarf, showing that her hair was mostly gone. The clumps that were left were a tinted red. She scrunched the scarf up in her hands. "I would bake bread. Knead, knead, knead, like this."

Pine sighed and glanced at Blum in resignation. She leaned in and whispered, "Just keep talking to her."

"What are you going to do?"

"Just look around."

"Agent Pine, the poor woman, I mean."

"Carol, I know. I feel for her, I really do. But if she has something in here that can help me find my sister, I have to look. I might not get another chance. I'll be quick and efficient."

Blum refocused on Evie and asked her what kind of bread she liked to bake. Pine quickly searched through drawers and bent down to look under the bed. If Evie noticed this she made no sign. She was still kneading her scarf.

Pine next started riffling through the closet and finally spied a cardboard box behind a mound of clothes, stacks of *People* magazines, and a collapsed walker. The box was packed with papers.

She pulled it out of the closet. "Mrs. Vincenzo, do you mind if I look through this?"

She was now lightly tapping the scarf while Blum looked over and shrugged at Pine.

"I don't think she can give informed consent," noted Blum.

"It's not like I'm going to use anything I find to put her in jail."

"But it might her husband."

"Don't go all lawyer on me, Carol. This could be my only shot."

Pine sat down and went through the box while Vincenzo had set the scarf aside and now stared happily at her pink lampshade, seemingly having forgotten that they were even there.

There was so much in the box that Pine ended up giving Blum a stack to look through. "Old photos of her kids. Here's one of her and Ito, I think. Looks to be on their wedding day."

"These photos have the names on the back. Here's Teddy," said Blum as she went through a stack. "He looks to be a teenager. And this one is of Tony when he was a baby; someone's written his name at the bottom. He looks so innocent. They all do at that age, of course, because they are."

"And then some of them grow up to be felons."

"Keeps us gainfully employed," said Blum.

"Look," Pine said excitedly. "Here's an article on Bruno Vincenzo's conviction. This is his picture." She showed Blum the clipping with the photo of Bruno.

Blum recoiled a bit at the image. "He looks like he'd kill you over a piece of chewing gum."

Pine scanned the article. "It says he was convicted of murdering two people, one of them a witness for the prosecution. The trial was in New Jersey, which still had the death penalty back then. He got a death sentence, but then it was commuted to life after he agreed to cooperate."

"And then he was later killed in prison?" said Blum.

"Right. He was in solitary at the prison, but apparently somebody paid off a guard, and an inmate knifed Bruno." She pulled a folded, yellowed newspaper out of the box, and when she opened it something fell out from between the folds. It was a piece of paper with writing on it. Pine started to read it and her eyes widened as she did so.

"What?" asked Blum, trying to read over her shoulder.

"This is a letter from Bruno to Ito. From the date on it he must've written it after he went to prison but obviously before he was killed there."

"What does it say?"

"Bruno says he discovered a snitch but didn't out the person to his mob bosses."

"Why not?"

"I don't know. He told his brother that the snitch had screwed him over somehow and that's why he'd been arrested and was in prison now. He asked Ito to come see him."

"Maybe he didn't want to write down anything too sensitive. He wanted to tell his brother in person."

"Yeah, to tell him that it was my *mom* who screwed him over. But this letter still doesn't tell me how Bruno found out where we were living. Because he had to know. That was the only way Ito would have known."

"I guess this confirms once and for all that he was the one to take Mercy."

"I can't think of another possibility. But what did he do with her?" She looked over at Evie Vincenzo, who was still staring in fascination at her lampshade. "And this poor woman isn't going to be able to answer that question."

"But maybe her son can."

They finished searching the box but found nothing else nearly as earth-shattering as the letter. Pine slipped it into her pocket along with a few other items, including photos of various family members.

She rose and said to the woman in the bed, "Mrs. Vincenzo, thank you for seeing us."

"I so miss my stove."

She started kneading her scarf again.

Blum watched Evie for a moment, her eyes glistening, and then she followed Pine out.

CHAPTER

7

IT WAS MUCH LIKE EVERY other prison that Pine had been in: loud, reeking of foul odors, chaotic and at the same time rigid in organization mainly because of the walls and bars. It was a sophisticated chess match between the imprisoned and the guards, but sometimes the guards shirked their duties in exchange for the profits associated with allowing access to drugs, girls, and other things that made whiling away years of one's life in a cage somewhat bearable.

While Fort Dix's classification topped out at medium security, such was the state of the inmate population at federal facilities that men who would otherwise have deserved maximum-security status had been relegated to installations like Fort Dix. Maybe the authorities hoped that the prison's being on a military base would keep the inmates in line. That was wishful thinking, she believed.

She and Puller cleared security together, reluctantly giving up their weapons. Then they were led to the visitors room.

"He won't give things up easily," noted Pine as they took their seats.

"Never assumed otherwise. The reverse, actually. He's apparently got a brain, at least my sources say. He'll want his pound of flesh for cooperating."

"What else can you tell me about him?"

"He's a bad guy through and through. Been in trouble since he was a teenager. Petty stuff to start, and then he rapidly graduated to more serious crimes. He's in here after being busted for heading up a burglary ring that was targeting senior citizens. One of them was nearly beaten to death when he showed up at his own house unexpectedly. Teddy's got a good lawyer, but he'll still be in here for another eight years at least."

"Does he have a relationship with Tony?"

"From what we've found, Teddy would never qualify as father of the year. He wasn't around much. His mother did what she could with Tony before she called it quits and got the hell out of Dodge, but he nonetheless seems to have followed in his father's footsteps."

"Crime runs in the family. Teddy's uncle was a mobster."

"Right, the Bruno Vincenzo you mentioned before."

Pine nodded. "And now here comes the mobster's nephew."

Two guards escorted Teddy Vincenzo to a seat at the table across from them.

He was about five nine, his frame hard and wiry. Corded muscles lined his forearms. He carried himself with as much confidence as anyone in leg irons could. At over fifty, he had hair that was more gray than black, and coarse in texture.

From his expression Pine could read the man clearly. He was curious but guarded. He was looking for an advantage. For anything to get him out of here at the earliest possible moment so he could get on with his criminal career.

"They said FBI and CID," began Vincenzo, and then he stopped right there, sat back and eyed them. "To what do I owe a visit from so many alphabet letters?"

He had selected his opening move with a pawn, thought Pine. Nothing too dramatic. He was here for info, too.

Puller said, "We're interested in your son, Tony."

Vincenzo said nothing to this, but he also didn't seem surprised by the statement. He looked at Pine. "And you?"

"I'm actually interested in your father, Ito."

The inmate showed a glimmer of surprise at this request. He folded his arms over his chest. "Why?"

"I'd like to talk to him."

"Same question."

"He's a person of interest in a case I'm looking into."

"You sure you ain't after the wrong Vincenzo brother?"

"Bruno's dead."

"That's right. He took a shiv in prison for being a snitch." He looked over his shoulder, making his point. "Is that what you want for *my* future?"

"Are there any other Vincenzo brothers besides Ito and Bruno?" asked Pine. "Because I couldn't find any."

"No, that's it. Big Italian Catholic family, but the rest were girls. What case?"

"A kidnapping that Ito was involved in."

"Bullshit. My old man ran an ice cream shop here in Trenton, about a half mile from our house on the strip where they had all the mom-and-pop shops. It was called Vinnie's Creamery."

" 'Vinnie' as in…?" said Pine.

"Just shortened from Vincenzo. What, you think *Ito's* Creamery has a nice ring to it?"

"Okay."

He smiled. "My old man was as pure as the driven snow. Only sold vanilla." Vincenzo showed white teeth as he smiled at his little joke. "Sound like a kidnapper to you?"

"Circumstances can change people," interjected Puller.

"What, you mean like Tony?"

"Like a lot of people. But, yeah, like Tony."

"You're Army, he's not."

"He works here at Fort Dix. That makes it my problem."

"Tony's a good boy. It's probably a misunderstanding." He looked dead eyed at them as he said this obvious falsehood.

"You have any idea where he might be?"

"I'm in here, he's out there."

"You're saying he's never come to visit you even though he works here?"

"I don't remember saying anything like that."

"How'd you come to inherit Ito's house?" asked Pine.

Vincenzo's gaze swiveled back to her. He seemed to enjoy the back-and-forth between the two federal officers. "I was the oldest. And my siblings couldn't have cared less about it."

"What about your mother?" said Pine.

"What about her?" said Vincenzo sharply.

"She's not doing very well."

He shrugged. "My sisters put her in a place. I wasn't in a position to have a vote. I was locked in my own dump."

"I've been to see her."

"So, she's really not doing good?"

"She has dementia."

"Lot of that going around, I hear. Got some of that in here, older guys. They talk funny."

"Your siblings live around here?" asked Puller.

"Nowhere near. I don't think Jersey agreed with them. They got out quick as they could. Me, I like it just fine, only not so much in this place."

Pine had a sudden thought. "Did your dad ever use the nursery rhyme 'eeny, meany, miney, moe' with you and your siblings while you were growing up?"

Vincenzo grinned. "How the hell did you know that?"

"So he did?"

"Yeah, with six kids he used it to pick one of us."

Pine licked her lips and tried to prevent her nerves from running away from her. "Pick you for what? To…reward?"

Vincenzo shrugged. "Sometimes. But other times to punish. When one of us did something wrong and the others wouldn't rat him or her out."

Pine sat back, disappointed and trying hard not to show it. Ito Vincenzo had used that nursery rhyme in deciding whether to take Pine or Mercy that night. She wanted to know if being picked in that manner was a good or bad thing. Vincenzo's response had obviously not helped.

Puller glanced at her briefly and said, "Back to the house. Tony's living there."

"Okay."

"You knew that?" asked Puller.

"I know it now."

"When's the last time you heard from your dad?" asked Pine.

Vincenzo took a moment to scratch his cheek and then rub his nose, which gave him an opportunity to think things through, Pine knew.

"I don't know. What's in it for me?"

Finally, we're getting somewhere, she thought.

Puller sat forward, taking charge. "Let's cut to the chase, Teddy. You help us, then you help yourself."

Vincenzo sat forward now too, all business. "How much? And it has to be in writing. To my lawyer. I'm taking no chances with you feds screwing me over."

"The time you got left here? We can make eight years six."

"And you can also make eight years four. I'm not getting any younger."

"Five. But it depends on what you can tell us. Bullshit gets you zip. Deal goes off the table and does not come back."

Pine could tell by the declarative way Puller said this that these negotiation parameters had been preapproved in his chain of command.

"Oh, tough guy, are we? I'm shitting my pants right now." Vincenzo said this with a smile that again came nowhere close to his eyes.

"I'm waiting," said Puller.

"What do you want to know?"

"Where is Tony? And where is Ito?"

Vincenzo glanced at Pine. "Why the hell do you give a shit about my old man?"

"Sometime in 1989, he was gone from home. For several months, maybe? Spring, summer? Ring a bell?"

"That's a long time ago, lady. I get hung up on stuff from last week."

"And three years off your time here is a damn good reason to try to remember."

Vincenzo nodded and his manner turned less flippant and more focused. "Okay, look, I want to help, but I'll need to give it some thought."

"Only think in facts. I know enough that the bullshit Chief Puller mentioned applies fully to me as well."

"Okay, your point is clearly made, lady. I'm not looking to extend my stay here any longer than I have to."

"He talk to you about Bruno?" she asked.

"Sometimes; they were brothers. He was my uncle."

"What did he say? I'm talking about what happened to Bruno, when he went to prison the last time."

"Well, one thing my old man told me stuck with me. He said his brother made a deal that never came through. Cost him his life." He glanced sharply at Puller. "Which is the position I might find myself in. Snitches don't have long life expectancies in prison. You walk from this, I'm dead."

"We can throw in solitary if that'll make you feel better," said Puller.

"Did Ito say he was going to do something because of what happened to his brother?" asked Pine.

Vincenzo refocused on her, his expression calming. "Nothing specific that I can remember. He was pissed, that I know."

"Your father was clean. Not even a traffic ticket. Bruno was mob. Why would he care?"

"It was his own flesh and blood. That means something or used to. Yeah, my old man knew what Bruno was. But Bruno went to prison and he died when he shouldn't have. Somebody had to pay for that."

"Ito told you that? Is that what you're saying?" asked Pine.

"Yeah, that's what I'm saying. He didn't talk much about Bruno, so what he did say was memorable, at least to me."

"And then your dad disappeared, we understand. Know anything about that?"

"Nope. I was actually a resident of another fine institution like this one at the time."

He looked at Puller now. "So what the hell has Tony done?"

"Thought you'd know all about it."

"I would never encourage my son to break the law, and I'm sure he didn't."

"Are we expected to laugh?" said Puller.

Teddy shrugged. "Look, I'm an asshole, sure, but selling out my own kid? Come on."

"Under no circumstances?" said Puller.

"You make the five years three, in my own cell, and I get private workout privileges and no probation. I'm clean and free when I walk out of here, no checking in with nobody. No peeing in a cup for the next five years. Call it a family discount."

Pine looked at Puller, who nodded curtly.

Vincenzo hunched forward and dropped his voice. "Okay, look, Tony is not complicated. He's a one-trick pony with not an original thought in his head. He does his little pill operation and he sells his shit and collects his share and he drinks his beer and bangs his women. But the situation he's in now *is*...complicated. He's way in over his head."

"We're listening."

"I think he's got himself involved with some people he shouldn't be. And at some point they're going to figure out he's a liability and not an asset."

"How do you know all this?" asked Pine.

"He came by to see me a while back. He was worried. Stuff he mentioned, didn't add up to me. I told him to watch his back and look for an exit before it was too late."

The man, Pine thought, looked deadly serious about that.

Puller said, "Okay. What exactly did he tell you?"

At that moment the door opened, and three guards and two suits entered the room.

"Interview is over," said one of the suits.

Puller barked, "It was fully authorized, and we're not done yet."

"You're done now," said the other suit.

The guards grabbed a startled Vincenzo and started to pull him from the room.

"Hey, hey!" The inmate roared as he struggled futilely against them. He looked bug-eyed at Puller and screamed, "You screwed me over! You son of a—"

And then the door slammed shut and Teddy Vincenzo was gone.

CHAPTER

"THAT WAS IT?" said Carol Blum when Pine returned to the hotel and reported what had happened at the prison.

"John made inquiries and ran into a stone wall. He'll keep at it, but I don't know what the result will be."

"But I don't understand. Why would anyone care that you were talking to Teddy Vincenzo?"

"Maybe the people his son was involved with do. Teddy seemed to think his son was way out of his league."

"And these people can influence the goings-on at a prison? I mean, how would they have even known you were there?"

Pine looked at her. "Apparently they have connections, at a pretty high level."

"Well, that's a scary thought."

"And it also means we don't have a way to get a lead on Ito or Tony. So we're back at square one."

Pine slumped down in a chair and looked out the window at the backs of buildings perched on the rear of the hotel property.

One tiny step forward, four jumps back.

"Did Teddy tell you *anything* that was helpful before the interview was stopped?"

"He did confirm that his father was pissed about what happened to Bruno."

"Did Teddy know his father was even in Georgia back at that time?"

"He would have been an adult by then, so he might not have been living at home. He started getting in trouble with the law even before then. But even so, I would imagine he would know if his father was missing, particularly for an extended period. But in any case, he said he didn't remember, and would have to think about it. Now I guess we won't get the opportunity to ask him again."

"Not unless Puller can work some magic."

"He didn't sound hopeful from the last email he sent." She grew silent and then said, "Vinnie's Creamery."

"What?"

"Ito had an ice cream shop in Trenton named that. He said it was only a half mile from their house. I wonder if it's still there?"

"If it is, wouldn't Teddy have mentioned it?"

"I didn't ask him. And they don't deliver ice cream where Teddy is."

As it turned out, Vinnie's Creamery was no longer there. The entire area had been razed and an apartment building and other businesses had been put up in place of the old shops that had lined both sides of the street. Pine and Blum asked around and found Darren Castor, a middle-aged man who had worked at Vinnie's and was now head of maintenance at the apartment building.

Castor was about to take his coffee break, and Pine bought him a cup at a shop around the corner from the apartment building. Castor was in his fifties, had a string bean frame, a thick crown of gray hair, and weathered features. He sipped his coffee as he reminisced.

He grinned. "Ito Vincenzo. Haven't heard that name in a long time."

"You liked working with him?"

"Oh, yeah. It was fun. Happy customers. Who doesn't like ice cream? In my job now all I get are complaints."

"I guess so."

"We sold gelato, too, of course. I mean, he was Italian, after all. And desserts and bakery goods. Ito made them himself. He was really good. The business did well."

"Yeah, I understand he was a good cook." Pine took out a

picture of Ito that she had gotten while in Georgia. "And just to confirm we're talking about the same person."

Castor looked at the photo and nodded. "That's Ito, all right."

"Did you know his son, Teddy?" asked Blum.

"Bad news. He's been in and out of prison. Ito couldn't do anything with him. Kept giving him second chances, and when his back was turned, Teddy would put his hand in the till and the money would disappear. Ito never learned with that piece of trash."

"When was the last time you saw Ito?" asked Pine.

"Hell, I don't know. It was a long time ago."

"Just think about it for a bit. Work it through in your head. Tie it to major events in your life, that will help."

"Well, I started working for him when I was eighteen. I remember that because I was just out of high school and answered an ad Ito put in the paper. So that was back in 1985. I was there full-time through…okay, yeah, I started at the auto body shop in, I think…2001."

"So you worked for him for over fifteen years?" said Blum.

"I know, ice cream, right? But it went by fast. He taught me a lot. Learned about dealing with people, which has come in handy down the road. Heck, I became his partner in a way. He treated me well. Never got rich, but I got by and it was enjoyable work. We had a lot of regular customers. It was a popular place, packed on Fridays and the weekends. All word of mouth. His stuff was just that good."

"Then I understand that Ito just disappeared one day?" asked Pine.

Castor nodded, looking sad. "Yeah, that's right. It's the only reason I changed jobs. Strangest thing. One day he was there, the next—poof—the guy was gone. His wife, Evie, tried to keep the business going. She could cook, too, especially her baked goods. I helped out as much as I could, but I needed a steady paycheck. I had a family then. Competition started coming in and people stopped eating as many sweets and the business just kept going down. Evie ended up selling it."

"Any idea what happened to him?"

"Nobody knows. Least that I heard of. They looked for him and all. The police, I mean. But as far as I know, no one ever saw hide nor hair of him again."

"So before he went missing did you notice anything unusual? Was he troubled or anything? Did he get a letter or a phone call that upset him?"

Castor drank his coffee while he thought about her questions.

"Well, first of all I didn't know he was going to disappear, so I didn't pay particular attention to the time leading up to it."

"Still, anything you can recall."

He shook his head. "Not that I can recall, no. I'm sorry. It was just so long ago."

"Okay, so you left there and started work at the auto body place?"

"That's right. I was always good with cars. Then that place went under and I got this job."

"So Ito would have disappeared some time shortly before that?"

"Yeah. In 2001, I'm pretty sure."

"Okay. Let me ask you something else. During the spring and summer of 1989, was Ito absent from the business?"

Castor finished his coffee. "Nineteen eighty-nine? Whew, now you're really getting in the weeds with me, lady."

"Take your time and think it through again," said Pine. "And I'm not talking about a day or even a week. This would have been a chunk of time that he was gone, I'm talking months. You should be able to remember that."

Realization finally spread across Castor's face. "That's right. I remember now. It must've been 1989, 'cause I'd been there about four years then and that was the only time he was gone for more than a few days. Said he was going to Italy, you know, the old country. That's what he told Evie, too. They still had kids at home, so I guess she couldn't go. He was gone for about two months, maybe more. And it was a busy time, too, the spring and all. Scared me to death because I had to make all the ice cream and stuff. But Ito had taught me well. Evie stepped in and helped out.

So it worked out okay. But still, I wish he hadn't left us in the lurch like that. If he hadn't come back when he did, I'm not sure he'd have had a business to come back to. If that had happened in 2001 we probably wouldn't have made it. Like I said, there was a lot more competition for customers in 2001 than in 1989, at least around here."

"Yeah, I can see that," said Pine. "And when he came back?"

"He had a bunch'a stuff from Italy, all right, and everything seemed okay."

"Until he disappeared?"

"Yep. He got back to work and ran the business, and everything was normal. Until that time he left and never came back. Damn shame. I enjoyed working for him. It was fun. What I do now, it's just a job."

"Did you know his brother, Bruno?"

"Can't say that I did, no. I did hear about him, though. Apparently, he was some kinda criminal like Teddy is. Maybe it ran in the family. He never came around the shop, least that I knew of. Bruno got killed in prison or something, right?"

"Yes. Did Ito tell you that he was a criminal?"

"No. Evie did. She didn't like him one bit, I can tell you that. Told me she wouldn't have that man in her house. I think she was afraid he'd rub off on Teddy. Well, that strategy didn't work. But some people are just born bad."

"Did Evie have her husband declared dead at some point?" asked Blum. "I think they have to wait a certain amount of time, seven years or so."

"Not that I know of, but I would've moved on long before then."

"Anything else you can tell us? Focusing on when he came back?" asked Pine. She leaned forward and her voice grew tense. "Did he seem nervous or upset, or troubled in any way?"

Castor scratched his head. "Not that I recall specifically. But again, it was a long time ago. He brought me back a bottle of wine from Italy. And some chocolates. Never had nothing like that before."

"So he just seemed the same?" asked Pine, clearly disappointed.

Castor thought some more. "Well, I don't know if it means anything, but I do remember him telling me something not that long after he got back."

"What?" said Pine sharply.

"He said you never know what you're capable of until you have to do it. It was such a weird thing to say that it stuck with me."

Pine glanced at Blum.

"Did he elaborate?" asked Blum.

"Well, I asked him did he have to do something in Italy that surprised him."

"And what was his answer?"

"He said he hadn't done something that surprised him. He'd done something that *shocked* him. But he never would say what that was."

"I'm sure he didn't," muttered Pine. She handed Castor her card. "You've been a big help. If anything else occurs to you, give me a call or shoot me an email."

CHAPTER

9

JOHN PULLER WAS NOT a man easily intimidated. A many-times-decorated soldier and two-time Purple Heart recipient, he carried physical scars from being in a war that were harsh to look at, but he nonetheless carried them with pride. The internal trauma he endured from humans trying to kill other humans in often the most barbaric ways possible was difficult to confront. So he often chose not to. Whether that would come back to haunt him at some point, as it had others, he didn't know. But right now he had a job to do. And right now that job was causing Puller considerable stress, or at least the man sitting across from him was.

Barney Moss was taller than Puller but flabby, his skin a sickly white. His drab brown suit was ill fitted, either because he'd lost weight or because he didn't give a crap about his clothes. His hairdo was a stringy, greasy comb-over. He looked like the villain in every bad 1970s-era movie ever made. His necktie was undone, and his open collar showed off his neck wattle. He was the government suit repping Fort Dix so, technically, he was a fellow fed. Yet from the moment Puller stepped into the office, Moss's manner had Puller fantasizing about pulling his gun.

"So just to be clear, you are not to ever approach Theodore Vincenzo again for any reason," said Moss, for the third time now. He apparently thought repetition equated with substance. "If you do, there will be hell to pay and you'll be the one footing the bill, buddy."

He stared straight across the width of the scarred and cheap wooden desk, like it was a stretch of battlefield and Puller was the enemy firmly engaged.

Puller cleared his throat, inclined his neck slightly to the right, and was rewarded with a satisfying pop and release of vertebral pressure.

"Well, now let *me* be as clear as I can be, Mr. Moss. I'm investigating a case and I talk to the people I need to talk to, and Teddy Vincenzo is one of those people." Puller kept direct eye contact with the man, searing every detail of his countenance into the part of his memory that he reserved for "special people."

Puller continued, "And, despite your calling me and *ordering* me to come here, I still don't have a clue as to why you're even involved in this, since you don't happen to be in my chain of command. That also means that legally, technically, and every other way in which the United States Army does business, I have no obligation to follow any order you attempt to give me. So I'm just here as a courtesy. You might or might not be familiar with the concept." He added, "Just so we're clear."

Moss sighed and rested his palms on his paunch. "So that's how it's going to be, is it?"

"From my perspective, it's the only way it can be."

"What, you need to hear from your buddies playing soldier in the sandbox?" he said with a sneer. "Will that make you feel better if it comes from a guy with pretty ribbons on his chest?"

Puller's features remained inscrutable even as he inwardly seethed at this inane insult. "I need to hear from my chain of command. It goes up to the commanding general at the U.S. Army's Criminal Investigation Command and then tops out at the Army's Provost Marshal General. Just like you have a chain of command." Puller cocked his head and eyed the man more closely. "So can you tell me who ordered *you* to do this?"

"To do what?"

"Feed me a bunch of bullshit."

"Sorry, but you're not cleared for anything else."

"On the contrary, I'm cleared for everything up to TS/SCI with polygraph. How about you? What are you cleared for?"

Puller eyed the wall behind the man where photos and mementos were hung. They looked to be of local politicians, business leaders, a few national pols whom Puller recognized, shaking hands and grinning and doing what elected officials are often compelled to do. He didn't even know if this was Moss's office. There had been no name on the door.

"That's none of your business," said Moss, an ugly expression on his face.

"For somebody with all the answers, you don't seem to have any."

"Don't push me!" barked Moss. "You think you're something special because you wear a uniform?"

Puller rose and looked down at the man.

"I've got better things to do with my time than sit here."

Moss pointed a finger at him. "You work for the federal government. Your loyalty lies there. You follow orders. Well, here's your order: Stay away from the Vincenzos."

Puller flinched slightly. "So father *and* son, then?"

To Puller, who was observing Moss closely, the man seemed to have regretted his words, not because of their harshness, but because of their *carelessness*. He composed himself and said, "You'll learn I don't make threats lightly."

Puller closed the door quietly after him, even though his initial impulse had been to slam it.

Don't give the idiot the satisfaction.

As Puller walked outside the government building he saw a column of dark clouds shaped like anvils creeping across the Delaware River as a storm rolled in over the water.

It definitely fit his mood.

Before he got to his car he phoned Pine and filled her in on his meeting with Moss.

"What the hell is going on? Why is all this happening?"

"Teddy did mention that his son was involved in something way over his head. Maybe the people behind that got me called on the carpet with Moss."

"But that would mean the folks involved in a criminal enterprise have connections to the government."

"Corruption is the number one business for some politicians. Serving the country faithfully doesn't even run a close second."

"Well, it's certainly plausible that Tony Vincenzo or the people he was working with could have connections to some powerful people."

"We just have to find out who they are. Hey, how about some dinner tonight and we can plan our next moves?"

"Sounds good."

Puller gave her the time and place.

"But we need to tread lightly, Puller. It's all well and good not to be called off by a jerk like this Moss guy. But there have to be people behind him who carry a lot more clout."

"It's one of the reasons I didn't shoot him. See you tonight."

CHAPTER

10

Pine took a shower, changed into jeans and a sweater, gunned up, and slipped her badge and creds into a bag, which she slung over her shoulder. She caught her reflection in the mirror.

I do look like my mother.

The mother who had abandoned her. That was not a motherly thing to do. It had tainted everything that Pine felt about her. Yet she still wanted to know where her mother was. Whether she was alive or dead.

She drove to the restaurant, which was in a suburb of Trenton. She had looked it up online. It served Italian cuisine without breaking the budget of two federal stiffs like herself and Puller.

He was already waiting in the small foyer when she got there. He was dressed in jeans, a gray V-neck sweater with a T-shirt underneath, and a windbreaker.

The waiter took them to a back table, something Puller had requested. He sat with his back to the wall, which was something Pine liked to do as well.

The restaurant had the usual decorations for that kind of place. Fake vines growing out of old Chianti bottles, framed prints of yachts and beachgoers on the Mediterranean hanging on the wall, red-and-white-checkered tablecloths, and menus thick enough to be novellas.

They ordered Peroni beer and opted to share a pizza with Greek salad starters. Each of their gazes had already taken in all the patrons in the place, and all possible exits. It was in the DNA. It should be in everyone's DNA, Pine thought, particularly these days when any building could, at any moment, become a shooting gallery.

"I didn't ask you before, but how's your brother and your father?"

"Bobby's doing great. Running a chunk of the country's cyber-security now."

"And your father?"

Puller's father was "Fighting John" Puller, a legendary Army three-star with more medals than almost anyone. He was now in a VA hospital suffering from dementia.

"Hanging in there" was all Puller would say. "Just hanging in there. How's Arizona?"

"Hot. And dry. How about you? Are you still in Virginia?"

Puller said, "Yeah, but I spend most days on the road."

"Our jobs don't leave much time for pleasure."

"No they don't. You still doing the Olympic weightlifting and MMA tournaments?"

In college Pine had competed to be on the women's weightlifting team for the Olympics but had missed out on a slot by a kilo. She was a black belt in multiple martial arts and had competed in MMA matches.

"I still lift just to stay in shape. I'm getting too old for the MMA stuff, but I can still kick over my head," she added with a grin.

"I hear you." He paused. "So, I dug a little into this Moss guy, but I didn't find much. I don't think he's been in the job long."

"He hasn't" was Pine's reply.

He looked up at her. "You scored something?"

She nodded. "Called in some contacts. Up until a year ago he was a bigwig attorney in Manhattan. Then he joined a lobbying firm. He went right from there to working for the Bureau of Prisons. He's currently the northeast regional director, which puts Fort Dix under his jurisdiction." She paused. "If you met the guy, didn't he tell you that? Or wasn't the title on his office door?"

"No and no. I don't think it was even his office. There were a bunch of photos on the wall, but he was in none of them. He's probably not based in Trenton. He was just the closest attack dog they could sic on me."

"That's interesting."

"It's also informative. And infuriating. He obviously doesn't hold the military in high regard."

"Why'd you even bother to meet with him?"

"I got the call and was told to meet with the guy."

"Who told you to do that?" she asked.

"A guy two levels up from me at CID. He didn't seem happy about it. I think he was just grudgingly passing the request along. But his tone made it clear I had to go."

"So Moss ordered you to stand down?"

"Which I told him he had no authority to do."

"Bureau of Prisons is under DOJ."

"Still not in my chain of command," Puller replied.

"But DOJ can make it really hot for you."

"I haven't heard any blowback yet from my side, which I take as a good sign. My folks want whoever's behind this drug ring Tony Vincenzo's involved in. Like I said, if they're selling to soldiers, it diminishes their military readiness. If soldiers are selling the drugs, it opens them up to blackmail by enemies of this country. So it ultimately strikes right at America's national security. If DOJ wants to make the argument to the DoD that something takes precedence over protecting this country, I'd love to be in the room to hear what it is."

"At the end of the day, politicians do love the military, at least publicly, so you might have both right and might on your side there."

"Maybe," Puller said. "Did you find anything else about your mom and your sister?"

She took a few minutes to fill him in on what she had discovered in the box in Evie Vincenzo's closet and also her conversation with Darren Castor, the man who had worked for Ito at the ice cream shop.

"So Ito *did* go down to Georgia, abducted your sister, and

almost killed you. That seems to be confirmed, or as close as is possible at the moment."

"Looks to be."

"In revenge for his brother, Bruno?"

"It seems the case, yes."

"And Ito told his employee that he was shocked by what he had done?"

"I don't know if that refers to almost killing a six-year-old girl, me. Or…" Pine could not bring herself to say it: *Or murdering my sister.*

Puller, obviously sensing her distress, gripped her hand and said, "One thing I've learned over the years, you have to hope for the best, and plan for the worst. But it's also true that until we know everything we really know nothing. There is no evidence that conclusively shows your sister was killed, correct?"

"Correct," said Pine, finally meeting his eye after twice trying and failing. She felt her adrenaline spike and tried to hide the fact that she was taking deep breaths to keep her nerves from running away from her. The last thing she wanted to show to Puller was that she was not in control. The man would be understanding, but his confidence in her would also be lessened.

"Okay, then we have to proceed in the belief that she's still alive."

She said, "The odds are not with that assumption, you know that."

"I also know how many times the *facts* have proved my best assumptions wrong. There are a number of things that Ito could have done with her. And from everything you've learned about the guy, he was not a violent criminal, not like his brother. He owned an ice cream shop."

"Everyone I talked to pretty much described him as being nice and kind…and normal."

Puller slowly let go of her hand. "It's hard to kill someone, Atlee. We both know that. It's harder still to kill a child."

Pine touched her head where Ito had struck and shattered her skull. "He managed to nearly kill me."

"And maybe that's what could conceivably have saved your

sister. He could have killed you, easily. But he hit you and then fled without knowing whether you were dead or not."

Pine slowly lowered her hand.

Puller continued. "And the nursery rhyme he used, presumably to choose between you two? You asked Teddy about that to see whether it was good or bad for your sister, but his answer cut both ways."

"Yes, it did."

"But that could have been a guy out of his depth who's stalling for time before he has to do something he doesn't really want to do."

"You're not just trying to make me feel better?"

"I would never do that in a situation like this. That would be crueler than anything else I could think of." He paused and fingered his beer. "The fact is, a guy going there to do what he ultimately did, why choose at all? Why not kill both of you right then and there? He took Mercy when he didn't have to. Getting out of town with a small child? Then transporting her to some other place? What could be harder than that?"

Pine shook her head, looking unconvinced. "He wanted to make my father suffer. He got into a fight with him, accused him of attacking his own daughter and killing the other daughter."

"But I thought it was presumably your mother Bruno had the beef with, not your father."

"My mother was at the hospital with me. Maybe my dad was the only one he could reach at the time."

"Maybe."

"And then, years later, my father, probably suffering from overwhelming guilt, took his own life, on my birthday."

"Damn, I didn't know that," said Puller.

"I haven't told many people."

He took her hand again. "I'm really, really sorry, Atlee."

Their salads and pizza came, and they ate in silence for a few minutes.

They each ordered a second beer and took their time drinking it as the restaurant emptied out of customers.

"You like it out there in Arizona?" asked Puller.

"I like it fine."

"Only fed for miles around?"

"No, the DEA has an office in my building. But the closest FBI agents are in Flagstaff. Then we have offices in Tucson, Lake Havasu, and of course Phoenix, among others. But for day-to-day stuff in the Grand Canyon area, it's just me."

"You have any support?"

"I have the best admin in the Bureau, Carol Blum. She's traveling with me and helping me on this." She put down her fork. "So what's our next move?"

"I'm running Tony down and I haven't given up on Teddy yet, either. He obviously knows stuff that's relevant. And he may know more about Ito and where he might be."

"How are you going to take a run at him?"

"Carefully. Like you said, the DOJ *can* make my life miserable."

"I'd like to know why any other agency even cares about this."

"It only takes one bureaucrat, Atlee."

They paid their bill, splitting it down the middle despite Puller's trying to pay for it all.

"It's the least I can do, Atlee."

"I blew your collar. I should pay for all your meals for the next month."

"You're the real deal, all right," he said with a smile.

He couldn't have paid her a higher compliment, thought Pine.

They walked outside.

"Where are you staying?" she asked.

"Motel a few miles from here. We're limited on vehicles so Ed McElroy dropped me off and he's coming to pick me up."

"I can drive you back," said Pine.

Puller pointed to a green sedan with government plates parked at the curb a few feet away, with McElroy leaning against the front fender.

"He's already here."

They walked over to McElroy.

"How was the food?" he asked, pushing off the fender and walking toward them.

Before Puller could answer, the bullet slammed into McElroy's back, dropping him right where he had stood alive and well a second before.

11

PULLER AND PINE CROUCHED DOWN behind the sedan as more rounds sailed past them. A bullet smacked into the window glass of the sedan, shattering it. Another caromed off a metal windshield support, sending bits of shrapnel spinning away.

Puller and Pine drew their weapons and returned fire at the mouth of the alley from where the shots were coming.

Terrified people had dropped to the pavement and were screaming.

When no more shots came their way, Puller quickly checked McElroy's pulse. There was none. The man's pupils were fixed and turning glassy. His life was over.

"Shit," muttered Puller. He dialed 911 and told the dispatcher what had happened. He put the phone away and said, "You stay here with the body. I'm going after the shooter."

"Not alone, you're not."

"Don't argue. Someone has to stay with the body." He peered over the hood of the car. "Cover me."

He raced across the street while Pine did so, aiming her gun toward the alley.

When Puller disappeared down it, Pine snagged an older man in a private security uniform who was crouching behind a mailbox, showed him her badge, and told him to stay with the body until the police arrived. Then she raced after Puller.

She hit the entrance to the alley and peered down it. The space was ill lighted, but she could see about fifty feet ahead where Puller was crouched next to a dumpster. He looked behind him, spotted her, and frowned and pointed for her to go back.

She waved this look off and pointed ahead of them into the darker recesses of the alley.

Puller held up one finger and then pointed to her and then at the spot beside him.

She gave a thumbs-up. The alley was dark and quiet, with numerous places where someone could be waiting to ambush them, which meant they had to tread with care.

When he beckoned to her, she scurried forward until she was squatting next to Puller.

He snapped, "I told you to stay with the body. When I give an order I expect it to be followed."

She barked right back, "Well, in case you missed it, I'm not under your command, Puller, because I don't happen to be in the damn *Army*."

He calmed as quickly as he had angered. "Right, sorry."

She explained what she had done to protect the crime scene and McElroy's body.

"Okay, I heard one set of footsteps," he said quietly. "About a hundred feet ahead. They've stopped. No door opened, no car started."

"So he's still in the alley. It might be a dead end, then."

"Funny selection for a shooter," Puller said ominously.

"Yeah, it is."

Puller eyed the access ladder bolted to the brick wall and then looked up to see where it went.

"I'm taking the high ground. You stay down here."

"I can take care of myself," she said bluntly.

"Which is why I'm leaving you alone, down here."

"What are you going to do up there?"

"In a fight or a chase high ground is always better ground."

He hustled over to the ladder and quickly started to scale it. Pine watched him go until he reached the roof and slipped over the edge.

Pine started moving forward, in her mind's eye trying to parallel

Puller's movements above. As she left one building and moved to the next, she looked up and saw Puller leap effortlessly from that rooftop to the next. There were alleys between the buildings, but two had high chain-link fences with padlocked gates and barbed wire on top. Pine peered down a third one but it was clearly a dead end.

Three rooftops and blind or gated-off alleys later, she stopped. Her phone buzzed.

It was a text from Puller.

Dead end. A set of trash cans. He's behind them. Flush him.

Pine edged forward and peered at the line of battered trash cans.

She looked up and could see a shadow slightly darker than the night around them.

It was Puller. His gun was aimed downward right at the target.

Pine knelt down and pointed her pistol at the cans.

"FBI, throw your weapon down and come out with your hands up, fingers interlocked behind your head. Do it. Now!"

Pine could see one of the cans shaking and couldn't think of a reason why that would be. And, like Puller had pointed out before, why had this person shot McElroy from a blind alley where his escape would be cut off?

"I said to come out now. Do it. This is your last warning before we open fire."

She wasn't going to open fire because she was in no imminent danger, and Bureau rules would forbid her taking life-threatening action in such a situation.

But the guy they were chasing didn't know that.

She aimed her gun as the person slowly rose from behind the cover of the garbage cans.

He looked like a teenager. He was black, small of frame, and he was shaking, which might explain the vibrating nature of the trash can. In his right hand was a gun. The weapon was Pine's main focus because it had to be. Once that was neutralized, she could work the situation any number of ways.

"Put the gun down," she said. "You've got no chance, so you've got no choice."

The kid looked wildly around, as though he couldn't believe he was in this situation.

"Don't shoot me," he cried out.

"No one's shooting anyone," said Pine. "If you put the gun down."

"I didn't do anything."

"Put the gun down and we can talk about it. You can tell me your side of things."

He shook his head. "Nobody's going to believe me."

"I can promise to listen, if you put the gun down."

"No, lady, I can't do that. We're in deep shit."

"You'll be in a lot deeper shit if you don't put the gun down."

The kid seemed to be considering this but was obviously unsure of what to do.

"What's your name?" asked Pine. "I like to know who I'm dealing with, that's all."

"My…my name's Jerome. Jerome Blake."

"Okay, I'm Agent Pine. That's a good start, Jerome. Now if you put the gun down I can listen to your side of things."

Jerome started to tremble, and tears slid down his face. "You don't understand, lady."

"I'm trying to."

He waggled his gun hand. "Please, I—"

That was when the shot rang out.

Pine cried out, "No!"

Jerome looked over at her as though surprised by the hole that had suddenly appeared in his chest. Directly over his heart.

She looked up at the roof of the building. She couldn't see Puller up there but there was no way his position would have allowed for a shot like that.

She looked back at Blake in time to see him topple first into the trash cans and then to the dirty asphalt.

The next moment a uniformed policeman raced past Pine, his gun drawn. He was in his midforties, tall and broad shouldered, with dark hair and darker eyebrows.

He knelt next to Jerome and felt for a pulse. He looked at Pine and shook his head.

"He's gone. He was going to shoot you, ma'am."

"No, at least I didn't think he was."

The cop pointed his gun over at the building as Puller scrambled down a ladder there.

"Hold it right there," barked the cop.

"He's with me," cried out Pine. "I'm FBI. He's Army CID."

"Let me see some ID," said the cop in an edgy tone. "Now."

He looked at their creds and badges and then handed them back.

"We got a 911 about shots fired and somebody being down. Guy back on the street."

"That was us," said Pine.

"Who's the dead guy on the street back there?"

Puller said, "An Army CID agent named Ed McElroy."

"Why the hell would a kid be targeting an Army CID guy?" asked the cop.

"Wish I had the answer to that," replied Puller grimly. "But I plan to find one."

CHAPTER

12

"WELL, THANK GOD YOU WEREN'T HURT," said Carol Blum.

She was sitting in Pine's room and had just finished listening to her account of the evening's adventures.

Pine had taken off her jacket and flung it on her bed. She was sitting next to it, her gaze downcast. "But two people did die tonight, one of them an Army cop. And the other was what looked to be a sixteen-year-old kid."

"I wouldn't exactly call him a kid if he had a gun and shot someone intentionally. But why would he target McElroy?"

"Or was he actually aiming at me or Puller? Right before he was shot, McElroy stepped forward in front of us."

"I suppose that could be possible. You *are* investigating a case that might make some people nervous. And the shooter might be connected to Tony Vincenzo and his drug ring."

"The kid was scared, Carol. And something just felt off about the whole thing."

"I suppose the local cops are handling the situation?"

"Yes, but Puller's involved, too, because the victim was one of his agents."

"What did Blake say to you?"

"That he was in deep shit. That no one would believe him."

"Believe what?"

"He never got a chance to tell me." She shook her head. "But there was something, something in his features. I don't know. It just didn't fit with the situation. It was like he had no idea why he was even there or how to even hold a gun."

"What do you plan to do about it?"

"Blake probably has family around here somewhere. Maybe we can talk to them."

"But I'm sure the locals will be doing that. Won't you be encroaching on their investigation?"

"Probably," conceded Pine.

"And I can't see how what took place tonight is connected to our search for what happened to your sister."

"I can't see that it is, either," admitted Pine, gazing determinedly at her.

"But I also know that look," said Blum.

"That kid died violently right in front of me, Carol. I know stuff like that happens every day pretty much all over this country. And it's not the first time it's happened to me. But again, something just feels off and I'd like to know why."

"But you let a series of murders in Andersonville interfere with your search for your sister."

"And I helped solve them and at the same time learned a helluva lot about what happened to her. I can multitask, Carol. You should know that better than anyone."

"But still."

"Carol, the only reason I'm an FBI agent is because I want to see people who destroy other people's lives brought to justice and pay for what they did. I want the families of their victims to have closure. I want…" Pine's voice trailed off, and she slumped over and stared at the floor.

Blum said gently, "You mean you want for others what you never got for yourself?"

Pine let out a long breath and said, "I can't let this go. I can't."

"Well, as you said, we can find out who his family is and go ask questions."

"Dobbs would have a stroke if he knew I was getting involved in *another* murder case. He wants me back ASAP."

"Well, Clint Dobbs will just have to wait."

"I don't like putting you in situations like this, Carol. You work at the Bureau, too."

"I chose to come on this…mission with you. I put myself into every situation we've faced so far. And I'm fully prepared to continue doing so."

"You're going way above and beyond the call of duty."

"You're not just my boss. You're my friend, Agent Pine."

"I wish you'd just call me Atlee."

"I've been at the Bureau too long. Protocols like that are hammered into me. How will you go about finding any relatives of Jerome Blake?"

"Well, I can call Superman."

"Superman?"

"John Puller. Didn't I tell you? He's able to leap tall buildings in a single bound."

CHAPTER

13

THE FOLLOWING AFTERNOON THEY set out to visit Jerome Blake's mother. She lived in an old part of Trenton that was being gentrified. They saw this in numerous homes being remodeled and expensive late-model cars parked in the driveways of some of the newly renovated homes.

"It's good to see old neighborhoods getting new life," said Blum. "But the downside is the people who've lived here a long time get pushed out because their taxes go up. Or the home prices get out of control and a working-class family can't afford to buy."

"Nothing fair about that," said Pine.

Despite the cold, a group of young men played pickup basketball on a cracked asphalt court, pouring in three-pointers and slamming dunks through a rim with no net. As Pine and Blum passed by, some of the men stopped to watch them, their expressions not exactly friendly.

Blum said, "It's the next house on the left."

Pine pulled into the driveway of a one-story bungalow with a metal carport, under which was parked a Buick two-door. A pair of flowerpots were on the stoop. In the distance they could hear a dog barking.

"So how come Superman didn't come with us?" asked Blum. "I'd like to meet the Man of Steel."

"You will, Carol. But the fact is he's got a ton on his plate right now and superiors to answer to. I can only imagine the debriefings and paperwork John's having to do right now, what with losing an agent like that. But I told him what I planned to do, and I'll report back to him what we find."

Pine noted that the house had a fresh coat of paint and what looked like a fairly new shingled roof. The colorful curtains in the windows were warm and inviting.

They got out and walked up the sidewalk to the front stoop. Before they could knock, the door opened and a black woman in her forties stared back at them. She looked over their shoulders and said brusquely, "Come on in."

Before she stepped through the opening, Pine looked back and saw a small knot of young men gathering outside on the street in front of the house.

"Are those friends of Jerome's?" asked Pine.

"Just come on in," said the woman. After they did, she closed the door firmly behind them and locked it.

She settled them in the front living room, where the large picture window overlooked the street. Pine kept one eye there and observed that the young men were coming closer.

"You're Mrs. Blake?" began Blum.

The woman nodded, her expression both grief stricken and nerve-racked. "Cheryl Blake. Just call me Cee-Cee, everybody does."

"We're very sorry about Jerome," said Pine.

"On the phone you told me that you were there," Blake said, her voice cracking. "When it happened."

She pulled a tissue from her pocket and dabbed at her eyes, which were red and angry looking. She had on a long sweatshirt and black running tights and tennis shoes with ankle socks. She was about five four with a strong, athletic build. Muscles in her neck flexed and receded as she spoke.

Pine said, "Yes, I was there. I tried to talk him into putting his gun down."

"But you wasn't the one to shoot him."

"No. That was a local police officer. But another man was killed. An Army investigator. I'm trying to understand what, if any, connection Jerome had to that."

"The police came by late last night. To let me know about Jerome. And to ask questions. And they came by again this morning. They took stuff from his room."

"Do you have other children?" asked Blum.

"Two. My oldest, Willie. He's on his own now. Living and working in Delaware. And then I got Jewel. She's in middle school. Only fourteen. She's upstairs sleeping. Cried her eyes out all night. She loved her brother."

"I'm sure she did," said Blum.

Pine interjected, "Jerome had a gun last night. A Glock. Have you ever seen that weapon around here?"

"Cops asked the same thing and I'll tell you what I told them, Jerome didn't have no gun. He never wanted a gun and he didn't have one," she added fiercely.

"Well, he had one last night. I'm just trying to piece things together."

Blake eyed her suspiciously. "You say you're with the government? You got something that says that?"

Pine pulled out her cred pack and badge and showed them to Blake. "I'm with the FBI. I was meeting with another Army investigator when the shooting happened. We're working the case together."

"What you want me to tell you?"

"What did you tell the police?"

"The truth, but they don't want to believe it."

"I'd like to hear it," said Pine.

Blake settled back in her chair and rubbed her eyes and blew her nose into the tissue. Then her softened features turned hard and her expression became fierce.

"Look, I'm not stupid, okay? I know the police come here and think, 'Okay, here we damn well go again. Same old shit. Black man kills a white man, so he got what he deserved.' But see, the picture here is different. Way different."

"Tell me," said Pine.

"For starters, Jerome was smart, real smart, the smart that you're born with and then you get smarter by sucking up all the information you can. He got straight As in school. He was going to college, already getting scholarship offers and he's still a junior. Because of his *brain*," she added sharply.

"Okay," said Pine. "Keep going."

"Now, the police came here and start telling me that what happened last night is because Jerome was doing some gang thing. Kill someone. Kill a fed, they said. Initiation shit."

"They actually said that to you?" asked Pine incredulously.

"Sure as I'm sitting here talking to you."

"And you didn't believe that?" said Blum.

"Course I didn't 'cause it isn't true. There are gangs all over this damn place. Everybody knows that. Look out the window, they're out there right now. My oldest boy, he was in a gang. But he got out. Only reason Willie moved away. Hell, I *made* him go. I don't want that for my kids. Too many getting shot and buried before they're even grown. My husband's dead now fourteen years. He was just coming home from the grocery store with ice cream for me 'cause I was pregnant with Jewel and I needed something cold. He went out for damn ice cream and ended up in a box just 'cause he was walking down the street late at night with a brown paper bag and some cops driving by had a problem with that. They said he resisted arrest, that he was going for one of their guns, and they shot him. Yeah, he was going for their guns all right. Bullshit."

"Was there an investigation?"

"Oh yeah. Took all of like a week. Justifiable shooting, they said. Feared for their damn lives, even though it was four against one. Those cops went right back to work. They might still be out there for all I know. Shooting people for carrying damn ice cream."

"I'm so sorry to hear that."

"But Jerome never wanted no part of any of that. He was home every night doing his schoolwork. He was on the Honor Roll. He wanted to be whatchacallit when he graduated. You know, number one?"

"Valedictorian?" suggested Blum.

"Yeah, valedictorian. And he was gonna be, sure as I'm sitting here. So he didn't have time for gangs. They got a robotics team at the school. Jerome was head of the whole damn thing. They won the state competition last year."

"That's all very impressive," said Pine. "But it doesn't account for him being in an alley across from where a man was shot. Or him running from the scene with a gun. That's what I want to work through. How was he when he came home from school yesterday? Did he seem troubled or anything?"

Blake nodded her head. "He came home looking all upset and worried. I asked him what was wrong. He said, 'Momma, I messed up on a test. Missed a couple questions.' I told him that ain't the end of the world. He looked at me funny, like…like maybe it was." She pulled a fresh tissue from her pocket, dabbed at her eyes, and looked down, shaking her head. "I can't believe this is happening. I can't believe my baby's gone. Not Jerome." She started to rock and moan. "Lord help me, not Jerome."

"Momma?"

They all turned to see a tall, athletic girl around fourteen at the bottom of the stairs. She was dressed in a set of two-piece pajamas and her eyes were red from crying.

"Momma, please don't cry."

Blake jumped up and wiped her eyes. "Oh, baby, Momma's okay. Just blubbering a little bit." She turned to Pine. "This is Jewel. Jewel, these ladies are with the FBI. They're here to help find out what happened to your brother."

Jewel looked at Pine and Blum, turned, and fled back upstairs.

Blake watched her go, her lips trembling. "Poor baby. Poor baby. Our lives just turned upside down. I didn't let her go to school today, of course." She shook her head. "I don't know when I'll send her back. I don't want to let her outta my sight."

Blum rose and put her hand on her shoulder and gently rubbed it. "This is every mother's worst nightmare," said Blum. "I am so sorry."

Blake sniffled and said, "You got kids?"

"Yes. All grown, some with children of their own and their own problems. Some I can help with, some I can't, so I just worry. You never stop being a parent. Not until you take your last breath."

"That's the truth, honey. That is the truth." She patted Blum's hand and composed herself while Blum retook her seat.

"When did he leave the house yesterday?" asked Pine after a few moments of silence.

"After dinner. He told me he got to run back to school to work on a robot. It's just down the street from here. He said the principal said it was okay. I don't like him being out at night around here. But Jewel was feeling sick and I was taking care of her, so I just told him to call me when he got there and call me when he was leaving. But I was still worried about him."

"So he had a cell phone?" asked Pine.

"Oh, yeah. He bought it himself. Worked for a company over the summer building gadgets and such."

"No cell phone was found on him," said Pine. "Did he call you last night?"

Blake's eyes filled with tears and she shook her head. "He *texted* me around seven. Say, 'Momma, I'm at the school.' And he'd let me know when he was coming home. When he wasn't back by ten, I texted him. Then I called. No answer. I was starting to get real worried. I was gonna go looking for him. Then the police showed up to tell me my baby boy was dead."

She jumped up and hurried into the adjacent room, where they could hear her sobbing.

Blum rose and said, "I'll see if she has any tea or coffee and make her a cup. Give me a few minutes alone with her."

Pine nodded as Blum walked into the other room.

Pine went over to the window and looked out. The young men had now surrounded her car and were showing it uncomfortable interest.

She walked out the front door to face them.

CHAPTER

14

"CAN I HELP YOU?" asked Pine as she stood on the front side-walk staring at the group. To a person they all stared back at her. The oldest looked to be early twenties, the youngest fourteen or so. It was one thirty in the afternoon, so Pine wondered why the school-aged among them were not where they should have been. She could read in their eyes and attitudes one very clear reality: They didn't trust anyone who wore a badge.

She asked her question again.

None of them answered her. Again. They just stared.

She took a few steps forward, acutely aware of the delicacy of the situation. She didn't move her hand close to her Glock, though it was visible to all of them, as was the shiny FBI shield that she had pinned to her belt. Pine knew it was not impenetrable protection, not here, maybe nowhere anymore.

"Did any of you know Jerome Blake?"

"He's dead. Cops shot him."

This came from a boy in the back, around fifteen, hair cut near to the scalp, wiry build, features hardened beyond his years. But not for a place like this. For a place like this, he was probably just right.

She said, "Jerome had a gun. He might have shot someone."

"Jerome didn't shoot nobody."

This came from the oldest looking of the group.

"Okay, tell me why you think that."

"Who the hell are you anyway?" said the man.

"I'm a federal cop. And I was there when the man was shot and Jerome was killed. Now I'm looking into it."

"You kill him?" said the man, with menace in his tone and tensed features. The rest of the group, taking their vibe from him, assumed that same angry posture. Pine could sense the mob mentality emerging just enough to make her situation grow increasingly untenable.

Pine said calmly, "No, I was trying to talk him into dropping the gun. Because he *had* a gun. I saw it. I'm not saying he did anything with it, but he had it. A Glock. His mother says Jerome never had a gun."

"She's right about that. Robot man ain't never had no gun."

The rest of the group chortled at this remark.

Pine nodded. "Right. He built robots. He was smart. He said he was going back to school last night to work on robots. Only that apparently didn't happen. I'd like to understand what *did* happen. Did any of you see anything? Do you know where he might have gotten the gun?"

"Cops already got their story. They ain't looking nowhere else."

"Gang initiation, you mean?" said Pine. "Jerome's mother told me that's what the police said. You apparently don't believe that."

In a scoffing tone the man said, "'Cause it's not true. Jerome ain't in no gang."

"But was a gang trying to get him to join?"

"Why would they?" said the man. "They got all the meat they need. And you got to look at things smart."

"How do you mean?"

"Jerome was strong up here," said the man, pointing to his head. "But with books and robots and shit like that. Thing is, gangs got all the sorts of smarts *they* need. Jerome ain't smart that way. Not street way. So what they want is muscle, someone who's tough and don't give a shit, and brothers willing to carry a gun and do what needs doing with it. That's not Jerome. No gang would want him. To them, he's just a book punk they got no use for." He grinned and added, "Shit, be like hiring Bill Gates to guard their stash, see what I mean?"

"Okay. Anything else you can tell me? Did any of you see Jerome last night? Did he text or phone any of you saying what he was going to do?"

The people in the group looked at one another. Finally, the youngest of them took a hesitant step forward. "He texted me last night."

"What time and what did he say?"

The boy pulled out his phone. "Seven ten. He said he got something to do but he didn't want to do it."

"Did he say what that was?"

"No. I texted him back and asked him, but he said he can't tell me. But he said he was worried 'cause it might go all bad."

"That what might go all bad?"

"He didn't say."

She looked at the others. "No one else saw Jerome last night, or talked to him?"

No one said anything in response, though Pine did focus for a moment on a guy around sixteen who stood off to the side. He had been staring at her but then glanced down when she'd asked her question.

"Anybody have the name of someone I should talk to about this? A friend of Jerome's? Someone he might have confided in?"

Again, no one said anything.

"Well, thanks for the information," she said.

"Now what you gonna do with it?" snapped the man.

"Follow it to the truth. If Jerome did nothing wrong, then I'll clear his name. For what that's worth."

"Sure you will," said the man sarcastically. "Cops are cops. All stick together."

"I'm more of a loner. I'm actually stationed out in Arizona. I'm usually the only cop around out there. I go my own way and sometimes, for better or worse, make my own rules."

"What you doing here then?"

"Looking for answers." She eyed him. "Story of my life."

As she turned and headed back to the house the man called out, "Hey, good luck, *Arizona.*"

She looked back at him. "I'll take all the luck I can get."

15

When Pine returned to the house, Blum and Blake were sitting in the front room and Blake was sipping on a cup of tea.

Blum eyed Pine curiously.

"I was just having a chat with some of Jerome's 'acquaintances,'" she explained as she sat down. "They don't think he was involved in any gang thing, either."

Blake bristled. "That 'cause he wasn't, like I told you. But the police don't see it that way. I told them Jerome was top of his class. That he was going to college. They looked at me like I was speaking Chinese."

"That must have made you very upset," said Blum.

"Damn right it did. But they just gonna sweep it under the rug, you mark my words."

"Not if I have anything to say about it," said Pine.

Blake looked at her squarely. "What you gonna do about it? Your boss say back off, then you gonna back off, right?"

"Wrong," Blum answered for her. "That is not how Agent Pine operates. And she is not part of the local police. She will see this through."

Pine said, "Is there anything else you can tell us? Did Jerome ever mention someone named Tony Vincenzo?"

Blake shook her head. "Never heard that name. He Mexican?"

"Italian-American."

"No. Nobody with that name lives around here, least that I know of. And Jerome never mentioned him to me."

"Until yesterday, did Jerome seem okay?"

"Yeah. He went off to school all happy and everything."

"But when he got home he was upset. And you don't think it was about missing questions on a test?"

"I know it wasn't that."

"So whatever made him do what he did last night, it happened between the time he left here yesterday morning and when he came home?"

"Must have been," agreed Blake.

Pine looked at Blum. "So we need to find out what that was."

"Do we go to his school then?" asked Blum.

"It's a start."

The high school was about a half mile from where the Blakes lived. A new football field had been erected, and the façade of the building had been power-washed. And a new adjacent building was set off from the main building. The landscaping looked abundant and well planned out. She hoped the classroom, students, and teachers had gotten the same level of support.

They headed to the main office and Pine's badge got them in to see the principal.

Her name was Norma Bailey. She was a tall black woman with iron-gray hair pulled back in a severe bun. She had the no-nonsense manner of someone long used to having to corral and attempt to control and finally to teach legions of teenagers.

"I heard about poor Jerome," she began, her expression full of sadness. "I wish I could say I can't believe it, but shootings have become so frequent. People just see one on the news and the next day there's another. People are becoming desensitized to the whole thing, and that is an abysmal development."

"But you would be surprised it would involve Jerome?" said Pine.

"Yes, I'm afraid I wasn't clear on that point. Jerome..." She shook her head and touched her trembling lips with a shaky hand before regaining her composure. "He was one of the brightest students we had. He was destined for an important role in life. He would have gone very far. He was an absolute genius in math and science. He could understand things even the teachers couldn't, and we have two math PhDs here. A certifiable prodigy."

"We understand he was the head of the robotics team," said Blum.

"Yes. That's housed in the new building on the school grounds. They won the state last year. It was very exciting. Jerome...he loved his robots, that was clear. He could build them with such...*flair*." She dabbed at her eyes with her fingers and said, "How can I help you?"

"We've learned from Jerome's mother that he was fine when he went to school yesterday, but he wasn't when he got home. He mentioned something about a test and that he had missed some questions."

"No, that couldn't be. There were no tests in any class yesterday. It was a prep day for upcoming exams."

"Okay, then he wasn't truthful with his mother. Something else was bothering him. And from the timeline it seems that it happened while he was at school."

"I can't imagine what that might have been."

"Can we speak with his teachers?" asked Pine.

"Certainly, I can arrange that."

"Have the police been in to talk to you?" asked Blum.

"No. They haven't been by."

Pine and Blum exchanged a troubled look.

An hour later they had spoken with all of Jerome's teachers. None of them could recall anything that might have led Jerome to do what he allegedly had. They all expressed shock and sorrow, but provided no useful information.

As they left the school, Pine glanced to her right. "I know him. He was outside the Blakes' house this morning."

The person Pine was referring to was sitting on the fence surrounding the new football field.

Pine and Blum walked over to him.

Pine said, "You looked like you knew something but didn't want to say earlier."

The young man jumped down and faced them. He was about Pine's height, lean, and looked as tough as a piece of iron. His face held a jagged scar, and part of one of his fingers was missing.

"Did you know Jerome?"

"Yeah."

"What's your name?"

He shrugged.

"You followed us here, didn't you? So you must have *something* to tell us."

He looked over her shoulder.

"We think Jerome met someone yesterday who made him do whatever he did last night. Do you know anything about that?"

"Maybe."

"Maybe you do?" prompted Pine.

"See a man talkin' to him yesterday."

"Here at the school?"

He nodded.

"Do you go here?" asked Pine.

He shook his head. "Ain't go to school."

"You graduated?" asked Blum.

He shrugged, grinned, and said nothing.

"Did you recognize the man he was talking to?"

"Uh-uh."

"What time of day was it?"

"'Bout two." He pointed. "Saw 'em talkin' over there."

"What did the man look like?"

"White dude. Tall guy with big shoulders."

"Age?"

"Forties, maybe. Dark hair."

"How was he dressed?"

"Pants and a shirt."

"Tie?"

He shook his head.

"You think he worked here?"

"Don't know."

"If we can get some pictures together, do you think you could recognize him again?"

"Maybe."

"What's your name?" she asked again.

"Peanut. What they call me on the street."

"How well did you know Jerome?"

"We real tight till a while back."

"What happened?"

"I quit going to school and he didn't."

Pine said, "How did Jerome seem when he and the man parted company?"

"Jerome, he walked off, looking at his shoes. Seemed jumpy to me. Weird, y'know?"

"Do you think Jerome would have shot anyone?"

He cracked a smile. "Shit, lady, Jerome don't know how to kill nobody."

CHAPTER

16

THEY HAD GONE BACK INTO the school and asked Norma Bailey if she could put together a photo book and background information of the school employees. She told them that they had it digitally, but it would take her some time to get the necessary permissions to release that information. She added that she would contact Pine when it was ready.

After that they climbed into their car and drove off.

Three minutes later Pine said quietly, "We picked up a tail. Silver Mercury Marquis. Don't look, Carol!"

Blum caught herself halfway through turning around. "Sorry, Agent Pine. Can you tell who it might be?"

Pine slowed down a bit to let the car catch up and she eyed it through the rearview mirror. "Okay, now I can make out the plate. It looks like a New Jersey state plate."

"Can you make out the tag number?"

"Yes. Write it down."

Pine told her the plate number and Blum inputted it on her phone.

"Just a driver or more?"

"A pair."

"You're sure they're following us?"

"Well, we can find out."

She hung a sharp left, hit the gas, roared through an intersection, and then hung a right.

She peered into the rearview again. "They got caught at the light, but they were following us all right."

She hit a speed dial on her phone. Puller didn't answer.

"Why do you think they were tailing us?" said Blum.

"They want to see what leads we're following up."

"Did you notice them while we were at the Blakes'?"

"No, but I wasn't looking, either."

"So someone from the state government is interested," opined Blum.

"That guy who gave Puller the third degree was with the *federal* government, not the state."

"But still the 'government.' Talk about a dog biting its own tail."

"There might be more to it than that, Carol."

"This doesn't have the feel of the typical government turf fight."

"It has the feel of criminal *collusion*."

Her phone buzzed. It was Puller.

He said, "This case has thrown another curve at us."

"Why, what happened?"

"Teddy Vincenzo was found dead in his cell this morning."

"What! How?"

"Prelim is suicide or drug overdose. They found him dead when they were doing a head count."

"You can't believe that."

"No, I don't believe it. I checked his records and photos of him when he went into prison. Not a needle track anywhere on his person, no tooth, nostril, or gum decay, no indication that he was a user. And when we saw him in person, he had no signs of being a user. Second, and most importantly, the timing is a little suspicious."

"Don't they have cameras in the prison?" asked Pine.

"They do. I asked about that. Unfortunately, the camera in question was not in operation. They apparently have a maintenance backlog."

"That's highly convenient. And if they were doing their head count, he died presumably early this morning, but you only found out recently."

Puller said, "I doubt they care about keeping me in the loop. I only found out because I was working another channel to get back in to see him. That's when I was told it was a no-go because he was dead."

"Damn, that is definitely a curveball all right."

"So they took out the father," said Puller.

"Which means the son now sits squarely in the crosshairs."

"We need to find Tony Vincenzo fast, before he bites it, too," he said.

"FYI, we picked up a tail today. Whether it was at the Blakes' home or at the school where we went to see if anything there might have precipitated what happened, I'm not sure. But it was a silver Mercury Marquis with New Jersey state government plates."

"You get the tag number?" Puller asked.

Pine read it off to Puller from Blum's phone screen.

"I'll check that out."

Pine said, "The people I spoke to, including Blake's mother, said the cops think it was some gang thing, maybe an initiation. But these same people were also pretty sure Jerome didn't even know how to fire a gun, much less make a shot like that last night."

"It all stinks. The local cops have pretty much closed the case. They're not looking anywhere else."

"You know we could have been the targets last night, right?" pointed out Pine.

"The thought had occurred to me, yes."

"His mother said he was going back to school to work on a robotics project, but that wasn't true. And he lied about messing up a test to explain away why he was worried when he got home from school. And then an old friend of Jerome's told us that Jerome had been approached by some guy at school, and it made him upset and nervous. I'm trying to run down a lead on that now."

"What if someone got to him and made him show up in the alley, gave him a gun, and told him to run after he heard the shots?"

"How could they make him do that?" wondered Pine.

"That's for us to find out."

"Have they even confirmed that the gun he had was the murder weapon?"

"Not that anyone's told me," said Puller in disgust.

"Wait a minute, who's doing the post and forensics? Surely CID people."

"All I can tell you is that the local cops took the gun and Jerome Blake's body and left us with McElroy's remains."

"But, Puller, how could that happen? A CID agent was the vic; that makes it *your* case, or at the very least gets you in the loop."

"I made that argument last night and this morning and ran into a stone wall. Something about working with local cops to build trust and camaraderie."

"That's bullshit," snapped Pine.

"It *is* bullshit. And my superiors up the line at CID think the same thing. But apparently orders on this came from up high, maybe past the uniforms and into the land of the suits."

"What in the hell is going on here, Puller?"

"A cover-up of epic proportions. And for that to happen, there has to be a matching motivation. On a scale of one to ten, I'd put the possibilities here squarely in the double-digit range."

"We need to find out what that is."

"I hope I get the chance."

Pine's jaw eased down. "You mean—"

"I wouldn't be surprised in the least if I get pulled from the case."

"What will you do if that happens?" she asked.

"I'm not sure. This has only happened to me once in my career. I never expected that it would happen again."

"What did you do when it happened the first time?"

"Something I shouldn't have," he replied.

"And what will you do if it does happen again?"

Puller didn't answer.

CHAPTER

17

Superman might have just gotten a dose of kryptonite," said Pine quietly as she put her phone down. "He's afraid he's going to get pulled from the case."

Blum absorbed this worrying information. "Anything else?"

"Yep, and it's a stunner. Teddy Vincenzo's dead. They say it's a suicide or a drug overdose. Puller obviously doesn't believe it. And neither do I."

"I gathered that he was dead from the snatches of conversation I heard."

"And the local cops have taken over the Jerome Blake case and they have the gun. John was left with McElroy's body and that's it."

"Will he let that stand?"

"He got pushback from high up, perhaps beyond the military." She glanced at Blum. "The suits outrank the uniforms in our system."

"Well, it seems the cover-up has started, big-time."

"I think it started a long time ago, actually."

"What do we do now while Puller is trying to figure this out and we wait to get the photos for our witness to look at?"

"I've got a resource I can call on."

"Who's that?"

"The FBI has an RA in Trenton," said Pine. "I know one of the agents, Rick Davies. Let's see what he can find out for us."

She brought Davies up on her list of phone contacts and made the call. Davies answered, and she told him the situation and what she wanted.

"You officially engaged in this?" Davies asked. "I thought you were in Arizona."

"I was there when the shooting happened. I'm working with Army CID on the case."

"Oh, okay. I'll see what I can find out. Just to warn you, the Trenton cops positively do not like feds sniffing around their backyard."

"Show me a local cop who does."

She put down the phone and looked over at Blum.

"Now what?" asked Blum.

"Until we hear back from Puller or Davies or the school principal, we focus on another Vincenzo. Ito."

Blum put her hands together and looked attentive.

Pine began, "Let's look at this logically. Either Ito killed Mercy..." She paused, stiffening at her own words, and clenched her hands for an instant before relaxing and turning to Blum. "Or he abandoned her somewhere."

"Or he gave her to someone," added Blum.

Pine looked startled by Blum's suggestion but quickly moved on. "Now, Mercy's DNA is in a database at the FBI. Samples of all unidentified remains discovered anywhere in the U.S. are sent to that database for comparison checks. None have turned up that matched Mercy's. I know that for a fact."

"Was that your doing?" asked Blum.

"Yes."

"What did you give them for Mercy's DNA sample?"

"I'm her twin, Carol. I gave them a sample of *my* DNA. They put it in the database."

"Of course, that was stupid of me. But that's good news, then. No remains have matched her DNA."

"Yes. But her remains might not have been found yet. And we can't be sure that every agency across the country sends samples into the database. I'm sure some of them don't, or a processing mistake was made. Or maybe she was taken out of the country and killed there."

"Still, the odds are with you on that."

"Now, if he *had* abandoned her, you would think someone would have found her, either dead or alive. She might have died from exposure or from animal attacks if she was left in some wooded terrain, which they have a lot of in rural Georgia. She could have starved to death or died from an accident."

"But if so, you would think her remains would have been found by now."

"Bodies out in the elements tend to disappear fast, Carol. Natural decomp, animal intrusion, if she fell into a river and got lodged on something at the bottom, lots of factors."

Pine suddenly looked like she might be ill.

Blum said quickly, "But once more you have to look at the odds. And unless Ito had checked out a place beforehand to leave her, I doubt a guy from Trenton, New Jersey, and who had probably never been to Georgia, knew very much about places to abandon or get rid of her down there."

"Well, according to what we found out while we were in Andersonville, he was in Georgia for a few months at the very least."

"So are you leaning towards her having been abandoned?"

Pine rubbed her head and looked uncertainly at her friend. "That wouldn't dovetail with the letter we read from Bruno. He was clearly pissed. He wanted revenge."

Now Blum looked uncertain. "The only thing that cuts against that is everything we've learned about Ito thus far. It takes a lot to kill someone. It takes a lot more to kill a defenseless child."

"He could have been driven to it by his love for his brother. By what happened to him."

"May I play devil's advocate?" said Blum.

"Please do."

"How do we know that Ito loved Bruno? We've found no evidence of that."

"Well, he went down to Georgia and took my sister and nearly killed me and then accused my father of the crimes."

"Okay, let's assume that is true. But the life he led before was polar opposite to his brother's. And remember what Castor told us. He *knew* Bruno was a bad guy."

"But he said he learned that from Evie, *not* Ito."

"And you don't think husband and wife were in agreement on that? I think they clearly were, from what we've learned."

Pine thought about this for a moment. "Castor also told us that he never met Bruno."

"That's right. He worked for Ito all those years. Was with him every day all day, and Ito's brother, who presumably lived in the area, or at least in New York City, never came by for a visit?"

Pine said, "And Evie's neighbor didn't like Bruno, either. And she said Evie hated him. Wouldn't allow him in the house. And Ito didn't object to that. The neighbor said Ito didn't like Bruno."

"Exactly my point."

"Then why go down to Georgia at all and do what he did?" said a puzzled Pine.

"It might come down to what we read in the letter. It didn't say much, but it did tell us that Bruno had maybe tried to do the decent thing for once in his life—not turn in a mole that was going after the Mafia families—and he ended up getting screwed. Maybe that just snapped something inside Ito. That sounds more plausible than trying to make Ito some cold-blooded killer on a rampage. Because that does not square with what everyone has told us about him."

Pine sat back and pondered all of this. "I checked the police records. Before Ito came down to Georgia, Teddy was charged with grand theft auto and got prison time."

"So Ito perhaps had in his mind that Teddy was going down the same path that Bruno had?"

Pine said, "It's possible. And that might have fueled his fire to do what he did. Remember what he told Castor, that he'd done something that 'shocked him.' "

"So it was a confused and perhaps conflicted man who came down to Georgia, then?"

"I can't feel sympathy for him, Carol. Never."

"I'm not asking you to. But we need to understand the man at that moment in time because it will help us better arrive at what he might have done with your sister."

Pine's expression became agitated. "To finish our line of reasoning, if he didn't kill her or abandon her, he might have given her to someone, like you suggested."

"Human trafficking, then?"

"No, to take a page from your book, in coming to understand the man, I doubt Ito knew anything at all about human trafficking. Now, his brother might have, but he was dead by then. And I don't see Ito gabbing it up with the dregs of the organized crime family his brother once worked for in order to get input on where to sell little kids."

Blum said, "But if he gave her to, say, a family, wouldn't Mercy just tell the family who she was and that she had been kidnapped? The account of what happened I'm sure made the press all over Georgia, if not the country. Her picture was probably everywhere. They either would have taken her in and then called the police, or just called the police right off the bat when Ito came by with her." She hesitated and then plunged on. "So maybe Ito gave her to someone by *prearrangement*."

"We just discussed that—human trafficking."

"No, not human trafficking. Just a family perhaps in desperate need of a child."

Pine looked at her. "What? But they would know—"

"They would know only what Ito told them. He could have lied about her background, how he came to have her. Maybe they thought they were doing good by taking her in."

"But wouldn't Mercy have rebelled at that? Told them who she was, what had happened to her, just like you said, Carol? Now you're arguing against your own position."

"No, I'm just trying to look at it from different perspectives. Now, even a precocious six-year-old can be made to believe and accept things that no adult ever would," said Blum. "We don't know what Ito told her. That her life could depend on her accepting her conditions. Or he could have threatened harm to you or her parents if she didn't do as she was told."

Pine sighed and slumped back against the car seat. "All of that makes perfect sense. Maybe more sense than any other explanation." Pine fell silent, but as she sat there her expression changed, evolving from hopeless to curious.

"What?" said Blum, who knew her so well.

"Two questions. First, in the letter Bruno Vincenzo said he got screwed over. What do you really think he meant by that?" When Blum shook her head, Pine said, "I think he didn't rat my mom out because he wanted to cut a deal and save himself. Only that deal didn't happen. I wonder why."

"And the second question?"

"One I've voiced before: How the hell did Ito Vincenzo know we were in Andersonville, Georgia?"

CHAPTER

18

THIS SHOULD NEVER HAVE HAPPENED. You shouldn't be dead.

John Puller was staring down at the body of CID Special Agent Ed McElroy.

My agent, my responsibility. Buck stopped with no one other than me. No excuses.

His wife, and now widow, had been notified of his death and was on her way here to confront the absolute worst reality a spouse would ever have to face.

Puller left the facility and returned to his car. He drove across town to the police building, where he had been informed the investigative unit that was handling the shooting and Jerome Blake's death was stationed. He met a stonewall at the front reception desk despite showing his creds, badge, clear connection to the case, and earnest manner in wanting to understand what was going on with the local side of the investigation.

The sergeant, who was called in to handle the situation when Puller had deemed the first two officers insufficiently senior and uninformed, seemed finally to take pity on him.

"Army, huh?" said the man, giving Puller the once-over with a pair of scrutinizing eyes.

"Chief warrant officer."

"West Point?"

"No. I'm enlisted. Noncommissioned officer. My father went to West Point, but I chose another path."

"My youngest boy's in Iraq now," the sergeant said, letting his guard down a bit. "Been there about six months now. Did you fight over there?"

Puller nodded. "Came back with metal inside me I didn't start out life with. But it was a privilege and honor to serve my country."

The cop, hefty and broad shouldered but with a softening expression on his features, nodded. "Hope my boy comes back in one piece."

"Nothing about combat is safe, but the Army takes great pains to train their people for every situation and provide the best equipment to do the job."

"Good to know, Agent Puller. And we all appreciate you serving our country." He looked around. "Um, look, let me check on something. You hang right there, sir."

While he stepped away Puller eyed the small space. It had photos of the current police commissioner, mayor, governor, and president. They all smiled at him from their official portraits. He had nothing to smile back about. What was happening to him right now made no sense, but it apparently made perfect sense to others. And that disturbed the hell out of him.

"Can I help you?"

Puller turned to see a petite young woman who looked to be in her late twenties standing behind the desk, the hefty cop nowhere in sight. She had large brown eyes and short dark hair that revealed a slender, freckled neck. The ID lanyard around that neck identified her as being with the public affairs office. The large eyes were looking at him questioningly.

Puller came forward and put out his hand. "CID Special Agent John Puller."

She didn't shake his hand. "I know who you are, Agent Puller. I'm just wondering why you're here. I'm very busy, so I hope it's nothing complicated because I really can't spare the time. I'm sure you can understand."

Every hair on the back of Puller's neck stood up at her mindless and condescending statement. "One of my men was shot last night here in Trenton. I'm working the case in conjunction with the local police here."

"I'm aware of the unfortunate death of Agent McElroy." She stopped there and continued to stare at him as though challenging him to come up with a reason why their conversation should be extended.

"We're doing the post on him now. We'll have a bullet to provide to your unit to match to the murder weapon, which you have in your custody."

"There's no question about who killed your agent and what gun was used to do it," she pointed out.

"There are a great many questions to resolve," replied Puller. He took a step forward, cutting in half the distance between them. He glanced at the name on the lanyard. "So, Ms. Lanier, I'm here to discuss the investigation with your people. That's how it's done on a joint case like this. Surely you're aware of that."

"I wasn't *aware* it was a *joint* case."

"How can it not be?" Puller shot back in a harsher tone than he probably intended at this point in the sniffing-out exercise that was taking place between the two. "A federal agent was shot and killed. One of your men shot the alleged killer. I'm sorry if you don't want to hear a complicated case, but this clearly is one."

"He shot the shooter—saving an FBI agent in the process, if I recall correctly."

"Maybe."

"What do you mean, 'maybe'? It's clear that's what happened."

"I wish it were as clear to me. But that's why we investigate. So I'd like to talk to him and—"

"Why?"

"Why what?"

"Why do you need to talk to him?"

The question was so odd and out of bounds that it gave Puller, a seasoned investigator if ever there was one, pause. "He fired his weapon. He was involved in what happened. He might have seen things pertinent to the investigation."

"I believe he filed his report."

"Can I see it?"

"I'm not sure that's possible."

"And I'm not sure what you're saying makes any sense at all. You can't deny me a look at his report."

She shrugged off this rebuke. "Difference of opinion."

"Difference of reality," said Puller, taking the kid gloves off because it was clear that approach was akin to attacking an aircraft carrier with a jet ski.

"I don't like your tone."

"And I don't like being cut out of an investigation in which I have a clear reason to be involved."

"You may not understand how we do things here."

"On the contrary, I've worked two cases with the Trenton police and three with the New Jersey State Police and one case with the Newark cops. I received nothing but the highest professionalism and the fullest cooperation, with the result that we successfully cleared every single case."

"Well, I think we have things well in hand on this one. We have the shooter. He's dead. Case couldn't be clearer. It's over and done with."

"Excuse me, are you a trained investigator? Because your ID says 'public affairs.'"

"I have been briefed on the matter."

"Which is more than I can say," retorted Puller.

"I think you know all you need to know about the case. It's been resolved, Agent Puller. You can freely move on to other *unsolved* cases."

"Your opinion on the matter, unfortunately, carries no weight with me since you were clearly plucked out to come here and tell me absolutely nothing."

"I'm doing my job," she shot back.

"So am I—at least I'm trying to, but you're not helping."

"I didn't know that it was my job to help you. But, regardless, I wish you good luck in whatever you're doing."

Puller held out his card. "If anything occurs to you, I'd appreciate a call."

She didn't take it. Lanier turned and walked back through a doorway, closing it hard behind her.

A moment later the hefty cop appeared from another door.

"How did it go, Agent Puller?" he asked hopefully.

"It didn't," replied Puller as he turned and walked out into a gathering storm. It was not nearly as intense as the one going on inside his head.

CHAPTER

19

Over the phone Jack Lineberry sounded weak and a bit depressed. He'd known both of Pine's parents for decades. Pine had recently learned that he'd worked with a government agency back then on the sting operation against the mob in which Pine's mother acted as a mole. Lineberry had been sent to Andersonville to watch over them, a mission at which he'd failed. Since then, he'd become extremely wealthy through an investment company he had started.

And Pine had also learned that Jack Lineberry was her and Mercy's *father*, having conceived them with their mother before she met the man Pine thought had been her father, Tim Pine.

"Jack, are you okay?" asked Pine in a worried tone.

She had put her phone on speaker so that Blum could listen in.

"Just a bad day. Some infection, they said, and a bit of pain accompanying."

"Wait a minute, are you still in the hospital? I thought they were releasing you."

"They've assured me it's nothing serious, but they are keeping me a while longer, as a precautionary measure."

"Are they *sure* it's not serious?"

"Yes, just typical postsurgery stuff, but I'm feeling claustrophobic. I just want out of here. Hence, my mood is not all that good."

"Hang in there, Jack. They need to make sure you're good to go."

"Where are you?"

"Trenton."

"Ito Vincenzo, then?" he said.

"Yes. We've found out a few things and had some curveballs thrown our way."

"Such as?"

Pine said, "Such as Ito's grandson, Tony, is a fleeing fugitive. And Ito's son and Tony's dad, Teddy, was just murdered in prison shortly after I spoke with him."

To his credit, Lineberry did not sound shocked by any of this. "Life is full of curveballs, Atlee," he said quietly. "And I surely speak from experience on that."

"Which is why I'm calling you for some help."

Lineberry said, "Your call could not have been better timed. It will give me something to do while I wait for the next bad meal they're going to serve me today."

Pine told him about the letter they had found in Evie Vincenzo's closet.

"What?" gasped Lineberry. "That sounds like Bruno knew about your mother's working with us."

His heavy breathing was making her worried. Pine said, "I don't think you're in a condition to hear any more."

"No, no, I'm…I'm fine, please go on."

"I take it you didn't know that Bruno might have known about my mom."

Lineberry said disgustedly, "Bruno Vincenzo was a cold-blooded killer. If I had known that, I would have pulled the plug on the whole op in a New York minute."

"He said he didn't rat out my mom, but that *he* was screwed over. He made it sound like he had worked a deal where he would get some sort of immunity but that it didn't come through."

"I can't believe that, I really can't. But you have to understand that I was kept out of the loop on the legal end of things. I'm not a lawyer. My job was to watch over your mother. Any deal would have to have been made with the prosecutors, the folks at the FBI, and ultimately the Justice Department. Not with me. But still, I would have been made aware of it, or at least I should have been. Bruno knowing about your mother's real role comes squarely down on the operation's side. That was my jurisdiction. If the lawyers did cut such a deal and didn't tell us? Well, it would have been incredibly stupid. If we had known we would have changed how we engineered the whole op. I guess we could have used Bruno as an asset. Not that I would have ever trusted the son of a bitch."

"He eventually *did* turn state's evidence," pointed out Pine.

"Right, only to save his own ass. And he failed at that, and you won't find me crying over it. That guy probably had the blood of at least fifty people on his hands. Good riddance."

"But assuming that Bruno's having found out about my mother's undercover status *was* relayed to the prosecutors, why *wouldn't* they have struck a deal with him? I mean, he had leverage. He could have blown the whole investigation, like you said. He could have put my mother's life in danger. They might not have had a choice but to go along."

"Her life was already in danger," noted Lineberry.

"In *more* danger, then."

"I don't know what to tell you, Atlee. I wasn't in those discussions, if they did occur."

"It seems clear that was why Ito did what he did. To avenge Bruno."

"Look, don't assume that Bruno was telling the truth in that letter. It could have just been sour grapes on his part. And he deserved what he got. Like I said, the number of people he killed while he was in the mob? And *how* he killed them? It was nauseating. The bastard!"

"Okay, Jack, just calm down. The last thing you need is to get all worked up."

She could hear him take several deep, calming breaths. "I'm sorry, I don't usually let it get to me like that. I'm good now. Continue on with your questions."

"You're sure?" she asked.

"Yes. Quite sure."

"Okay, moving on, you said that, at least initially, my family was in witness protection?"

Lineberry said, "That's correct. After your mother served as an inside source for law enforcement, her identity was leaked, and threats were made. The decision was made to put all of you into witness protection."

"How was her identity leaked?" asked Pine.

He didn't answer right away. "That is something we never determined, although we did an exhaustive investigation."

"Did you make the assumption that her identity had been leaked because of the threats?"

Lineberry coughed and said, "Exactly. That was the surest proof of all."

"What was the nature of the threats?"

There was a long moment of silence.

She said cautiously, "We can do this another time, when you feel better."

"No, let's just push on." He cleared his throat. "The first threat came in the form of a letter that was mailed to the apartment in New York where you were living at the time. The location of that apartment was a secret, but nonetheless there it was. It was a clear death threat. The decision was made to move all of you into witness protection."

"Why send a letter and essentially warn us, instead of coming there and trying to kill my mom?"

"I could never figure that out. It might have been done to intimidate, which it did. And also cause us to move you, which we did. We never determined why that was advantageous for whoever sent the letter."

"So they knew of her identity even though she never testified in court?" she asked.

"Your mother 'testified' to federal authorities in quite a few lengthy interviews, which in turn led to other witnesses who *did* testify in exchange for plea deals. She also provided recordings she took secretly while in the presence of numerous mob bosses. Those recordings were validated by other sources and entered into evidence. It was all legal and aboveboard, but we took great pains to keep her identity secret. She was our best shot at taking the families down. We had to keep her safe. And in the end, many of the mob just took deals because the evidence was overwhelming. Most of the older members we arrested ended up dying in prison. As far as I know, the younger ones are still *in* prison, right where they belong."

"Okay, tell me about the first witness protection experience."

"You were relocated to Hudson, Ohio. It's a suburb of Akron. It was far removed from New York City. We thought you all would be safe there."

"But we weren't."

Lineberry said, "No. One night, about two months after you arrived, there was a home invasion. Two men with guns."

"What happened?"

"You had a dog back then, a lab named Molly."

"I don't remember a dog," she said.

"Well, you were very young, Atlee. Anyway, the dog barked and woke up your parents. Your father kept a shotgun. He fired at the intruders and managed to scare them off. The decision was made to move you the very next day to a temporary safe house pending the readiness of a more permanent location."

"And where did that turn out to be?"

"Colorado. It was rural and any strangers in town would be instantly noticed. We really thought it would work."

"But it obviously didn't. What happened?" she asked.

"This time it wasn't a home invasion. It was an attempted carjacking. They ran you off the road. It was only by the grace of God that two state troopers were coming the other way. They intervened and saved you and your family. One of the carjackers managed to get away. The other was killed after a shootout with the troopers."

"Did they manage to ID him?"

Linberry said, "They did. He was Giovanni Colletti, part of a Colorado-based crime family. We obviously couldn't interrogate him, but we did subsequently learn that a contract had been put out on your family by one of the Mafia families that had been destroyed by your mother's work."

"Okay, the big question becomes: How did they keep finding out where we were? There had to be a leak, Jack. And it *kept* leaking."

"A fact we were well aware of. But we took every precaution, dug through the background of everyone who knew about your relocations. We could find nothing, no common denominator that would lead us to the mole. We constantly changed personnel, so that the inner circle was different, so that those who knew the most were limited. It was the most puzzling and infuriating phase of my career. After Colorado, the decision was made to take you out of witness protection and move you to Andersonville, Georgia. I was assigned there to personally look over you and keep you safe." He paused to clear his throat once more. "I clearly failed at that." A single cough followed this last comment, and then turned into a series of wracking ones.

"Jack, are you all right?"

As the spasm subsided, he said, "I'm fine. Just…tired."

"Look, you clearly need to rest, but can I ask you a favor?"

His tone instantly became alert. "Certainly. Anything."

"Can you provide me with information about who was in the loop with my family's experience back then? I mean, anyone you can remember, no matter how attenuated their connection was?"

"Atlee, a lot of them are long since retired or even dead."

"I still would like to go over them."

"I don't see the purpose."

"Then I'll tell you. Ito Vincenzo came to Georgia. He tried to kill me, and he took my sister. Whoever leaked our locations in Ohio and Colorado did the same in Georgia. That person must have communicated either with Bruno or Ito or someone close to them. If I can find that person, they may lead me to Ito."

Silence followed for a few moments.

Lineberry said, "I'll see what I can do. But I've been long since removed from that world. My contacts are largely no longer viable."

"If you run into obstacles, call me and I'll see what I can do to help," she said. "I told you back in Georgia that we had to try to do this together. And I haven't changed my mind."

"And sometimes dredging up the past can be more devastating than people realize."

"I need to know the truth. And I need to find my sister, and your daughter, Jack! Ito is really the only connection I have right now."

"He may not even be alive," said Lineberry.

"No one has seen him since 2001, apparently. But that's not proof that he's dead. Until I know that for sure, I have to keep looking for him."

"It's quite ominous that Teddy Vincenzo was murdered right after speaking to you. You don't think..." Lineberry's voice trailed off.

"No. I don't think it's connected to my case. I think Tony Vincenzo was into something far more serious than simply drug dealing. And I think he told his father. And his father paid the price."

"Then Tony Vincenzo is a target as well."

"And I just hope we find him before the people who killed Teddy do," replied Pine.

CHAPTER

20

A SMILING PINE SAID, "John Puller, Carol Blum."

Puller shook Blum's hand. "Nice to meet you, Carol. I've heard quite a bit about you."

They were standing in the lobby of Pine and Blum's hotel. It was the following day, and the weather had turned chilly and rainy.

Blum stared up at the tall, ramrod-straight, and good-looking Puller. "I can say the same about you, Agent Puller."

Pine said, "Let's grab a coffee and talk about our next steps."

They followed her into the small café off the lobby and ordered coffees. Then they took their drinks over to an empty seating area, sat down, and looked at one another.

"How's your case coming?" asked Puller.

"We've learned a few new things but we're still trying to gain some traction. My priority is to find Ito Vincenzo. I spoke with someone who might be able to help me find out what happened to him, but it's a long shot. So let's talk about your case. If that will lead me to Ito faster that's where I need to go."

"Meaning Tony might know where his grandfather is?" said Puller.

"It's the reason we came to Trenton in the first place."

Puller nodded. "Well, I can't say I'm gaining much traction, either. I tried again, but the Trenton police have now completely closed me off from the investigation. I can't see any reports. I can't talk to the cop who shot Jerome Blake. They have closed ranks and left me on the outside."

"You said the Bureau of Prisons guy, Moss, warned you off. Maybe he talked to the Trenton folks and told them to stonewall you."

"I'm not surprised that Moss might have told the Trenton folks to stand down, particularly after he had that meeting with me. I'm just wondering why the Trenton folks are going along with it. It clearly stinks of a cover-up."

"And how about your side?" asked Blum.

"Disappointing because there's been very little support. And I don't expect that to change. There's a hush coming from the uniforms that I don't understand. I expected someone to show some backbone, but it's extraordinary how they all seemed to have fallen in line." He paused, his gaze rooted on his knees. "It's not the Army way to just stand aside meekly when an injustice is being done. Why the hell do we even wear the uniform or take an oath?"

"Preaching to the choir. But let's talk about the shooting that killed Agent McElroy," said Pine.

Puller looked up at her. "It clearly wasn't a gang thing, as you've shown. I'm not even convinced Blake fired the shot. If not, who did? And was Ed even the target? Or was it you and/or me, as we discussed before?"

"Or was he the target but only as a warning to us to back off the case?" suggested Pine.

"All good points," interjected Blum. "But if they were willing to kill a federal agent in cold blood? The reasons to do so must be quite something. And so would having such a broad conspiracy to cover everything up."

Pine said, "Teddy Vincenzo told us his son had gotten in way over his head. So maybe we're not just talking about a basic pill-mill operation. There could be more to it. A lot more to it. Could it be that the folks behind the drug ring have political connections high up?"

"I guess that's possible because there's definitely something weird going on," agreed Puller.

"You said they wouldn't let you talk to the cop who shot Blake?" said Pine.

"That's right. I didn't even get his name."

"You said Tony had military personnel involved in the scheme?"

"Yes."

"Have you arrested any of them?"

"Two. Bill Danforth and Phil Cassidy. They're sitting in a holding cell right now at Fort Dix."

"Not the prison part of Fort Dix?" said Pine.

"No. What happened to Teddy Vincenzo is not going to happen to them. They're being held by the Army in a secure facility nowhere near the prison. MPs handpicked by me are guarding them."

"I assume you've interrogated Danforth and Cassidy."

"Until they both asked for military counsel," said Puller. "Once they lawyered up, the interrogation stopped."

"In that regard I guess military law isn't that much different from civilian law," noted Blum. "My son is an MP. Stationed in California."

Puller nodded. "Not an easy job. And it's good of him to serve his country. And yes there are similarities, but the Uniform Code of Military Justice can be an odd-looking bird to outsiders. Soldiers take an oath. Consequently, we hold them to a higher standard than laws do with civilians. Burdens of proof and punishments can be very different. Now, in this case charges have already been handed down. Danforth and Cassidy will both be up for general court-martials. No way this is being dealt with through an Article 15." Puller glanced at Pine and Blum. "Sorry, I tend to automatically fall into military jargon. Article 15 allows the soldier's commanding officer, or CO, to punish personnel for minor offenses without need for a trial. It's like a civil action, although it lands in their record and can impede their careers, promotions, and the like. But drug dealing is not a minor offense. And we have all the evidence we need to get convictions. They're looking at long prison sentences."

"Then they may want to cut a deal," said Pine.

"I'll cut deals so long as I get the big players behind this. If I'm allowed to do so," he added.

"Did you ever talk to Danforth and Cassidy about the possibility of a deal?" asked Blum.

"Not yet. My plan was to get that authority and go after them hard to give us names further up the line. Right now, everything's in limbo since they lawyered up."

"Can we speak to the prisoners if their counsel is present, or is the military different on that, too?" asked Pine.

"No, we can. I'll make a call and try to set it up. But don't get your hopes up. Everything about this case is screwed up."

"I would suppose they have every incentive to make a deal to lessen their punishment," said Blum.

Puller glanced at Pine before saying, "But they also have one very important reason to keep quiet."

"Namely, what happened to Teddy Vincenzo might happen to them," said Pine.

Her phone buzzed. It was her contact at the Trenton FBI office, Rick Davies.

She answered it, and Davies said, "I'm sending you a photo that I got from a cop bud of mine who knows someone assigned to the case. It's the gun that was used to kill the CID agent."

"Okay."

"And I've learned that there were six surveillance cameras in the area in question. I believe the cops have grabbed all of them, but I couldn't verify that. I'm sending you the locations of each one in case you want to check them out."

"That's great, Rick, thanks."

She clicked off, explained to Puller what was going on, and waited for the email to pop into her queue. When it did she opened it and looked at the photo of the gun.

She caught a breath and glanced up at Puller.

"What?" he said.

"That's not the gun Jerome Blake was holding."

21

THE POLICE PRESENCE HAD GONE, the only remnants being yellow police crime scene tape flapping in the wind. With the rain and wind there were few pedestrians brave enough to be outside.

Their umbrellas braced against the brisk breeze, Puller, Blum, and Pine looked around the area where the shooting had taken place. In the daytime it seemed far different to Pine, larger and more complex. That night it had seemed like a long, narrow tunnel with very little life present. She eyed the alleyway.

"Puller, where'd you learn to jump across buildings like that?" she asked, while Blum hiked an eyebrow at this odd remark.

"Ranger School," he said off-handedly before adding, "You're sure it wasn't the right gun?"

She glared at him. "Blake was holding a Glock 26 subcompact. The gun in the picture is a *full-sized* Glock 26 with a black stainless steel slide."

"I didn't get a good look at it, like you did. And it was dark in that alley," cautioned Puller. "And the gun frames look alike."

"I know my weapons," retorted Pine. "Somebody switched guns. This was all a setup and they used Blake as the scapegoat."

Puller said, "But you have to have extra muscle in very high places to pull off something like this."

"And I think we've seen clearly that they do," said Pine. She thumbed her phone screen until a new page appeared. "Six locations for surveillance cameras," she said. "Let's start knocking on doors."

Two banks, a laundromat, a pawnbroker's shop, a convenience store, and an office supply store later, they found that all the footage from that night had already been confiscated as evidence by local police.

Pine, Puller, and Blum stood on the sidewalk outside the pawnbroker's shop in the driving rain, determining what their next steps might be.

"They worked extremely fast taking all the camera feeds," said Puller. "That leaves us with zip video for that night."

"And it's doubtful they're going to actually use it as evidence," said Blum.

"More likely they'll bury it in a landfill," said Puller.

"People were around during the shooting," noted Pine. "Maybe someone took video on their phones. That happens all the time these days."

"Do we return later tonight and start asking around?"

"Well, right now, we could go back to the place where we ate. Someone who worked there might have seen something. We were standing right out in front of it when McElroy was shot."

They headed over to the Italian restaurant. They sat at a booth and ordered some food. Pine recognized the waitress from when they had been there before and called her over. She was in her twenties, with light brown hair, sharp blue eyes, and a slim figure.

Puller and Pine showed the young woman their badges and asked her about the shooting.

The waitress, whose name tag read DAWN, instantly became rigid. Her blue eyes grew wide. "That's right. You two were here that night." She glanced outside. "It was horrible. I mean, this is a nice neighborhood. We've never had a murder right outside."

"Can you tell us what you saw?" asked Puller, taking out his notepad.

Pine interjected, "And have the local police been by to talk to anyone here?"

"Not that I know of."

Pine and Puller exchanged a look. Puller said, "So anything you can remember, no matter how trivial it may seem."

She pulled up a chair and sat down. Glancing out the window again she said, "I heard some pops. Like firecrackers, only it's not July."

"Right," said Pine. "Then what?"

"I ran over to the window and saw the two of you and the man…he was lying on the pavement by then."

"Did you see where the shots came from?" asked Puller. "Or the shooter?"

She shook her head. "I was just looking at the body. It was…" She paused. "I did see something, in the alley across the way."

"What was that?" asked Pine.

"It was something, a flash of something, maybe a person turning and running."

"In which direction?" asked Puller.

"Back into the alley, I think." She looked up at them with a hopeless expression. "I…I'm sorry, I just can't be sure."

Puller drew a photo from his pocket. "Did you see this person that night?"

It was a picture of Jerome Blake.

Dawn studied it and then shook her head. "No."

"You're sure?"

"Yes." She looked out the window again. "They must have cameras out there. You could check those."

Pine explained, "We tried that. They…weren't available."

"Well, you could check with Karl."

"Karl?" said Blum.

"He's one of the short-order cooks here."

"Why would he know anything?" asked Pine.

"Karl lives in the building next door to this one. There's a fire escape overlooking the alley on this side. He's had two break-ins into his apartment in the last year, both through the fire escape. So he put one of those camera things out there. You know, it notifies him if there's any movement there. But it's pointed in a way that it might have filmed what happened across the street."

"Do you know where Karl is now?" asked Puller.

"Probably home. His shift starts at five and runs to midnight."

They paid for their food and had Dawn give Karl a call to verify he was home and that they were coming over to check the camera feed.

As they headed out for the short walk Pine looked at Puller. "Could this be the big break in the case?"

"I'm not sure even a smoking gun would be enough. It's not that sort of a case, apparently."

"But we have to get to the truth."

"Only reason I signed up for the job."

"Me too."

"Count me in on that," chimed in Blum.

CHAPTER

22

"THERE IT IS," said Pine, pointing up at the second-floor fire escape landing where a small camera was attached to one of the support posts. It covered the entire fire escape outside the window and looked like it would also have a sight line to the alley across the street.

They continued on into the building and took the steps up to the third floor, then went down the hall to apartment 311.

Karl Shaffer was in his late forties, balding, grizzled, and tired looking. He seemed a man who had looked at life and life had looked back at him, and neither had been satisfied by what they had seen.

He wore a T-shirt despite the chill in the room. They showed him their official creds and he invited them inside.

"My wife works during the day, office job," he said as he moved a basket of laundry and some other odds and ends so Blum and the other two could sit down. "So, Dawn called and said you needed to see my camera video?"

"From the shooting the other night."

Shaffer shook his head. "Damn, that was some crazy shit, wasn't it? But why not, I guess. Shootings happening all over the place. You're not safe in your own house or apparently eating spaghetti bolognese at our place."

"So the camera?" prompted Pine.

"Yeah, burglarized twice in the last ten months. I said enough was enough." He turned to Pine and Puller and took out his phone. "The camera live-feeds to my phone through an app. It records all the time. It's on some cloud loop or something that I don't understand, but I don't have to; it just has to work."

"But can you pull up a video feed from the shooting?" asked Puller.

"I think so. The guy who set it up showed me. Give me a sec. It's easier to do it on the laptop."

He got up, went out of the room, and returned with the computer. He set it down on his lap, accessed the app, and hit some keys.

"Let's see, I'm putting in as close to the time as I can. I remember it pretty damn well. I was making a batch of chicken marsala when I heard the shots. I'm not sure I can ever make it again. Okay, here we go."

He turned the computer around so they could see the screen. He hit a key and the video started to run.

They all watched as Pine and Puller exited the restaurant and met up with Agent McElroy. A few moments later a shot rang out on the video. Though they'd been expecting it, they all flinched. McElroy dropped to the pavement, and Pine and Puller ducked down behind the car as more rounds sailed past.

"Okay, back it up until I tell you to stop," said Puller.

Shaffer did so.

"Freeze it there."

They were now watching the mouth of the alley where pops of gunfire were erupting from. And, just as Dawn the waitress had said, there was a blur of something. A sleeve, a leg, a hand. Even with Shaffer zooming in, they couldn't see any more than that.

"Run it now," said Puller.

They watched on the screen as first Puller and then Pine ran into the alley and vanished.

A minute went by and Pine visualized herself running down the alley, paralleling Puller's movement from above. They had reached the end—the dead end, in many ways—of the alley.

Jerome had risen up from behind the trash cans. Pine had talked to him, tried to coax the gun from his hand. He had said what he had.

The next instant she heard the shot. The shot that had ended Jerome's life. She visualized the surprised look on his face, and then his seemingly slow-motion descent to the alley floor. In reality he had dropped instantly.

But that dramatic vision was instantly overshadowed by something else, something both terrible and inexplicable.

Stunned, she looked over at Puller. His expression was granite, a knot in his jaw was flexing and unflexing.

She leaned over and whispered to Puller, "The cop who shot Jerome never appeared on the camera running into the alley."

"No, he didn't," he replied in an equally low voice.

"Which means he was already in the alley."

"Which means *he* was the one who killed Ed McElroy," replied Puller.

CHAPTER

23

Unlike that night, it was quiet in the alley. With death came a stillness unlike any other, thought Pine. You could be in a crowded plaza teeming with the sounds of the masses, and a dead body would suck in all the noise around you and turn it into grim silence.

Puller and Pine bracketed Blum as they entered the space.

"The question is, where was the shooter hiding that we didn't see him," said Pine.

They walked to the end of the alley and noted the line of garbage cans, behind which Jerome Blake had been hiding. They glanced down at the bloodstains on the ground where he had been shot and died.

In those splotches Pine saw a young man who could have gone on to make the world a better place. Now he was lying in a morgue accused of a murder he had not committed. Something harsh and deep and unyielding burned in Pine's gut. The world was filled with enough injustices every day to make you want to pull out your hair and scream at the country's leaders to *do something*.

"You came down from the roof using that ladder," noted Pine, coming out of her musings and speaking to Puller.

Puller eyed the same spot. "Right. Let's run through what happened."

Pine said, "The cop came running up after he shot Jerome. Said Jerome was getting ready to fire his gun. I told him I didn't think so. He checked his pulse, then almost drew down on you when you came down the ladder."

Puller took up the recollection. "He asked for our creds and we showed him. Then he said he was responding to your 911 call, which was clearly a lie, since he was already here."

"You asked if he knew Jerome and he said no. He asked who the dead guy was back there, and you told him."

"And he asked why a kid would be targeting an Army CID guy."

"Then more cops showed up and things got frenetic," said Pine. "We both got pulled away to make statements."

"He was about six one and broad shouldered. Never really saw his face clearly. How about you?"

Pine took a moment to answer. "I'd definitely recognize the guy if I saw him again."

"What happened to him?" asked Blum. "How did he get away?"

"I remember looking over at Jerome's body and then gazing around the area. Puller was talking to a sergeant."

"Right. He was in charge and jotting down notes and then he called in the tech team."

Pine said, "Then I turned and looked back down the alley. I couldn't swear to it, but I thought I saw the guy heading out. But there were a lot of uniforms around at that point."

"Which made it the perfect disguise," interjected Blum. "And also the only way you wouldn't have jumped the guy and arrested him for shooting Jerome."

Puller said, "He might have been a real cop. Which would make this situation even more of a nightmare. Did you see his name tag?"

"No. And I would have. I always look at that. Which means he wasn't wearing one. Which should have been a dead giveaway that something was off," said a sheepish Pine. "I blew it."

"I think you can be forgiven for not noticing, Agent Pine," said Blum.

"I can't forgive myself, Carol. I'm trained to notice what other people don't." She thought for a moment. "His uniform looked legit, except for the name tag. He kept his cap on, so I don't know if he had thinning hair or a bald spot. His forearms were pretty hairy. Like I said, I'd definitely recognize him if I saw him again."

Puller looked behind them. "We just have to find out where his hidey-hole was."

They walked back down the alley, taking it slow and looking at the blank walls. There were no doors or windows anywhere. No one could have come silently over the barbed wire that topped the locked gates going into the side alleys. A few spots looked to have once had either windows or doors but had either been bricked or boarded up. They checked these places and ensured that they were fully mortared or solidly nailed shut.

Puller said, "They probably closed up all the side alleys and nailed all these doors and windows shut to keep out drug users and prostitutes and burglars hiding their stash. Some of these buildings are abandoned or are being renovated. Big temptation for certain elements like that."

"Could he have come via one of these roofs, like you did?" said Pine.

"He still would have had to access a building somewhere. And folks running across roofs are sort of conspicuous. I'd think he'd want to keep a lower profile, no pun intended."

They walked back to near the mouth of the alley.

Pine said, "Jerome must have come into the alley earlier, before the video feed we saw."

"But what made him do that?" asked Blum.

Pine took a few steps forward. The sounds of her boots hitting the ground changed slightly, from a thump to a hollow sounding *clink*.

She looked down at the manhole cover.

Puller followed her gaze. When they both looked up, each smiled resignedly.

Puller ran back to his car, grabbed the lug wrench from the trunk, and rejoined them. He inserted the shaped end of the wrench into the notch in the center of the cover and exerted leverage. The metal slowly gave way, and then Puller and Pine lifted it out and set it aside.

Pine pulled out her Tac light and shone it down into the hole.

"Carol, you stay up here while we check this out. We'll text you with what we find."

Puller went first as Pine illuminated the way for him.

Then she slowly followed into the darkness.

24

W HEN SHE GOT DOWN TO THE BOTTOM, Pine shone her light around. There were copper and PVC pipes running along the walls, along with what looked to be valves and power boxes and rubber hoses.

"Looks like an access tunnel for the utility companies," observed Pine. "Probably servicing this whole block." She pointed her light down.

On the concrete floor they saw fresh footprints outlined in the grime.

"Two sets of footprints, one big, one smaller," noted Pine. "Maybe the cop and Jerome came together. And the prints only head in one direction, towards the alley."

"And none going back. So the cop brought Jerome in this way because it was the only way he could guarantee that the kid would show up and that he could control his movements. They go up the ladder and the cop shoots McElroy and then tells Jerome to run down the alley, which he does."

Pine added, "Then the cop probably hid behind some of the junk in the alley until we passed by, or maybe just went back down the hole he came out of."

"Then he comes out after we pass, follows us down the alley, waits until we finger Jerome, and then shoots him before he can tell us the truth. Neat and tidy."

Puller used his phone camera to take shots of the prints. They were careful to walk to the side to avoid impacting what was now evidence at a crime scene.

"And you know what we're *not* seeing?" said Pine.

"Any evidence that the local cops have been down here."

They followed the dual set of footprints along the passageway, which was long and curved in numerous places. It finally ended in a blank wall and another ladder. They climbed it back to ground level, pushed open the manhole cover, and found themselves in a large room *inside* a building. It was full of machinery and dull gray panels on the wall, behind which were switches and circuit breakers.

"This must be one of the power company's control rooms for the energy being provided to the area," noted Pine.

The footsteps in the dust led to the only door in the place.

They headed over to it. Using a latex glove he pulled from his jacket, Puller tried the knob. It was locked, and there was no way to unlock it from in here.

"No surprise there," he said. He pulled out a small leather kit from his other pocket, opened it, and took out two slender pieces of shaped metal. He examined the lock and then inserted the pick tools into it and started working away, his ear close to the lock.

"The military has taught you some impressive skills," said Pine with a sly smile.

"That's the Army way. I'm sure you're not lacking there, either."

There was a click, and he turned the knob and the door opened. They cautiously peered outside.

"Shit," said Pine.

They were staring at the back of a police station.

Puller checked to see that no one was in the vicinity, then they stepped out and he closed the door softly behind him.

"Pretty ballsy of them to make their entrance right next to the cops," said Pine.

"Unless he really is a cop," replied Puller. "In which case it makes perfect sense. Jerome was never going to live to point the finger at him."

As they walked back toward where Blum was waiting for them, Pine said, "Okay, are we looking at a rogue cop or something more than that?"

"A rogue works alone. Nothing I've seen so far indicates this guy is a loner. Quite the contrary."

"I was hoping you were going to say that, because I personally think we're dealing with one of those conspiracies you hear morons online pushing all the time."

"Thinking the same thing."

"So if the locals are in on it, and the feds are in on it?" said Pine expectantly.

"That leaves little room for us to operate. So we have to watch our p's and q's like we've never done before."

"You said before you didn't know what you'd do if you got called off the case."

"Every time the phone rings, I dread answering it because it might be that call." He hesitated. "But I can't leave it like this."

"But you're in the military. If they reassign you to another case, you have to go."

"What about you? You work for a big, unforgiving bureaucracy, too."

"I'm working on a short leash there. In a few days I expect to get an order to hightail it back to Arizona and be a good agent and forget all about this."

"And?" he said expectantly.

"And I'm like you. I can't leave it like this."

"This isn't really your fight, though. You need to work on your sister's case. I can plug my thumb in the dike and hope it holds."

"Nice try, my knight in shining armor, but you know me too well to think I'm going to sign off on that. It's both or none."

"Then can I make suggestion?"

"Please do."

"Let's attack both at the same time. You want to find Tony Vincenzo for your own purposes, and so do I. One thing I haven't told you is I had a surveillance team on Tony before we tried to arrest him. He went to New York a few times. To one place in particular, a skyscraper on Billionaires' Row."

"Billionaires' Row?"

"It's around the Fifty-Seventh Street corridor. Splinter-in-the-sky buildings where the apartments are owned by the überwealthy. Some of them are purchased by Russian oligarchs, foreign strongmen looking to move money out of their country, Arab sheiks, that sort of thing."

"What was Tony Vincenzo doing at one of those places?"

Puller said, "We don't know, but we need to find out. And on two occasions he drove up there in an Aston Martin."

"An Aston Martin? How much money was he making from his pills?"

"The car wasn't registered to him. It was registered in the name of a shell company. We tried to trace it back but hit a dead end. Only people with money and/or connections can do that."

Pine mulled over this. "Okay. So this thing just went to another level."

"I'm going to give you some names at Fort Dix in the motor pool. And other people he worked with there. I want you to talk to them and see what they can tell you. That way they can't ding me for investigating it."

"In the meantime, what will you do?" she asked.

"When you're outnumbered on the battlefield, and the other side is preparing to come right at you with the thought of over-running your position and wiping you out, there's really only two things to do." He looked at her inquiringly.

"Okay, one is to retreat," said Pine.

"And the other one is to attack. And in this case, my moving forward is the best choice because it would be the last thing they would expect me to do under the circumstances."

"But *who* are you going to attack?" she asked nervously.

"My chain of command. But not in the way you or they might think."

"Care to elaborate?"

"No, otherwise I might inadvertently make you an accessory

before the fact. And that would be highly inconvenient for both of us. You're gonna just have to trust me."

And on that Puller picked up his pace, and Pine had to hurry to keep up.

CHAPTER

25

So you know Tony well?" asked Pine.

She and Blum were sitting across a café table with a young woman named Lindsey Axilrod. She was in her midthirties, medium height, wiry, and fit, with sandy brown hair and pretty features accentuated with a freckled complexion. Axilrod had been on the list that Puller had given her.

"Yeah, he's a nice guy. I like hanging out with him."

"And you met him at Fort Dix?"

"Yes. I'm not in the Army. I'm a civilian, like Tony. I do back-office stuff. I'm in IT, so I basically troubleshoot any technology problems we have."

"You will never be without gainful employment then," noted Blum. "Folks with your knowledge rule the world."

Axilrod smiled and folded the paper wrapper she had taken off the straw for her iced tea. "I don't know about that, but it's challenging work, which I like. Every day is different, so there's not much monotony." She paused and looked up at Pine. "So, why is the FBI interested in Tony?"

"When was the last time you saw him?"

"About a week ago. He hasn't shown up for work lately. Did something happen to him?"

"He's actually gone missing," said Pine.

"So something *has* happened to him, then. I thought so."

"We're trying to find him. So whatever you can tell us would be appreciated."

"I'm not sure what I know that would be helpful."

"You've gone out with him?"

"Yes, both in groups and just the two of us."

"Any place you've frequented over others?"

"No, not really. We went bowling once. He's a really good bowler. Bars, clubs, basketball games, restaurants, that sort of thing. Nothing really regular."

"We understand he visits a place in New York?"

Axilrod's eyes widened. "Oh, right. So you know about that?"

"We'd like to know more."

"It belongs to some guy. They became friends. Real tight."

"This friend have a name?"

"Randy, at least I think. He founded some company and then sold it to Google or somebody like that for a gazillion bucks. He's not much older than me, but he's set for life, lucky bastard. Place has a doorman, and a private elevator that opens into the foyer." She shook her head. "I've only seen stuff like that in the movies."

"So you've been there?"

"Oh, yeah, a number of times. I go with Tony. Only way I can get in."

"How did a guy like Tony meet a guy like Randy?"

"Randy wasn't always rich, apparently. He and Tony knew each other before. Tony was like only eighteen or something. I don't know particulars, but after Randy hit the big time, he didn't forget his old friends."

"Where is this place?"

"Fifty-Seventh Street."

"Billionaires' Row, maybe?"

"Yeah. It's a pretty new building. The parking spot fee is probably five times what I make in a year."

"And I heard he drives up there in some sort of *exotic* car?"

Axilrod smiled. "The Aston Martin. Yeah, that belongs to Randy, too. He lets Tony drive it sometimes. If you'd asked me a year ago if I thought I'd ever be driving around in an Aston Martin, well, the answer would have been no! But what a sweet ride."

"Did you ever meet Randy?" asked Blum.

"No. Tony said on any given day he might be in Beijing or Paris or Rio. He has his own jet. I can't even imagine a life like that. But apparently the guy likes to share the wealth, so that's cool."

"So you drove up there to the penthouse and...?"

"Just hung out. Did some drinking. Played some video games. It's got this whole room just for gaming. We're both big gamers, although, not to toot my own horn, I'm a lot better than Tony."

"So you two are dating, then?"

Axilrod frowned. "I'm not sure I'd call it that. We were just hanging out. There were no plans to get married, if that's what you're asking. I'm about ten years older than Tony."

"So you were never intimate?" asked Pine.

Axilrod's frown deepened. "I don't feel comfortable answering that. And what does that have to do with finding Tony? And why all these questions?"

"We're just trying to get a fuller picture of his life. I wouldn't want anyone to ask me that question, but it is standard protocol for the Bureau."

Axilrod still looked put out. "Well, I'm just sticking with 'we were friends.'"

"Okay, was he 'friends' with anyone else?"

"I don't know if he was...*intimate* with anyone. He never said."

"When you went there each time was it just you and Tony?"

"Oh, no. There were lots of people there."

"Friends of Tony's?"

"Maybe some of them."

"The others were associates of Randy's?"

"I guess. Or friends of his. Look, it's not like anything weird is going on there. People with too much money like Randy like to play the big man, right? We go there, we drink and have fun, and we do gaming and fool around some. That's all. There's nothing more. Stuff like that goes on in New York all the time."

"Maybe it does and maybe it doesn't."

"Well, I don't know what to tell you other than everything I've seen there is legit. Just harmless fun."

"Does Randy let parties go on there every day?"

"Of course not. Tony told me he'll get a call that tells him it's party time there. It's not that often. Once or twice a month. But I always look forward to it. I mean, come on, how else would I ever get into one of those places?"

"Okay, let's switch gears. Have you seen anything unusual at Fort Dix?"

"Unusual how?"

"Just out of the ordinary?"

"No, never."

"Because Tony was manufacturing and selling drugs, Lindsey."

Axilrod shook her head and said vehemently, "No way you could get drugs on the installation. They have dogs sniffing for stuff like that, and vehicle searches."

"Okay, this place in New York. You could find it again?" Even though Pine knew the address, she didn't want to let on to Axilrod that she had that information.

"Why?" she said warily.

"I'd like to check it out for myself. We can go together."

Axilrod shook her head, looking nervous. "I don't think I want to be part of anything that's going on here."

"If you don't I can have a warrant issued and a team can be there within an hour. But I'd prefer not to have to go down that route."

Axilrod tensed. "You're putting me in an impossible situation. If you do that and Tony finds out I talked to you, he's going to be pissed."

"I thought you said nothing was going on up there."

"Nothing that I *know* about. But what if there is? Then I'm stuck right in the middle of it. And I'm not stupid. If the FBI is nosing around, something must be off."

"And all you have to do is get me into the building. I can take it from there. You know the doorman?"

"Well, yeah."

"So? Are they having a party tonight?"

Axilrod glanced at Blum and then looked at Pine, and her expression appeared resigned. "Actually, they are."

"How do you know they're having one tonight?" Blum asked.

"Because Tony told me about it last week. We were supposed to go together. But I haven't heard a word from him since."

"Well, you and I can go together. Okay, Lindsey?" said Pine.

Axilrod finally nodded. "Okay. But if things get hairy, I'm outta there."

CHAPTER

26

Axilrod and Pine shared an Uber into the city. They had met up in Newark and ridden in from there.

Axilrod had on tight, dark dress jeans, a white blouse open at the neck and showing a bit of cleavage, a short denim jacket, and three-inch heels.

Pine was dressed in jeans as well, and a black bomber jacket with a dark blouse buttoned all the way up. For obvious reasons she had left her guns and creds back in her hotel room.

"What are we going to do when we get up there?" asked Axilrod nervously.

"Mingle, listen, and watch. Try to find a lead on Tony. I don't expect to hit the jackpot, but anything we learn will be more than I have now."

"Hey, do you think Tony will be there? He hasn't answered any of my texts or calls."

"Let's just say I would be surprised if he is, but I've been surprised before."

They got out at the address and Pine looked up. They were on the south end of Central Park between Seventh and Eighth Avenues, and the building they were about to go into was twelve hundred feet high.

After Puller had told her about this building, Pine had done some digging. The cheapest apartment in the place went for forty-three million dollars. The most expensive unit was the penthouse, which took up the entire top floor and also the entire floor below it. They were connected by both a grand stairway and a private elevator. Pine had learned that this two-story mansion had been purchased by a Saudi prince for one hundred and ten million bucks, and he spent less than three weeks there a year.

There were no vacant units. There were also no full-time residents. These places were not homes; they were safe-deposit boxes, a way to move money out of a country where the government sometimes took things from the rich without paying for them. Or, they were a perfect way to launder money that had been made in illegal ways overseas.

The uniformed doorman, who, to Pine's discerning eye, carried more muscled bulk and keener observation skills than most doormen in the Big Apple, led them into a small but palatial lobby and over to the concierge desk. There they were met by a broad-shouldered young man with thick, wavy hair, an expensive blue suit complete with white pocket square, and a helpful, inquisitive look.

Pine figured he had a tricky balance here. He couldn't afford not to be suspicious, but he also couldn't afford to piss off a VIP, either. She assumed he had been rigidly trained to perform that duty as well as it could be.

"Yes?" he said, looking between Axilrod and Pine.

"I'm Lindsey Axilrod, remember me? I'm usually here with Tony Vincenzo."

"Oh, yes, of course, hello, Ms. Axilrod, good to see you again. I'm afraid Mr. Vincenzo is not here."

"I know, but he told me to meet him here. I, um, I think he's coming later. I'm assuming there's stuff going on up there, like usual."

He said diplomatically, "There are others in the unit tonight, yes." He turned to Pine. "And your friend?"

Pine put out her hand. "I'm Angela. Lindsey said it would be okay to come with her."

"Tony thought so, too," added Axilrod quickly. "He wanted Angela to come tonight."

"Come on and I'll get you on the elevator, then."

He pressed his thumbprint to the scan pad next to the elevator and then punched in the floor number. The doors slid open, and Pine and Axilrod stepped on. The doors closed and the car lifted off, swiftly traveling ninety floors up, where it opened into what could only be described as a raucous scene unfolding over some of the most expensive real estate on earth.

Pine could see about forty people, most of them under thirty, many of them drunk and getting drunker. They were standing in small pockets of conversation, or draped over the massive furniture, or leaning against a wall, or sitting on tables, or heading off, hands on firm asses, to more private spaces.

The next thing she noticed were the two burly men dressed in dark clothes with bumps near the chest for their weapons.

One of them put out a large hand. "Purses."

It wasn't a question.

They handed the men their purses and they were thoroughly searched and then handed back. Next, they were efficiently patted down by the men.

"Names?" one asked.

They gave them.

"I'm usually here with Tony Vincenzo," said Axilrod. "I've seen you before."

The burly man swept out a hand and said, "Right. Enjoy."

They walked over to a bar that was set up along one wall. Beyond that were sweeping views of the city. On the streets far below were the winks of thousands of vehicles. A slim jet cruised past their line of sight to its final descent into LaGuardia. Next to them was another splinter building where the überrich lived far above the rabble, at least in their own minds.

Pine and Axilrod ordered drinks, a rum and Coke and a champagne cocktail, respectively.

Pine's gaze kept sweeping the room like radar sucking up as much information as possible. She checked out Burly One and Burly Two at the door. They were not paying her any more attention than they were anyone else.

"Recognize anybody?" asked Pine. "Specifically someone who knows Tony?"

"The two guys over there," said Axilrod. "I've been here with Tony and talked to them. They seemed to know him, but just to say hello and talk sports."

"Okay, anyone else here from Fort Dix you recognize?"

Axilrod slowly surveyed the room. "That woman over there, in the corner doing a lip-lock with that guy."

Pine looked to where she was indicating. The woman was petite and in her twenties with stringy ash-blond hair. She was too thin, and her skin was pale and unhealthy looking. Her legs, encased in black jeans, looked like pencils flowing down into red high heels that raised her height to about five four.

"Her name?"

"Sheila Weathers."

"What does she do at Fort Dix?"

"She works at the commissary."

"She looks like a drug user. The eyes, twitchy limbs. You know anything about that?"

"No."

"How does she know Tony?"

"He eats in the commissary. I've seen them talking. A lot."

Pine put her drink down. "Let's go then. She looks like she wants to be rescued from that guy."

CHAPTER

27

HEY, SHEILA," said Pine as she strode over to the couple and inserted herself firmly between them. "I'm Angela."

Weathers looked up blankly at Pine but then saw Axilrod and said, "You're at Fort Dix. I've seen you there."

"Yep. I'm Lindsey. I'm in IT. I think we both know Tony Vincenzo."

"Hey," barked the man. He was around five eight with broad shoulders, a loose gut, slicked-back dark hair, and a pissed-off expression. "Do you mind?"

Pine looked down at him. "No, we don't mind if you have to head off. We want to catch some girlfriend time with Sheila here anyway."

The guy squared off with Pine. "That wasn't what I meant. I meant for you two to back the hell off."

"Is that what you want, Sheila?" asked Pine.

Weathers glanced at the guy and smiled. "I'll catch up with you later, Ryan." Before he could reply she kissed him. "I promise," she added.

He glared at Pine and said to Weathers, "I'll hold you to it."

He stalked off as Weathers turned to them. "God, what a creep. Thanks."

"You're welcome, but you know he's coming back for more," said Pine.

"I hope to be long gone before then. I have to get in to work early. Did you really want to talk to me, or was that just a way to get him away from me?"

Pine said, "No, we really wanted to talk to you."

"Okay. I was hoping Tony would be here. I got a text to come up here tonight and the text said Tony was coming, too. That's how I started coming here, through Tony."

"Me too," said Axilrod.

"Who texted you?" said Pine sharply.

Weathers said, "I don't know. But I've gotten them before to give a heads-up about parties here."

"You and Tony dating?"

She smiled. "Kinda, yeah."

"Well, it's Tony I want to talk to you about," said Pine.

She led the way into another room that was miraculously empty. She shut the door and turned to Weathers. "Tony is missing, and we'd like to find him."

Weathers glanced at Axilrod, who nodded. "It's true."

Weathers said to Pine, "Do you know Tony?"

"We dated. It was serious. I'm from Newark. I wanted to get back together with him."

"Don't get me wrong. But you're a little old and a little tall for Tony. He likes them petite, like me."

"Then his taste has changed."

"He never mentioned an Angela to me."

"Do guys mention old girlfriends to their new girlfriends?" pointed out Pine. "When was the last time you saw him?"

Weathers bit her lip. "Look, I'm not sure I want to talk to you about Tony."

"What if something has happened to him?"

"Nothing has happened to him."

"You can't know that for sure. And we both know that the stuff he's involved in can be dangerous."

"What, you mean the motor pool?"

Pine gave her a hard stare. "Is that really what you think I'm talking about?" She glanced at the woman's eyes and nose. "I'm not judging, Sheila. I'm just saying you have to be smart. I know the Army. They come down like a ton of bricks on drug users."

"How dare you! I'm not a drug user."

"Oh really. Well, your eyes and nose and your twitches tell me otherwise. Again, I'm not judging. But I've been down that road before. I've spent enough time in detox to know, so don't bullshit me."

"Okay, okay," snapped Weathers. "But it's also impossible to get off the shit once you're on it. I've been in rehab four times now. If the Army could find any more bodies to wash dishes and empty the trash, I'd be long gone by now."

"Did Tony supply you as well?"

Weathers gave her a look. "Why? Are you really a cop feeding me a load of bullshit and you're looking to bust him? And me?"

She stared pointedly at Weathers and tapped her flat belly. "This is why I want to talk to Tony."

Weathers sucked in a breath. "You're—?"

"Not showing yet, but it won't be long."

"And he's the father?"

"Oh yeah."

"I don't know where Tony is. I really don't."

"Okay, but you've seen him?"

"Yeah. At work."

"He hasn't been to work in a while."

"I know."

"So have you seen him other than at work?"

"Maybe."

"Either you have or you haven't," said Pine. "And anything you can tell us will be more than what we know now."

"Okay, he came to my place a few days ago. Said he got rousted from his house by the cops looking for him, and he needed to lie low for a bit."

"You mean his dad's old place?" said Pine.

"Yeah, I guess. How'd you know about that?"

"I've been looking for him. He told me about the place. I went there. It was empty. How long did he stay with you?"

"Just the night." She glanced at Pine and added hastily, "We didn't do anything. He slept on the couch."

Pine waved this comment off. "I'm not looking to marry the guy, Sheila. I just thought he'd like to know he's going to be a daddy. Did he say where he was going to go after he left your place?"

"No, but afterwards he texted me and said his father had died in prison. I think that really spooked him."

"Did he say why the cops were after him?"

"No, and I didn't ask. I know better."

"And he said nothing that would lead you to know where he was going?"

"Not really." She paused and looked around the room, as though checking for eavesdroppers. "But if he can't go back to his house and he hasn't come back here, there aren't many places left."

"But do you know of any?" asked Pine.

Axilrod looked around as the door opened and some folks walked in with drinks and cigarettes in hand. She said, "Look, I don't think we want to talk about this here."

Pine said, "Okay, we can go somewhere else. Drinks on me."

"You can't drink if you're pregnant," Weathers pointed out.

"Don't I know it. I meant I'd spring for drinks for you."

Axilrod said, "There's a place in Chinatown, Lucky Thirteen."

"Let's go," said Pine. "We can cab over together."

Axilrod said, "I'm not sure we should leave together. If something weird is going on here…" She looked worriedly at Weathers.

Weathers said, "I know where Lucky Thirteen is. I can meet you there."

Pine didn't look pleased. "Okay. But Sheila, if you don't show, I'm going to be pissed."

"Okay, okay. I'll be there. I swear."

Pine and Axilrod headed out past the two guys at the front door, who barely acknowledged their departure.

Pine said, "If she doesn't show, do you know where she lives?"

"No, but it's in the files at Fort Dix. I can access it."

"Good."

Before getting on the elevator Axilrod ordered an Uber.

A dark SUV pulled up front as soon as they hit the street.

"That's it," said Axilrod, glancing at her phone.

Pine got in first.

And that was the last thing she remembered before waking up in a dark place with a dead body next to her.

28

PINE ROLLED TO HER RIGHT and slowly came to. The next moment she was violently sick to her stomach and retched on the floor.

"Shit."

She sat up, rubbing her head and her belly. And froze.

Sheila Weathers was lying next to her. And unlike Pine, the lady would not be getting back up. The deep, wide gash right under her chin went from ear to ear. Pine looked around for her purse, but it wasn't there. She had no phone, no light. She had no idea where she was. Or how long she'd been unconscious.

There was blood everywhere, the floor, the body. She'd been killed here, and the arterial spray had coated the floor and the walls, and the corpse.

The woman was wearing the same clothes as earlier. Pine touched Weathers's hand. It was cold, but not ice cold. She moved her arm. No rigor. The woman's death hadn't happened all that long ago.

This made Pine think of something. She examined every inch of herself she could. Someone had taken her shoes and her bomber jacket, leaving her in just her jeans and shirt. There was blood on her shirt, her jeans, and her arms. She ran a hand across her face and felt the coagulated blood there. She touched her hair and felt it matted down with blood, too.

They must have killed her while I was lying here. She died right here, and her blood sprayed all over me while I was unconscious.

Her stomach lurched again, and she took deep breaths to keep the bile in her gut and her nerves from running away from her.

Okay, this was a crime scene, and she had to treat it as such.

And I'm part of that crime scene.

That was when she saw it. The knife. It was within a foot of her leg. She drew closer to it. She looked at the bloody handle and then at her bloody hand. She drew even closer, trying to see if…Shit, what if they had placed her hand around the knife while she was unconscious?

Then my prints will be on the murder weapon.

She scooted away from the body, sat on her rear, and took a long look around, trying to find some way out.

The walls were wood, and so was the floor. There were no windows that she could see. Pine continued to run her gaze around the walls until she came to a single door. It was made of wood and looked stout.

She got up and padded over to it in her bare feet.

She tried the door. It was locked.

Of course it's locked.

Then it occurred to her. Where the hell was Lindsey Axilrod? She'd gotten into the Uber with her.

Or had she?

Pine tried to recall every moment, but it was a complete muddle. Whatever they had used on her must have had an amnesiac component because her memory was blank.

So had they killed Axilrod, too? Was her body in one of the darkened corners of this room? Had her throat been slashed? Was Pine covered in her blood, too?

But then her thoughts recalibrated as she considered the matter more closely. She recalled that Axilrod had ordered the Uber and then identified the vehicle as being their Uber, which was the only reason Pine had gotten into the vehicle. Well, it had not been their Uber. It had not been an Uber at all, which left one obvious conclusion.

She set me up and I fell right for it.

Axilrod must be in on whatever was going on. Pine had gone to her, thinking she was simply a potential witness or lead to get to Vincenzo. And she played that role well, trying to convince Pine that nothing nefarious was going on. Then, she probably became afraid that if she didn't play along Pine would make good on her threat to send a search team to the apartment. She had no doubt arranged for there to be a "party" after she had met with Pine. Otherwise, it would have been a coincidence indeed that on the same day she had met Axilrod such an event would be scheduled. And when Weathers had started to talk, it had been Axilrod who suggested leaving the place. And to have Weathers leave separately.

Pine groaned at her gullibility. But she had been so fixated on finding out information, and, to her credit, Axilrod had played her role to perfection. She was clearly experienced in the art of deception.

And now I'm probably being framed for Weathers's murder.

She had to get out of here. She slammed her shoulder against the door. It didn't budge.

Then she froze as the sounds of footsteps reached her.

"Here, kitty, kitty," said a voice. "Here, kitty cat."

Pine backed away into the darkest corner she could find.

"Come out come out wherever you are," said the man tauntingly, which made Pine's blood burn.

The confident footsteps grew closer and suddenly a beam of light shot out and across the warehouse space.

"It will be faster if you don't run," said the voice. "If you run, I'll make it slow. If you stand still, it'll be over in a second. One little cut and it's over. I promise, kitty, kitty."

The man came around the corner. Pine squinted to see him better. He was tall, lean, broad shouldered. Maybe around her age. And the knife he held was serrated and glistened in the light. It had a curved blade and looked like something a ninja warrior might use to finish off a foe.

"I know you can hear me, kitty cat."

"Why did you kill Weathers?" Pine said as she slipped away and took up position in another corner.

"Don't be slow on the uptake. You told her you were pregnant with her boyfriend's baby. She got pissed. You met up here. Got in a fight. You killed her, kitty, kitty, but not before she cut you with the knife I'm holding right now. It just took longer for you to bleed out. Then it's case closed."

"No one is going to believe that."

"That's not my department. I'm a specialist. I'm sure you know in what."

"Bullshit." As soon as she spoke, Pine moved again. Her movements weren't haphazard. They were methodical. And she was now glad they had taken her shoes. She could move silently.

And the man was now moving toward where the sound of her voice had come from.

"You're running away. I told you not to do that."

"Help me, someone help me," cried out Pine, drawing his attention to the spot, but she had already moved.

"There is no one to help you."

He crept forward. No more talking. He was focused and wary, and maybe a little nervous that things were not going exactly to plan.

The powerful kick to his back sent the man headlong into the opposite wall. He slowly rose but Pine had already charged forward and struck him with a thunderous right hook, followed by a whip kick to his neck. He toppled to the side, cursing and moaning.

She barked, "Come here, *kitty, kitty*. So I can finish this."

He staggered up, grabbed a box, and threw it at her. She dodged out of the way, but that gave him time to grab the knife that he'd dropped.

"Now we'll see how good you are, bitch—"

A second later the knife was flying out of his hand as Pine crushed it with another whip kick and then locked the man down in an arm bar. She pitched forward, taking his limb to an angle that it had never been designed to go, and they landed on the floor. She jerked back with all her strength on his arm.

He screamed as multiple bones and tendons in his arm snapped all at once. He kicked at her, slamming a knee into her arm, which sent pain rocketing up and down her right side. Then he did it a second time, which made her let go. The two scrambled to their feet. As Pine was preparing to attack again, her foot slipped and she went down, hard.

He took the opportunity to run away, holding his ruined arm and sobbing in pain.

In a few seconds he had disappeared. Somewhere in the distance, Pine heard another door open and then slam shut.

"And I hate fucking cats," she screamed in his direction.

Pine slowly rose and shook out her arm where a stinger she'd gotten from the right hook she'd struck him with had gone all the way up her shoulder. She turned to the door again, backed up a bit, then ran forward, pivoted, and kicked her right leg out, smashing her toughened heel against the wood. The door buckled under the thunderous blow but did not open.

She set her feet, studied the door, and then fired off a front knee kick right below the lock. The shaft broke free from the doorjamb, and the weakened portal swung loose on its hinges.

She peered out to see an ill-lighted set of stairs leading down. She listened for a few seconds, for footsteps, breathing, words, anything that would give away the presence of someone other than her being here.

She went down the steps tentatively, reached a landing, turned, and kept going down. At the bottom of the stairs, she paused in front of the door. There was a window next to it, but it had been blacked out. She could hear noises outside, cars, what might have been a conversation, the screech of a cat, more cars.

She reached out and turned the doorknob. To her surprise the door was unlocked.

She drew a long breath, and swung the door open. She looked out onto a darkened street, where it was raining steadily. She saw no passersby, which made sense on such an inclement night, and she had no idea how late it was.

A car passed by and was gone before she could step outside. She went down a short flight of steps and reached the ground.

An instant later she was hit by a strong spotlight.

"NYPD. Get down on the pavement, hands behind your head. Do it. Now."

Pine sank down to the pavement and put her hands behind her head.

"Don't shoot," she cried out.

Damn, this night is just getting better and better.

29

JOHN PULLER HAD GRABBED a bumpy ride in a jump seat on a military transport plane into Andrews Air Force Base. From there he'd bummed a ride with an agent in the Air Force's CID with whom he'd worked a joint case. This ride dropped him at the metro, and he rode the subway to his final destination. The Pentagon was the largest office building on earth.

It had been in the middle of a renovation when one of its five sides had received a gut punch on 9/11 in the form of a hijacked American Airlines jumbo jet piloted by Saudis intent on bringing down the country. In addition to all the passengers on the jet, more than a hundred people had died sitting behind their desks or walking along a corridor or just chatting with colleagues. A small memorial chapel had been erected at the spot where the jet had hit. But the facility had been quickly repaired and was now stronger than ever. It would have to be, thought Puller. Because the world kept getting more unpredictable by the minute.

He cleared security after showing his cred pack and relaying to the guards that he was armed. He walked down a labyrinth of corridors without an escort, keeping tightly to the route he knew well. The Pentagon had nearly eighteen miles of halls, with Rings A to E and Corridors One to Ten on the main level. You could work here your entire career and still get lost, although the way it was designed a trip between two points shouldn't take longer than seven minutes. Puller had never gone awry in finding any location in Afghanistan or Iraq, but he had become lost multiple times here. Each one had been a humbling event, especially the one time when an elderly woman, a veteran and visitor that day, had taken him by the hand and guided him to where he needed to go. Almost the reverse scenario of the vintage image of a Boy Scout helping an older person cross the street.

He entered the office suite, where the spacious anteroom and displayed flags denoted the ultrahigh rank of the man he was meeting tonight. This was the vice chair of the Joint Chiefs. He was the second-highest-ranking person in the U.S. military world. The vice chair received his fourth star upon elevation to the position. By law he could not be in the same military branch as the chairman. Currently the chairman was Air Force; the vice chair wore the same uniform as Puller, which was one of the reasons Puller was here.

The junior officer greeted Puller and led him into the interior office, which was of a size befitting the man's lofty position. On one wall was the "wall of love," as the Army liked to call it. It was a photo array of the VIPs smiling, shaking hands, and rubbing shoulders with the current occupant of this office.

And that would be Tom Pitts, around five eleven, built like a chunk of granite, with facial features to match. The grip of his handshake equaled that of Puller, who was around twenty-five years younger. The four stars rode well on his broad shoulders. He was one of only fourteen four-stars in the entire Army, and one of only forty-two in the entire Armed Forces of the United States. A combat veteran, Pitts had more than earned every medal and ribbon.

"I went by to see your old man the other day," began Pitts.

Puller was a bit surprised by this, and his face showed it as they sat down across from each other on matching couches set next to Pitts's desk.

"I didn't know that," said Puller.

"I would have given you a heads-up, but the fact was it was a spur-of-the-moment thing. We were passing by the VA hospital and... I just wanted to see Fighting John Puller."

"You don't need my permission, sir. I'm sure he enjoyed seeing you."

"Your father's forgotten more about leading soldiers into battle than I'll ever know."

Puller looked down. "He's forgotten a lot, sir. Too much."

Pitts's features clouded. "A poor choice of words on my part. I'm sorry. I understand his condition is not…going to improve?"

"No sir, not unless there's a miracle."

Pitts nodded slowly, his features somber and faraway. Then he snapped back, like a crisp salute. "But you didn't come here for that. What can I do for you?"

It took Puller about two minutes to fully bring Pitts up to speed. The general's face grew longer and longer as Puller went on. When he was finished Pitts said, "I'm not sure I've heard anything that extraordinary. It's inexplicable."

"I thought the same. But with the roadblocks being thrown up, and as you used to be the head of CID, I thought you might want to be made aware."

"And your chain of command?"

Puller cleared his throat and took a few moments to compose his response with great care. There was nothing so sacred in the Army as the chain of command. A soldier who went outside of it better have a damn good reason, and even that wasn't always enough.

He ended with, "So, you can see that I went through all the usual channels, sir."

"Yes, I can. And?"

"And none of my issues have been resolved. And my superiors seem to be as perplexed as I am."

"That is not acceptable."

"I thought you might see it that way."

"You're investigating crimes involving military personnel. You have every right to pursue whatever lead and whatever evidence comes your way. There is no provision for anyone blocking your access, civilian or military, and certainly not the government."

"Well, some folks apparently have not gotten that message."

"I will follow that up. You have a job to do and you should be allowed to do it."

"Thank you, sir."

"Leave it with me for now. But come back to see me in twenty-four hours. I'll know more by then."

Pitts stood and so did Puller. He knew the general probably had ten more meetings before he was going to call it quits for the day, and every one of them almost certainly dealt with far more pressing matters.

Puller departed and hurried back down the hallway. He had debated long and hard on whether to call in the chit represented by Pitts, but then decided he had nothing to lose.

Outside he stared back at the building that, ever since its construction during World War II, had been synonymous with the might of the American military. It had taken some heat during unpopular wars and been heralded when things turned out okay. Puller knew that was just the way the world worked. But at least the building was still here. Puller never hoped for war. No soldier he'd ever met did. But if it came to it, the country needed a place just like this.

Unfortunately, in a little over an hour he would be back in combat.

CHAPTER

30

Puller jumped back on the metro and rode it to the Reagan National stop, where he had left his personal car in long-term parking. He drove south on Interstate 95 to his apartment, where he found his cat, AWOL, lounging on the kitchen counter, his tail flicking back and forth like a furry metronome.

He leaned against the counter and spent ten seconds rubbing AWOL's ears, which was the length of time AWOL allotted him before wanting to be left alone. An elderly neighbor came in and took care of the cat while Puller was away. And with Puller's schedule, the neighbor probably saw more of AWOL than he did.

AWOL suddenly turned his luminous green eyes toward the window. Puller was on the second floor of an apartment building not that far from Quantico. CID headquarters was located there on Telegraph Road in the same complex as the Marine Corps base. He watched as AWOL crept over to the kitchen window and looked out. The cat's tail went down and its back went up. Puller heard AWOL hiss.

Puller had been in the Middle East where the most innocuous sounds often led to the most deaths and destruction. Because of that, his internal antennae had been fine-tuned to such an extent that what he could hear and discern from it was almost otherworldly. He would use a different phrase for it.

It makes you a soldier who survives.

And it really helped when you had a cat with even better antennae than a human would ever have.

His M11 came out of its holster and he nudged AWOL with the pistol's butt. The cat leaped off the counter, landed silently on the floor, and disappeared into another room.

There was only one door into and out of the apartment. There were two windows facing the street. There was no outside deck. It was just nine hundred square feet of a typical American apartment. Puller's government salary was good, higher than the median pay, though far lower than he would have made in the private sector. He could have afforded a more luxurious place, but why pay for something he barely used? And it wasn't like AWOL cared what his accommodations looked like.

He slipped over to the side of one of the windows and eased the curtain back. It was dark outside, but his eyes had been trained to see in the dark.

In the lighted parking lot were lots of darkened cars. But there was one where he could see steam rising off the hood because the motor was on and the falling rain was being heated. The car's lights were out, so why sit there with the engine running?

Then he saw two shadows about fifty feet from the car and moving toward the building. They were moving slowly. That was a telltale sign because it was raining, and normal people hurried to get out of the rain. These were obviously not normal people.

He moved across the small space to his front door, opened it a crack, and peered out.

Stealthy footsteps scraped the steps.

Puller grabbed a to-go knapsack that he kept in the closet by the front door and threw it over his shoulder. He eased out of his apartment and closed the door behind him. He moved noiselessly down the outside corridor and took up position behind an ice-maker unit.

He took aim and waited.

The first figure appeared at the top of the stairs, stopped for a moment to look around, and then motioned to his partner to follow him up. They reached Puller's door just about the time that Puller pushed two sound mufflers into his ears.

They checked the lock. Puller hadn't left it open. He didn't want to make it too easy for them. The first man pulled something from his pocket and worked away at the lock while the second man kept watch.

The lock was defeated, and the first man pushed the door open an inch at a time. A few moments later both men disappeared inside. Puller moved from his position, pulling something from his knapsack as he did so. He put on a pair of night-vision goggles right as he reached the door. He peered inside the front room and saw the backs of the men. He pulled the pin on the object he was holding, held it for two seconds, and then tossed it inside. He stepped away and placed his back flat against the outside wall.

The flashbang did exactly what it was designed to do. The blinding flash robbed both men of their vision. The simultaneous bang robbed them of their senses. Puller heard both men cry out and fall to the floor.

Puller waited two seconds and then stepped inside.

The men were writhing and moaning on the floor of the small kitchen. When one tried to get up, Puller tapped him rather hard on the back of the neck with his fist, and the man went down for the count. The other fellow tried to raise his gun, but Puller quickly disarmed him and then laid him out with an M11 slap to the head.

He was about to call the police when a burst of machine-gun fire from the front-door area made him dive for cover behind a couch. The guys he had already dealt with were apparently only the advance team.

Both M11s were out now and he fired back at the doorway. Another burst of bullets tore into the couch, and a second after it ended Puller sprinted to the right, kicked open his bedroom door, and slammed it shut behind him.

He dove to the floor right as more machine-gun rounds shred-ded the door and ripped into the far wall. He flipped on his back, and with both pistols he fired back through the torn-apart door. Next second he heard the sirens. Machine-gun fire that wasn't happening as part of an exercise at Quantico drew the attention of the legion of military and FBI personnel who called this place home. Still, Puller was thinking:

What the hell took them so long?

He slammed in spare mags, moved to the left, listened to the sounds of slight movement, and then emptied one mag through the thin drywall connecting up with his front room. He was rewarded with a grunt and someone falling and hopefully dead.

He dove into the small attached bathroom as multiple bursts of gunfire tore through the wall and ripped his bedroom to shreds.

Then he heard feet stumbling from the front room, a door being banged open, and now running feet rushing away.

He got up, went back into his bedroom, and cautiously peered out.

There was no one in the room. He ran over to the window and saw men running toward the vehicle with its engine on and lights off. They were half-carrying another man, who might have been the one Puller had shot. They climbed into the SUV and the driver hit the gas.

Puller slid his window open, took aim, and fired his other M11 at the fleeing vehicle until his hammer clicked dry. At this range, he couldn't have expected to stop it with a pistol shot.

In another few seconds the SUV had turned the corner and was gone.

As the sounds of the sirens drew closer, Puller went in search of and found AWOL. He was on the top shelf of the closet, behind a plastic bin where Puller had kept some of his winter clothing. There was a bullet hole right through the bin.

An unhurt AWOL meowed and jumped down onto Puller's shoulder. Puller left the closet and sat on his destroyed bed while he tickled AWOL's chin. The cat didn't budge. He apparently didn't want to be alone.

Puller couldn't blame the feline.

He surveyed what was left of his apartment. The two guys he

had laid out were gone. Their buddies must have revived them and they had fled in the SUV.

He glanced down at his twin empty M11s and let out a long, relieved breath.

I thought I left the Middle East behind.

CHAPTER

31

Pine could smell the stink of her own sweat as she sat, alone, in the holding cell handcuffed to a metal bench which, in turn, was bolted to the floor.

Never thought I'd see the world from this side of the bars.

She was still shoeless, still covered in blood, and she was freezing.

She looked up to see a man standing there. He was in his fifties, paunchy, balding, and holding a manila file folder. His expression alternated between grim and bored.

"You the one who keeps saying you're an FBI agent?"

"I do because I am. And I'd like to make a phone call."

"Absolutely. We just got a few people ahead of you in the line. Busy night tonight. Must be a full moon."

"Who are you, anyway?"

He tapped the badge riding on his belt. "Detective Milton Barnes. Your case got dropped in my lap, lucky me. Who's the dead girl they found you next to?"

"I told the cops that already. And also about the guy in there who tried his best to kill me."

"We didn't find any guy, but tell me about the woman."

"Her name, at least I was told, was Sheila Weathers. I was also told she worked at the commissary at Fort Dix."

"You were *told*?"

"Can I get these cuffs off, clean up, and get a blanket? And what, did you not pay your heating bill? It's like forty degrees in here."

"Sure. I can pay for your lawyer, too. And you'll get a free car and a trip to Antigua if you're acquitted of murder. What, you think this is *Wheel of Fortune* or something?"

"I'm Special Agent Atlee Pine of the FBI. Take a picture of me and email it to the Bureau. They'll confirm I am who I say I am."

"Where are your badge and creds? That would move things along a lot faster than a picture."

"I was undercover. Highly inconvenient if they'd found them on me. I didn't even bring my phone."

"Uh-huh. Turned out to be dangerous anyway. For the dead lady. Your prints are all over the murder weapon, by the way."

"Then somebody squeezed my hand around it while I was out. Maybe the guy who was going to cut my throat. They were obviously going to frame me for her murder."

"Cops got a call about a fight in that building. Screams and stuff getting knocked around."

"Right, that was me and the guy. I broke the jerk's arm in about six places. I gave a description of him to NYPD. Try going around to the emergency rooms. The asshole's probably in one crying like a baby."

The man continued. "They go there and out you pop all covered in blood and your prints on the knife. What do you think I'm thinking? That you're undercover FBI like you say, or you're a killer. This ain't TV, lady. This ain't a plot twist, okay?"

"Just take the picture and send it to the Bureau." She had a sudden thought. "To Special Agent Eddie Laredo, of the New York Field Office."

"Okay, while we're waiting, you can come with me."

He had a uniformed cop unlock the door and her cuff and led Pine to an interrogation room. The cop then pushed her down into a chair set at a table, locked her leg into a bolt in the floor, and left. Barnes sat down across from her and put the file down on the table.

"We haven't identified the vic yet."

"I told you who she was."

"Who you were *told* she was. What were you doing in that building?"

"I was knocked out and taken there. I woke up next to the body."

"Where were you taken from?"

She gave him the address of the building on Fifty-Seventh Street.

"Ritzy neighborhood," he said.

"You might want to pay attention to it. You might find a lot of international crooks live pretty well there."

"Tell me something I don't know. And they got twenty lawyers for every one we got, so who's gonna win that battle? So keep talking. What happened next?"

"I confirmed that she was dead and then kicked the crap out of the guy who'd been sent there to finish me off. And then I broke out of the room. That's when the cops showed up and almost shot me."

"You're covered in *her* blood, you know. They checked you for wounds and found none."

"My arm has twin bruises about the size of Rhode Island. What do you call that?"

"So you beat this guy up and he just ran off? Doesn't seem likely."

"Why, because I'm a girl? Give me a two-by-four and I'll show you how hard I can hit."

"I'll take your word for it. You know, we could have put all of you in a giant evidence bag. We're going to need to take those clothes and run swabs all over you."

"I'm surprised you haven't done that yet."

"We need the suits to paper it first. Don't want you running around screaming about your Fourth Amendment rights being violated, do we, Ms. FBI Agent?"

She calmed and studied him, sensing an opportunity. "You have two exceptions to the Fourth Amendment protection against unreasonable search and seizure, at least with respect to my situation."

Barnes watched her closely, suddenly looking intrigued. "Oh yeah? What's that?"

"Plain view, which the blood on me obviously is."

"And the other?"

"Search incident to a lawful arrest with a condition being the preservation of evidence. Again, a condition my situation meets perfectly. I won't charge you for either one of those. It's on the house. Fed to local cop. Want to return the favor?"

Barnes sat up straighter and his confrontational look slowly dissipated. "So, what case you working, Agent Pine?"

"It's a long story."

"What was that name again at the FBI?"

"Eddie Laredo. So now you believe me?"

Barnes stood. "You said you were a cop and I gave you the chance to prove it. Plain view and incident to with all necessary criteria laid out just like it is on the detective's exam? You passed with flying colors. Only a cop's going to know that stuff."

He left and was gone far longer than a minute. Pine had actually put her head down on the table and fallen asleep. Whatever they had used on her to knock her out had really kicked her ass.

She woke up when the door opened.

"Well, well, so we meet again."

FBI Special Agent Eddie Laredo looked down at her, an incredulous grin on his face.

As Pine looked up at him, she was both extraordinarily happy to see him, but also wanted to strangle him just to wipe the smirk off his features.

It might have been a very good thing that she was bolted to the floor.

CHAPTER

32

This sounds like some serious crap you're involved in," said Laredo as he drove Pine back to Newark where her car was. It was late the following morning, and Pine had spent much of the ride filling Laredo in on what had happened.

Pine had given her statement to the NYPD, turned over her clothes for evidence, had photos taken of the blood spatter on her body, and then been released. They had given her blue hospital scrubs and flip-flops in place of her clothes, and she had left the precinct with Laredo.

"Story of my life, Eddie."

"And this CID guy you're working with?"

"John Puller, yeah."

"You talked to him?"

"I haven't talked to anyone, other than Carol Blum on your phone."

"All this pushback you've been getting from the locals and the feds, that's really troublesome, Atlee."

"You think I don't know that?"

"And this lowlife Tony Vincenzo playing with the big boys in that penthouse? How does that make sense?"

"I don't know. Maybe they like to keep the foot soldiers happy. Hell, it's probably empty except when they let the riffraff come up to play. But it is bizarre."

"Well, I wish you luck. Sounds like you're going to need it."

He dropped her at her car, where Blum was going to meet her.

As Laredo pulled away, Blum drove up in an Uber. She got out, walked over, and gave Pine a hug.

When Blum stepped back, Pine saw the other woman's strained features. "I'm fine, Carol, I really am."

"I know," Blum said in a hushed voice. "But it was close, wasn't it?"

"It was," she conceded.

She held up a spare set of car keys for the rental. "Now, let's get you back to the hotel and cleaned up."

They drove back to the hotel and Pine did just as Blum had suggested. The hot water took off the blood and grime. She stood in the shower for at least thirty minutes, letting both the stink and another woman's blood flow off her. As she watched the red swirl down the drain, she leaned her forehead against the tile of the shower wall and started to sob. She wasn't sure why—no, maybe part of her did know.

Lindsey Axilrod played me like a fiddle. And Sheila Weathers is dead because of it.

She toweled off, dried her hair, and changed into fresh clothes after throwing the scrubs and flip-flops into the trash.

Starving, she took the elevator down to the lobby and walked into the hotel restaurant, where she ordered coffee and a sandwich. She pulled out her phone to check her messages. There were three from Puller in her mailbox.

She quickly called him. "Everything okay?"

"I guess it didn't warrant the national news pipeline," he said.

"What are you talking about?"

Puller filled her in on the attack at his apartment.

"Oh my God. How did you get out of that alive?"

"My cat alerted me."

"Wait a minute, you have a cat?"

"AWOL. He sensed them before I did. Not sure how, but I pay attention when he gets riled. So when they came in, I wasn't there. I was waiting outside my apartment with flashbangs and my M11s. Got the jump on them. But some reinforcements showed up and they all got away."

"Thank God for AWOL."

"I've been trying to get ahold of you," he said.

Her coffee and sandwich arrived, and she took a sip of her drink. "You got a few minutes? I had my own little adventure." She filled him in on what had happened to her the previous night.

"You're lucky to be alive, too," he said.

"I know."

"So this Lindsey Axilrod was a setup?"

"Yes."

"I gave you her name. So this is on me."

"You had no idea. I'm normally suspicious of everyone, but Axilrod played it just right. She put me off my guard with her dumb-girl routine, and letting me think I was leading her around, when it was actually the reverse. I can tell you I'm never getting into another Uber again."

"So the odds are very good that Axilrod does not show up for work today."

"And I highly doubt we'll find her at home, but I'm going to check there anyway."

"I can send you the address. I have it in my files."

"How did your 'attack' plan go?"

"I met with him yesterday, drove home, and got ambushed. I have no idea if the two events are connected. I hope they're not, because that would suggest a mole inside the Army at a pretty high level."

"I think Teddy Vincenzo was spot-on when he said his son was in way over his head."

"The son might not even be alive at this point," noted Puller.

"If not, there goes my only lead to Ito. So what's your next move?"

"I should wait for my command to get back to me. But I don't think I will. I don't like it when people come to my home and shoot it up. I take that personally."

"What are you going to do about it?"

"Somebody must have seen something last night. It's not like they were bothering to keep quiet; they brought full artillery. What about you?"

"I also don't take kindly when someone pulls the shit they did with me last night. So shoot me her address and I'm going after Axilrod."

"Let's compare notes later, and Atlee, I know I don't have to tell you, but I am anyway."

"I'm going to watch every flank I have. And trust nobody."

"Copy that."

The phone went dead. Pine finished her coffee and sandwich and then had another cup.

When she saw Blum enter the restaurant, she waved her over.

"I'm sorry, Carol, I should have invited you to eat with me."

"No, it's fine. I already ate." She sat down and looked at her boss.

Pine read everything in the woman's eyes. "I know, Carol. I know. I have to be more careful." She took a few minutes to fill Blum in on what had happened to Puller.

"My God! So I assume you've talked to him?"

"Just now. He said his cat saved him."

"Good cats do, you know," replied Blum matter-of-factly.

Pine's expression darkened. "A woman is dead because of me, Carol. And I have to make that right."

"I had already anticipated that you would say that. But I'll tell you what I told you back in Andersonville. You're here to find out what happened to your sister. And while the two cases may have some tangential connections, you could spend all your time on one, solve it, and make no progress on your sister."

"I *had* thought about that. But I can't just let this go. A young kid with a great future is dead. I saw him die. A young woman who was out at a party had her head nearly cut off. And I think she was chosen as a victim so that I could be set up and found dead with the body. So that's on me, too. I am not going to let these assholes get away with this. I'm an FBI agent. This is my wheelhouse. And it always will be."

"Another thing I anticipated you saying. And I'm not disagreeing with you. I just want you to move forward fully informed. Including my two cents."

Pine reached out and gripped Blum's hand. "I appreciate your two cents. It always turns out to be far more valuable than that."

"So what now?"

"I have *two* people to find. Tony Vincenzo and Lindsey Axilrod. And who knows, one might very well lead me to the other."

CHAPTER

33

PULLER EMAILED LINDSEY AXILROD'S home address to Pine. In it he also verified that Axilrod had not shown up for work that morning. She and Blum drove over to the small bungalow situated in a quiet neighborhood about five miles from Fort Dix.

"No car in the driveway," observed Blum.

"Front door closed. No lights on that I can see, though it is daylight. No one lurking in the bushes."

They pulled to a stop at the curb, got out, and walked up to the front door. Pine rapped on the wood and waited. No answer. She rapped harder, with the same result.

Pine eyed the doorbell. "She has a doorbell with a camera, so she's probably watching us right now from wherever she is." They walked to the backyard, where there were two listing and rusted poles set in concrete and the remnants of a rotted clothesline, which was hanging down to the ground. A wooden and shingled utility shed sat back against the fence.

Pine walked over to it and peered in one of the windows. "No dead bodies hanging from the rafters. Just a lawn mower and some gardening tools."

"What do we do now?" asked Blum.

"I'd really like to get into her house."

"But without a search warrant we have no legal standing to do so. And if you're thinking about breaking and entering again, I would advise against it."

"Maybe I can do something that would allow us *legal* entry then."

She made a call and said, "I'm FBI Special Agent Atlee Pine. I was supposed to meet with a woman named Lindsey Axilrod about a matter I'm investigating. She did not show up for work today and we're at her home now. She is not responding to my knocks. I'd like you to do a welfare check on her because I'm worried that something might have happened to her." Pine gave the address and put her phone away and looked at Blum.

Five minutes later a cruiser pulled up in front of the house and two uniforms climbed out. One was in his forties, overweight with a flushed face and a bored look. The other was about a decade younger, tall and thin with a runner's build, who looked far more animated than his partner at having been called in by the Bureau.

"You the FBI agent?" said the older cop. His name tag read DONNELLY, and he looked like a man going through the motions until his pension kicked in.

Pine produced her badge and creds and introduced Blum.

The younger cop, who had excitedly identified himself as Officer Brent Tatum, said, "What were you investigating with the lady who lives here?"

"Not something I can disclose, really, but I can tell you that she was a potential witness for something critical to national security that was going on at her place of work."

"Which was where, exactly?" asked Donnelly.

"Fort Dix."

"But that's military."

"I'm working the case with Army CID."

Donnelly rubbed his chin and shot a glance at the house. "Locked?"

"Yes. She has a doorbell camera, but she didn't respond, which she could have even if she wasn't here."

"We better check this out, Dan," said Tatum.

His partner didn't seem inclined to do so, but he hitched up his gun belt and led the way up the walk. He knocked on the door and got no answer. Then he bent down to the doorbell and said, "Ms. Axilrod, are you here?"

"Hello, who is that?"

Donnelly straightened, shot a look at Pine, and said, "Officer Donnelly with the Trenton Police Department. Is this Ms. Axilrod?"

"Yes it is. What do you want?"

"We have an FBI agent here, Agent Pine, who said she was supposed to meet with you."

"Oh, I think I remember that. But I was called out of town on a family emergency. I'll have to get back to her when I return."

Pine strode past Donnelly and said, "Axilrod, I need to know where you are, right now."

"I'm sorry, but I have to go. I'm at the hospital with my mother. I'll call you later."

"Axilrod!" barked Pine, but the door camera remained silent.

"Well, that's that, she's got a family emergency," said Donnelly. "She'll call you when she gets back, like she said. You sure she didn't say anything from the camera when you knocked earlier?"

Pine gave him an incredulous look and he said quickly, "Well, least she's okay. Have a good day."

They got back into their cruiser and pulled off, leaving Pine and Blum standing there.

Pine leaned down to the camera and said, "Hey, Lindsey, I'm really looking forward to seeing you again. And next time you send somebody to kill me, better make it a girl. The guys keep coming up short. And just so you know, however long it takes, one day I'm going to put my cuffs on you and read you your rights. And you're going to get a lifetime supply of prison food."

They walked back to the car and got in.

"Can we trace her from that door camera? It must be tied to her phone."

"Yes. If I could get a warrant. But I'm not even officially

working this case. Puller could try, but by the time he gets a warrant it'll be too late."

Her phone rang.

"Jack?" said Pine. "How are you feeling?"

"Better," said Lineberry. "There's talk of letting me go home tomorrow or the next day. But I was calling because I came up with an old contact for you. His name is Douglas Bennett. He's in his early seventies now and lives in Annapolis."

"What was his involvement?" she asked.

"He was my handler."

"So he was with the CIA then? As were you? You were never clear on that."

"And I'm not admitting to anything now, Atlee. But Doug was intimately involved and knew both your parents, and he actually met you and your sister. You wouldn't remember that, of course. He's long since retired and spends his days sailing, taking long walks with his prized Labradoodles, Finnegan and Guinness, and puttering around his garden."

"Is he married?"

"He was. Joan died two years ago. A car accident. He lives alone now, except for his dogs, his books, his boat, and his memories."

"So you kept in touch all these years?"

"Yes. He's a good man. A good friend."

Pine, who was already in a bad mood because of Axilrod, barked, "Which means you should have thought of him off the top of your head when I asked you for old contacts, but you said you had to *think* about it."

"The fact is, I had no idea if Doug would talk to you. I wasn't going to give you his name until I cleared it with him."

"So he's agreed to meet?" Pine said in a calmer tone.

"We wouldn't be having this discussion if he hadn't. I'll text you his address."

"And how much does he know of my situation?"

"Some. I thought I'd leave it to you to explain the bulk of it."

"Okay, Jack, thanks. And sorry for snapping at you. It hasn't been a great twenty-four hours for me."

"Good luck."

He clicked off, leaving Pine lost in thought.

"Well?" asked Blum.

Pine glanced up. "Looks like we're heading to Annapolis."

CHAPTER

34

THEY PULLED INTO ANNAPOLIS after a nearly four-hour car journey and were driving down one of the main streets of the town, a quaint shopping area also filled with exclusive and nicely tricked out bed-and-breakfasts and small inns.

The twin heavy smells of fish and salt air from the nearby water fell thickly on them.

"The Naval Academy is down that way," said Pine, pointing to her right. "I had a friend who graduated from there."

"Pretty prestigious," said Blum.

"And right down here is Doug Bennett's house. He has a place right on the harbor. Nice location."

They parked in front of a gray, shingled Cape Cod. They could see the mast of a docked sailboat rise up from behind the house.

They walked up a flagstone path to the front door.

Blum noted the neat, mulched flower beds, healthy lawn, and trees, and said, "A disciplined, methodical person."

Pine had called ahead, and the door opened as soon as she knocked. Facing her was Doug Bennett. He was about six feet tall and beefy of build, with a shock of white hair and a tanned, weathered face. He had on khaki pants and a white polo shirt with the Naval Academy's insignia printed on it.

Two large and curly-haired dogs stood on either side of him, as though at attention. One had a white coat, and the other was black and tan with a bit of orange around its muzzle.

An unlit cigar was perched in one corner of Bennett's mouth.

He looked gruff, but when he saw Pine he smiled. He took the cigar out.

"My God, Lee. Last time I saw you, I held you in one arm."

"Mr. Bennett, thank you for agreeing to meet with me. This is my associate, Carol Blum."

"Ms. Blum, very nice to meet you. Please come in."

He backed away and the dogs moved with him.

"And who are these handsome boys?" asked Pine.

"The tall white one is Finnegan, Finn for short. The black and tan, of course, is Guinness."

"Labradoodles?" said Blum.

"Yes. I have allergies. These boys do not shed. They have hair, not fur. And they keep me company," he added quietly. "We take long walks together. They are…sound friends."

Blum glanced around the front room and saw it was decorated in blues and golds and whites. The room had a nautical feel, organized with a place for everything and everything in its place. A wall of built-in cabinetry was filled with photos and books. She saw several photos of the same woman always standing next to Bennett.

Pine noticed this, too. "Jack told us about the loss of your wife. We're very sorry."

Bennett's features clouded and one of his hands reached down and started to stroke Finn's head.

"Yes. It was…a shock."

"Do you have children?" Blum asked.

He shook his head. "Please sit down. Would you like something to drink? This is about the time of the day where I have a finger or two of scotch."

"I'll just take water," said Pine.

"I'll join you in the scotch," said Blum, drawing a surprised look from Pine.

Bennett led them through to the rear of the house, where he poured out the drinks, and they settled in comfortable chairs overlooking the water. Finn and Guinness lay on either side of their owner and friend.

"Is that your boat?" asked Pine.

"Yes. The *Saint Joan*." He smiled sadly. "A little joke between us. It's taken on new meaning now, at least for me."

"Do the dogs go with you?"

"The dogs go everywhere with me. The two best first mates I've ever had." He added in a pensive tone, "I spent much of my working life alone, just because the mission called for that. Now I don't like to be alone." He took a sip of his scotch and looked out at his boat.

"I'm sure," said Blum.

"So, Jack said you'd talk to me about what happened all those years ago?"

He focused on her. It seemed to Pine that the man was once more assuming a professional veneer over his long-since-retired features. "I'll tell you what I can. I don't think it will be everything. Some of the things have never been declassified."

"You know what happened to me and my sister?"

"Yes." He swallowed with a bit of difficulty, and Pine thought she could see his eyes glisten before he looked away and rubbed at them. "Yes. It was unfortunate and unforgivable. It was the worst failure of my professional life. Jack's, too." He paused and added, "But that was nothing compared to what happened to your family."

"Thank you," said Pine. "What can you tell us?"

"I spoke with Jack, of course. He filled me in on what he had told you. Thus, you know what your mother's role was in all that. She was the inside source in our sting operation against the New York Mafia back in the eighties."

"Yes. Her real name was Amanda. I never knew her real last name."

"Doesn't matter. All that was officially changed, so the Pine family you all became."

"And my father worked as a bartender at the Cloak and Dagger bar in New York, where part of the sting took place. I was surprised that all of the people working there wouldn't be law enforcement."

"We didn't have enough bodies to fill all the roles," explained Bennett. "Your father had no idea what was going on, of course. He just poured the drinks."

"But then he and my mother became intimate. And she confided in him?"

Bennett slowly nodded. "Damn nuisance, that was. But your mother was so young and under so much pressure. I could hardly blame her for reaching out to Tim. She must have felt very alone."

"You're right, they were both very young. So did they have any family?" asked Pine. "Were their parents still alive? Siblings? Grandparents?"

"They both told us no."

"But did you check?"

"Checking would have led to a possible trail and opened doors that someone could have followed up on. We made the decision to take them at their word."

"It would be unusual for both of them not to have any family," noted Blum.

"I'm sure they *did* have family. But again, we didn't push it. And to my knowledge neither of them tried to contact anyone while they were under our watch." He looked at Pine. "Did you ever meet any of their 'family'? Or I guess your family, too."

"No."

Bennett frowned. "In WITSEC, that's the sacrifice one makes. All ties severed. It's the only way to keep the protectees safe."

"But it didn't work in our case," said Pine. "Two attempts were made on our lives. We had to be taken out of WITSEC."

Bennett's frown deepened. "I know. That drove me nuts."

"There had to be a leak," said Blum.

"I agree, but we could never find it. And we looked, long and hard. Checked and rechecked everything."

"After we left WITSEC, we resettled in Andersonville, Georgia."

"Yes, I know. Jack and I worked on that."

"And he was sent down to keep watch over us."

"Yes."

"But a man named Ito Vincenzo found us."

Bennett sat up and drilled her with a fierce stare. "Vincenzo?"

"As in Bruno Vincenzo's brother. Jack didn't tell you that part?"

"No, he didn't. You're sure. You're sure it was Bruno's brother?"

"Yes. Without a doubt."

"But why would this Ito — ?"

"Bruno found out that my mom was a spy for the feds, but he didn't turn her in. I found a letter that Bruno sent his brother, Ito. In so many words, Bruno intimated that he'd gotten screwed. I'm speculating that he expected some type of sweetheart deal for keeping his mouth shut. Only he went to prison and was killed there."

"I never knew about any deal offered to Bruno. And I sure as hell didn't know he knew about your mother working for us."

"Jack didn't know, either. He said he would have stopped the op if he had."

"We would have, yes."

"If my mother had found out that Bruno could have outed her, could she have offered a deal to him without you knowing about it?"

"She had no authority to do that. She was a mole, she didn't represent the government," replied Bennett. He paused and looked pensive. "But I came to know your mother pretty well. She was smart and cunning beyond her years, and what we were asking her to do made her even more so, simply to survive. I think it's possible that if Bruno approached her and let her know that her cover was blown, she might have pretended to promise him a deal in order to keep her secret. God, she must have been scared. Bruno Vincenzo was one of the mob's heavy hitters. No one knows how many people that bastard killed."

Pine considered all of this and said, "I think you're probably right. So Bruno kept his mouth shut and thought he had a deal. But that deal didn't come through. Meantime, my mom, my dad, my sister, and I go into hiding. Then Bruno gets arrested and jailed. But before he goes to prison, he writes Ito a letter laying out some of his grievances. And he asks Ito to see him in jail. I think it was at that time that he told Ito we were in Andersonville, which we probably were by then."

"Do you think Bruno also knew about your locations while you were in WITSEC, and was the catalyst for those attacks?"

"I don't know. It's possible. But the mob has long arms. They could have paid off people connected to WITSEC to reveal our locations."

"What do you know about Ito Vincenzo?" asked Bennett.

"He ran an ice cream parlor in Trenton and was never in trouble with the law. But then I have proof positive that he came down to Georgia, almost killed me, and took my sister. She's never been seen since."

"What happened to him?"

"He came back to Trenton after a few months' absence. He explained that away to his wife and workers by saying he'd been to Italy. Then years later he disappeared again, and this time he never came back."

Bennett sat back, looking like he had aged ten years in the last couple of minutes. "This is all so extraordinary. It's like waking up from a bad dream to find yourself in a nightmare. A real one."

"So the question becomes, how did Ito, a man with no criminal or other helpful connections, find us in Georgia?"

"I think it's obvious, like you suggested. His brother told him where you were."

"I agree," said Pine. "But how did *Bruno* find out?"

Bennett shook his head. "As I said before, we could never determine the leak."

"One other thing, Mr. Bennett, did Jack tell you…about him and my mother?"

Bennett stiffened and set his drink down. "I'm not sure what you mean?"

Pine drew a long breath, glanced at Blum for a second, and said, "Well, for instance, that Jack is my father?"

Bennett's expression was one of total shock. He abruptly stood and swayed a bit. His agitation was so great that both dogs started to whine, perhaps sensing their owner's distress.

"Your father? But that means—"

"Yes, he and my mother were together right before she met Tim."

Bennett slowly sat back down. "Jesus, maybe *that's* why he broke up with Linda. I never could figure that one out."

Now it was Pine who looked stunned. "Linda? Who's Linda?"

"Well, back then she was Jack's fiancée."

35

JOHN PULLER KNOCKED ON THE DOOR of General Pitts's office suite, but when the door opened it was not the aide who had previously greeted him.

"I'm CWO John Puller with CID. General Pitts asked me to meet with him today," said Puller. He looked over the woman's shoulders and froze when he saw the moving boxes piled up.

The aide was a woman, in her late thirties, with short dark hair and a trim physique.

"General Pitts has been reassigned, Chief Puller."

Puller's jaw went slack. "Reassigned? He's vice chair of the Joint Chiefs."

"Not any longer."

"Where was he reassigned to?"

"That is classified."

"Who took his place?"

"I'm not at liberty to say."

"Why not?"

"I'm not at liberty to say."

"You're not at liberty to say why you're not at liberty to say?"

His pointing out the utter absurdity of what she was saying seemed to have an effect on her. She looked down, pursed her lips, and composed herself. "I freely admit that this situation is unusual."

"It's off-the-charts unusual. I met with General Pitts on an extremely sensitive matter one day ago. He was going to investigate this matter and told me to meet him here. Well, I'm here. And he's not. What does that tell you?"

"I was just assigned to this post this morning. I'm not even sure who the new vice chair will be."

"This whole thing stinks to high heaven," said Puller. "What the hell is going on? And don't tell me you're not at liberty to say." He never once raised his voice, but his calm, professional manner seemed to unnerve the woman.

She looked over his shoulder, motioned him into the office, and then closed the door.

"Chief Puller, I don't know what's going on, but I agree, it does stink to high heaven. However, keep this in mind, if they can pull a four-star like General Pitts at a moment's notice, what can they do to someone like me? Or, more to the point, someone like *you*?"

"Well, I'll tell you what they tried to do to me. They came to my apartment with machine guns and shot the hell out of the place. And it's only by the training the Army provided me that I'm standing here talking to you."

"Oh my God."

"Yeah, I would take some help from God right about now. So maybe you'll get off easy. They'll just ship you off to Antarctica instead of trying to kill you like they did me."

"I don't know what to tell you except I'm sorry."

"I represent the uniform. I represent the Army and by extension the American people. This is not a cliché to me. We all took an oath."

"And I worked hard to get where I am. I don't want to lose my job, or my career."

"Well, that's good," said Puller. "Because you've already lost everything else, including your self-respect. For me, no job is worth that."

He left and walked briskly down the hall.

He had always loved coming to the Pentagon. He felt safe, comfortable, reassured simply by walking around here. He was surrounded by people who were on the same mission he was: keeping America safe, doing the right thing in a selfless manner. It might have seemed corny, but it was how he had led his life. Yet now Puller felt like he had just parachuted into North Korea or Iran. Everyone he passed could be the enemy, an informer, part of the "them," whatever them was.

Okay, Puller, it's time to get really serious.

He ducked into a restroom stall, took out his phone, turned it off, took out the SIM card and put it in his pocket. Then he dumped the phone in the trash.

He picked up his pace, hit the exit, and picked up his pace even more. He grabbed the first metro car he could, later changed trains, and rode it to Vienna, Virginia. Along the way he kept up a vigilant watch for anyone attempting to keep him under surveillance.

There, he walked through the station, reversed course, took another train, switched trains at another station, headed toward Springfield, found a nearly empty train car, jumped off at an interim station, stopped and watched for anyone else getting off there, then grabbed a cab and directed it to an electronics store on the Reston Parkway.

Inside he purchased a GSM network prepaid phone. Outside he called the number to activate the phone, without giving any personal information.

He punched in a number well-known to him. It was a number that could not be traced or hacked, or at least it would not be easy to do so. Right now, he had no choice. He needed help.

"Bobby?"

"Hey, little brother, how's it going?"

"I've got an issue."

"Not Dad?" Robert Puller said quickly, his buoyant attitude instantly turning serious.

"No. Give me two minutes to fill you in. No interruptions, just listen, then give me some advice on the other side."

Puller actually took a little more than three minutes to tell his brother everything. From the disappearance of Tony Vincenzo, to the murder of a CID agent, to the death of Jerome Blake, to the murderer being a cop or impersonating one, to the stonewalling of his investigation by folks at the state and federal levels, to the yanking of a four-star general from his position as vice chairman of the Joint Chiefs. To being attacked and almost killed in his apartment.

When he was done Robert Puller said nothing for about thirty seconds. John Puller could almost hear the wheels of his brother's formidable intellect absorbing all of these facts and putting everything together, almost like an FBI profile, or a string of DNA, before arriving at if not a solution, then at least some sound advice. But his first response surprised Puller.

"Why the hell didn't you call me after you got attacked? I've been off the grid in a bunker the last two days doing cybernuke drills. But you could have tried to call, dammit."

"I survived, what was there to tell? I just need you to focus on what I just told you and help me, Bobby."

More silence passed between them. Finally Robert said, "Okay, the level of influence required to take out a four-star right from the Pentagon twenty-four hours after you met with him is sky-high, John. There aren't many suspects to consider, the players are very few."

"If they can yank Pitts I can't be far behind."

"They tried to punch your ticket, permanently, at your apartment. At the same time they were yanking Pitts's assignment. They could do that and no one's going to care for very long. There are enough four-stars. And a CWO in the field was expendable. But ironically, if they tried to reassign you when you're working on an investigation, guess what?"

"What?"

"That has whistleblower status written all over it. You'd be in front of a congressional committee telling the whole country what these people don't want anyone to hear."

"I hadn't thought about that angle."

"Because you don't give a crap about politics, but in my position I have to pay attention to that." He paused. "Hold on, John."

"What?"

"A story is coming over the wire with your name on it."

"What does it say?"

Robert responded after reading through the article. "Okay, that was smart on their part. There's reporting based on anonymous sources that the attack on you was orchestrated by elements of a Mexican cartel, high-ranking members of which you helped put in prison three months ago after they tried to infiltrate an Army base in Texas and recruit soldiers as operatives for the moving of drugs into the U.S."

"Anonymous sources?"

"It'll be all over the web in a few minutes. Trolls will swarm it, people on every conceivable side will slice and dice it. By the time they're done half the country will think you tried to shoot yourself with a machine gun."

"But where does the truth come into all this?"

"It doesn't. Social media has absolutely nothing to do with the truth. It has to do with making shitloads of money off ads trying to sell people crap they don't need. But the terrible by-product of that is giving a global platform to the absolute worst elements of society. The result is that 'truth' is whatever you can convince people it is. It's exactly what Orwell wrote about."

"How does this country survive, then?"

"If you want the truth, John, unless a lot of things change, I'm not sure we do, at least not as the free society we all want."

"Thanks for the pep talk, Bobby. I really needed it."

"You asked. And I'm not going to lie to you. So what are you going to do now?"

"I'm not working this case alone. You remember me telling you about Atlee Pine?"

"Yeah. FBI. You think very highly of her."

"She's on leave from the Bureau working a personal case that crossed over into mine by virtue of a connection with the Vincenzos." He went on to tell his brother about Pine's working undercover at the penthouse, being abducted, waking up next to a dead woman, and almost being killed.

"And this Lindsey Axilrod is in the middle of it?"

"Seems like she set Pine up. And now she's disappeared."

"Give me the address of the penthouse."

"Why, what are you going to do?"

"Don't ask. And don't worry, this will not have my personal prints on it."

"Just make sure it doesn't."

"You and Pine are going to remain targets so long as you're investigating this."

"We've been targets ever since we signed up."

"This is different."

"Not to me."

"Watch your back."

"You do the same. I have to tell you, I had some trepidation about pulling you into this."

"Blood is thicker than anything, John. Or it should be. But let's try not to spill any of ours."

Puller thought back to the near massacre in his apartment. "Easier said than done, Bobby."

36

LINDA HOLDEN-BRYANT?" Pine said into the phone. She was sitting in her car outside of Doug Bennett's house with Blum next to her.

Jack Lineberry said, "Doug told you about her?"

"Yeah, he did," snapped Pine.

"Why did he mention her?"

"Why the hell didn't *you* mention her before now?"

"There was no reason to."

"There was *every* reason to," retorted Pine.

"Why?"

"You were engaged?"

"Well, yes. For a time."

"Did you live together?"

"Yes, in New York."

"When did you break up?"

"Why do you need to know this?"

"I think it's obvious, Jack, don't you?" she responded sharply. "In fact, I think when you gave me Bennett's name, it had occurred to you that her name *would* come up. Maybe you had thoughts that she could be the mole."

He started to cough but that wasn't a deterrent for Pine, not this time.

The coughing subsided and he said, "You give me more credit than you should if you think that."

"Did you ever talk to her about your work?"

"Of course not. Never!"

"Did you ever work from home?"

"I suppose I did on occasion."

"Back then there were no smartphones, no computers, no internet really. How did you work from home?"

"I used the phone. A secure line."

"What else?"

"I wrote memos. Sometimes people came by to see me."

"While Linda was there?"

"Not always."

"So some of the time, then?"

"Some of the meetings were on short notice and late at night. What did you want me to do, push her out in the street in her nightgown?"

"Are you sure she was asleep?"

"Atlee—"

"Are you sure she never looked through your briefcase, or eavesdropped on a phone call? Or followed you to wherever you were going to see what you were up to?"

"She knew I worked for the government. And she knew it was...secret."

"But you trusted her?"

"Of course I did, but I took all appropriate precautions. I would never want to put her in danger because she inadvertently discovered some information about what I was doing."

"There may have been nothing inadvertent about it. So let me ask you again: Why did you break up?"

Lineberry didn't respond. Pine thought she could hear the quickened beats of his heart over the phone; they seemed to match her own. She glanced at Blum, who was watching her intently.

"Jack?"

"She found out about...about what happened."

"What does that mean exactly?"

"She found out about me and Amanda."

"How?"

"I was never exactly sure. But she confronted me."

"Jack, if she found out about it, she must have taken steps *to* find out. Like having you followed."

"I took precautions."

"Screw precautions," barked Pine. "They obviously didn't work."

More silence.

In a calmer tone, Pine said, "Did she know that my mother was pregnant? And that you were the father?"

When he said nothing, she added, "Jack, I really need to know this. And you know why. That's the only way we can find out what happened to Mercy. Just like I told you back in your hospital room. We have to do this *together*."

"She knew."

"So she knew about my mother? I mean, who she was?"

"I never told her about the circumstances."

"But she knew my mother's identity?"

"Yes."

"Did they ever meet?"

"Not to my knowledge. At least your mother never mentioned anything like that."

"If Linda didn't tell her who she was, my mother may not have known the connection."

"That's...true," Lineberry said haltingly.

"You know where this is leading, Jack."

"She was *not* the leak, Atlee. She couldn't have been."

"You don't know that. And from where I'm standing, she is the most probable source of the leak. And she had the motive to sic the Vincenzos on my family."

"How would she even know about the Vincenzos?"

"Wasn't it in all the papers back then? After the arrests were made?"

"Well, yes."

"And you're telling me that Linda was so oblivious to what you did for a living that she couldn't have made that connection? Or was she that stupid?"

"No one would accuse Linda of being stupid. Quite the opposite. She was a brilliant woman."

"Then you're proving my point. Did you ever have my mother over to your place?"

"Not while Linda was there."

"But she could have seen her there if she had been suspicious. She could have left and then come back."

"I just don't think that's possible."

"What did she do for a living? Did she have a profession?"

"She was a lawyer."

"Oh, great. Don't tell me she was a criminal defense lawyer?"

"She was, actually, yes."

"And you still think she couldn't have possibly made the connection with the Vincenzos? Hell, she might have had mob clients."

"No, no, I'm sure she didn't."

"Did she share her work with you?"

"No, she was as guarded as I was."

"Then you can't possibly know who her clients were, can you?"

"Now *you* sound like a lawyer cross-examining me."

"Good, that's my intent. Where is she now?"

"I don't know. It's been over thirty years."

"Do you know what happened to her after you two broke up?"

"I...I heard she got married. To a very wealthy man. He died a few years later, leaving her very rich. She might have gotten married again after that. But I'm not sure."

"And she never made any effort to contact you? After you became superwealthy? You probably moved in the same circles."

"I moved to Georgia. She was more of a big-city girl."

"She should be easy enough to trace."

"Are you going to do that?"

"I *have* to do that, Jack."

"Even if she had anything to do with what happened, do you really think she'll just confess it to you?"

"I'm not expecting that, no. But I still need to talk to her."

"Look, despite what I said, I know that it could be possible that Linda was the leak. I...I guess I just didn't want to even entertain the thought."

"I'm not saying she's a bad person, Jack. I'm not even saying she wanted to hurt my family. But for someone who was engaged and then found out her fiancé was going to be the father of another woman's children? That might have been enough to make her do something she otherwise never would have done."

"I guess I can see that."

"I'll make my own inquiries. But if you come up with anything, let me know."

"I will."

Pine clicked off and dropped her phone on the car seat.

Blum said, "I heard most of the exchange. He's a man clearly in denial."

"Yes, he is."

"Chances are very good this Linda Holden-Bryant was the leak."

"I know."

"When you find her and confront her, what will you do? How will you work it?"

Pine closed her eyes and took a long breath.

She opened her eyes and said, "When I figure that out, you'll be the first to know, Carol."

37

P INE WAS STANDING ON BILLIONAIRES' ROW, this time with Blum, staring up at another splinter of a building as a weather system bringing chilly temps and rain passed over the city. They were one block down from the building where Pine had been abducted and very close to the sweeping vistas of Central Park.

"She must have done really well for herself if she lives in there," noted Blum.

Linda Holden-Bryant had not been difficult to track down. She went by her maiden name, though she had been married twice. Once to a man in his seventies who had died four years into the marriage, leaving his thirty-something widow a fortune worth hundreds of millions of dollars. Then the woman had hit the real jackpot with her second husband, an heir to a French cosmetics empire. After their divorce, she had walked away with more than three billion dollars. Another decade had passed since that divorce, and Pine figured if the woman had just put the money in the stock market she was probably worth over ten billion now.

"Yes she has."

"Are you surprised she agreed to see you?"

"Not really. She must be as curious to see me as I am to see her."

"Did you tell her...everything?"

"I told her I know Jack Lineberry. I didn't tell her how."

"So why does she think you want to see her?"

"I'm working a case that has to do with Jack. I'm sure that's what got me in the door."

"Are you going to tell her that you're his daughter?"

"Yes, but at the right moment."

"Which will be when?"

"When my gut tells me."

They cleared the doorman and concierge after a video of Pine and Blum was shown to Ms. Holden-Bryant, and she cleared their coming up in the private elevator.

The elevator car opened right into the vestibule of her apartment, which they had been told occupied three levels of the building.

"She seems to be even wealthier than Jack," murmured Pine, more to herself than to Blum.

A butler in full livery greeted them in the vestibule and escorted them down a marble-floored corridor that was lined with paintings that looked like they could have hung at the Met or the Louvre.

They were ushered into a room that they assumed was the library, since it held thousands of volumes on two walls. A fire smoldered in the grate that was bracketed by a soaring wall of stone.

Blum drew near to the flames and put her hands out.

"Arizona never feels this raw," she said. "That wind cut right through me out there."

Pine perched on a settee that looked like something Napoleon would have favored and tapped her fingers on the wooden arm.

The fourth wall was covered with photos. Pine rose and went over to study them more closely. There were a number of A-list actors from the previous decade, two Yankee baseball players from another era, and photos of rock stars from the seventies and eighties, each signed by the musician. But all the others were of politicians, both past and current. There was a photo signed by a past VP with "warmest wishes to a real friend." Translated, Pine knew that Holden-Bryant had donated/raised a shitload of money for the man.

Blum joined her and started to say something, but Pine put up a cautionary hand and then waved at a black lens that occupied a space near the ceiling where two walls were joined.

To the camera she said, "Anytime you're ready, Linda. Thank you."

About thirty seconds later another door opened, and a young woman dressed all in black with blond hair in a ponytail, tortoiseshell glasses, and an efficient expression poked her head in and said, "Please follow me."

They walked up a grand staircase made of marble, metal, and wood to the floor above. They passed along another long hallway, where yet more Picassos and Dalis and Monets hung, until they arrived at twelve-foot double doors painted sparkling white. The woman knocked, received an "Enter," and opened one of the doors.

Pine and Blum stepped through. The woman shut the door behind them, and they heard her heels tap-tapping efficiently back down the hall.

They looked around. They were in a bedroom. Only it was the size of a large condo. The bed was at the far end. And lying in it was, presumably, Linda Holden-Bryant.

She lifted herself off the pillows. "Please, come closer."

They walked over, and Holden-Bryant pointed to two chintz-covered chairs set next to an enormous bed on which six adults could have slept without touching one another.

She had on a thin, long-sleeved satin lavender robe that was closed in front. The woman settled back against the plumped-up pillows as Pine introduced herself and Blum. Pine ran her gaze over the woman. She was in her midsixties, toned and fit. Her hair was dyed blond with just a trace of silver roots evident. Her features were sharp enough to hurt someone. The green eyes looked electrified. The mouth was a slash, the chin jagged yet elegant. She was very attractive, so put together it was easy to think of her as ten or even fifteen years younger than she was. She lay under the covers, but a glance at her long legs told Pine that Holden-Bryant was only a few inches shorter than she was.

"I'm sorry to see you in here, but the fact is I have some sort of bug," she began. The woman's voice was deeper than Pine would have imagined it would be.

Holden-Bryant glanced at Blum. "Oh, I'm not contagious, no worries there. Full course of antibiotics and recovering fast. But still not quite all there. And it's so dreary out today. Crushes one's spirits."

"But I would suppose living in this place, your spirits won't be crushed for long," said Blum in a disarming tone.

"Aren't you sweet. And very right. I've been very lucky. Privileged. Right place, right time."

"I haven't seen a butler in a long time," said Pine.

Holden-Bryant tittered at that. "A holdover from my last marriage. I could have let most of the staff go because I actually live a simple life. But that wouldn't have done them any good or been fair to them. The divorce wasn't their fault, so I kept them on."

"Very nice of you," said Blum.

"They thought so, too. Now," she said, turning to Pine, "you wanted to speak with me about Jack Lineberry?"

"Yes."

"I understand he's done very well for himself. Investments, right?"

"Yes. But I think you have him beat on the financial end."

"I wouldn't say that. His jet is bigger than mine, although I have *two* of them."

"How do you know that?"

"We have some mutual friends. They keep me informed. But he earned his money."

Blum said, "Well, I think you earned yours, too."

"If you keep that up, you might be my new best friend," she said. When she turned to Pine her expression grew far more serious. "So, what did you want to talk to me about?"

"Jack is in a hospital in Georgia."

She tensed. "Is he all right?"

"He's going to recover, but he was shot."

Her features collapsed. "Oh my God. Jack shot. Who? Why?"

"The who is known. The why is also known. The person was actually aiming for me, but Jack was in the wrong place."

"Why was someone trying to kill you?"

"I'm an FBI agent, it sort of goes with the territory."

"And how do you know Jack again? Is he involved in some FBI thing?"

"No. I met him down in Georgia recently. I actually knew him as a child but didn't remember him."

Holden-Bryant's features grew strained. "You knew him as a *child*?"

"It was only later that I found out he was actually my father."

Holden-Bryant, to her credit, remained absolutely quiet. For about five of the longest seconds of Pine's life.

"He's your father?" she said in a hushed tone.

"Me and my sister, Mercy. Yes. My mother was Julia Pine. But back then she went by Amanda. Perhaps you knew her?"

Holden-Bryant took a moment to fluff her pillow and draw her covers up above her chest, as though she were burrowing in for a long winter's nap.

"No, no, I can't say that I did."

Pine held the woman's gaze for one long second. "I know that you and Jack were engaged back then."

The woman suddenly flung the covers off her, pivoted her feet to the floor, and got out of bed. Under the robe she was wearing pajamas in a striped pattern. She marched over to a wooden cabinet against the wall and opened its door, revealing a full bar.

"You want something?" she asked.

"Little early in the day for me," said Pine. "And if you're on meds, should you be drinking?"

"Oh, I just feel like living dangerously right now," shot back Holden-Bryant.

"I'll have a glass of sherry, if you have that," said Blum.

"I have everything, sweetheart. And I can use a belt right now."

She brought over a glass of sherry for Blum, then sat down on the bed with a glass of bourbon. She crossed her legs and took a healthy sip. She primly wiped her mouth, sighed, and said, "I was engaged to Jack. For well over a year. We dated for years before that."

"Then it must have come as a shock to you that he was fathering another woman's children," said Pine.

"God, I wish I still smoked," barked Holden-Bryant. She eyed Pine shrewdly. "Why are you really here?"

"I'm going to tell you something. Something startling. It will probably shock you, at least I hope that it does. And then let's talk about it."

Holden-Bryant stared at her for a moment, then swallowed the rest of her bourbon and rose to pour out another one. After she resettled on the bed Pine told her some of what had happened to her family, though she didn't go into great detail and she didn't mention the Vincenzos' involvement, not by name. She was saving that revelation. Even so, as she spoke Holden-Bryant seemed to grow smaller and smaller on the enormous bed.

When Pine finished, she folded her arms over her chest and watched the older woman.

Holden-Bryant finished her second shot of bourbon and put the empty glass down on her nightstand.

She sat back against her expensive and plumped pillows. "This was all a long time ago."

"Old sins cast long shadows," remarked Blum.

"Is that what you think, I'm a sinner?"

Pine said, "I don't know or care. I just want to know what you might have done back then when you found out about Jack and my mother."

"You have no proof that I found out or did anything."

"Then let me ask you directly: Did you know that Jack had slept with my mother and that she had become pregnant?"

"And I could answer that by saying you have no way to make me respond to that question."

"You're right about that. And the only thing I have to fire back is I would like to know what happened to my sister. Wouldn't you, if our positions were reversed?"

"I was a criminal defense lawyer. I lived in hypotheticals, but that doesn't mean I have to answer one."

"Is it really a hypothetical?"

"I don't know," said Holden-Bryant coolly.

"Did you know about Jack and my mother?"

Holden-Bryant glanced at Blum. "You look like a mother."

"Six times over."

"I never had kids. Wanted them. But I was too busy professionally. When I got married, the men I married had been married before. They had kids and even grandkids. They didn't want a do-over. So, I lost out there."

"But my mother had two daughters," said Pine. "At a very young age."

"Jack always wanted children. If we had married, I'm sure we would have had kids together."

"But you didn't. You broke up. Why?"

She gave Pine a whimsical smile. "Why does anyone break up? There was an issue. A problem. A falling-out."

"And specifically for you?" said Pine. "What was it?"

Holden-Bryant got up and started to pour herself another drink. "Sure you don't want one?"

"All right. I'll have what you're having."

"Now you're talking."

"But the thing is, I want *you* to start talking."

She finished making the drinks and slowly walked back to them.

Now maybe we'll get somewhere, thought Pine.

38

J ACK AND I JUST MOVED in different directions."

Holden-Bryant had settled back on the bed after handing Pine her drink.

"Did anything prompt that?" Pine asked.

"Look, let's cut to the chase. We all know what men are like."

"And for at least one person here who may not know what you mean by that?"

"It's hard enough to get men to commit. It's virtually impossible under one circumstance."

"Which is?" asked Pine.

Blum answered, "When the man no longer loves you because he loves someone else."

"Bingo," said Holden-Bryant, though her expression did not match the triumphant word.

"Jack loved my mother over you. And you were aware of that?"

"I had my suspicions."

"Based on?"

The woman pointed her sharp chin at Pine and gave her a triumphant look. "I was a lawyer. I know how to find out things."

"You had Jack followed?"

"I took steps to find out why the man I was going to marry suddenly didn't want to marry me."

"Did that include telling mobsters where to find me and my family so attempts could be made on our lives while we were in witness protection?"

Holden-Bryant slowly lowered her glass. "What?"

"And when that failed, did you tell Bruno Vincenzo where my family was so that he could shame his brother, Ito, into coming down to Georgia to hurt my family?"

"I don't know what you're talking about," sputtered Holden-Bryant. "I have no idea what you're blabbering on about. Who is this Bruno person?"

"Do you think I look like my mother?" Pine asked suddenly.

"What?"

"Do I look like my mother?"

Holden-Bryant hesitated for a moment and then said, "You have her height, for sure."

She realized too late what she had just done. She sat back and said in a chagrined tone, "Well, that was neatly done, Agent Pine, I'll give you that."

"You saw my mother, then. Did you ever talk to her?"

"I don't remember."

"There's no liability for you. Whatever exposure there was, the statute of limitations has long since passed. Being a lawyer, you know that."

"I haven't really thought about it, frankly. I haven't practiced law since my first marriage."

"So you won't have a problem telling me about what you might have done."

"Why do you care?"

"Because I have a twin sister who may be dead or may be alive. But I need to know either way."

This seemed to affect the woman more than Pine thought it would.

"Tell me more about that," she said in a low voice tinged with curiosity.

And Pine did, every detail from that awful night in Andersonville. And then all that she had learned about Bruno and Ito Vincenzo.

"That is quite horrible," Holden-Bryant finally said in a breathless gush.

"Yes, it was. So anything you can tell me would be more than I have now."

The woman once more got out of bed. But this time not for a drink. She pulled a chair up to them and sat down. She stared at the carpeted floor as she spoke. "I loved Jack unconditionally, with everything I had. He was absolutely everything I wanted in a husband. I had planned out our wedding, our first few years of marriage together. I was a driven, independent woman, don't get me wrong. I wanted a very high-powered legal career and I worked my ass off for it." She paused. "But that wasn't all I wanted. I wanted a life with Jack. I wanted children with him." She paused again and looked around her to-die-for bedroom. "And instead I got this. And I can tell you it doesn't come close to making up for it." She bowed her head for a moment before looking up. She eyed Blum. "I suspected Jack was seeing someone else. A woman can just tell, you know?"

Blum nodded. "I had that happen to me. And I agree with you. There are telltale signs."

"What did you do to validate your suspicions?" asked Pine.

"I hired a private detective and had him followed. I used a guy who worked with me on my legal cases. He was good, very good. He got details, photos, everything."

"Of Jack with my mother?" said Pine.

"As soon as you walked in that door over there, I knew you were Amanda and Jack's daughter. Amanda was the most beautiful woman I'd ever seen. I could understand why Jack would fall for her. But I was also furious with him. Angry beyond belief."

"And what did you do about that anger?" asked Pine quietly.

"I knew that Jack worked for the feds. He never talked about that work, and I never pressed him. I knew all about confidences. I exercised those in my line of work. I never talked to him about *my* cases." She got up, went over to the bar, and poured herself a glass of club soda. Returning to her seat she said, "I followed the mob cases going on in New York at that time. I never repped any of the mob bosses, but from time to time I did represent some of the foot soldiers. I knew they were scum, but that was part of the challenge. And I happen to believe that everyone deserves good legal representation. But it was more than that. The bosses expected undying loyalty from the guys down below. But they never extended that same level of loyalty. They'd throw them under the bus to save their own asses. That didn't sit well with me."

Holden-Bryant paused and seemed poised to lapse into a sea of old memories.

"Go on," prompted Pine.

"There was one foot soldier who came to me for legal representation in connection with the string of RICO cases going on then. His name was Amadeo Bertelli. You can't get more Italian than that, and the guy filled every awful stereotype of the Italian mobster. He was up to his elbows in blood. He was not a man I would have spent one minute with on a personal level. But he had a story to tell and I listened to that story. And the more I listened the more things started to make sense to me.

"He had a friend who had gotten embroiled in this whole thing. The friend had tried to do the right thing but had gotten screwed by someone. He'd already been arrested but had made bail for some reason. I met with this person."

"Bruno Vincenzo," said Pine. "The man you just denied ever hearing of?"

"Yes. Bruno Vincenzo," she parroted bitterly. "He was even worse than Bertelli. Just being in the same room with the guy gave me the creeps. Anyway, Vincenzo told me everything. And I mean everything. He was hoping I could work a deal with the prosecutors to put him in WITSEC. But before any of that could happen his bail was revoked, and another lawyer took over the case. Bruno ended up going to prison. And I learned he was killed in there some time later."

"And that should have been the end of it," said Pine.

"Should have been but wasn't," said Holden-Bryant in a heavy voice.

"How did you find out where my family was being relocated?" asked Pine. "You said Jack never talked about his work."

Holden-Bryant glanced up at her, her eyes slits through which tears were seeping.

"He didn't always lock up his briefcase. He didn't check to see if anyone was listening to his phone calls, meaning he didn't check to see if *I* was listening to the phone calls he made from our apartment. I suppose he trusted me. And when he'd been drinking heavily, which was quite often back then, his lips got looser around me than they should have. It didn't take me long to find out that the person Bruno said had screwed him over and Jack's *Amanda* were one and the same."

"And what did you do with that information?" asked Pine, keeping her gaze directly on the woman.

"I must have been mad with jealousy. I really must have."

"You somehow got the information on our whereabouts, our new names, and other details to Bruno," said Pine. "Didn't you?"

"Yes."

"How?"

"I passed it to his attorney of record, who passed it to Bruno when he visited him in prison. Guards can't mess with notes passed to prisoners from their attorneys."

"And did this attorney know what the notes were about?"

"He never asked, and I never said."

"We received a threatening letter, which caused us to be moved. Shortly after that two attempts were made to murder us, and then Jack got paranoid and pulled us from WITSEC. He moved us to Andersonville under the last name Pine. And he went down to personally watch over us." She paused. "And then Ito Vincenzo, Bruno's brother, came calling, shortly after his brother was killed. Because you also told Bruno about us moving to Georgia, didn't you? Before he was killed in prison for being a snitch."

Holden-Bryant wouldn't look at her now, but she nodded her head. "When Jack finally broke it off with me and told me he was moving, I knew what was going on. I knew exactly what he was doing. He was following your mother, the woman he really loved. And leaving me...alone."

"He wouldn't have told you the details, surely," said Blum. "How did you find out what you needed to tell Bruno?"

"Jack told me nothing. And he stopped drinking and stopped making calls from the apartment. I don't think he ever suspected me, but he was just taking an abundance of caution. But he did make a big mistake. He had gotten a phone call that made him rush into his home office and check something in his safe. Our relationship was on the ropes, but we were still sharing the apartment, and I was trying to turn it around. Now, normally when I was there, he would shut and lock the door when he went into his office. But he was in such a hurry he left the door ajar. This allowed me to spy on him from the doorway when he was opening his wall safe, and I learned the combo. I checked it periodically while we were still living together. One day, when it was clear he was leaving town, I waited until he was gone, and then got into the safe and found a letter in there that had been sent to him by someone at his agency. It was all there. Andersonville, Georgia. Tim and Julia Pine and their two lovely daughters, Atlee and Mercy. I got that info to Bruno, and I guess he told his brother about it, because I suppose, by then, his mob connections had dried up. I believe he died shortly after he got that information."

"But not before he got that info to his brother." Pine paused. "Did you ever hear what happened to us back in the late 1980s?" she asked.

"I don't really recall."

"But you didn't tell anyone what you had done?"

"And put myself in prison? No, I didn't do that."

"I read a letter that Bruno had written to his brother, Ito, complaining about his unfair treatment. As if a man who had killed scores of people had a right to complain. He basically guilt-tripped his law-abiding brother, Ito, to come after us. Ito almost killed me, and he took my sister and she's never been seen since. My father killed himself, and my mother has vanished. I don't know if she's dead or not. So if your goal was to destroy my family, you succeeded. You wiped us out. As far as I know, I'm the only one left."

Holden-Bryant put a hand to her face and sobbed quietly into it. She said shakily, "I'm sorry, Atlee. I never imagined—"

"Sure you did. You told a murderer where to find us. What exactly did you think was going to happen?"

Holden-Bryant dried her eyes on her sleeve and looked at Pine with a sober expression. "I guess, in a way, exactly what did happen. I guess it would be absurd and trivial and even cruel to say that I'm sorry for what happened, though I sincerely am."

"Did you ever meet with Ito Vincenzo?" asked Pine.

"No, I never even knew he existed until you mentioned him."

"You're sure you never communicated with him?"

"Never."

"When did you and Jack officially break up?"

"When he moved down to Georgia. There didn't seem to be a point to continuing."

Pine rose and handed her a card. "If anything else occurs to you, please call me."

She took the card. "I know what you must think of me."

"It doesn't matter what I think of you. It's far more important what you think of yourself."

Holden-Bryant pulled a tissue from a box on the nightstand and sniffled into it. "Well, right now, I don't think much of myself at all."

"Okay."

"Will Jack be all right?"

"It seems that he will, yes. He's lucky to be alive, actually. As am I."

"You really just found out about his being your father?"

"Yes."

"It must have been a shock."

"Everything about this has been a shock."

"I hope you find your sister."

Pine didn't respond to this.

"Will…will you tell Jack about what I did?"

"Not unless I have to, no."

"I appreciate that."

Pine didn't answer. She was already headed to the door. A moment later she was gone.

Holden-Bryant looked at Blum, who still stood next to the bed. "I guess love makes fools of us all," she said.

"Oh, I think we do a pretty good job of that all by ourselves," said Blum. She looked around. "Well, at least you have all this...to keep you happy. Aren't you lucky?"

She walked out and closed the door softly behind her.

CHAPTER

39

PULLER HAD JUST FINISHED a six-mile run at Quantico, keeping pace with a couple of long-legged Marine recruits still in their teens. He returned to his "new" apartment, since the other one was still a crime scene, took a shower, and was about to put on civilian clothes when his phone buzzed.

It was a text from his brother.

Tonight twenty hundred, ANC, Remember the Maine. Salt. Four bars and a star.

Anyone not knowing the brothers, or the military in general, would be hard-pressed to decipher this message. But it made perfect sense to Puller, up to a point.

He checked his watch. He would have just enough time because he needed to make a stop first. He went to his closet and pulled out his set of dress blues. It was for the meeting tonight, though it wasn't exactly required. But it was also for where he was going right now.

For a long time the Army had stuck with dress greens and dress whites. But now blue was the thing. It was the color of America's two greatest military home-turf victories. The bluecoats against the redcoats in the Revolutionary War. And the Union blue against the Confederate gray in the Civil War.

Why mess with success?

He checked his row of ribbons to make sure they were all where they were supposed to be—the military allowed no margin for error there—picked up his dress cap and headed out after allowing AWOL to give him the once-over and purr his approval.

He drove to the VA hospital and was escorted to the memory care unit. Along the way he saw and saluted soldiers sitting in wheelchairs, lying on gurneys, and roaming the halls using walkers. They had all served their country well and honorably. Now they were here, the last deployment of their careers: a nursing home provided by Uncle Sam.

The escort left him, and Puller tapped on the door to the room. He waited for a moment and then entered.

The space was small, and held very few things, chief among them a bed with an old man in it. That old man was Puller's father and namesake. John Puller Sr.

It used to be that his father, upon seeing Puller, would bark out, "XO, what are you doing here?"

Puller was not his father's executive officer, or XO, but he had played along with it because the doctors said it was probably for the best.

That was then.

That was no longer the case. Now was very different from then.

His father lay curled in the bed. Once six three, he had been robbed of several inches by age and bad health. He was bald except for small pockets of hair the color of clouds strewn around his scalp. His clothes these days were not combat fatigues or dress blues. They were hospital scrub pants and a white T-shirt, where curly white chest hair poked out from the front.

Puller came around to the side of the bed so he could face his father. He stood there flagpole straight and looked down at the man who had helped create him, giving him half his DNA and other attributes, some good, some not so good.

"Reporting in, sir," said Puller, a bit half-heartedly. He did not expect an answer. The last five times he had come to visit his father, the man had never even woken up.

Alzheimer's was the worst thing that could happen to a person, Puller thought. It eventually killed you, like other bad diseases. But before it did that, it took away the one thing that made a person a person, leaving their physical husk reasonably intact. And that wasn't much of a comfort, not for the family and friends. It just made one wonder how a person could look normal, and yet no longer be anywhere close to who they had been.

To his surprise, his father stirred. The eyes blinked open for a moment before closing again. Puller thought that would be the end of it. But the eyes came open a second time and stayed that way.

Puller leaned down and decided to forego the subterfuge. "Dad?"

"Bobby?" he said gruffly.

His father now often got the brothers mixed up.

Puller Senior had endured his oldest son going to military prison for a crime that he didn't commit. He had seen Robert Puller freed and fully exonerated. He had also endured learning what had happened to his wife, Puller's mother, who had vanished decades before. That had been the hardest for the old man, Puller knew. Nothing could be worse than that. But at least he had closure on that.

At least we all have closure.

Puller glanced at his father's still-broad shoulders and visualized seeing the three stars on them. There should have been a fourth star, but politics had gotten in the way of that. And Puller knew there wasn't a four-star in the Army who felt Fighting John Puller didn't deserve that last bit of shiny career acknowledgment. But it wasn't to be. Just like the Medal of Honor wasn't to be, another sacrifice to politics over merit. But his old man was a legend, and legends didn't need stars or medals. They lived on in the thoughts and memories and myths of everybody who came after them.

"It's Junior, sir. Not Bobby."

His father straightened in the bed, sat up against the pillow, and looked around at probably the last room he would occupy on earth. By his expression, he didn't seem to recognize it at all. He lay back, stared at the ceiling for a moment, and then turned his head to the side and stared at his youngest son.

"You in the Army, soldier?"

"Yes sir. Chief warrant officer."

"What are those?"

Puller's heart sank because his old man was pointing at his rows of ribbons. Puller had been a combat stud. He had earned every major wartime commendation the Army offered, several more than once. And with all that, his rows of "guts and glory" would have paled in comparison to his father's, whose commendations had run to a dozen horizontal rows. They could have made a blanket out of them. But then again what did you expect from someone who had tried to enlist to fight in a war while in his sixties?

"Just something that came with the suit," replied Puller.

"They're nice," said his father.

"Yeah, thanks. I think so, too."

"Who are you again?"

"I work here. Anything you need?"

"Better chow. The crap they serve here I wouldn't feed to a damn dog, that is if I had one. Do I have a dog?"

"No sir."

"Well, the food still sucks."

"Yes sir, I'll check on that."

"I don't know how I even got here. I was at work and now I'm here."

"Yes sir. I think it was complicated."

"And they put this here and I have no idea who she even is."

Puller glanced at the framed photo of his mother, Jackie.

"You know her name, son?" asked his father.

"I...No." Puller didn't know what his father's reaction might be if he mentioned his mother's name.

"Doesn't seem right, putting a strange woman's picture in here. My wife might get angry."

"Do you remember your wife?"

"What?"

"Your wife?"

His father turned the photo on its face and settled back against his pillow.

Puller glanced at the window and hurriedly changed the subject. "Your bird still around? Outside the window. There was a nest last time."

His father looked at him blankly. "Bird?"

"Yes, I...Do you need anything, sir?"

His father stared more intently at him. "You look familiar. You remind me of somebody."

Puller's gut clenched. "Is that right, sir? Who might that be?"

"Guy I went to school with, least I think. Didn't like him very much. Can't recall the name of the place right now."

"You went to West Point."

His father looked confused. "You sure?"

"Pretty sure, sir," said Puller quietly.

"Yeah?"

"You did very well there. You became quite the leader of men."

His father just grunted at this.

Fighting John Puller had never lost a battle. He had taken enormous risks, thrown out the Army playbook when it suited him, demanded everything from his men and given even more of himself. He pissed his superiors off beyond belief, and then handed them one improbable victory after another to take credit for. There were two generations of warriors in this country who would fling curses at the mere mention of the name "Fighting John Puller," and those who would go anywhere he would lead them, convinced of victory because of the man at the helm.

And the two groups would be one and the same.

"The men respected you, sir. We...we all do."

Another grunt was the response to this. And then his father curled up and fell back asleep while his son was standing at attention next to him.

Puller would take the father he remembered, the screamer, petty and vindictive at times, relentlessly pushing his sons when he was home, which was almost never, the iron man of the Army, but also the man of smiles and encouragement and moments of pride in his sons, over this disoriented shell of a man.

Puller covered up his father with a blanket and then marched out with his heart split right in half. But with his face unblemished by tears, his spine still straight, and his focus back on the mission at hand. Coming to grips with the fact of his rapidly failing father was the only enemy John Puller had ever been afraid to face.

40

Puller valeted his car at the front entrance to the Army and Navy Club on Seventeenth Street in northwest DC and headed inside. The building was old, with architecturally classic lines that mirrored the interior he was just about to enter. It was run efficiently and quietly by a devoted team, with many serving here for decades. There was a large dining room on the main floor, private meeting rooms and more intimate dining areas on the second, and, because this was a military outpost of sorts, a bar. Of course.

He checked his watch. He was early, which he always wanted to be. A Confederate Army general had once said that you almost always win if you get there first with the most. There was definitely some truth in that. And maybe the person he was meeting here had thought the same thing. He went to the glass doors of the bar and peered through. Three men and two ladies were seated at the bar. Only two were in uniform. One woman and one of the gents. The man was a lieutenant colonel in the Army, the woman a Navy commander, an O-5, which meant she and the man were of equal rank. But Puller was looking for an O-6, a *Navy* captain, right below a rear admiral lower half. That had been what his brother had meant by the term "salt."

A captain in the Navy was of equal rank with a major in the Army, a senior officer.

Puller headed up to the third floor, where there was a library. And in the library was a table that was full of bullet holes from when it was used as a shield by American soldiers during a firefight in Cuba over a century ago. This was Robert Puller's reference to Remember the Maine. That ship had been blown up in Havana Harbor, prompting the Spanish-American War. The military led the world in historical props, Puller knew. And they made more of them with every battle.

He looked around but saw no one, until a voice broke the quiet.

"I see you like to be early, too, Chief Puller."

From behind a high-back chair turned away from him rose a woman. She was medium height with her dark hair done in a ponytail. Her dress whites rode well on her trim physique. Puller put her age at about forty, which was young for a captain. It normally took twenty years from graduation at Annapolis to get the four bars and a star and the full eagle spread on your uniform. That also explained Robert Puller's reference.

She walked over to him and put out her hand. He shook it and felt the strength in her grip as he looked down at her from nearly a foot gap.

"Captain…?"

"Gloria Miles, Chief Puller."

"Please, make it John."

"Then you can call me Gloria. My father was a master sergeant in the Marine Corps. He named me. You know what his nickname for me was?"

Puller shook his head.

"Glory." She smiled but her eyes held a wistful look. "Can you imagine the teasing and bullying I got with that one?"

He looked her over. "It seems to have made you stronger. And if you're as young as I think you are, then an overachiever as well."

"Right on both counts. I made O-6 three years early. But it felt six years longer than that."

"I can see that. How is your father?"

"No longer with us. How is *your* father?"

To that question Puller almost always answered, *Hanging in there.* But there was something about Miles that made him say, "He's seen better days, unfortunately."

"It's hard to see your father grow old," said Miles. "It's harder still when your father was a soldier, a leader, tough as nails. You expect him to live forever."

"Where are you deployed now?" asked Puller.

"For now, I'm working out of the Norfolk Naval Station, so I can oversee my baby being born."

Puller looked confused for a moment and glanced at her unadorned ring finger.

She noted this and laughed wistfully. "I'm waiting to take command of a Freedom-class LCS they're just about to launch, the USS *Seattle*," said Miles, referencing the acronym for a Littoral Combat Ship. "That's my *baby*."

"Yes ma'am. That must be quite a thrill."

She glanced over his shoulder. "Why don't we find a private place to talk?"

Puller turned to see a group of suits and uniforms come into the library and take up seats.

They found an empty room at the end of the hall on the third floor. Puller closed the door behind them, and they sat across from each other in fold-up chairs. Miles placed her cap on her lap, Puller did likewise with his.

She ran her gaze over his rows of ribbons and her eyebrows hiked. This was the military's equivalent of bragging rights. Guts and glory on full uniform display on one's chest. The earning of them had been anything but uniform. Puller had endured violent intrusion of metal into his body and been thrown into hellish situations that no human being should have to endure. In other words, just a day's work for a soldier.

"The DSC, Purples, Bronze, twin Silvers, along with everything else. Very impressive, John. You've served your country faithfully and well."

"I do my duty, like everybody else."

"There's nothing wrong with acknowledging exceptionalism."

"Why would my brother contact you?"

"I think he contacted a number of people who he thought might be helpful to you."

"But you're the only one he asked me to meet with."

She nodded. "I think my relevance to your investigation has nothing to do with my being in uniform."

"Okay."

"It has a lot to do with someone I know quite well."

"Okay."

"As I alluded to, I have no children. But I am a godmother to someone."

"Who is that?"

"Jeff Sands."

"I don't know who that is."

"He's the grandson of Peter Driscoll."

"Peter Driscoll, the Senate majority leader? Why would that knowledge be of use to me?"

"Jeff just turned twenty-one years old. Because of his grandfather's connections he got into Georgetown, where he's a junior. He could not have gotten in on his own merit."

"Okay. Still not getting what this has to do with my case."

"Jeff is a drug user. He is also probably a drug dealer. I don't know that for sure, but that is my best guess."

"So a drug dealer, maybe. Why haven't I heard anything about that?"

"Why would you?"

"So Grandpa has kept it out of the courts and the news?"

"Like I said, I don't know about the drug-dealing part. But Jeff has a lot of wealthy and well-connected friends at Ivy League colleges who could be customers of his."

"So a network of elite drug users? And what have you done about it?"

"I'm his godmother, which is usually an honorary rank. I knew his mother, Jennifer. She died when Jeff was eight. It was a big blow to him. His father is a hedge fund guy. He works and lives in New York. After Jennifer died, he married a much younger woman. They have two little kids. He's written Jeff off. I tried to step into the breach, so I've spent a lot of time with Jeff over the years. Not as a second mom, or anything, but just as a friend, someone to talk to."

"Jeff have any other siblings?"

"No."

"And what does he tell you when you two talk about his issues?"

"I've confronted him a number of times. He tells me that things are fine. He had a problem but has it no longer. And that anything else I've heard about him is just wrong."

"Did he look like he was using?"

"Not when he was with me."

"And did you tell my brother this?"

"Yes."

"How did he even come to contact you? Were you friends? You didn't say."

"No. I knew of him. But he told me he had never heard of me. He said it had to do with the results of an algorithm he had come up with for the purposes of your investigation."

Puller cracked a smile. "An algorithm? Now that sounds like Bobby, all right. Are you sure Driscoll knows about his grandson's wayward ways?"

"I know he does. I told him, numerous times."

"And what did he do?"

"He said he would handle it."

"And did he?"

"I doubt I would be here talking to you if he had."

"When was the last time you spoke with Jeff?"

"About two weeks ago."

"Did he ever mention a man named Tony Vincenzo?"

"No, not to me. I would have remembered that."

"How about a penthouse on Billionaires' Row in Manhattan?" Puller gave her the street address.

Miles looked puzzled. "You know, I think I dropped him off there once when we were in New York together. This was about a month ago. He said there was going to be a party. I remember telling him that he needed to be careful. And I also remarked that he must have some really, really rich friends. Do you know who owns the place?"

"We tried to track it and failed, which means it might be a global criminal enterprise with mega-deep pockets."

"Oh my God. Who the hell is he mixed up with?"

"I intend to find out. But I need to talk to your godson, ASAP."

"Do you want me to reach out to him and arrange something?"

"No, that won't work."

"Why?"

"Because he'll either disappear or someone will be sent to kill me. And since that's already happened once very recently, I'd like to avoid it again if possible."

Miles had turned pale as he was speaking. "Then what do you want me to do?" she said in barely above a whisper.

"Send me his contact info and a picture. I'll take it from there."

"And what should I do in the meantime?"

"Do not contact him. Go back to Norfolk, keep your head down, and when your ship is commissioned, get on it and don't look back."

"You're really scaring me, John."

"Then my mission is accomplished."

"Are you working this case all alone?"

Puller took out his phone. "No. I've got a partner who I'm just about to call."

"I hope this person is good."

"She's far better than good."

41

THE NEXT EVENING Pine met Puller outside the Eighth Avenue exit from Penn Station in New York City. He had ridden an Amtrak regional train up from DC, arriving in about three hours. The weather was overcast and chilly as they walked along the street, Puller's small duffel slung over his shoulder. His dress blues had been exchanged for jeans, a sweater, and a dark blue blazer. As they walked they filled each other in on their respective developments, including Robert Puller's algorithm netting them Gloria Miles and through her, Jeff Sands.

"So have you told Lineberry that Linda Holden-Bryant was his mole all those years ago?" asked Puller.

"I should, but I haven't. I'm not exactly sure how to go about it. Plus, he's still recovering from being shot."

They grabbed a cab that took them up the West Side to a condo building in the Eighties, near Riverside Drive.

As they passed the top-hatted and uniformed doorman and walked into the soaring marble-and-chrome lobby Puller asked, "What are we doing here?"

"This is where we're staying. Carol is in the condo now making dinner."

"Whose condo is it? I usually crash on a friend's couch when I'm in New York. The CID's per diem for lodging doesn't cover anything in the city lodging arena, and that includes sleeping in your car in a parking garage."

Puller eyed the smiling concierge seated behind a desk that would not have looked out of place at Versailles and added, "And

I don't have to be the world's greatest detective to deduce that this is also out of the Bureau's lodging per diem."

Pine looked uncomfortable. "This...this is Jack Lineberry's pied-à-terre. He generously allowed us to stay here."

"Weren't you staying at a hotel in Trenton?"

Pine thumbed the button for the elevator and said, "He called yesterday. I told him I was in New York and he insisted that we stay here."

"Was this before or after you spoke with his old flame?"

"After. But I didn't tell him that. He was just being kind."

They rode the car up to the tenth floor and she led him down a wide, luxuriously carpeted hallway lined with stout wooden doors and paintings that looked original. She used her passkey to enter the apartment. Puller followed, set down his duffel, and looked around.

"Wow, Lineberry is really loaded."

"Yes. He has his own jet, a mansion in rural Georgia, a penthouse in Atlanta."

"And this place," added Puller. "And he's your father."

"He's my biological father, but Tim Pine raised me," she retorted. "As far as I'm concerned, *he's* my father."

"I get that. But does Lineberry have any other kids?"

"No, he never married. He had me and...Mercy."

"Well, don't be surprised if he leaves all of this to you."

Pine looked surprised. "I never even thought about that. And I don't want it!"

"But he can still leave it to you. And you can do with it what you want."

"I'll worry about that if and when it turns out I have to."

A moment later Blum walked into the room wearing an apron and a smudge of flour on her cheek. She was rubbing her hands on a cloth.

"I thought I heard you come in. This place is deceptively large, and very quiet. I hope you're hungry. Dinner will be ready in about ten minutes."

"I am," said Puller. "It was slim pickings on the train."

"Let me show you to your room," said Pine.

She led him down a hall to the last door and opened it. She stepped in and looked around at what was clearly a high-dollar, professionally decorated space, just like the rest of the apartment.

"Lineberry has good taste, or hired someone who has good taste," remarked Puller as he set his duffel on the four-poster bed.

Pine sat in a chair in front of a reproduction desk all primed with stationery and pen and a large, leather-handled magnifying glass.

"So, Jeff Sands?"

Puller nodded and sat on the bed. "His grandfather is one of the most powerful men in the country. But his son-in-law has apparently written Jeff off and has a new family to focus on."

"So he might be a drug dealer in addition to being a user? How has that not hit the news?"

"I did some research on it. Sands is one of sixteen grandchildren and he has a different last name. And from what I could gather, not many people are in the loop on this. And maybe folks don't consider it newsworthy. I mean, Sands's dad was the absent parent. I can't believe many people will ding Peter Driscoll because one of his many grandchildren turned out bad. He raised his own kids and they all seemed to have turned out okay. It's not exactly his responsibility to look after another generation."

"Okay, that certainly makes sense. So what do we do?"

"I've got Sands's address. We set up surveillance and see what we see."

"And why not go directly to question him?"

"No. I want to reconnoiter this sucker a little bit first."

"The federal government and the Trenton police have come down on us like a ton of bricks. I can't see how Jeff Sands could have made that happen. But I can see someone like Peter Driscoll having a hand in that."

"I can't answer that one way or another. I hope to be able to shortly."

"But people have been killed. Sheila Weathers and Jerome Blake and Ed McElroy. Call me hopelessly naïve, but I also can't believe that a U.S. senator would be involved in that." When he didn't answer she said, "Puller?"

"I'm trying to decide if you're hopelessly naïve or I'm a confirmed cynic."

"But you think it's possible he's involved somehow?"

"I think there's so much money in politics today that anything is possible. Guys like Driscoll are a hot commodity, Atlee. They can be worth billions or even trillions of dollars to certain folks." He paused. "What do you think someone would do for a trillion bucks?"

"Anything," she said. "And looking at it that way I guess we're fortunate that only three people are dead."

"But I think that number is going to go up."

"Including you and me? It's already been a close call for us both, you especially."

"From the minute we put on the shield—"

"—we accepted that possibility," Pine finished for him.

"But, again, this is not your case, Atlee. You really should just focus on finding your sister."

"Very chivalrous of you to give me such an easy out."

"Which you're not going to take?"

"My answer is the same as the last time you asked. Let's go eat. You're not the only one who's hungry."

CHAPTER

42

IT WAS THE HOUR OF NIGHT when most people were already in bed. A marine fog had rolled in off the Hudson and been met by a twin mist burning off the East River. They met in the middle of Manhattan like secret lovers on a nighttime tryst.

Pine was fully dressed as she gazed out the bedroom window and saw nothing. Any activity going on at street level ten floors below was currently invisible to her.

She checked her main weapon and her Beretta for the fourth and final time. She moved down to Blum's bedroom door and listened for a few moments until she heard the woman's gentle snores. Puller was waiting for her in the front room. He was dressed all in black, and she noted the bulges along his waistline where his twin M11s sat.

Puller took out his phone and scrolled through some screens. "I've had a team of CID agents up here tracking Sands all day and night."

"What has he been doing?"

"Apparently, the twin workloads of being a student at Georgetown and operating a drug ring got to be too much for him. He's taking some time off from academia to fatten his wallet and expand his market share."

"So it's confirmed that he's dealing?"

"Pretty much, yeah."

"Have we ruled out his father being a partner in all this?" she asked as they stepped into the elevator car and headed down.

"Not definitively, but from all we could ascertain the guy is legit rich. And he's a prick for a father, at least to Sands. So I doubt father and son are in this together."

A taxi dropped them three blocks from their destination in Brooklyn.

"It's a club where Sands hangs out," explained Puller.

"What kind of a club?"

"An expensive one."

"You want front or back?" she asked.

"Up to you."

Pine headed to the back.

She settled in behind a line of dumpsters about twenty yards from the rear exit of the place that was called, simply, the Club.

Now that's either really lazy or really ingenious, thought Pine.

Puller had emailed her a picture of Sands. He was handsome, with an arrogant glaze to his features. He looked like a child of privilege to Pine. But then again, his mother had died while he was a child and his father had abandoned him. Pine could relate to that, but it didn't absolve the man from the consequences of being a drug dealer.

A light rain began to fall, and Pine moved back so that she was under the cover of an overhang. She pulled up the collar on her jacket and kept her gaze on the back door of the Club. She stiffened at one A.M. when the door opened and two men stumbled out. But neither one was Sands. They quickly moved off, picking up their pace as the rain came down harder.

Twenty minutes more passed, and Pine was wondering whether this stakeout would turn out to be a bust when the door opened once more. She stiffened and then relaxed as the woman appeared. She looked to be in her twenties, short, voluptuous, and wearing barely anything at all.

A moment later Pine came to rigid attention as the man appeared in the doorway and looked around. Jeff Sands then stepped out, smiled, and coiled his hands around the woman. His hands dipped to her buttocks and took up purchase there. They kissed and he maneuvered her back against the wall.

Pine wasn't sure she wanted to see what was coming next, until the two men appeared from a darkened corner of the rear of the building. The woman darted away, and it was just Sands and the two gents with pistols pointed at his handsome and now terrified face. He put his hands up and backed away. She could see him pleading with the gunmen, even as she knew these pleas would not cut it. She had already texted a one-word alert to Puller. She slipped out both pistols and moved forward. Her Glock was aimed at one assailant, her Beretta at the other.

They had backed Sands up to the same wall as he had the woman.

She would normally call out her presence and FBI authority, but this situation did not ideally allow for it. Rushing silently forward, she clubbed the first man on the back of the head with the butt of her pistol; he dropped to the ground with a yell. The other man whipped around, his gun leveled at her chest. The next moment he was on the ground after being slammed there by Puller, who had rounded the corner and hit the fellow with a full head of steam.

They quickly disarmed the men and then ordered them to get up.

The man Pine had clubbed had blood streaming down his face. "I need a doctor," he screamed.

"What you need," said Puller, holding out his shield, "is to start answering questions. Beginning with why you were just about to kill this man."

Sands had collapsed against the wall and was panting with tears in his eyes.

"We weren't going to kill him," said the other man, rubbing a bruise on his cheek where it had slammed into the pavement. "We were going to talk to him about some delinquent bills."

"And you do that with guns?" said Pine.

"Mr. Sands usually needs some persuading."

Puller took out his phone and punched in a number. "Well, you can explain your technique to NYPD, how about that?"

"You don't really want to do that."

They turned because this came from Sands, who had regained his composure and was looking at them imploringly. "These are business associates of mine. They really weren't going to hurt me."

"Which I can't say for you two," the same man said, rubbing his cheek again.

Pine said, "Either one of you know Tony Vincenzo?"

The men glanced at each other until the bleeder said, "Who?"

Puller put his phone away and looked at Sands, who said, "This has nothing to do with Tony. They don't know him."

Pine turned her attention to him. "But you do?"

"I know him, yeah," he said grudgingly.

Puller glanced at the two men. "Beat it."

The men looked in surprise at each other and then hurried off, disappearing into the mist as quietly as they had emerged from it.

Sands pushed off the wall and straightened out his clothes. "Thanks for the help. I'd buy you a drink, but I have someplace I have to be."

Puller hooked him by the arm. "You do have a place to be. Speaking with us. Let's go."

Sands strained against him. "This is a free country and I've done nothing wrong. So get your damn hands off me."

Pine stepped forward. "Or we can call up your grandfather and let him know what our investigation has uncovered about you."

"You think he'd care?" sneered Sands. "Why don't you call the asshole who happens to be my father and see what you'd get there?"

"Maybe they won't be interested, but the police probably will. Those guys weren't collecting for a charity. How much do you owe them?"

"Why are you guys giving me such a hard time?"

Puller remarked, "We know what you're involved in, Jeff. And people have died. What makes you think you're special?"

"Who's died?"

"Tony Vincenzo's father. And a woman named Sheila Weathers."

Sands looked panicked. "Sheila! You're lying. She was just—"

"Just what? Just at that penthouse the other night? So was I. She's dead. I saw her body."

"You're lying."

"We can take you right now to the morgue to see her corpse. It won't be pretty because they've already autopsied her. I have the report on my phone. You want to see the pictures?"

Sands shook his head and put a shaky hand to his face. "No…I…"

"Let's go get a cup of coffee. There's an all-night place right around the corner," said Puller.

They walked off into the darkness.

CHAPTER

43

IT TOOK ONE FULL CUP OF COFFEE before Sands would even look up at them.

The place was a dive, but pleasant enough, and not too crowded at this hour. Both Pine and Puller had kept an eye out for the two men who had gone after Sands. If they were out there, and they probably were, they were good at staying invisible.

"You want something to eat?" asked Pine, who cradled her coffee and let the steam rise to her face, helping to cut against the rawness outside.

Sands shook his head, dumped some sugar into the cup the waitress had just refilled, and said, "Sheila was nice."

"She told me she was sort of dating Tony."

Sands pushed a hand through his thick, tousled hair. He looked like a Kennedy, thought Pine. Handsome, charming, connected, and sometimes getting into serious trouble.

"I guess she was. But we all hung out."

"She worked at Fort Dix, in the commissary," said Pine. "At least that's what I was told."

"Yeah, something like that."

"So why did a girl like that warrant a pass to Billionaires' Row?"

"Because *I* said she could. Same as Tony."

"Same as Lindsey Axilrod?"

"Lindsey? Why are you mentioning her?"

"Because she was the one who set me and Sheila up. She helped whoever killed Sheila."

"No way, I don't believe that," he said heatedly. "Lindsey's cool. She wouldn't do something like that."

"And how do you know Lindsey?" asked Pine.

"We...we just met. The way people do."

"Why do I think she sought you out?" said Pine.

"Why would she do that? She's just an IT worker at Fort Dix."

"I went to the penthouse with Lindsey. She got in because of her connection to Tony. Or at least I thought that then. She pointed out Sheila to me there. We arranged to meet with her later. Lindsey and I were getting into what I thought was an Uber that Lindsey ordered. The next thing I remember I was waking up next to a dead Sheila, and Lindsey was nowhere to be seen."

"Maybe they got her, too."

"No, I later went to her house. No one answered my knocks, so I called the cops to do a welfare check. When they got there she spoke to them through a doorbell camera setup and told a bullshit story about her mother being ill and her having to go out of town. She never mentioned what happened that night. She's in this up to her eyeballs. And she's not just an IT person. She fooled me and she apparently fooled you."

Puller put his coffee down and leaned forward. "So what exactly is going on, Jeff?"

Sands looked nervously at him. "Look, I don't know what you want me to say."

"The truth would be really good."

"How'd you even find out about me?"

Puller said, "I had a talk with your godmother. She was very worried about you. She asked me to check on you. So here I am, checking on you." He paused. "She really does care for you, Jeff."

"Yeah, I know Aunt Gloria does. She's really the only one, after my mom died," he added miserably.

"Lots of people have shitty lives, Jeff," said Pine. "But you're young, you've got money, unless those clothes you're wearing are knockoffs. You're attending one of the best colleges in America."

"I got in because of who my grandfather is, that's the only

reason. I didn't even want to go, but he insisted. He said I had to make something of myself."

"Maybe he genuinely means it."

Sands chuckled.

"What's the joke?" asked Pine.

"The only thing he's 'genuinely' concerned about is that I might do something to mess up his good name."

"I heard that he plans to retire after his term is up," pointed out Puller.

"He's also planning to join this big-ass lobbying firm to fund his golden years. Anything messes that up, he's SOL."

"I thought members of Congress had to wait before they could lobby the government," said Pine.

"The way it was explained to me, he won't be directly lobbying anyone. But a wink, a nod, a phone call, a whispered word. That shit's easy to get around. It's why they wrote the law that way. To make it look like they were doing something positive, only there are holes in it big enough to drive a semi through."

"You seem to have checked that out pretty thoroughly," noted Puller.

"I like to know what I'm dealing with," said Sands.

"Meaning what exactly?"

"Meaning exactly what I just said."

"So would drug dealing qualify as besmirching the family's reputation?" asked Pine.

"Who says I'm dealing drugs?"

"You say you're not?"

"No, I'll just sit here and confess to two feds. You want it in writing or is verbal okay?"

Puller leaned in even further. "I'm going to tell you something and I want your opinion, all right?"

Sands looked surprised by this but nodded. "Okay."

"Tony Vincenzo is a pill maker. That's beyond doubt. I've got two of his stooges cooling their heels in the stockade at Fort Dix. Plus, we found a ton of evidence at his dad's old home. That's the first point. The second point is we have encountered extraordinary opposition from both state and federal platforms to our investigation. My question to you: Why would a run-of-the-mill drug op trigger so many players on the other side with the intent of burying the truth?"

Sands took a sip of coffee before answering. "I don't know. Maybe it's not a run-of-the-mill drug operation."

"So is that penthouse on Billionaires' Row a heroin silo or what?"

"No, that's just a playpen, a perk for the faithful."

Pine noted that Sands's despair had faded and his confidence bolstered as the conversation had veered to this topic. But his features betrayed that maybe he had said too much.

"Then you must be one of the faithful. So tell us, where do you direct that faith?" asked Pine.

Sands leaned forward. "I don't want any part of this, okay?"

"Do you want part of prison?" said Puller.

"You have no proof of anything."

"I've got witnesses ready to rat your ass out, Sands."

"Who?"

"You really think I'm going to tell you that?"

"You're bluffing. You've got nothing."

"Then walk out of here right now," said Pine. "There's the door. Keep in mind, they got to a guy in a federal prison. Keep in mind they got to your friend, Sheila. Keep in mind that Lindsey is in on it and she strikes me as a 'survive at all costs' kind of gal. So now that you've been seen with us, how long do you think you have?"

"You're trying to scare me."

"I'm giving you facts. If the facts scare you, so be it."

Sands glanced at the door. "You'd really just let me walk out of here?"

"Sure," said Puller. "But before you go, you have any idea where Tony Vincenzo is?"

"No. I haven't seen him in about a week."

"And how do you know him? You didn't say."

"We met a while back. Hung out. He's cool."

"And why do you have access to the penthouse if you're not contributing to the cause?" said Pine. "It didn't strike me as a freebie sort of place. What's the price of admission?"

Sands shrugged and stared down at his coffee.

"You can understand our skepticism that you're clean, Jeff, right?" said Puller. "Do you know who owns that penthouse?"

"No."

"Who told you about it? Who said you could go there?"

"Some guys. I forget their names."

"I doubt they'll forget yours. Well, I think we're done here, Jeff. Have a nice life, however short it might be."

Puller rose, and Pine did likewise. Sands looked up at them.

"You're just going to leave me here by myself?"

Puller looked at Pine and then said, "You said you're clean, we have no grounds to hold you. What do you expect us to do? You said before you had someplace to go. So *go*."

They moved toward the door.

"Look, hey, guys."

They turned back.

A pale Sands, the jauntiness struck clean from him, rose and joined them. "I don't want to die, okay?"

"So what do *you* do about it?" said Pine. "Because the only way we can help you is if you help us. You're a college boy. You're smart enough to grasp that concept."

Sands glanced nervously around. A few of the customers were staring at him. "Can we go somewhere and talk about this? Maybe we can figure something out."

"Sure," said Puller as he laid some cash down for their coffees. He gripped Sands by the arm and nodded at Pine. "Check the back. We can't take any chances with him."

Pine cautiously exited out the back door, and did a recon of the area behind the restaurant. Her gaze took in all sectors, sight lines, and hiding places. Satisfied, she crept back to the door and called out, "Clear."

Puller came out with Sands.

"We can go back to my place," said Pine.

Sands said, "Where's that—"

He didn't finish due to the rifle round slamming into his head. It passed through the back of his skull and plunged right into Puller. Both men dropped to the ground.

"John!" cried out Pine.

Sands was clearly dead.

And it looked like John Puller might be, too.

CHAPTER

44

Pɪɴᴇ ʜᴀᴅ ɴᴇᴠᴇʀ ʟɪᴋᴇᴅ ʜᴏꜱᴘɪᴛᴀʟꜱ ever since she nearly died in one as a child back in Georgia. She had been in and out of consciousness in the ambulance that had taken her there. Bright lights, masked people, tubes and lines being inserted in her.

Her anguished and sobbing mother.

The race down the hallway on the gurney, the white, antiseptic room, strangers hurtling around her, machines beeping, overhead lights like a cluster of suns, so intense they hurt, so she closed her eyes and then there was a prick of something, another something covered her mouth.

Dark.

Then she rose again, like Jesus, or at least her tired mind had remembered this little tidbit from vacation Bible school.

Her mother had been there. Her father. Others. A man with a white coat, a smiling nurse.

She would live, it seemed.

Now she sat in the visitors room at the hospital where the ambulance had taken Puller. She had ridden over with him, every memory of her own frantic ambulance ride coming back to her in waves conjured from thirty years ago.

She held his hand, whispered encouragement into his ear, unsure if he could hear her, whether he was actually conscious. But she had felt him squeeze back, however weakly. And then he was whisked off for emergency surgery.

When Mercy had vanished, six-year-old Pine had prayed every

night for her sister's safe return. She had prayed all the way until the eighth grade. And after that, she had prayed no more.

Until now.

She got down on her knees and pressed the palms of her hands together.

God, this is a good man. A just man. Please, don't let him die. Please. We need him. I need him. Please save him.

She quickly rose when Blum bustled in. "How is he?"

"Still in surgery. They said they'd come in when they were done and let me know how it went."

"Have you reached his family?"

"His father has dementia. I left word for his brother at a number I scrounged up. I don't know if it's good."

"Do you know his father and brother?"

"His father is an Army legend and John's namesake. His brother, Robert, is a lieutenant colonel in the Air Force, a once-in-a-generation talent with computers, according to Puller. I've never met either of them."

"It must have been awful last night."

"It was...pretty awful, yes."

"Did you see the shooter?"

"No. I covered Puller with my body when he went down. I knew Sands was dead. Half his brain ended up on Puller's clothes. I fired in the direction of the shot, but they didn't return fire. By the time the police got there, it was way too late. The shooter was gone."

"And did Sands tell you anything helpful before he was killed?"

"He was going to, I think."

"So you were being followed last night?"

"Yes. We ran into two thugs earlier who were going to come down heavy on Sands, probably over drugs. We chased them off. I don't think it was them."

"So maybe whoever Sands was going to finger?"

"I guess we'll never know for sure."

The door opened and they both turned to see who it was. Pine was expecting the surgeon and praying it would be good news.

But the tall man in his late thirties was wearing Air Force ABUs, that service branch's camouflage version.

"Are you Atlee Pine?" he asked.

Pine rose and looked at the man. He was an inch shorter than Puller and not as muscular, but the face and the eyes didn't lie.

"You're Robert Puller," she said, shaking his hand.

"I came as soon as I got your message." He glanced at Blum, who nodded at him, a sympathetic expression on her features.

"This is my assistant, Carol Blum."

"What's his condition?" asked Puller.

"He's still in surgery. They promised to come in here after it was over."

"You said you were there. How bad is it?"

"Had to have been a rifle round. Went through Jeff Sands's skull before it hit your brother, so that was good. A lot less kinetic energy."

"Where did the round hit him?"

Pine touched her upper torso on the left side. "Here. In and out, which I hope was good. But he bled a lot. I stopped it as best I could. Then the paramedics arrived and took over. He was in and out of consciousness, then they put him on a drip, and he went under. His vitals on the ride were critical, but stable."

Pine had to sit down because recounting all of this so clinically and impersonally had suddenly run up against the fact that the person she was discussing was a friend and that he might still die.

Puller sat down next to her and gripped her shoulder. "He's the toughest man I know, Agent Pine. If anyone can pull through, he will."

Pine leveled a far calmer gaze on him. "Please, make it Atlee." She paused, desperately wanting to change the subject. "John mentioned you used an algorithm to turn up Gloria Miles, which led us to Jeff Sands. How did you do that, Colonel Puller?"

"I go by Robert." Puller sat back and brushed at his regulation short hair. "From what John explained to me, I concluded that we were operating in exalted circles. No run-of-the-mill drug dealer can get a vice chair removed from his assignment at the

Pentagon on a day's notice because the man was making inquiries. That narrowed things down quite a bit. I ran a script on possible connections between highly ranked politicos and any connection at all to criminal activity, including drug dealing, because it seemed to have a nexus to what you were looking into. I ran a series of calculations and the one name that kept popping out was Jeff Sands and his grandfather, Peter Driscoll. Next, I looked for any connection to them that John could use as an investigative point of contact. That's how I got to the godmother, Gloria Miles."

"How long did all of this take you?" asked a wide-eyed Pine.

"I did it over lunch. I'm not that fast, but the computers I use are, and the databases they have access to are truly immense."

"Can the FBI borrow you for like the rest of your life?" interjected Blum.

Puller added, "But now Sands is dead. So that lead is dead, too."

"At least we know more now than we did," said Pine. "But all I want right now is to hear that John is going to be fine."

At that moment the door to the visitors room opened once more. The woman was in her fifties and she wore blue scrubs and spectacles. Her hair was salt and pepper and her expression was one, it seemed to Pine, of relief.

"Agent Pine?"

"Yes," she said, jumping up. Robert Puller did likewise.

"He's out of surgery and stable. He's going to make it. He's quite a strong young man."

"Yes he is. This is his brother, Robert Puller."

Puller shook hands with the surgeon. "Thank you, Doctor."

"I noticed that he had several previous wounds that had healed."

"He's Army. Middle East."

The doctor nodded. "That explains it. Well, he just added another one to the collection."

"When can we see him?"

"He's in recovery and needs to rest. I would say later today or tomorrow even. He's strong, but he's been through a lot."

Pine said, "Will...will he make a full recovery?"

"I think he'll be fine."

"I mean, physically and all. Like he was before. He's a CID agent in the Army."

"Oh, I see." She looked from Pine to Puller. "Well, I can't make any guarantees, but I hope that he will. I can't say one hundred percent. There was some internal damage. But from the looks of him, and from what you just told me, I wouldn't bet against him, either."

She left and closed the door.

Pine and Puller collapsed into their chairs. Pine put a supportive arm on Puller's shoulder. "He's going to make it, Robert, that's what's most important."

"Thank God," Puller said quietly.

To herself Pine added, "Yes, thank you, God. Thank you."

CHAPTER

45

A few hours later Pine and Blum left the hospital and returned to Lineberry's condo. Robert Puller had opted to stay at the hospital. Pine texted him her address. She planned to be back at the hospital later that day. Hopefully, they could see John Puller then.

An exhausted Pine slept until two in the afternoon, then sat in her bedroom and looked out the window. The day looked like it would be warmer than the previous ones had been, and free of rain. Her belly was empty, and she had a hunger headache, but she didn't want to waste time eating right now. She felt terrible guilt for what had happened to Puller. She knew all about the company line—that it came with the territory— but still…she felt immense responsibility for the man's nearly dying.

And with Sands dead, they really had no leads to pursue.

She phoned Robert Puller. He told her that his brother seemed to be doing as well as possible. She thanked him for the info and said she would come to the hospital later.

She showered and changed into fresh clothes. When she came out, Blum had a meal on the table.

"Carol, thank you, but you don't have to do this. I'm perfectly capable of taking care of myself."

"It gives me something to do, Agent Pine. I don't like feeling idle and useless."

Pine's phone buzzed. She didn't recognize the number, but it was a New Jersey area code. She answered it.

The voice said, "Agent Pine, this is Norma Bailey, I'm the principal at Jerome Blake's school."

"Yes, Mrs. Bailey?"

"I wanted to let you know that I have the photos of the school employees ready for your review."

"Can you email them to me?"

"Yes. I can do that right now. Have you made any progress on what happened to Jerome?"

"A little, but things are getting very complicated very fast."

"I hope you find the truth. Jerome deserves that."

"I'll do my best."

Pine gave her the email address. A minute later the photos were deposited in her inbox.

She looked at Blum. "I just got the photos of the school personnel from Norma Bailey at Jerome's school."

"Terrific. Now we just have to find that young man, what was his name again?"

"Peanut. But I have a shortcut that I hope will save us some time."

They left New York and drove back to Trenton, arriving at Jerome Blake's home about ninety minutes later. His mother answered their knocks.

"Have you found out who killed my boy?" she said.

"Not yet, but we're still working on it," replied Pine. "We met a friend of Jerome's, he said his name was Peanut?"

Blake nodded, looking thoughtful. "Jerome and Peanut were real tight when they were younger, then they went their separate ways."

"Do you know where we might find Peanut? And what's his real name?"

"Donald Washington. His grandma lives on the next block over. What does he have to do with what happened to Jerome?"

"He told us he saw a man speaking to Jerome the day of the shooting, at school. He said Jerome looked really weird afterward. I've got some pictures of employees at the school to show him. To see if he recognizes the man. Can you give us Peanut's address so I can do that?"

"Peanut don't live at home anymore. Just his grandma there now, and she's doing poorly."

"So where might we find him?" asked Pine.

"He hangs out over at a gym on Broad Street. Calhoun's."

"Why a gym? Does he like to work out?"

"A few guys box there. But I don't think most folks who go there care nothing 'bout working out. It's just a safe place to go to and hang out. You find the guy who owns it. His name's Gerald. He's a good man."

"But other business happens there?" said Pine.

Blake held up her hands. "Not in the gym, no. Gerald don't allow for that. But outside? I ain't getting in the middle of that. I got my Jewel to raise. She needs her momma."

"How's she doing?"

"Not good. Still crying her eyes out."

"This must be so traumatizing for her. I...I know what it's like to lose a sibling. If we can do anything, please let us know."

They drove off and quickly found Calhoun's. It was an old, dilapidated building with ancient boxing posters plastered across its front, many of them ripped or faded by the sun. Some young men were hanging around outside. The area was run-down, with boarded up storefronts and a general air of decay. She parked at the curb about a block down and told Blum to wait in the car and to get in the driver's seat, which she did.

"Are you sure you don't want me to go with you?"

"Very sure, Carol. And keep the doors locked and the engine running. Anything starts looking hinky just leave."

"If you're not out in twenty minutes, should I call the police?"

"I'll be okay."

Pine walked past the groups of young men who gave her long stares and some catcalls. But they otherwise ignored her. She went into Calhoun's, which turned out to be built out like a warehouse. There were high, angled ceilings, industrial support columns, three boxing rings, and thousands of square feet of workout equipment that looked old and shabby. There were a few guys hoisting iron, and others expertly skipping rope and still others going after speed and heavy bags, but most were congregated around one of the boxing rings.

Pine walked over there and joined the crowd. Several young men tried to bar her way but a broad-shouldered man, with curly gray hair and wearing an old-fashioned three-piece suit and a brilliant red tie, said, "Show some respect, let the lady through."

The men obeyed and Pine came to stand next to him.

"Thanks, Mr. . . . ?"

"Just call me Gerald. And you are?"

"Atlee Pine."

"Had an aunt down in Alabama named Atlee, God rest her soul."

"Quite the gym."

"Really? Forgive me, but I thought you'd be one of them folks who like the juice bar and the Peloton and that yoga stuff." Then he ran his eye over her, not in a sexual way, but in a way of a person experienced at gauging fitness. "But then again, looking at your shoulders, thighs, and core, I would be wrong about that, wouldn't I?"

"I'm a powerlifter. The gym where I work out in Arizona has no AC, just a lot of iron and a lot of sweat and no juice bar need apply." She looked around. "And from what I can see of this place, I think I'd fit right in."

"Well, come back anytime to work up a sweat. Now, what can we do for you?"

"I'm looking for a young man named Peanut."

"And why would you be doing that?"

Gerald's tone was still very polite, but his smile and gaze had hardened just a bit.

"He told me he could help me on a case. I wanted him to look at some photos I just got."

"A case?"

She showed him her FBI badge. "Jerome Blake's death. Did you know him?"

Gerald took a moment to look at the throng of young men around them and said, "Hey, fellas, give us space so me and this lady can have a private talk, okay?"

The group fussed a bit over this directive, but they all moved away.

Gerald looked back at Pine. "I knew his brother, Willie. Would've made a fine light heavyweight."

"His mother said she got him to move."

"So she did. And Cee-Cee made the right call. He was heading down the wrong path."

"Cee-Cee told me to look you up here. That you were a good man."

"She's a nice lady. Had a hard time, like a lot of folks around here." He looked at the two men in the ring, both in their twenties, muscled, wearing head protection gear and bobbing and weaving as they danced around the ring. "Like those two right there. Maybe their mommas should get them outta here, too."

"So what keeps them here? You?"

He put his hand on one of the ropes. "Lived here my whole life. Fought in the ring a lot in my day. Was pretty good. Marine Corps champion for my weight class. Served my time in Nam. Got a lungful of Agent Orange, which derailed any athletic career I might have been contemplating. I'm seventy-one years old and feel like I'm a hundred. You have days like that?"

"I think we all do, even without breathing in Agent Orange."

"Anyway, I started this gym in 1977. Been running it ever since. Try to teach the young folks around here the art of pugilism. But really, I'm just trying to give them a safe space to go to. Learn some discipline. Learn about working hard, setting goals, getting together in groups without pursuing any illegal activity, if you get my point."

"All good things. So, Peanut?"

"He's usually around here this time of day. Let me go check."

Gerald walked off and the situation changed immediately. She could sense the heightened tension, the more focused gazes of the men who had once more clustered around her.

The men in the ring stopped what they were doing and leaned over the ropes. One took out his mouthpiece and snarled, "What you doing here?"

"Just asking about someone."

"You ain't got the right to ask 'bout nobody," barked the other man, spitting out his mouth guard. "You can't come in here and ask nothing."

"And why is that?"

"She's a cop," said one of the men in the crowd. "Saw her flash her badge."

The first fighter said, "Then you ain't welcome here. You just good for shooting us in the back."

Pine sized him up. "I'll make a deal with you. If you can kick *my* ass, I'll leave. If I kick your ass, I stay and get my questions answered. Deal?"

The two fighters looked at each other and belly-laughed. The crowd of men behind her closed ranks and did likewise.

"You gonna get in this ring with me?" he said with an incredulous look that eased to a grin.

"Unless you want to come out here."

"No, step right up. Which teeth you want to lose and which ones you want to keep? I'll try to be accommodating."

The other man split the ring ropes so Pine could duck under.

She stood to her full height and drew closer to the man she was about to combat. He looked a little surprised that she was taller than he was.

Pine took off her jacket, revealing the Glock in her belt holster.

"You want me to hold your piece for you, lady?" said one man in the crowd.

"That would be a no." She looked at the man in the ring. "How much do you weigh?"

"One-sixty."

"Wow, almost as much as me. I'm five pounds heavier, for the record." Pine had on a short-sleeved shirt underneath, and her ropy, corded muscles were clearly visible. The man glanced over at his friend, who shrugged and looked a little nervous as he stepped out of the ring.

"Okay, what are the rules?" asked Pine.

"Shit, ain't no rules in here," the man laughed.

"Great." In a blinding move, Pine slammed a foot into his gut, and when he doubled over, she laid her right leg against the side of his head with such stunning force that it knocked him right through the ropes, where he was caught by several of the onlookers below.

She walked over and looked down at him. "Okay, warm-up's over. You want to start now? Or just answer my questions? Your call."

They heard someone clapping and all turned to see Gerald walking back to the ring, alone. Gerald stopped next to the boxer Pine had laid out and knelt down. "Okay, Ty, remember what I keep telling you about disrespecting the women?"

Ty nodded dumbly. Gerald helped him to his feet and looked up at Pine.

"Peanut ain't here." He turned to the others. "Anybody here know where Peanut is?"

Pine looked over the crowd one by one until a young man around eighteen stepped forward.

"Seen him over at Duke's," said the man. "Before I come here."

Pine glanced at Gerald. "Duke's?"

"When you leave here, go right, three blocks, then go left. It's a...store."

"What do they sell?" she asked.

"It depends," said Gerald. "It just depends on what you want. But if I were you, I wouldn't be buying."

46

DUKE'S WAS A STOREFRONT that looked abandoned, just like every other storefront around here. Pine peered through the glass doors, but it was too dark inside to make out anything. She rapped on the glass. Then she rapped again.

"What do you want?"

She looked up to see a man staring down at her from the second-floor window.

"I'd like to talk to Peanut. I heard he was here."

"Who'd you hear that from?"

"A guy over at Calhoun's."

"And you are...?"

The man was in his forties with wiry dark hair and a stern, suspicious countenance. As he leaned out she could see he was wearing a compression-fit sleeveless athletic shirt showing arms and shoulders that were both heavily muscled and tatted.

"Just a friend. I met him over at the school."

"Peanut don't go to school."

"But his friend Jerome did. I'm trying to find out what happened to him."

"Then you a cop?"

"I have some pictures to show Peanut. He agreed to look at them."

The man disappeared from the window.

A minute later the shop door opened and there stood Peanut.

"You got them pictures?" he said.

"Yeah." She looked over his shoulder to see the man standing about ten feet farther back in the room.

Pine said quietly, "So what sort of business goes on here?"

"This and that."

"Right. Is that guy in there Duke?"

"Maybe."

"You don't know?"

"I don't know much. Works fine for me."

They got into the car and Peanut was shown all the photos one by one. At the end he said, "He ain't in there."

"You're sure?"

"Real sure. Ain't nobody in there look like he did."

Pine sat back, enormously frustrated. She looked at Blum. "We keep running into dead ends and I'm really getting sick of it."

Peanut said, "See, what I can't figure is, why Jerome do it at all. I mean, why he let a man do that to him? Give him a gun and set him up, 'cause that had to be what went down. And then he get shot on top of it. Why do shit when you know you gonna die? Why not say no and take your chances?"

"Maybe Jerome didn't know he was going to die," replied Blum.

Pine glanced at Peanut. "You said you haven't been friends with Jerome for a long time?"

"Yeah, so?"

"Would you know about any close friends he might have?"

"Not really. Maybe somebody at school. Why?"

"Because in the alley that night he told me, '*We're* in deep shit.' I'm just trying to think of someone they could have threatened to get Jerome to do what he did."

"Shit, lady, only ones he might do that for is his family. Nobody closer than that to him. They all real tight."

"You know, I think you might be right about that. Thanks, Peanut."

He opened the door. "And, yeah, that's Duke in there."

"This and that?" said Pine.

Peanut smiled. "Little'a this and a little'a that."

"Give me your cell phone number in case I can get some more

pictures to show you. I won't have to look you up in person." He did so and then climbed out of the car.

After he went back into the shop Blum said, "Where are we going now?"

"Back to Blake's house. I've got a hunch and I'm praying that it pays off, because if it doesn't we have less than zero right now."

47

"DID YOU FIND PEANUT?" asked Cee-Cee Blake when she answered their knock.

"We did. Turns out he really couldn't help us, but I was wondering if we could speak to your daughter."

Blake looked confused. "To Jewel? Why?"

"We wanted to ask her a few questions about her brother."

Blake shook her head. "She's really upset. Can barely get her to eat anything. And she won't come out of her room."

"We will be very gentle, Cee-Cee. We have experience speaking with young people. And I really think it might help with finding out what happened to your son."

"Well, okay. I guess you can try. You want me to go with you?"

"Just to introduce us. Then we'd like to speak with her alone."

"No guarantee she'll see you, though, and I ain't gonna make her."

They followed Blake up the stairs and down the short hall to a bedroom door. She knocked.

"Honey? It's them two ladies from the FBI again. They want to ask you some questions about your brother."

"No!" a voice screamed out. "Tell them to go away."

Before Blake could answer Pine stepped forward and said, "Jewel, it's really important."

"I said no."

"I'd like to know why your brother did what he did."

"Go away."

"Because I think he did it to protect you."

Silence.

Blake looked astonished. "What the hell do you mean by that? Protecting Jewel? From what?"

They turned when they heard the door start to open. And then there was Jewel, tall and beautiful and well-developed for her age, with long dark hair swirling around her shoulders. She had on pajamas, with characters from *Mulan* on them. Her eyes were reddened and swollen.

"It's okay, Momma, I'll talk to the lady."

"You sure, baby?"

Jewel nodded. "Yeah, I'm good."

Blake gave Pine a disapproving look. "Well, okay, but don't take too long, honey, you need to rest."

She slowly walked back down the stairs.

"Can we come in?" asked Pine.

Jewel stepped back and let them pass through.

The bedroom was cluttered, with clothes on the floor, books lying around, an iPad on the unmade bed, and a smartphone on the nightstand. And used tissues littered over seemingly every available square inch. The walls were painted with a mural of what looked to be female superheroes.

"Who did that?" asked Blum, motioning to the wall.

Jewel rubbed her nose. "Me and Jerome."

"It's really excellent. You're both wonderful artists."

"Jerome ain't anything anymore 'cept dead."

Pine leaned back against another wall and folded her arms over her chest. "That's what we want to talk to you about."

Jewel slumped on her bed and looked down at her bare feet.

Pine began. "A man met with Jerome at his school. After that meeting Jerome was totally changed. Then that same night he ends up in an alley holding a gun. And then he's shot by a cop who might not be a cop." She paused and glanced at Blum, who was standing rigidly by the mural wall.

"Jerome said something to me right before he died, Jewel. Do you want to know what he said?"

Jewel didn't look up, but she nodded. "What'd he say?"

"He said that no one would believe him when I asked what he was doing there. Then he said something else. And that's why we're here to see you."

Jewel looked up now. "What did Jerome say?"

"He said, '*We're* in deep shit.' Why would this man be able to make him do something that would end up getting him killed?" She stopped and looked at Jewel, who seemed to be withering to nothing under the gaze. "It must've been someone very important to him. Like maybe *you*, Jewel?"

Tears spilled down the girl's cheeks. Blum sat down next to her and took her hand.

"I know this is so hard, Jewel. So very hard. But we're trying to find out who took your brother's life. And any help you can give us would be very appreciated."

Jewel wiped her eyes and stared up at Pine with a composed expression.

"Jerome knew."

"Knew about what?"

"The man who came to get me."

"What man?"

"Just a man. He would come at night. When Momma's at work."

"Where does your mother work?"

"She cleans buildings at night. Then she comes home in the morning and goes to sleep for a few hours. And then she has another job at Subway for the lunch crowd."

"Okay, maybe you should start from the beginning," suggested Pine.

Jewel collected herself. "It started one night. I went somewhere I wasn't supposed to. Momma had to go see Willie, my other brother in Delaware, cause he was sick. Jerome was supposed to be home, but he got called to do this thing with the robots. I told him I'd stay in. But I didn't."

"Where did you go?"

"A party in Newark. I look a lot older than I am. I had a fake ID showing I was twenty-one. I went with a couple of friends from school. We got a ride with another friend."

"Where was the party?"

"At some guy's parents' house. I was there for a while, had a couple of drinks. And then someone said there was a van taking people to a place in New York. A guy came over and said I'd been picked to go."

"How? What guy?"

"I don't know. He was older than me, early twenties. Tall, good-looking. Said he was in college."

"White or black?"

"Oh, he was a white dude."

"Color of his hair?" asked Pine.

"Brown, sort of wavy. I mean, he was real handsome."

Pine pulled out her phone and brought up the picture of Jeff Sands that she had gotten from Puller. "Was this the guy?"

Jewel looked at the screen. "Yeah, that was him. How'd you know that?"

"I didn't, until just now."

"Do you know his name?"

"I do. Did he give you one?"

"Just said it was Charlie or something like that."

"Did he tell you why you were picked?"

"No."

"And you just went?"

"Well, it was a bunch of us, so I felt safe. And…and it sounded exciting. Charlie even said there would be some real celebrities there. I mean, some A-listers, not like old dudes. And I could meet them. And then he said I'd be given a ride back to my house."

"What happened after that?"

"We drove to this building in New York."

"Do you know where?"

"I don't know New York. I'd only been to the city one time when I was a kid. But the building they took me to that night had a doorman and a private elevator and stuff like that."

"So you went up there with all the others?"

Jewel shook her head. "See, the thing was, everybody got sort of separated. I ended up by myself heading up in the elevator. I was scared, but what could I do? I mean, I was already there."

"What about Charlie?"

"He sorta disappeared. I didn't see him in the van. Everything happened so fast."

"Then what?"

"The elevator opened right into someone's apartment. I never seen a place like that for real. I mean, it was like being in a movie. I mean, Jesus. I didn't know nobody lived like that, not really."

"And then what happened?"

"A woman came out to greet me."

"Describe her," said Pine.

"She was maybe thirty-five, sandy hair. Shorter than me. I...she just looked normal."

"Lean and fit with freckles?"

"Yeah, that sounds like her, and she did have freckles on her face."

Pine looked at Blum, who said, "Probably Lindsey Axilrod."

"Okay, what happened next?" Pine asked Jewel.

"She said that I was to make myself comfortable and someone would be out shortly. She asked me if I wanted a drink." Jewel stopped for a moment. "I...I didn't know what to do. I mean, I'm only fourteen. So I told her just a Coke. She came back with it and I sat down and drank it."

"And then what happened? Did someone else come out to see you?"

Jewel shook her head, her eyes filling with tears. "The...the next thing I know, I woke up in bed. I was naked. And..." She bent over and sobbed.

Blum put her arm around the girl's shoulders. "I know this is so terribly hard. So painful for you. Just take your time, Jewel, take all the time you need."

A minute later Jewel composed herself, wiped her eyes, blew into the tissue Blum handed her, and continued. "There was a man lying next to me in the bed. He was naked, too."

"Do you remember what he looked like?"

She nodded. "Older, white guy, maybe sixty with gray hair. He was snoring really loud." Jewel wiped at her eyes. "I was totally freaked out. I didn't know what the hell had happened. I mean, I was drinking a Coke and then this? But then when I sort of looked around, and the sheets...I...I knew that..." She seemed unable to say it.

"That he'd had sex with you while you were unconscious?"

She nodded, her eyes filling with tears. "I got out of bed really quiet, I didn't want to wake him. I ran to the door and opened it...and..."

"Was someone there?"

Jewel nodded. "The same woman. She had my clothes, all ironed and on hangers. She helped me get dressed. She calmed me down. She got me a ride home."

"So they drugged your Coke, and the man had sex with you?"

"I was so scared."

"And when you got home, did you report this to the police?"

"I was going to, but..."

"But what?" said Pine.

"I got a call on my phone. I don't even know how they got the number. It was a man."

"And what did he say?"

"That if I told anyone I'd get in big trouble."

"Jewel, you were raped. You were drugged and then raped."

"I know, but—"

"But what?"

Looking even more miserable, Jewel stuck her hand under her bed and pulled out a pillowcase. She held it up and dumped the contents on the bed.

It was cash, a lot of it.

"Where did you get all that?" asked Blum.

"That's the part I didn't tell you. The lady who helped me, she gave me two thousand dollars that night. Said it was to help me get over it."

Pine looked at the money. "Jewel, that looks like a lot more than two grand."

"It is. Because—"

"Because you went back?"

Jewel started talking fast. "They told me they'd pay me every time. Pick me up and take me back. I'd be home before Momma would get off work. One time they even flew me on a helicopter to New York, and we landed on top of the building. It was, like, unbelievable."

"And Jerome?"

"He didn't know. At first. But then he caught me coming back in one night. I tried to blow it off. But then he'd been asking around. He knew I suddenly had money. I bought some stuff, a ring and some earrings and a real Prada bag and a new iPhone and some cool clothes. I never let my mom see them. She would've been all over me. But Jerome found out. He got on my case about it big-time."

"And did you tell him the truth?"

"Some of it. He was real upset. Told me to stop going. And I did. I really did."

"But after the first time, they didn't still drug you, did they?"

"No."

"Was it the same man each time?"

"No. It was always different guys. But they all looked the same to me. Old white guys. But…"

"And what?"

"But once I did it with a woman. She was old too, maybe forty."

Pine said, "Did you recognize her, or the men?"

"No."

"Did they talk to you?" asked Blum. "Mention a name, anything about themselves?"

Jewel looked down and shook her head. "I wasn't there for them to talk to. They just wanted me for one reason."

"You're underage. That's statutory rape," said Pine.

"They might not have known. Look at me, you think I'm fourteen?"

"Doesn't matter. That's why they call it *statutory*."

"You really think they got Jerome to do what he did because of me?"

"I think it's a safe bet, yeah," said Pine.

"Then I'm the reason he's dead."

"No, you're not. But you can help us find out who did it."

"I've told you all I know."

"No, you haven't. When did you stop going to that place?"

"They called the day before Jerome got killed."

"Can I see your phone?"

"Why?"

"I want to run the number they called from."

"I already checked. It's blocked. No number comes up."

"When they called, what did they say?"

"That they weren't going to bring me anymore."

"Did they say why?"

"No."

"Can you tell us the address of the place in New York?"

"I don't remember."

Pine sat forward. "How many times did you go there?"

Jewel shrugged. "Maybe a dozen, maybe more."

"And you don't remember the address?"

"I never paid attention. I was usually sleeping in the car."

"Can you describe the area of town? What the building looked like? The street it was on?"

"Like I said, it was real what you call high dollar. I mean, everything about that area was dope." Jewel thought for a few moments. "But it was a number street."

"Like Seventh Avenue?"

"No, higher than that."

"Fifty-Seventh Street?"

"Yeah, that's it."

"Was it near Central Park?"

"Yeah, that's right. I saw it one time when they were driving me back to Trenton."

Pine glanced at Blum and then pulled out her phone again. "Would this be the building?"

Jewel looked at the screen. "Yeah, that's it. That's the one."

Pine looked at Blum again. "Well, they don't just use that place for parties, then." A text came over her phone and she said, "We have to go. But thank you for being so honest with us, Jewel. I know it wasn't easy for you. But what you told us will help us catch whoever killed your brother." She gave Jewel a card. "Call me if you think of anything else."

As they were leaving, Cee-Cee Blake tried to ask them what was going on. Pine said simply, "Keep an eye on your daughter and have someone come over here to stay with her when you go to work at night."

She jogged out to the car and Blum followed as fast as she was able.

"What's up?" asked Blum as Pine started the car and drove off fast.

"Puller's fully conscious and is out of post-op and they're getting him a room. By the time we get back there the attending physician will be able to brief us on his status."

CHAPTER

48

IT WAS LUCKY THAT HE'S YOUNG and in tip-top condition," said the doctor, a white-haired man with the calm manner of an airline pilot. They were in the visitors room at the hospital. Robert Puller had been the one to alert Pine about his brother.

"So you said he's fully awake," said Robert anxiously. "And doing well?"

"He's on a lot of pain meds, so he's in and out. That bullet went clean through, but it hit some things along the way."

"The surgeon mentioned that. Will he suffer any permanent damage?" asked Pine just as anxiously.

"Well, it's too early to tell that yet. We'll need to do follow-up with tests, X-rays, and other imaging. But I can tell you that right now he's resting comfortably, and his condition is stable."

"When can we see him?" asked Robert.

The doctor studied him. "You're family, correct?"

"His brother."

The doctor looked at Pine. "And you're...?"

"His sister," said Robert quickly. He turned to Blum. "And this is his aunt Carol."

The doctor didn't appear to believe this, but gave a weak smile and said, "Okay." He looked at his phone. "They just found him a room. I'll walk you down, but only for a few minutes."

When they got to the room John Puller was lying on a bed with tubes and lines covering him. His eyes were open and he looked over at them and waved with his good hand.

Pine's gaze went directly to the monitor recording his vitals.

They all looked reasonably okay, particularly for someone who had endured what Puller had.

"You said the bullet had hit some things?" said Robert in a low voice to the doctor.

"Well, there's a lot around that region. Bone, blood vessels, ligaments. It could have been far worse if the bullet had pinged around in there."

"But the surgeon fixed it?"

"Katherine is an excellent surgeon, and she did the best she could. But understand that this may not be the last surgery he has, though. And his rehab will be intense."

"I see," said Robert, glancing nervously at Pine.

Pine said, "Well, he's going to come out the other end just fine. Probably better than he is now."

"Hey, I can almost hear you," said John Puller weakly. "So stop talking behind my back."

They drew closer and the doctor said, "How are you feeling? How's the pain level?"

"When can I get out of here?" Puller said firmly.

"Well, that won't be for a while," said the doctor, eyeing Pine with widened eyes.

"I'm feeling okay," said Puller. "I should be able to leave. I have work to do."

Robert said, "John, you just underwent major surgery. You need to give yourself time."

"I don't have a lot of time to waste, Bobby."

Pine touched his uninjured shoulder. "John, we'll carry the ball while you're laid up here. All you need to focus on is getting better. Even Superman took days off."

While Pine was speaking, the doctor had manipulated the flow of meds going into his system by punching in a new dosage on the controller next to the IV stand.

The doctor then glanced at Puller, whose eyes fluttered and then closed. "I upped his pain meds to get him back to sleep. The last thing we need is for him to get agitated and pull at his lines or reopen the sutures. I think it's best we leave him to rest. You will be updated on his condition. And feel free to call in to the nurse's station during the interim." He gripped Robert's arm. "Don't worry, he's in good hands."

"Yes, I know. Thanks for everything."

As they were leaving the hospital Pine said, "His vitals were good. And the fact that he wants to get back to work is an excellent sign."

Robert nodded. "Yeah, he's going to make it. The only question is, in what condition."

"You mean, as a CID agent?"

"I mean, as a member of the United States Army. It's his whole life. If he can't cut it physically anymore?"

"Let's not get ahead of ourselves," said Pine.

"I saw your look back there. You were thinking the very same thing."

Pine changed the subject because he was exactly right. "Where are you staying?"

"Near the hospital."

"How long are you going to be in New York?"

"As long as it takes."

Later, Pine and Blum drove back to the condo, had a very late dinner, and went to their beds, exhausted.

After breakfast the following morning, Pine went back down to the street level and started to walk, her hands shoved deeply in her pockets and her heels striking the pavement with force.

Shit, shit, shit.

She knew that Puller had signed on for the risk when he joined CID. She knew that. She had done that when she suited up for the FBI. But, still, she felt deep guilt for what had happened. Could she have eyeballed that alley more intently? If she had focused more, could she have seen the shooter or maybe sensed his presence? Puller had relied on her to clear the alley, and she had failed him.

I failed John Puller. And now, maybe he won't be the same John Puller.

Utterly demoralized, she stopped and slumped down on a

bench. Slapping her thigh, she sat up straighter, rubbed her face, and thought, *Okay, this sorry-for-me shit is not going to cut it. Start dissecting this case. What are the holes and how do you plug them?*

Well, the holes were many. She was no closer to finding Tony Vincenzo and thus just as far away from any information about his grandfather, Ito. Teddy was dead. Evie could be of no help. She had no leads on finding the man who had murdered Jerome, although now she did know about Jewel's involvement, and the uses to which that luxury apartment was being put; only she didn't yet understand the motives behind it. And she doubted that Jewel was the only underage girl who had been recruited for whatever was going on there. And, last but not least, the vile Lindsey Axilrod was out there somewhere. She was up to her slender neck in this, including the murder of Sheila Weathers.

But what was the connection to Fort Dix? Tony Vincenzo and Axilrod both worked there. As did Weathers. If Weathers was involved only because Vincenzo had invited her to the penthouse, then that left Vincenzo and Axilrod. But what was so special about Fort Dix?

The penthouse on Fifty-Seventh Street was definitely a clue, but she just wasn't sure how she could follow it up. She didn't have enough for a search warrant.

But what about Jeff Sands?

She pulled out her phone and scanned the news sites. There was nothing. The grandson of the Senate majority leader was violently gunned down in New York City more than a day before, and not one news outlet had reported it? How could that possibly be?

Unless the NYPD was sitting on his ID for some reason. She figured if the Trenton cops could be co-opted, why not New York's finest? Or at least some of them.

She punched in a number and a few seconds later was transferred to the person she wanted at the Bureau.

"Sandy, it's Atlee Pine. I know, it's been a long time, right. Look, could you do me a favor? There was a shooting victim the other night outside a diner in Brooklyn. The vic's name was

Jeff Sands. He's the grandson of Peter Driscoll. Right, *that* Peter Driscoll. I haven't heard a thing about it in the press and I was just wondering what the hell was going on. Okay, yeah, whatever you can find out. Thanks."

She clicked off. Sandy Wyatt was an agent in the New York Field Office. She and Pine had gone to Quantico together. They had been close and had kept in touch over the years, even though Pine had headed west while Wyatt had stayed on the east coast. They were both members of WIFLE, which was an acronym for Women in Federal Law Enforcement. To her credit Wyatt had not asked about Pine's interest in the case. She would have afforded Wyatt the same courtesy if their positions had been reversed.

Pine got up and started walking again. Her path carried her to the building on Fifty-Seventh Street. Billionaires' Row. Billionaires' Heavenly Perch, more like it. They lived far above the rest of us, thought Pine. Behind doormen and concierges and trust funds and shell companies and the rules they created that gave them every possible advantage over everyone else.

Getting on your soapbox is not going to help, Atlee.

She stood across the street from the building when her attention was suddenly riveted. She quickly moved behind a parked truck and then peered around it to keep watching.

The man who had shot Jerome Blake was coming out of the building. He was wearing a suit and tie, and no cop's hat, but it was definitely him. He looked right and left, then headed down the street.

Pine followed.

CHAPTER

49

"Cheer up, I'm not dead yet, Bobby."

Robert Puller sat bolt upright in his chair, where he'd been dozing.

His brother was now staring at him from under the layer of tubes and lines.

"You're supposed to be heavily sedated," said Robert, drawing his chair nearer the bed. "Yesterday, the doctor said he upped your meds."

"I have a higher tolerance than most."

"Are you in pain?"

"Again, higher tolerance."

"Do you know what happened to you?"

"Just a guess, but I think I got shot."

Robert smiled. "Okay, jokes are good. That means you're functioning at a high level."

"And Jeff Sands?"

"He didn't make it. The shot that hit you killed him." Robert leaned forward. "It was close, John. Another inch here or there."

"Don't you have an important job to do really far away from here, or is that just a rumor?"

"Excuse me for caring."

Puller shifted a little bit in his bed. He stared at all the tubes and lines holding him down. "Why do I feel like Gulliver after he got jumped by the Lilliputians?"

"Do you remember anything about what happened?"

"We stepped out into the rear of the diner. Pine was in the

lead. I had hold of Sands. I think I heard a pop. And that's pretty much it."

"They were obviously targeting him."

"They must have followed us from the nightclub where we picked Sands up." Puller looked confused for a moment. "But the guys outside the club were a couple of thugs. I don't think they're involved in what happened to Sands."

"And who exactly do you think *is* involved?"

Puller looked at his brother. "Well, since it looks like I'm going to be laid up here for a bit, you want to pitch in?"

"Pitch in? As you said, I do have another job."

"Well, so long as you're here to hold my hand it might take your mind off other things."

"I'm listening."

"You got me to Gloria Miles and she led us to Jeff Sands pretty fast. Miles mentioned you found her through an algorithm?"

Robert went over the algorithm he'd used, as he had already explained to Pine.

Puller nodded thoughtfully. "I'll have to keep you in mind in future investigations."

"I have access to technology, databases, and computer networks that the average person doesn't. But I can't do that all the time, not even for you, Junior."

"But you had to feed the algorithm to get anywhere."

"I just explained to you the factors I loaded in. I pinpointed certain political leadership, and then degrees of separation vis-à-vis family members to see what would pop. Jeff Sands came up and then it was pretty easy to trace the connection to Driscoll."

"Sands popped up because of his criminal background?"

"As I'm sure you know, he's never been convicted. But he has been brought in and questioned a number of times. And he has certain business associates who *do* have criminal records, or at least questionable pasts. My data load factors covered those possibilities."

"But then his grandfather got the best lawyers involved, and nothing came of it?"

"Apparently so."

"He told us he didn't know Tony Vincenzo. Did that name ever pop up in your digging?"

"No. But I stopped pretty much after I got to Peter Driscoll. Then I looked for a connection to the military, and that's how I got to Gloria Miles."

"Do you think Driscoll knows his grandson is dead?" asked Puller.

"The Senate majority leader is not without his resources. And at the very least efforts would have been made by NYPD to notify the next of kin. It would take them all of ten seconds. Hell, his father lives right here in New York."

"Financial guy with lots of bucks."

"And a new wife and a brand-new family. Not sure how much he'll mourn his eldest child."

The brothers gazed at each other, silently communicating something important to both.

Puller said, "Yeah, if I had died, Dad wouldn't have even been able to process it. He doesn't know he has two sons."

"That's okay, Junior, *we* do."

"How soon can I get out of here? The doc didn't really answer me when I asked last time."

Robert didn't look surprised, but he said, "Not anytime soon. You are out of the game, John. Pine is carrying the torch now, just like she told you earlier."

"She can't do this by herself. And this wasn't even her case. She's working on something personal. She's only involved because she offered, and I accepted."

"Don't know what to tell you. From what I could see the lady is firmly committed to this. And also from what I've seen about the lady, I would not try to stop her."

"She's going to keep working this thing with no backup at all. That is not good, Bobby."

"John, I can hang around for a bit, but I'm in uniform. I don't get to call my own shots."

"I thought computer geeks could work remotely."

"This computer geek needs a super-secret SCIF to do his nerding," replied Robert, referring to a Sensitive Compartmented Information Facility. "So I can't just hop on my Mac and get to it."

"Am I really stuck in this bed? They had me patched up and back in the fight in Afghanistan in no time. And those wounds were worse."

"In case you weren't aware, you actually have blood in those veins and you lost a lot of it. Plus the surgeon and the doctor said the round did some internal damage. They've got you so patched up you can't even move your left arm. You're immobile and for a good reason. You're looking at a long rehab."

"To get fully back, you mean?"

Robert dropped his gaze. "To…just get better, John."

When he looked up his brother was staring dead at him.

"What are you not telling me?" said Puller.

"I've told you everything I know. You may make a full and complete recovery—"

"—but I may not."

"Can you predict the future? Because that gift somehow missed me."

"Good thing I shoot right-handed, then."

"You're not going to be shooting anything for the foreseeable future. Seriously, little brother, if you want a decent chance at getting all the way back, you have to follow doctor's orders."

Puller looked away. "You said you stopped at Driscoll?"

"What?"

Puller glanced at his brother. "Driscoll was low-hanging fruit."

"I just wanted to find a contact to help you with the investigation."

"Can you do another search, same sort of parameters, and see what else you get?"

"I'm not sure I understand."

"If Driscoll is involved in this in some way, what if he's just the tip of the iceberg?"

50

Pᴵⁿᴱ sʜᴀᴅᴏᴡᴇᴅ ᴛʜᴇ ᴍᴀɴ and took his photo when he turned around to cross an intersection.

Then he walked into an office building.

A government building. A *federal* government building.

Pine waited a few seconds and then stepped up to the door, peered through the glass, and then opened it. At the security checkpoint she flashed her badge and creds to the officer there. She watched as the man got on the elevator and the doors closed.

"Excuse me, but the guy who just came through here and got on that elevator?"

"Yes, what about him?" asked the officer, a woman in her forties with short brown hair and a friendly expression.

"I could have sworn he was an old friend of mine. Special Agent Simon King, used to operate out of Newark?"

"No, that's Adam Gorman."

"Is he FBI?"

"No, no, he's head of security for Congresswoman Nora Franklin. She's from an upstate district, but she has an office suite here she shares with some other politicos."

"Franklin? I know that name. She's a pretty big deal, right?" said Pine.

The woman smiled. "She's the ranking member on the House Ways and Means Committee. They write the checks, so yeah, a pretty big deal, all right."

"Is she in her office today?"

"Yes, she came in about twenty minutes ago."

"Well, Gorman is a twin for my buddy King. Sorry to trouble you."

"No problem. You have a good day."

Pine turned and left. She walked halfway down the block and Googled Gorman.

She found out he was born in Austria and had been a police officer and then a member of military intelligence there. He had immigrated to the United States when he was twenty-nine. He was now forty-eight and had earned a master's degree in political science from NYU. He had worked on political campaigns and briefly at a K Street lobbying operation in DC.

So a big-deal congresswoman had a former Austrian intelligence officer turned security chief who one night had masqueraded as a Trenton cop and murdered Jerome Blake.

And what do I do about that? It's really my word against his. John didn't get that good a look at him and is in a hospital bed. Jerome is dead and can't say. But I'm betting Adam Gorman was the guy who met with Jerome at school that day. And that means he knew all about Jewel and the encounters in the penthouse, a fact reinforced by the man's having just come out of the place.

She looked at her phone. She had Gorman's photo and his image from her Google search. And the last time they had met, Peanut had given her his phone number. She texted him the article on Gorman along with the photo and an accompanying message. Then she walked up and down the street waiting for his reply.

Fifteen minutes later it popped up on her screen.

Yeah, that's the dude.

Okay, at least it was confirmed in her mind. But it was still not enough. Peanut would not carry any weight with a prosecutor against a "respected" man like Gorman. And Pine really had no hard proof that he was the man who had shot Jerome, just a brief meeting in a dark alley under incredibly stressful conditions, or so would say the defense attorney.

She next Googled Nora Franklin. The face that popped up on the Wikipedia page was an attractive blond woman in her midforties. She had an impressive résumé. Born and raised in Colorado, she went to UVA undergrad, and law school at Duke. Her father, at seventy-three, was a long-serving and respected judge on the Fourth Circuit Court of Appeals. After law school she had moved to New York City and worked for a small law firm specializing in employment law and representing mostly workers. Then she moved to upstate New York, and then ran for city council. After that she had run a congressional campaign and won on her first try.

Since then she had won five more terms in Congress and made a swift run up the ladder. Her being the ranking member on Ways and Means at a relatively young age had surprised some, the article said, but she had been a loyal foot soldier and impressed leadership with her skills and knowledge. If the House flipped in the next election, she was expected to become one of the youngest chairpersons of arguably the most powerful committee in Congress. She had traveled widely, the article said. She had married young, but it had ended in divorce. According to her official bio she had practiced law only a few years. Pine checked an online database that listed the net worths of members of Congress. She was surprised that Franklin was listed as having a net worth of over twenty million dollars. After practicing law for a short period and in a field that was not known for huge payoffs for attorneys?

So where the hell had that kind of money come from?

Her phone buzzed. It was Sandy Wyatt from the Bureau.

"Hey, Atlee. I made some calls and checked some sources. As far as I can tell, NYPD has put a lid on this thing."

"I know they don't release vics' names until the next of kin are notified. But they've surely had time to do that by now."

"Only thing I can figure is maybe Driscoll asked them to hold it for some reason. And for him they probably would."

"Okay, thanks, I owe you." Pine put her phone away and pondered what to do next. She could stake out the building and follow Gorman to wherever he went next. But she had no idea how long it would be before the man came out of the building. And she couldn't call in another FBI agent, because she wasn't technically working this case. And other agents had their own matters to pursue. But she had one asset to deploy. She pulled out her phone again.

"Carol, I need you."

Within thirty minutes Blum stepped out of a cab and walked over to her boss.

Pine told her what she wanted her to do and showed her pictures of both Gorman and Franklin.

Blum eyed the café behind them with a picture window and an unobstructed view of the building across the street. "Then I'll just take up my position here. Where will you be?"

"Fort Dix."

As Pine climbed into a cab she thought, *What do I have to lose?*

When she got to Fort Dix, she would find out.

51

I DON'T UNDERSTAND," said Pine. "How could that be possible?"

She was standing in front of Tom Whitaker, a JAG lawyer at Fort Dix. He was a short man in his fifties, with rounded shoulders and a dour expression.

He said in a pedantic tone, "It's like I just said, Bill Danforth and Phil Cassidy each took Article 15s; it's akin to a plea bargain in a civilian court."

Danforth and Cassidy were the two soldiers whom Tony Vincenzo had been working with on the drug distribution. Puller had arrested them both and had them confined in the stockade under guard of Army MPs. Pine thought they would still be there. But they weren't.

"I know what an Article 15 is. I want to know *how* it happened."

"The concept is pretty straightforward, Agent Pine," Whitaker said in a bored tone. "It was offered and they took it. Most court-martial trials end up in conviction. They knew that. Then the penalties are a lot worse and they have a criminal record. With Article 15 that doesn't happen. No criminal record. Just like civilian courts, most cases in the military system don't actually go to trial. If every one of them did, we'd be clogged up for years."

Pine said impatiently, "I know that, too. I meant why would they be offered a plea deal in the first place? My understanding was they were caught dead to rights by the CID. They were involved in drug dealing. How does that get them a slap on the wrist? These guys should have been tried, convicted, and sent to Leavenworth."

The man shrugged. "That wasn't my call. The CO referred the charge, meaning it *was* going to trial. And I agree with you, the evidence was very strong. Had they gone to trial they would have almost certainly been convicted. But then the Article 15 popped up and everything got thrown off the rails."

"The Article 15 offer had to *pop* from somewhere, right?"

"Right."

"So where did it pop from?" said Pine, trying to keep her voice calm although she actually wanted to start yelling at the man.

"From their CO. That's the only place it could have come from. He referred the charges, but then he offered the Article 15."

"Why would he do that?"

"I don't know. And I had no reason to ask. I wear a uniform. I do what I'm told. When the CO talks, we listen. Pretty simple."

"When did all this happen?"

"Late yesterday."

"And who is the CO on this?"

Whitaker shuffled some papers on his desk and then looked at her curiously. "What exactly is your connection to this case again?"

"I was working it with CWO John Puller."

"Yeah, you told me that. He was the one who collected the evidence."

"For an overwhelming case that just got dropped," retorted Pine.

"I heard he got shot in New York."

"You heard right. Probably by the same gang that Danforth and Cassidy work for."

"I wouldn't know anything about that. Is Puller going to be okay? All reports on him are that he's a first-rate soldier and investigator."

"Right on both counts. And yeah, he's going to be fine. So, the name of the CO?" She took out her notebook and pen.

Whitaker deliberately glanced at both and said, "I'm really not at liberty to tell you that."

Pine put her pad and pen away. "Okay, what punishment did Cassidy and Danforth receive?"

Whitaker glanced at the paper in front of him. "Reduction in rank, lost some pay, and got eight days' confinement, but the CO suspended that for a year. They were in the stockade for a lot longer than that after they were arrested. He'll probably just let that ride."

"So they just walk away with fewer dollars and the loss of a stripe? For being part of a major drug ring inside *this* facility?"

"I admit it's unusual."

"You think? Where are Danforth and Cassidy now?"

"Back at the motor pool, as far as I know. I did hear some scuttle-butt that they've put in their discharge papers. Good riddance in my book."

"This is a clusterfuck, you know that, right?"

Whitaker looked at her wearily. "Ma'am, I've been doing this job for twenty years. Nothing surprises me anymore."

"Might be time for a new job."

"What my wife keeps telling me."

"If I were you, I'd listen to your wife. Do you at least have pictures of Danforth and Cassidy?"

"Yes, but why do you ask?"

"I'd like to see them."

"Again, why? The case is over."

"Not for me it's not. Their photos? Please? It's really important."

"You really think Puller getting shot was tied to these guys?"

"I think the connection is obvious."

The man opened his desk drawer, pulled out a bulky case file, and spun it around. The mug shots of Danforth and Cassidy stared up at her.

"Feel free to take their pictures."

Pine did so with her iPhone. "Surprised you let me do that."

"Ma'am, this *is* a clusterfuck, and in an ideal world these two pricks should be doing hard time courtesy of the United States Army. So if you can nail their sorry asses to the wall it's fine by me."

"Thanks," said Pine as she walked out.

52

DANFORTH AND CASSIDY WERE INDEED in the motor pool, although as Pine observed from a distance, they didn't appear to be getting much work done. Both were on their phones, texting.

She didn't confront them there.

She simply followed them when they left the base after their shift was over.

They drove together to a military dive bar about two miles from Fort Dix. They went in and she followed. The pair had found a table in the fairly crowded place.

The bar was called the Bunker. Unlike its name, the Bunker was large, open, and airy. Flags from all service branches hung over the walls. Helmets were mounted like trophy animals, along with ceremonial sabers, bayonets, and weaponry of all makes and sizes. Some couples in uniform were slow-dancing in the middle of the room to jukebox music. All bar seats were occupied, with most of the patrons draped in Army green.

Pine was one of the few not in uniform.

She eyed the pair and headed for their table after a waitress brought their longneck beers. She sat down next to Danforth, glanced at him, and then eyed Cassidy.

Danforth was big and beefy, and his expression was, to Pine, brainless.

Cassidy was small and cagey-looking, and he shot suspicious looks at her.

"Uh, don't remember inviting you to our private party, sweet cheeks," said Cassidy.

Danforth let out an inane belly laugh.

Pine shot him a look. "You really thought *that* was funny?"

Danforth clamped his mouth shut and scowled at her.

"So, Article 15, huh?" she said.

"Who the hell are you, lady?" snapped Cassidy while Danforth took a swig of his Bud.

"An interested party. Did you know your buddy Jeff Sands got his head blown off in New York the other night?"

Both men gave a visceral reaction to this. Cassidy composed himself and said, "Don't know who that is."

"Yeah, right. Like you don't know who Tony Vincenzo is, or Lindsey Axilrod? Did you wonder why Sheila Weathers didn't come back to work? She's dead, too. Also in New York."

Danforth shot Cassidy a worried glance, but the latter shook his head.

"We don't know what or who you're talking about."

"Sure you do, Phil. And so does your buddy here, because he looks like he's about to crap his pants."

Danforth grabbed Pine by the shoulder. "Look, you just need to shut up, bit—"

He stopped and looked at the badge she had just flashed him. Danforth slowly released his grip.

Cassidy said, "You're FBI? You got no jurisdiction over us. We're soldiers."

"I'll say this one time, dumbass. So long as you're in this country, I have every jurisdiction over you."

"But we got the deal from the Army. You can't touch us now. It's that double jeopardy thing." He looked triumphantly at her.

"Double jeopardy doesn't apply between military and civilian prosecutions. The Army cutting a deal with you has no impact on the FBI going after you. The only difference is you'll be spending your time at a max prison nowhere near here."

"Shit, are you serious?"

"Google it, if that'll make you feel better."

"Well, son of a bitch."

"That sucks," added Danforth, pounding the table with his huge fist.

She looked at their beers. "If I were you, I'd drink up. What I'm about to tell you will go down better with a little buzz."

"You're making no damn sense, lady," said Cassidy, but he downed his beer, as did Danforth, who wiped his face with a meaty palm.

When the empty bottles smacked the table, Pine leaned in and started speaking earnestly. "The CID agent who nailed you?"

"Puller?"

"Yeah. He also was shot up in New York when Sands bought it. He just got out of surgery."

"So? Why should we care?" said Cassidy, but he didn't look as confident as his words sounded.

"Do you know what Puller told me a few minutes before he got shot?"

"What?" This came from Danforth, who looked like he could use another beer.

"He said that he had to make sure you two were kept locked up and away from everybody."

"Why's that?" asked Danforth, sweat beads suddenly lining his wide forehead.

Pine looked shrewdly at Cassidy. "You want to answer your buddy? Because I think you know what I'm going to say."

"You're saying he wanted us in the stockade...for our protection?" said Cassidy.

She nodded.

"That's bullshit," barked Cassidy.

"Really? Let me ask you something. You two were caught dead to rights on drug dealing. I talked to the JAG. Ironclad case. No-brainer, slam dunk. CO's on your ass. You're both being court-martialed and sent to Leavenworth. Then, out of nowhere, you get an Article 15. The JAG said he'd never heard of such a thing. What do you think about that?"

Danforth eyed Cassidy. "Phil, you said it was 'cause we got friends in high places."

"Shut the hell up, Billy," barked Cassidy.

He looked at Pine, who said, "Or maybe you got the 'get out of jail free card' because you have *enemies* in high places."

"Are Jeff and Shelia really dead?"

"Then you *do* know them?"

"I asked you a question."

Pine took out her phone and scrolled through it. "Here's an email I got from NYPD on Jeff Sands." She showed it to him. "And here's another on Sheila. They're both dead. I saw their bodies."

Cassidy read the emails and sat back looking worried.

Danforth said, "What's this all about, Phil? What's she trying to say with all this crap?"

Pine turned to him. "What I'm trying to say is someone is cleaning house and you two are on the to-do list. That's the only reason you got the Article 15 and a suspended sentence on your detention. So instead of being in the stockade surrounded by John Puller's handpicked guards, you're out here as sitting ducks."

"You're saying we got sprung so they could pop us?" This came from Cassidy, who had forehead sweat bubbles of his own now.

"You know Vincenzo's old man, Teddy?"

"No, but Tony told us about him. He's squirreled away at Fort Dix Pen on a long ride."

"He *was*. Puller and I went to talk to him. All official and everything. Just as he was about to tell us something, they came and got him. No explanation, no nothing. Then before we knew it, he ended up dead in his cell. They say it was an overdose, though the guy wasn't a user. I'm thinking that they decided three prisoner deaths at the Fort Dix facility might arouse suspicion. So, you two got set free, and you'll come to the end of your lives on the other side of the bars. You see it any other way?"

Cassidy hunched forward and spoke in a low voice. "Let's assume all you say is true. What can *you* do about it?"

"I'm FBI. I can protect you. But this is a quid pro quo situation. I need something in return. Otherwise, you're on your own."

"Shit," muttered Cassidy as he looked around the place. "Let's take this outside."

Pine rose. "After you."

CHAPTER

53

THEY ENDED UP SITTING IN PINE'S CAR.

She said, "First things first. Where's Tony Vincenzo?"

Cassidy, who was sitting in the passenger seat, spread his hands. "Ain't seen him since we got arrested. Figured the locals would grab him when the CID arrested us, but that didn't happen, least that I heard."

"He was at his dad's house when I saw him last. Where he had the pill operation, right?"

Cassidy shrugged. "If you say so."

"The place used to be owned by Ito Vincenzo, Tony's grandfather. He ever mention him?"

"Once when we were over there and I was looking at some of the old photos in the basement. When I asked him, Tony said the guy just disappeared one day when he was just a kid. Said he didn't really remember him. Tony said his old man told him Ito was running from something."

"Why would he say that?"

"I don't know. I didn't ask. I didn't care. But that's just what he said."

"If Tony isn't at his old man's house, where else would he be?"

Cassidy and Danforth looked at each other.

"You guys know about the penthouse in New York?"

She didn't expect them to answer; Pine just wanted to see their expressions.

Danforth grinned stupidly and said, "Awesome place."

"Shut *up*, Billy," snapped his buddy. "You're gonna get us killed for sure."

"Then you *have* been there. What's the deal? Axilrod said it was a perk, at least that's what Tony told her, although I don't believe anything she says."

"Maybe."

"Your answers are not adding up to a quid pro quo, gents. Maybe I should end this now and let you get killed before the sun sets. I don't like my time wasted with bullshit. So, you can get out of my car. But run fast because they'll be coming for you."

"Wait a minute," exclaimed Cassidy. "Just hold on. I'm trying to process all this and it ain't easy. Just…just let me breathe, willya? I mean, Jesus."

"Okay, take all the time you need, keeping in mind that patience is not my virtue."

Cassidy chewed on a nail while Danforth slumped in the rear seat looking like he might start crying.

"Okay, look, we *were* working some drug deals."

"But no drugs can get into Fort Dix. Lindsey Axilrod told me that. She probably regrets it now because it was probably the only true thing she ever told me. They have drug-sniffing dogs at all entrances."

Cassidy grinned. "Yeah, but who said we were selling the drugs *at* Fort Dix?" He glanced at Danforth. "Right? *We* were at Fort Dix, but not the drugs, or the customers."

"Where were the customers then?"

"All around."

"How did you get involved?"

"Through Tony. He needed some guys. And he knew we were handy, and—"

"—didn't mind breaking the law?"

Cassidy shrugged but smiled.

"But again, why Fort Dix?"

"Tony worked there, so there was that."

"Who got him involved?"

"He told me once. His old man had a friend on the outside."

"This old friend have a name?"

"Ricky, or Johnny, or something like that. Anyway, Teddy was in the can, he couldn't do nothing. But he got Ricky or Johnny to ring up Tony."

"Nice of Dad to do that. So the Fort Dix connection is just because of Tony?"

"I guess so."

"No, I'm not buying that. Because you're leaving out Lindsey Axilrod. She's been at Fort Dix longer than Tony. I checked. So why do I think Tony was feeding you a bunch of bullshit about his old man's friend, Ricky-Johnny, and it was Axilrod who pulled him in? And then he needed a couple of guys and pulled you two in."

"I guess it could have gone down that way."

"What were your jobs with the drug ring? How did you two add value?"

Cassidy grinned, suddenly animated. "We drive Army vehicles. From here to there. Everywhere. Guess what happens when you drive Army rides?"

"The cops don't stop and search your vehicles for drugs," said Pine.

"Bingo. We'd drive outta Fort Dix, take a slight detour, and the vehicle gets filled up with the stuff. They were pros, took maybe ten minutes at best. Then we continue on our way. Right before we get to where we're going, we're met by another team and get unloaded. Then we head on. Simple, right?"

"So you two never dealt with any customers?"

"No. Tony did the pills. But Axilrod was calling the shots. She's a computer girl. Can do anything with that shit."

"Which also means she can move money digitally all over the world and leave no trail."

"I seen her working one time. This was at her place. Her fingers flying over the damn keyboard. After she was done, she turns to me and says, 'You know what you just saw?' And I said, 'no, what?' She said, 'You just saw a billion bucks go down a rabbit hole.'"

"Were Axilrod and Tony a thing?"

"They might'a hooked up now and then. Tony is slick. He knows how to talk to the ladies. Lindsey liked him. She got him the perk at the penthouse. That's how we got to go."

"So Tony *is* below her in the food chain. And who is Axilrod working for?"

"We never knew any of that."

"Come on, Cassidy, your deal is starting to fade to nothing."

"Swear to God. Swear on my old granny's grave."

Pine eyed Danforth, who was looking at her and nodding.

"Okay, I guess I believe that. I mean, why would they let you two knuckleheads have that kind of leverage."

"Leverage?" said Cassidy. "What does that mean?"

"It means it proves my point. Okay, I really need to find Tony. Any thoughts on that?"

Cassidy shook his head, but Pine was watching Danforth in the rearview mirror. His expression was such that an idea might actually be forming in his very small brain.

"Yeah?" said Pine expectantly.

"Tony and me were drinking one night. And he mentioned a place."

"What place?"

"His granddad's old place. It was on the Jersey Shore."

"His granddad? You mean Ito?"

"I guess so. Tony said the dude made money selling ice cream."

"That's the guy. Keep talking."

"Anyway, Tony would go there sometimes."

"You ever go with him?"

"Once. It was a nice little house on the beach. Really old, no AC, and they had space heaters, but then Tony had added one of them pellet stoves. Hell, they needed that in the winter 'cause you could see outside through cracks in the wall. We sat on the sand and had beer and buckets of wings. It was sweet."

"What was the name of the town?"

"I got it in my phone. I used my GPS to get there."

She had him text the address to her phone.

"Well, Jack Nicholson is from there," said Pine, reading a bit about Manasquan, New Jersey, which was located on the Atlantic Ocean. "Went to high school there."

"Cool," said Cassidy. "He was the Joker in that old Batman movie, right?"

"Okay, I'm going to make a call and you two are going into protective custody. You got that?"

"Hey, I just want to stay breathing," said Cassidy.

"Don't we all," replied Pine.

CHAPTER

54

IT WAS A LITTLE LESS THAN an hour's drive from Trenton to the borough of Manasquan, and it was dusk by the time Pine got there. Along the way she had called Blum and told her what she'd found out and also where she was headed.

"Neither Gorman nor Franklin have left the building," reported Blum. "I've had far too much tea and coffee, but every time I went to the bathroom, I left my phone camera on video so I could see if either of them left. It was the best I could do."

"That was quick thinking, Carol."

"I think the folks who work at the café are either wondering if I'm suffering from dementia and don't know how to get home, or thinking I'm interviewing for a job."

"Either way, just stay right where you are, and call me if anything develops."

"And you be careful, Agent Pine."

Driving through the quaint downtown, Pine saw it was full of small shops and restaurants. However, at this time of year, it was pretty well deserted, with many bars and restaurants closed for the season. But there were a few places open, and people were walking up and down the sidewalks while cars drifted past. Some parked, and people got out of them and went into several of the shops.

It looked like any other sleepy beach town in the off-season. The smell of salt air lay thick over everything, like a compression shirt. She breathed it in and felt comforted somehow. She didn't get those smells in Arizona.

Pine also spotted many large and elaborately constructed single-family homes on the beachfront. They looked fairly new and were undoubtedly expensive to build. But then again, it was oceanfront property and they weren't making any more of that.

She had loaded into her GPS the address Danforth had provided. She had taken both men to the RA in Trenton and explained what she wanted done. Neither of the agents on duty seemed inclined to take on this responsibility until Pine mentioned that they should call Clint Dobbs, head of the Phoenix Field Office, if they had doubts about helping. They told Pine that wouldn't be necessary and that they would see to the safety of the two soldiers, including contacting Fort Dix to let them know the men would not be back on base for the foreseeable future.

As she neared her destination, Pine slowed her car and looked for a place to park. She found an empty lot that had beach access and pulled in there. The Atlantic spread out gray and foamy in front of her. The wind was chilly, the skies as pewter in color as the frothy ocean, which was broken only by the slash of whitecaps and the folding of breakers.

She zipped her jacket up, looked around, and gained the lay of the land. Vincenzo's place was about a hundred yards down the street, a small beach bungalow that looked nearly identical to the neighboring homes. She walked on and gained a sight line on the place from across the street. She drew a pair of small optics from her pocket, glanced around to see if anyone was observing her, and then took a good look at the bungalow.

It was one and a half stories with dormer windows, saggy green shutters, a tan exterior, and no garage. Rotted and empty flower boxes clung to the underneath edge of the two windows bracketing the front door, which was painted black and badly weathered. A dark blue, rolling, rubber trash can was outside by the front stoop. An empty six-pack of beer bottles sat next to it. A black exhaust pipe piercing the roof was a definite add-on, she figured, because it looked relatively new. Danforth had mentioned a pellet stove, and the pipe must be its exhaust source, she thought. There was a car in the concrete driveway that was spiderweb-cracked in at least five places. The car was a Ford Focus with Jersey plates. As she kept looking it over, she spotted a Fort Dix parking sticker on the rear bumper. The yard in front was more sand than grass. She could have easily thrown a football from the backyard and hit the ocean at high tide.

She recalled that there had been no car in Vincenzo's driveway back in Trenton, but the man had been there. Either this was his car, or he had gotten a ride with someone, or a person was visiting him, or he wasn't here but whoever had driven this car here was.

She found a café open across the street with a good sight line of her target.

She ordered a coffee and a toasted bagel and watched the darkness thicken. No one came out of the house, and the car remained right where it was. She could hear the waves crashing on the beach as the tide rolled in. Normally a calming effect on people, it just made Pine more tense.

Two cups of coffee, a second bagel, and another hour of observation later, Pine took a moment to check her emails. Nothing from Robert Puller, and nothing from Blum. She expected Puller to stay until his brother was clearly out of danger. No word from him was good, at least from Pine's perspective. And Gorman and Franklin must still be in the building.

As a fog rolled in off the ocean, Pine's patience ran out. She left the shop, crossed the street, hit the beach, headed west, and came up on the sand side of the Vincenzo bungalow. There were no lights on in the house or in the residences on either side. There was a small, paved, fenced-in patio on which sat a set of rusty outdoor furniture and a tattered umbrella that was listing to one side. An empty beer can sat on top of one of the fence posts. Pine cleared this area and snuck up to the back of the house. She peered in a window and found herself staring at what looked to be the kitchen. She tried the back door. Surprisingly, it was not locked. She pulled it open slowly, prepared to face loud squeaks from a seldom-used door, but it opened silently.

She stole inside and took out her Tac light, and the thin beam cut through the still darkness.

She left the kitchen after seeing that there were stacks of dirty dishes and glasses in the sink. Apparently, someone, hopefully Vincenzo, had been here for a while. The air didn't feel musty, either, which was another sign this place was being occupied, even if the car wasn't parked out in the driveway. After searching the house, she planned to check the car next, when it was even darker. It was on the street side, which made it more perilous for her to search when people might still be walking down the street. Hopefully, it would be unlocked, too. The registration would tell her who owned the car. And there might be some other things of interest inside.

There was a small front room with decades-old furniture, a frayed carpet that looked ground down by sandy feet, and a small bookcase full of old paperbacks. The pellet stove Danforth had mentioned had been inserted inside the original fireplace. The black pipe went up into the ceiling and through the roof, as Pine had seen before. And, as Danforth had said, she could see tiny cracks in the old walls where she could feel damp air coming in. This place must be hell in the winter, she thought.

A small 5,000-BTU AC unit was perched in one window.

A fairly new-looking Samsung wide-screen TV hung on one wall, and there was an Xbox controller perched on the coffee table. Next to that was a virtual reality headset. That was a good sign that Vincenzo was in the neighborhood.

And next to the VR headset she struck gold.

It was a photo ID card for Anthony Vincenzo, allowing him access to Fort Dix.

There was one bedroom on this level. When she opened the door it was like she had stepped back forty years. The bed was made with a crocheted afghan on top, done in what could only be described as psychedelic colors. The bed and nightstands and bureau were all matching wood in a style from at least as far back as the 1970s. A tattered copy of Jacqueline Susann's *Valley of the Dolls* was on one nightstand along with an old-fashioned windup alarm clock. The bathroom attached to it matched the age of the bedroom. The small closet was empty.

She left the bedroom and approached the narrow staircase to the left of the front door. She ducked down as a car passed by outside. She cut off her light, stole to the window, and peered out. The car was already gone. The fog was thicker, and she could see no one passing by on foot. She clicked her light back on and took the stairs up.

The half-story must have been put on later, concluded Pine, because it was drywall instead of plaster, and the finishes looked more modern. There were two small bedrooms and a full bath up here, the latter with a one-piece fiberglass shower and double sinks. In one of the bedrooms, Pine found where Vincenzo was staying. A large duffel was on the floor, and clothes and remnants of fast-food meals were strewn all over. The stink of stale French fries assailed her nostrils. She searched through the duffel and found a nine-millimeter Sig. She popped the magazine, took out all the bullets, and cleared the breach before putting it back. If things went sideways later, Old Tony would be reaching for a useless weapon.

There was a smaller pink roller suitcase. She nudged it open. Inside were women's clothes, a box of tampons, and a fingernail file set in a small leather case. Inside the closet were about a half-dozen women's outfits on hangers. On the floor were three pairs of women's shoes, from heels to flats.

Okay, he was shacking up with a girl. Pine wondered who that might be.

On the nightstand was a bottle of Oxycontin that, despite the label, didn't look to be prescription. Probably street made with other shit in it, like fentanyl that could send you to the hereafter faster than any other synthetic drug known. There was also a wad of cash bigger than her fist, and two burner phones. And a bong with a full baggie of weed sat next to the phones.

Pine looked up and saw the dangling rope. She pulled on it and a set of folding wooden stairs came down, revealing the attic access.

She didn't expect Vincenzo to be hiding up there, but she wouldn't know until she checked. Still, she doubted he would have left his gun down here if he was up there.

She mounted the steps and shone her light around. There was no floor, only ceiling joists with pink insulation in between. But as she kept shining her light around, she saw that some large pieces of plywood had been laid over some of the joists. And there were some cardboard boxes stacked there.

The place smelled starkly of age, mold, and mildew, and Pine covered her mouth as she tread carefully over the joists to the boxes.

Sitting on her haunches she eyed the four boxes.

She opened the first one and saw that it contained nothing but old, mildewed clothes.

The next box was full of old photo albums. She quickly looked through them and saw a history of the Vincenzo family from the generation preceding Ito and his brother, Bruno, all the way to Teddy's time. Evie had been pretty and vivacious. Ito looked reserved and disengaged. Bruno, decked out in a three-piece suit with a yellow pocket square in one photo, looked larger than life, his smile huge, his eyes bulging with delight, his burly arm around his brother, who looked like he would rather be hugged by a python.

The next box contained business papers and copies of old tax returns from the ice creamery business.

The contents of the last box stopped Pine dead in her tracks.

55

ROBERT PULLER SAT IN THE OFFICE behind a large desk with a computer screen that seemed even bigger. The building was a secure one, the room was windowless, the insides of the walls were coated with a material that would block exterior electronic surveillance, so it qualified as a SCIF. Access to the place was restricted by RF badges, with certain rooms, including this one, requiring retinal portals.

Not many people could get into this building, and even fewer into this room.

Robert Puller was obviously one of them.

He had created algorithms—five of them, in fact—and unleashed them on all the databases at his disposal, which were some of the most exclusive ones in the world. He had also sent his search formulas, like charging armies, into every other database he could think of.

He sipped on a Coke and let both the carbonation and the sugar wash over him. He had been at this for a while now. It was something he was used to doing, but not for the purposes for which he was now doing it.

He stretched, stood, and did some light calisthenics. Though not yet forty, sometimes he felt twice that age. The pressure of his job, plus the countless hours bent over a computer, did not equate to a healthy posture.

His phone buzzed and he frowned. It was his brother.

He said, "What the hell are you doing using your phone?"

"I promised the nurse to be off in under a minute and she told me in no uncertain terms that she was coming to check, so talk fast. Anything yet?"

"If I had I would have contacted you. Now turn the phone off and go to sleep."

"I got a text from Carol Blum a little while ago. She's watching a building right now."

"Why would she text you?"

"She said she wanted to keep me in the loop."

"Why is she watching the building?"

"Because our shooter is in there."

"Shooter?"

"The guy impersonating a cop who killed Jerome Blake. His real name is Adam Gorman. He's head of security for a congresswoman named Nora Franklin."

"Nora?"

"You know her?"

"Just in her official capacity. She's the ranking member on Ways and Means. I've testified before that committee."

"What's your call on her?"

"Smart, dedicated, committed, patriotic."

"Which begs the question of why she's got a murderer as head of security. Can you dig up what you can on Gorman? Pine apparently did a fast and dirty, but we need more."

"Okay. And where is Pine?"

"In her text Carol said Pine's in Manasquan, New Jersey. She got a line on Tony Vincenzo and is running it down."

"Okay. I'll see what I can find while I'm waiting for my algorithms to do their thing. Now, your sixty seconds are up."

"I know, Nurse Ratched just stormed into my room with duct tape."

The line went dead.

Robert Puller turned back to his computer screen and typed in a search on Adam Gorman. He didn't expect to find much. The man would have been thoroughly vetted before landing a position with a congressperson. But background checks had been known to miss things. And the government had grown lax with doing them and allowed a backlog to accumulate. So maybe there was something useful that had slipped through.

His first search brought up the basics. Name, rank, and serial number. Puller did think it odd that the man had been a member of the intelligence services for another country before coming here. It was true that Austria wasn't exactly Russia, China, or Iran. It was a member of both the UN and the EU. A federal republic with a parliamentary-style government, Austria had proclaimed itself politically permanently neutral back in 1955. They obviously did not want a repeat of the Third Reich.

However, a country wasn't a person, and who knew where Gorman's true allegiances lay?

He did another search, read over the results, and then noticed something curious buried in the timeline background info on Gorman. He made a phone call to someone he knew in the State Department.

"Hey, Don, it's Robert Puller. Yeah, it's been a while. Look, I've been doing some digging on something and an issue popped up that I think you might be able to help me with."

Puller proceeded to tell him about Gorman and the possible issue he had found. His friend told Puller he would look into it and get back to him.

Then Puller turned his attention to the other person: Nora Franklin.

Accessing both databases available to the public and those available only to a handful of people like him, Puller quickly accumulated what looked to be significant material. Taken alone, none of it added up to much. But when it was all put together, Puller sensed something that was important. He sensed a *pattern*.

Later, his phone buzzed. It was his friend, Don.

"Got what you wanted. It was a six-month period. Best as I can tell Gorman went back to Austria for a sabbatical."

"Yeah, that's what I thought. But passport control records don't indicate that."

"Yeah, I know," said Don. "That puzzled me, too."

"And the airline he flew on after he got overseas was curious as well."

"Right, it's a sub of Aeroflot. Is this something we should focus on?"

Puller said, "I'll let you know the answer to that as soon as I can."

He clicked off and went back to the search on Franklin. He was looking at two things: financial disclosures and travel, going back fifteen years.

The financial disclosure forms required by the government were, to his mind, a joke. Everything could be placed into ranges. One million to fifty million. Assets could be hidden behind shell companies, or in relatives' names to avoid having to disclose. There were a million different dodges, and Puller had found that the politicians with the most money and assets worked very hard to hide their wealth. For electability reasons, they would much prefer to have the image of just being ordinary folks working for a living.

What he found with Franklin was a mountain of diversions and inconsistencies. He marveled at the fact that no one had called out the woman on this before. Then the truth struck him: Why would her colleagues call her out when many of them were probably doing the very same thing?

When he looked at the timeline of her history and travel, something seemed to click in the back of his mind. That's when he digitally laid Gorman's timeline over Franklin's. There was only one time period that matched.

A six-month sabbatical that both had taken at the same time. Only Franklin had not flown on a sub of Aeroflot. But she had ended up in Austria. And from there she could have gone anywhere by car or train or private jet, and Puller would have no accurate way to track that. The other thing that stuck out for him was the fact that shortly after Franklin returned to the States, she started her first bid for elected office. She had now won reelection multiple times and had a lofty perch on Ways and Means, and other committees, including—tellingly, for Puller— the House Permanent Select Committee on Intelligence, meaning she was privy to most of the important intel secrets of this country.

A feeling of dread rising up in him, he placed all this in a file and emailed it to Pine. Then he sat back in his chair and wondered what else he could do to help.

A phone call he got a few minutes later answered that question for him.

56

PINE HELD UP THE PAIR OF PAJAMAS as a whirlwind of memories engulfed her.

They were small, the size for a tall six-year-old, as Mercy had been. They had pink ponies on them. They were the PJs that Mercy had worn the night she vanished. Pine had a matching pair that their mother had bought them, although Pine's were not pink, but blue.

She held the cloth up to her nose, hoping that it retained her sister's scent. After all these years...there was none. It was just mildewed and smelled foul.

She picked up the packet of letters that had been underneath the pajamas. By her quick count, there were more than a dozen of them, faded and yellowed.

They were all addressed to Ito Vincenzo and had been sent from Leonard and Wanda Atkins in Taliaferro County, Georgia.

She opened the first one. It was dated three months after Mercy had been abducted.

She looked down at the signature at the end of the letter.

Len Atkins.

As she read the letter her mouth kept dropping and her eyes grew teary.

So happy we could give the girl a home.

They named her Rebecca.

The money you sent was a godsend.

And you more than paid me back for saving your butt in Nam.

Take care and we'll send pictures when we can.

Pine thought, *Rebecca? Pictures? Nam?*

She tore through the other letters, most of which had a similar theme. They were all dated a year apart. But there were no pictures in any of them.

Ito Vincenzo had apparently given Mercy to another family, the Atkinses of Taliaferro County, Georgia.

Pine did a quick Google search and learned that in 1990 Taliaferro only had 1,900 people spread over nearly two hundred heavily wooded square miles. She learned there were even fewer people living there now, making it the least populated county in Georgia and the second-least populous county east of the Mississippi. She did another search and found that Taliaferro was a three-hour drive from her old home in Sumter County.

Pine inwardly groaned.

You idiot.

She had learned on her trip back to her old homestead that a man she now knew to be Ito Vincenzo had gotten into a fight with her father the very next day after Mercy had been taken. Once Pine had also learned that he had been the abductor, it should have been clear that Ito had taken Mercy someplace relatively close by. Otherwise, he could not have been back the next day to have the altercation with her father.

She tore through the rest of the box. At the very bottom, under a layer of old clothes, was a metal box. Inside were two things: old check registers and a single photo, an old Polaroid.

Pine gripped the photo but didn't look at it. Not just yet.

It could be one of Ito and his family. But there had been all those photo albums for that. Why put one in here?

She set it down and picked up a check register.

The entries were neat and detailed. Ito had been a very organized man, apparently.

She scanned down the date column until she came to the relevant time period.

There it was. A check for $500 made out to Leonard Atkins. She quickly searched the other registers. She found a dozen more entries for $500 paid out to Atkins.

Five hundred bucks a year for a little girl's expenses? It didn't seem nearly enough, not even in Taliaferro County, Georgia. She glanced at the last check entry for the last register in the box. June 13, 2002.

And why had the money been paid at all? If Ito had gotten a little girl for the Atkinses, why hadn't they paid *him*, not the other way around?

And how did he even know the Atkinses? They presumably were from rural Georgia, and Ito had spent his whole life in New Jersey. *Vietnam?*

Pine slowly put down the check register and stared at the facedown photo. The moment of truth had arrived. She felt her adrenaline spike and a wave of anxiety sweep over her with such force that she thought she might be having a panic attack.

If this is a picture of Mercy, what would she look like? Will we still be identical?

Pine had lifted the photo off the plywood floor when she heard a noise outside.

She thrust the photo and some of the letters into her pocket, hastily put the things back in the box, clambered down the attic stairs, and lifted them and the ceiling door back into place. She hustled to the window.

A car's headlights were pointed straight at the house as a Subaru Outlander pulled into the driveway. Then the driver killed the lights and stepped out. The passenger in the front seat did the same. They were dressed in jeans and ski jackets against the foggy chill.

They both went around to the rear of the Outlander and the lift-gate rose. They pulled out some bags of groceries. The gate light illuminated both their faces.

The passenger was Tony Vincenzo.

The driver was a woman. And Pine quickly recognized her.

Well, well. Lindsey Axilrod had finally turned up.

57

VINCENZO AND AXILROD CAME IN the front door and went straight into the kitchen with the grocery bags. This gave Pine the chance to move to the top of the stairs and listen. The house was so small their conversation easily carried to her.

"I think this is enough food for now," said Vincenzo.

"How long do you plan to be here?" asked Axilrod.

"Long as it takes, babe."

"Aren't you afraid someone will find out about this place?"

"Only the family knows about it."

"Hell, Tony, they can check the real estate records. Is it in your dad's name?"

"I don't know. But he's dead now, so I guess it comes to me."

"You have two houses now, what a big deal you are," she said in a joking tone.

He laughed. "Come over here and I'll show you what a 'big' deal I am."

Pine heard Axilrod chortle. "Time enough for that, lover boy."

"It was cool you came to stay with me," said Vincenzo.

"Someone has to watch over you."

"I can take care of myself, okay?" His tone was not joking now.

"Those two cops were talking to your father in prison. Maybe he told them something."

"He had nothing to tell," replied Vincenzo.

"Come on, Tony, you told me you went to visit your old man. What did you tell him?"

Pine edged forward a bit. She didn't like how this conversation was going. Axilrod was digging for info, and Vincenzo sounded like he was totally missing what the woman was doing.

"I don't know, just stuff. Stop with the third degree, okay?"

She snapped, "My ass is on the line here, too. I need to know what's going on."

"I'm the one that got chased by this FBI chick."

"Right, Atlee Pine. She's definitely trouble."

"But you took care of that, you said."

"She killed Sheila, Tony. I told you that."

"Cops can't go around killing people and get away with it."

"It's the system, Tony. They cover for each other. Cops can kill people and there's no blowback for them."

"'Blowback'? Where'd you hear that word, Lindsey? You sound like a spy."

"The point is, Tony, things are getting tight here."

"You should let me get to know the people you're working with."

"Why would I do that?"

"I can help them, Lindsey. And I want to move up in the chain, okay? I don't always want to be the low man on the totem pole."

"Why so ambitious?"

"Look at my old man. He spent his life in the trenches, doing his own shit, carrying his own water. So when things went sideways, there he was; the cops grabbed him no problem. I'm thinking that a few layers between me and them is a good thing."

"Okay, maybe you're right about that," conceded Axilrod. "Let me think on it."

On the stairs, Pine's hand slipped to her pistol.

Vincenzo said, "Hell, maybe I can buy one of those penthouses one day."

"The penthouse is off-limits until further notice," she said sharply.

"Shit, why? I like that place. And the cops don't go there."

"Pine did. She went in undercover and almost wrecked the place. I had to think fast to get around that. So it's a no-go."

"So is it really just a perk, the penthouse, I mean?"

"I'm not following."

Vincenzo said, "I mean, it's a pretty expensive benefit if it is just that. I know the pill business is good and all. But you gotta push a shitload of it just to pay the monthly fees on that place."

"That's not your problem to worry about. And you're not the only pipeline out there."

"That's what I figured. Those guys probably have crews operating all around the New York and New Jersey metro areas. Probably coming up from Mexico and stuff, right?"

"Something like that."

"So maybe you can introduce me?"

"Sounds good. Now, why don't you go shower and I'll get to work on dinner?"

"Sounds good, babe. And then *after* dinner?"

"Sure, Tony, sure. Whatever my man wants."

He slapped her playfully on the butt and then went upstairs.

Axilrod waited for the shower to start. Then she made a phone call.

"You were right, he's getting to be a problem," she said. Axilrod listened for a few moments. "Yeah, I understand. After it's over, you know what to do."

She put the phone away and slipped a syringe from her purse.

She reached the bathroom and slowly opened the door. Steam had filled the room. She readied the needle, holding it in front of her like a knife.

She reached the shower curtain, steeled herself, threw aside the curtain, and raised the needle high to strike.

Only there was no one there. The shower was empty, the water simply running.

She whirled around to see a bare-chested Tony standing there.

And behind him and holding her gun to his head was Pine.

"Hey, Lindsey. I was really hoping we'd run into each other again. Now, put down the syringe you were going to use to kill Tony, and let's have a chat, *babe*."

58

Finally.

Blum stirred as both Adam Gorman and Nora Franklin came out of the building together. Blum hailed a cab right as a sleek black Mercedes-Maybach slid up to the pair and Gorman held the door for Franklin. He climbed in after her.

The cabbie, who was in his fifties and wearing a white turban and a maroon bindi on his forehead, turned to Blum and said, "Where do you want to go, ma'am?"

"I want to go wherever that Mercedes up there goes," she said, pointing to the vehicle as it pulled away from the curb.

"What is it that you mean by that?" said the man in a thick accent, which forced Blum to listen closely.

"I just mean to follow that car," said Blum.

He turned back around, whipped out into traffic, and settled in two cars behind the Maybach.

"Why do you follow them?" the cabbie asked.

"It's my job."

"Are you police?"

"I'm with the FBI."

"You are too old," he said dismissively. "You are older than me."

Blum took out her FBI ID card and held it up. The *F*, *B*, and *I* were quite prominent.

"Is this sufficient?" she asked him.

He turned to look at her again. "Do you have a gun?"

"Do you want to find out?"

He pivoted back around and made a left to follow the Maybach.

"Are those criminals up there?"

"They could very well be. That's what I'm trying to find out. Do you know the city well? I don't want to lose them."

"I have been in this country for ten years. I have driven cab for nine years all over this city."

"Is that when you came to this country, ten years ago?"

"Yes. But in Pakistan I was a doctor, not a taxi driver."

He turned the cab right as they followed the Maybach. "What will you do when they arrive at their destination?"

"I'll continue to watch them."

"Should you call the police?"

"No, it's not time for that. Not yet."

"You must find this work exciting."

"Sometimes it's too exciting. Sometimes it's incredibly boring. I've spent the last several hours drinking so much coffee I never want to touch it again."

"Yes, I can see how that might be."

He pulled up behind the car.

"Don't get too close," Blum warned.

"Every yellow taxi looks like every other yellow taxi."

"But they might see you."

"We all wear the turban. We all have the bindi. We all are either doctors or engineers who drive taxis." He glanced back at her. "Are those people dangerous?" he asked.

"One of them has shown himself to be very dangerous," replied Blum, keeping her gaze on the Maybach.

"That is not good. People like that are not good."

"I agree."

"I do not like it that you are following such people. You are a nice lady and they are dangerous people."

"Don't worry. I have other people supporting me who are not afraid of people like that."

"It is nice to have such people."

"I've always thought so."

Thirty city blocks later, the Maybach stopped in front of a hotel in a very upscale section of Manhattan. It wasn't Billionaires' Row, but it was close.

As Blum paid her fare, the cabbie told her, "You must be very careful now. I will no longer be with you."

"I will be very careful. Luckily, neither of them has ever met me."

"I wish you good fortune."

"Thank you."

As he drove away, Blum steeled herself, turned, and walked into the hotel.

A bellman tipped his cap to her as she went in. Blum bypassed the check-in counter when she saw Gorman and Franklin enter the bar lounge set off to one side of the lobby. They were led to their seats by a young woman. When Blum stepped up to the small hostess stand at the entrance to the lounge, another young woman dressed all in black with a name tag that read JULIET approached and asked her if she needed any help. Blum told her that she was meeting someone here but was early and just wanted to get a seat. The young woman led her into the substantial Art Deco–decorated lounge and deposited her at a table with two chairs. Luckily, it had a direct sight line to Franklin and Gorman, who had settled down at a table with high-backed upholstered chairs near the fireplace; the table had a RESERVED sign on it. The hostess helping them picked up the sign and departed.

As Blum pretended to consult her phone, she kept an eye on the pair. Gorman was leading the conversation and speaking energetically, but she could tell his voice was barely above a whisper, because Franklin had to lean in to listen. By her expression, she wasn't pleased with what she was hearing. Franklin glanced down at the drinks menu on the table and motioned a waitress over. She ordered something, but when the waitress turned to Gorman he waved her off and resumed speaking after the young woman walked away.

Blum positioned her iPhone so it looked as though she was scrolling through screens. But she had actually engaged the video feature and was recording the pair as they continued to talk.

"Ma'am, what are you doing?"

Blum turned and looked at the beefy man with squinty eyes dressed in a suit with a wired comm piece in his ear.

"Excuse me?" said Blum.

"You can't film guests without their permission."

Thinking quickly Blum said, "I'm not. I'm filming that fireplace. I want to get one like it for my home."

"I don't think so. I've been watching you since you came in here. You've had your eyes on that couple the whole time." He gripped her by the arm. "You'll have to come with me."

"I'm not going anywhere with you. I don't even know who you are."

The man lifted one of his lapels and showed the badge underneath. "Hotel security. And I'm also NYPD, off duty. So you're coming with me."

"General?"

They both turned as Robert Puller, in his full-dress uniform, strode up to them.

"General Blum?"

"Yes, Colonel?" said Blum instantly.

"General?" said the bewildered security man.

"Two-star, Air Force," said Blum, standing up and glowering at the man. "Colonel, this young man seems to think that I was spying on those people over there with my phone instead of taking footage of that beautiful fireplace. I think it will look great with the renovation I'm doing."

Puller immediately got this. "Absolutely it will. It fits right in with the design theme." He looked at the man. "We have a flight to catch to DC. General Blum is briefing the Joint Chiefs at the Pentagon late tonight."

"Jesus," said the man. With an embarrassed look at Blum he said contritely, "I'm really sorry, General."

"No need to apologize," Blum said kindly. "You were just doing your job. Now, if you'll excuse us."

"Oh, yes, absolutely." The man almost bowed.

As they walked out of the hotel Blum said, "Thanks for the assist, but how did you know where I was?"

"So long as you have a smartphone you have no privacy."

"Right. But why were you looking for me?"

"My brother called and told me you were watching Gorman and Franklin for Atlee. Then he contacted me again. He was worried about you tailing a killer by yourself and asked if I could check on you. I'm glad he did, actually, because I found out some troubling things about Gorman and Franklin. I went to the building where you were supposed to be, but you weren't there. That's when I traced you by your phone signal."

"You could have called."

"You were on surveillance. I didn't want to call at an inopportune time for you."

They turned down a side street and reached a spot where they could speak freely.

Puller said, "So what have you learned?"

"Agent Pine saw Gorman come out of the building where she had gone that night with Lindsey Axilrod. That told her he was in on whatever is happening there. Then he went to Franklin's congressional office. They were there for hours. He's head of her security team, Agent Pine found out. She asked me to pick up the surveillance, which I did. They left her office and came to this hotel and were having a very intense conversation in the lounge. He was talking and she was listening, and neither of them seemed happy. I think something big is going down."

She took out her phone and showed him the video.

"Wish I could read lips," said Puller.

"Me too."

"There's no need for that. I can fill you in."

They turned to see Gorman standing there, as a black town car slid up to the curb. There were two large and tough-looking men in the front seat. One got out and opened the rear door.

"Get in," said Gorman, who was now pointing a square-muzzled .45 automatic at them. "Or I'll shoot you both in the head right here."

59

Tony Vincenzo blubbered, "You were going to stick me with that?! I thought you loved me. I thought we were a team."

"Shut up, Tony." Axilrod lowered the syringe and stared at Pine.

Pine said, "Haven't seen you since you killed Sheila Weathers and left me to take the fall for it."

"I didn't kill Sheila."

"If you didn't kill her, you know who did and probably ordered it. And then you sent some asshole to kill me. Only it didn't work out that way."

"She told me before that *you* killed Sheila," blurted out Vincenzo.

"She says lots of things, Tony. But when she opens her mouth only lies come out." She glanced at the syringe. "What's in it? Morphine?"

"Just a little shot of Vitamin C." Axilrod looked at Vincenzo. "You would have felt so good, Tony."

"Put the syringe down, Lindsey."

Instead, she held up the syringe like a knife. "Make me, you bitch." She lunged at them.

Pine calmly altered her aim and shot Axilrod in the hand; the bullet passed through skin and bone before becoming lodged in the wall.

Axilrod dropped the syringe and doubled over, screaming in pain. Vincenzo tried to jerk free, but Pine's iron grip kept him from going anywhere.

"You shot me!" screamed Axilrod.

"You seem to be the only one surprised by that. And trust me, it was all I could do not to aim at your head."

Pine gave Vincenzo a hard shove, sending him sprawling face-first to the floor. "Stay there," she barked.

She pushed Axilrod out of the way, gingerly picked up the syringe, carefully wrapped it in toilet paper, and stuck it in the cabinet under the sink. "Whatever is in there, I'll leave to a bio-hazard disposal squad to deal with." She glanced at Axilrod, who was squatting next to the shower, holding her bleeding hand, and quietly sobbing.

Axilrod looked up at Pine through tear-stained eyes. "You have no idea who you're fucking with."

Pine tossed her a towel to wrap around the wound and leaned against the sink. "So enlighten me."

"You wish," said Axilrod as she tied the towel around her hand.

"How'd it feel feeding fourteen-year-old girls like Jewel Blake to horny old men, Lindsey? You get a kick out of that?"

"What?" said Vincenzo, staring at Axilrod.

"Yeah, your girlfriend plays pimp, too, as another sideline." She looked at the woman. "Girls who thought you were going to protect them? And you fed them to the wolves."

"I have no idea what you're talking about. And you have no cause to hold me. I'm outta here."

"You move to the door, the next thing I shoot will not be your hand. But if you talk, maybe we can work a deal."

"You will learn shit from me, okay?"

"Is this where you say you want a lawyer?"

"Go to hell."

Pine glanced at Vincenzo. "Hey, Tony, *you* want a great deal? All you have to do is rat this piece of shit out."

"You do that, Tony, and you are dead," snapped Axilrod.

"She was going to kill you anyway, so what's the difference?" noted Pine.

Vincenzo turned and looked up at Pine. "What do you want to know?"

"Tony!" screamed Axilrod.

Pine pulled out a pair of zip cuffs and handed them to Vincenzo. "Put these on her hands and ankles."

"But—"

"Now!"

Vincenzo pushed a struggling Axilrod down, flipped her over, put a knee on her lower back, and managed, with difficulty, to bind her hands and ankles.

"Good boy, Tony," said Pine.

When Axilrod started screaming a string of obscenities, Pine grabbed the scruff of the woman's jacket, slid her into the bedroom closet, and shut the door.

She returned to the bathroom and looked at Vincenzo.

"Okay, sit on the toilet. We're going to have a chat." Pine took out her phone and turned on the video with the lens pointed right at him.

Vincenzo sat down and rubbed the back of his head. "I can't believe she was going to *kill me*. I thought she loved me."

"Yeah, Tony, you need to get over that. She was using you just like she used everybody else. Now I need you to talk."

He looked at her warily. "Maybe *I* need to speak to a lawyer."

"Well, I haven't arrested you, which is why I haven't read you your Miranda rights, so technically, you're not entitled to a lawyer. But what the hell. You want a lawyer? Okay. I'll cut Axilrod loose and leave you guys to it. She probably has a second syringe in her purse. I'll go get her now and you two can work out your differences. I'm sure the murdering bitch would be willing."

Pine pocketed her phone and moved to leave the room.

"Wait, wait!" cried out Vincenzo.

Pine turned to look at him. "Well?"

"What do you want to know?"

She settled back against the sink, took out her phone, and turned on the video function. She recited the date, time, her and Vincenzo's names, and where they were located. Not exactly by the book, but the best she could do under the circumstances.

Pine said, "Do you want a lawyer?"

"No, I don't want a lawyer."

"Are you speaking to me of your own free will?"

"Yes."

"Okay, tell me everything. Starting with how you and Axilrod hooked up."

"She came up to me at a bar one night. She seemed to know all about me, where I worked, the petty crap I'd done."

"Meaning dealing drugs?"

"I don't deal, well, not technically. I just make the stuff."

"Okay, go on."

"She told me she worked at Fort Dix, too, in the IT department. Then says we can go big-time. She has it all planned out. She had a contact who could move a lot of product."

"Jeff Sands."

"Yeah, I met with him quite a few times while we were putting this together."

"He's dead, by the way. They blew his head off."

"Shit."

"Where did you get your ingredients for the pill making?"

"Lindsey arranged that. Then the boxes would come to my house, always late at night, so no one would see anything."

"Any idea where the boxes were shipped in from?"

"Not really. I did notice that some of the boxes had weird symbols on them."

"What, like another language?"

"Yeah. But not one I recognized. I mean, it wasn't Spanish or anything. I just figured that they came from some place overseas. Hell, just like everything else in this country."

"Okay, when you made the pills, Danforth and Cassidy would come into play, right?"

"Yeah. They would leave Fort Dix in military vehicles, stop at a designated place, pick up the pills I'd made, drive them to another location, and leave them there. Then they'd go on with their trip, drop the vehicles where they were supposed to, and come back to Dix in another ride."

"Do you know who Jeff Sands is related to?"

He shook his head.

"Peter Driscoll."

Vincenzo showed no signs of knowing who that was.

Pine sighed. "You really need to get off your Game Boy, Tony. Driscoll is the Senate majority leader."

"What, you mean like in the government?"

"Yeah, I mean, *like* in the government. A very powerful guy."

"Damn. And Jeff was related?"

"His grandson."

"Wait a minute, you don't think this Driscoll dude is involved with this, do you?"

"I don't know. Tell me about the apartment on Fifty-Seventh."

"Lindsey took me there. Said it was a bennie, you know, a thank-you for a job well done."

"And you never questioned how she would have access to a place that's reserved strictly for billionaires?"

"You want to know the truth? I thought maybe it was like one of those Mexican cartel guys. Pablo what's his name, or that Chapo dude."

"Pablo Escobar. Yeah, he was killed about twenty-five years ago, and El Chapo's in prison, but I get your drift."

"It was funny, though."

"What was?"

"I was at the apartment one time, late at night. Not for one of the parties. But there was a snafu with a drug shipment and I needed to meet with someone. They told me to meet them there. While I was waiting, I had to use the can really bad and went looking for a bathroom. But they were all taken. Probably people doing coke and shit. I looked around trying to find some place and then I saw this door, down a hall, out of the way."

Pine tensed a bit. "And?"

"And it was locked. But I was desperate and I had my knife and I jimmied it. Well, it was no bathroom. It was filled with computer screens and other equipment."

"Did you see what was on the screens?"

"Yeah, there were camera feeds from the apartment. I mean, like every room. I saw people screwing in the bedrooms and snorting coke and doing other shit that I didn't want to see." He paused. "There were men on men, women on women, and men with girls who looked way too young to be doing what they were doing, like you mentioned to Lindsey just now."

"So the whole place was wired for surveillance?"

"Yeah."

"So what did you do after you saw what was in that room?"

"I shut and locked that door and just prayed no one saw me. I had my meeting and then ran down the street to a restroom at a Starbucks."

"Did you ever tell anyone you saw that room? Like Axilrod?"

"Look, I'm not stupid, okay? I mean, I didn't think the bitch was going to stick me with a needle, but it's not like I trusted her all the way, either." He paused. "And there's one more thing."

"What?"

"I was in New York one night taking care of some business. I was near the building so I decided to walk past. It was late, around eleven."

"Did you go in?"

"No. The parties and stuff they throw up there are pretty infrequent. They send out a notice when they're on."

"So what did you do?"

"I watched the limo coming and going. Fancy-looking people getting out and going into that building."

"They could have been going to other apartments?"

"Nope."

"Why not?"

"'Cause I know the limo driver. See, it was the same driver and limo. He was just ferrying folks, because no one came at the same time. He sometimes comes up to the parties. I've talked to him. No, they were going to that apartment, for sure."

Pine thought about all this for a few moments. "Okay, let's move on. What about Sheila Weathers?"

"She was just a chick at the fort. She worked in the cafeteria. She was nice. She really knew nothing about the drugs. Why would they kill her?"

"Because they wanted to frame me for it and make sure I wasn't around to defend myself, that's why."

"That's really shitty."

"They killed your old man, you know. Because we talked with him. He knew something was going on with you. He said you were in over your head."

Vincenzo's head drooped. "Yeah, I figured out that he was right, a few minutes ago."

"Why did he say you were in over your head?"

"I went to visit him. I was getting freaked out. I mean, the strange writing on the boxes, this fancy apartment with all the cameras, Lindsey popping up at the bar like she did and coming on to a guy like me."

"And what did your father tell you?"

"He told me to get out while I still could. Only I couldn't figure a way to do it." He looked up at her. "So what the hell is going on here? It's not just about drugs, is it?"

"No, it's a lot more than that. But let me ask you something else, totally off topic."

"What?" he said curiously.

"Your grandfather, Ito?"

Vincenzo looked surprised. "My grandfather? What about him?"

"Did you ever meet him?"

Vincenzo's eyes narrowed. "If I did, I don't really remember. He…he just disappeared one day, or so my dad told me."

"Any idea what happened to him?"

"No. My dad said he just up and vanished. Not a word to him or my grandma. They were pissed. Why are you interested in him?"

"Just in connection with something else. What else did

your dad tell you about him? I know about the ice cream-ery. What else do you know about his past? Did he serve in Vietnam?"

"Yeah, in the Army. My dad told me Ito had a low lottery number and got drafted. Did his training at Fort Benning. You know that place?"

"Oh, yeah, I know it. You ever go up in the attic here and look through the boxes, old photo albums?"

"I only come here to drink beer and sit on the beach."

"You ever heard of a man named Leonard Atkins? Who might have saved your grandfather's life over there?"

"No."

Pine was about to ask another question when she heard a noise outside. She hurried to the window overlooking the front of the house and saw a black SUV pull in.

She ran back into the bathroom and grabbed Vincenzo. "I hope you can run as fast as you did when I was chasing you."

"What? Why?"

"Because your girlfriend's cleanup team is here. Move!"

Axilrod must have heard the sounds of the car, too, because she started to kick the wall of the closet and scream.

Pine jerked the door open, leaned down, and clocked her in the face with her fist. Axilrod slumped unconscious. Pine looked up at Vincenzo. "Damn, that felt good."

She and Vincenzo flew down the steps and then out the back door. They ran flat out toward the beach and turned right when they hit the sand. This direction, Pine knew, would carry them toward the police station she had passed on the way in.

As she sprinted along, Pine pulled out her phone, punched in 911, identified herself, gave the address of the beach house and what had happened there and their approximate current location. Then she put the phone back in her pocket, turned, and saw light skipping over the sand and coming toward them. A second later, bullets sailed past her.

"Go, Tony, go," she screamed at him, and he picked up his pace even more, as Pine slowed just a bit. She was going to keep herself between Vincenzo and the people after them.

To get to him, they'd have to kill her.

And right now, Pine wouldn't have bet on herself surviving the night.

60

I AM NOT GOING TO DIE on a beach in freaking New Jersey.

Pine was running as fast as she could in the tightly packed wet sand as the breakers pounded to the left of her and the tide was heading out. And if that wasn't enough, a storm was starting to rage off the coast.

Sweat was running down her face, though it was chilly. Out over the water a spear of lightning punched out of the dark clouds and headed directly to the Atlantic. Then followed an unholy crack of thunder that seemed to shake her right to her soul. She could see Vincenzo about fifty feet in front of her and running flat out.

"Keep going," she urged. "As fast as you can."

As more shots were fired at them she decided to do something. She stopped, pivoted, pulled her Glock and her Beretta, and opened fire, even as more bullets sailed over her. She was aiming at the dots of light coming her way. They stopped shooting and fell to the sand for cover. She turned and ran.

Where the hell is Tony?

He was no longer in front of her. She looked to the ocean and beach side and saw nothing. She sprinted full out. And fell flat onto the beach because she had tripped over something lying on the sand.

Pine felt wetness on her face, and it wasn't rain or ocean spray. She righted herself and flinched when she saw that what she had tripped over was Vincenzo. He was gasping for breath, and in the spike of another lightning bolt she saw both his contorted features and the bloody wound in his chest. She quickly felt under him and her hand came away all bloodied. He had apparently been shot in the back while running and the bullet had come out the front.

He suddenly focused on her and grabbed Pine's arm.

He gasped, "D-don't let me...die. P-please."

Tears streamed down his face and mixed with the raindrops that were starting to fall.

"Okay, Tony, just stay calm. Stay calm."

She knew this was pretty much impossible under the circumstances.

Pine felt the pulse at his neck and looked down at the ugly, bleeding wound in his torso. She put her hand over the wound to stop the flow of blood, but that wasn't going to work since he had holes in front and back. And he was no doubt hemorrhaging internally.

She eyed the pursuers behind her. They were still hunkered down apparently. She fired four more shots in their direction to keep them there.

She called 911 again, explained the situation, and put her phone away. As she looked down at Vincenzo, she knew they were never going to make it in time.

He seemed to understand this because he gripped her arm even more tightly and his eyes became even more panicked.

"I'm here, Tony. Help is on the way."

He shuddered and then shook his head stubbornly, now clearly aware that his death was near. He motioned for her to bend closer. She did so.

"T-tell my mom that I-I love h-her."

"Just hang in there, okay?"

She didn't want to give him false hope, but she didn't know what else to say. And what did any words really matter at this point?

The next sounds Pine heard were sirens cutting through the dark.

She looked back and saw the light dots swiftly moving to the street. They had evidently heard the sounds, too, and were beating a hasty retreat.

When she looked back down at Vincenzo another lightning burst revealed his face clearly.

He was dead.

She closed his eyes, rose, and sprinted toward the street.

Pine arrived there in time to see the men climb into the black SUV farther down the road and speed off in her direction. She ducked down behind a garbage can before it got close. As the vehicle raced past her she saw the person in the back seat.

Lindsey Axilrod was in there, her face heavily bruised where Pine had walloped her, and she was holding up her bloody hand. They had found and rescued her.

The SUV turned off and was gone.

Thirty seconds later she ducked behind the garbage can once more as police cars shot past her and pulled in down the street at Vincenzo's beach house. Pine jogged in that direction, but then broke off and went to the parking lot next to the beach, climbed into her car, and pulled out. She kept her headlights off and didn't gun the engine until she was two streets away.

She looked down and saw Vincenzo's blood on her. Everything had happened so fast. She had gone from searching the boxes in the attic to—

Shit.

She pulled into a convenience store, slid into a parking space, and put the car in park. She put her hand in her pocket and took out the photo. Her hand was trembling.

She clicked on the dome light and slowly turned the Polaroid over.

She first cast her eyes at the bottom, where in the white perimeter of the photo was written: "Len, Wanda, and Becky. July 1999."

Slowly, a millimeter at a time, Pine lifted her gaze. Her body was trembling like she was in the throes of a terrible chill, her breaths were painful, she felt sick.

Then she stopped. There were three people lined up in front of what looked like a mobile trailer set up on cinder blocks.

The man was of medium height, reedy, and bald. He was dressed in jeans and a T-shirt and held a cigarette. He was smiling at the camera. The older woman was rotund and short, wearing cutoff jean shorts and a sleeveless blouse. She was not smiling. She didn't look like someone who had ever smiled.

And next to her, and towering over both of them, at what Pine calculated was nearly six feet, was a young woman. She wore an old-fashioned gingham dress that looked to be handmade and that hung limply down past her knees. She was barefoot, and her hair was a mess of tangles and cowlicks. Her exposed skin was dirty and full of scabs. She was not looking at the camera. She was staring straight down at the ground, her shoulders hunched, her entire body looking uncomfortable, contorted—perhaps seized in pain, Pine didn't know. And even though Pine could not glimpse her face, she knew without a doubt that she was looking at her sister. It was mostly the height and the hair. The once beautiful hair that her mother had religiously brushed and endlessly braided into shapes and configurations that had made the tomboy Atlee giggle. But Mercy had loved it.

And now...this.

Pine started to quietly weep. She rested her forehead against the steering wheel as her body started to shudder and the sobs made her breathless.

The knocking on her window made her sit up and wipe at her eyes, her hand going to her holstered Glock. An old man in a baseball cap was peering in at her. He held a plastic bag full of things he'd presumably bought in the store. She hit the button and her window came down.

"You okay, ma'am?" he asked in a worried voice.

She nodded, cleared her throat, and brushed more tears away.

"Yes, just...just some bad news."

"Well, I'm real sorry about that. Is there anyone you can call to come be with you? Or is there anything I can do?"

"No, I'll be fine. Thank you for your concern."

He touched her hand with his. "Life can throw us some curveballs, can't it? I lost my missus six months ago. Always thought I'd be the first to go."

"I'm sorry for your loss."

"Well, I'm real sorry for what you're going through. But if it makes you feel any better, time does help. And you figure out you got other people who care about you." He held up the bag. "My son and my grandson are visiting. I told them this place here has the best durn grilled hot dogs in the whole state of New Jersey. They're excited to try 'em. I'm just happy I'm not alone tonight."

"Thank you. I hope they enjoy the hot dogs."

He gave her an encouraging smile, walked off, climbed into an old pickup truck, and slowly drove away.

Right when Pine had thought maybe there was nothing left that was good in the world, that old man had restored a little bit of hope to her.

She wiped her eyes again and put the car in gear.

I guess it really is all about timing.

She glanced down at the photo, at her beloved twin staring at the dirt, trapped in a life that was not hers.

"I'm going to find you, Mercy. Your little sister is coming for you. I promise."

61

No answer.

As she sped north, Pine had called Blum four times and gotten no answer; it had gone straight to voice mail as though the phone was turned off. She then tried calling Robert Puller and got the exact same result.

Panicking, she called John Puller. She gasped in gratitude as he picked up.

"Atlee?"

"I'm so sorry to bother you. But I can't reach either Carol or your brother. They both go straight to voice mail."

"Carol texted me. Said she was doing surveillance work on Gorman and Franklin."

"That's right," said Pine.

"I told Bobby about that. He was going to dig some stuff up on them."

"You think he and Carol might be together somehow?"

"They should be. I contacted Bobby and asked him to check on Carol. I didn't like it that she was tailing a guy like Gorman. And I really don't like it that neither one of them are answering their phones."

"I didn't like using Carol for that, either. And maybe I shouldn't have. But she doesn't take unnecessary risks. Sometimes I forget she's not a trained agent."

"But something might have happened."

"I'm going to have an APB put out on them both and have some agents go to the spot where Carol was doing her surveillance."

"I think that's a smart move, Atlee."

"And I have a lot to fill you in on." Pine proceeded to do that. She was only twenty minutes outside of the city when she had finished. She could hear Puller breathing heavily. It reminded her of Jack Lineberry. And for good reason. Both men had been shot.

"Puller, look, you just need to rest, okay? I can handle this. I shouldn't have called you."

She could hear him breathing fast for a few seconds and then came what sounded like him trying to sit up in bed.

"Puller, please, just lie still!"

"I'm fine. I don't know why I'm still in the hospital."

"You got shot, in case you forgot!"

Puller said, "Okay, okay. So, based on what you found out, what do you think is going on?"

"Let's start with the drugs. Tony and his two cohorts, Cassidy and Danforth, were making the drugs and getting them distributed. Jeff Sands was lining up buyers."

"And then there's the penthouse," said Puller.

"Sands was also involved in that, as was Axilrod. From what Tony told me that place could very well be a den of blackmail. He called them 'fancy' people, but they may be powerful people. And they could be buying drugs from them. Then they're whisked to this place for underage sex and more drugs and God knows what, and it's all captured on film."

Puller said, "And with the underage sex, like what happened with Jewel Blake, that would not only kill someone's reputation, it's also a felony."

"I just want to know how Nora Franklin fits into this. And Adam Gorman."

"I spoke briefly with Bobby about Gorman. He mentioned something in his background had set off warning bells, he just didn't tell me what."

"Look, are you sure you're feeling well enough to deal with this?"

"I'll be thinking about it whether I'm doing it with you or not."

"Then I'll be at the hospital in about twenty minutes."

"Well, I'm not going anywhere," replied Puller.

When Pine hurried into Puller's hospital room, he was sitting up in bed and looking at his phone.

"First, how are you feeling? Really? And don't bullshit me," added Pine as she sat down next to the bed.

"I can't jump tall buildings in a single bound right now, but I don't have to." He held up his phone. "Interesting."

"What?"

"Read it."

Pine read down the screens for about a minute and then looked up.

"Nora Franklin's opponent in her last election dropped out at the last minute even though he was ahead in the polls. She ran unopposed and won reelection. There was no explanation given by her opponent except to say it was a personal decision."

Puller nodded. "I think we might have drilled down to what that personal decision might have been."

"You think he was a visitor to the penthouse?"

"I wouldn't bet against it. And I'm wondering what she's done to repay 'them' for winning the election for her?"

"And how many other Nora Franklins are out there?"

Puller said, "And I doubt it's just politicians. You can have judges, bureaucrats, cops, military, CEOs, folks in the media, and a slew of other targets."

"And maybe that explains why a four-star got reassigned and you got shoved off the case and the local police cut us off and every other infuriating thing that's happened."

"It would explain a lot," agreed Puller.

"Axilrod said something to Tony that made me pause. She used the term 'blowback.' He called her out on that, in a joking way, saying she sounded like a spy."

"Spies, huh? Any word on your APB?" asked Puller anxiously.

"No."

"Then I might have to call in some reinforcements."

"From where?"

"You can leave that to me."

"No, I want to be part of the hunt. At the very least I want to get to Lindsey Axilrod."

"Okay. But I need to make some calls."

"While you do that, I need to make a call, too."

"Who to?"

"To a man who said if I needed a favor, to give him a ring. Well, I think it's time I called in that favor."

CHAPTER

62

THERE WERE EXHALATIONS OF BREATH mingled with the dripping of water coming from somewhere. There was consistency in the sounds, but no comfort.

Robert Puller looked down at his feet and winced a bit as the movement made the injuries in his shoulder and arm throb even more. They had interrogated him efficiently if not effectively. He was sure they would try again, with even harsher techniques. He was not looking forward to that. The car had driven them to a van in an underground garage somewhere on the outskirts of the city; the van had tinted windows. They had been restrained, and bags had been placed over their heads. They had driven around for about an hour. Then they had been taken from the van and hustled into somewhere; he didn't know where. The bags had not been taken off until they were inside. Blum had been taken somewhere else. A classic "divide and crush the confidence" technique.

Punching him in the face, cranking his arm behind his shoulder until nearly the breaking point, and breaking two of his fingers, they had questioned him for about an hour. He had no idea who the questioners were; Gorman was not among them.

He had thrown up during the course of the interrogation and had noted with some amount of satisfaction that he had sent his inquisitors jumping and diving out of the way from his projectile vomiting. That had been worth the two punches in the face he had gotten as punishment.

He had been called every filthy name in the book and been threatened in every way imaginable. That had been simple to endure. He merely did math calculations in his head while they were verbally pummeling him. That had been harder to do when the punches started flying, but he had done the best he could.

Puller had received SERE training during his time in uniform. That stood for "survival, evasion, resistance, and escape." Well, he had failed miserably in evading, resistance had gotten the crap kicked out of him, and he saw no way of escape.

So focus on survival.

Now he sat staring at a grimy floor and hoping that someone would come to help him.

He had endured years in prison for a crime of which he was innocent. But this was different. Those guarding him then were never going to kill him.

These men clearly were.

He had mentioned Nora Franklin's name once, after a question about what he was doing at the hotel with Blum.

"I hope Nora was worth what's going to happen to you assholes," he had said. This had gotten him a smack in the jaw by a man about the size of a small car that had knocked him out of his chair.

Now he sat slumped over, waiting for them to come back.

"Do you want to die? Because we will kill you."

The man towered over Carol Blum, who sat at a small table. Her shoes and jacket had been taken from her, and she was shivering, because the room was icy cold. The three men in here were all wearing overcoats.

Blum was scared, more scared than she'd ever been. She had the unshakable feeling that her life was about to end.

Blum looked up at him and said quietly, her voice trembling, "You're going to kill me anyway, so what does it matter?"

The men held up her FBI credentials.

"You are in admin. A secretary," he added derisively.

"I prefer the term 'support personnel.'"

That earned her a backhanded slap across the face that would have knocked her out of her chair if a second man had not held her in place. She choked back blood and tears. She was shaking uncontrollably and moaning in pain.

"Okay, have it your way, *support personnel*," said the man. "How did you learn about Ms. Franklin and Mr. Gorman?"

Through the one eye she could see out of, Blum stared at him. And then anger swelled up inside her. If she was going to die, she was not going out meekly. She felt her spine stiffen and her composure return. "The Bureau knows everything. All of you are in imminent danger of arrest."

"You are lying." He raised his hand to strike her again.

"Hitting a woman nearly twice your age won't take away the truth of what I just said. And if a lowly 'support personnel' knows as much as I do, what do you think the actual agents know?"

One man said, "Agents? How about *one* agent. Atlee Pine."

Blum was ready for that one. "And Army CID?"

"John Puller is no longer on the case."

"Do you really think he's the only agent CID has?"

"That has been taken care of. And if the Bureau was all over it, why have a secretary conducting surveillance?"

"Absolutely right. If I'm just a *secretary*."

"You are too old to be anything else."

"Absolutely right again. I'm just a secretary, nothing more. And I am with the FBI, no one else."

The man started to say something and then he stopped and stared warily at her. "What does that mean? 'No one else'?"

Now Blum allowed herself to look confused and uncertain. "N-nothing. I…I just meant what I said."

The man looked at his colleagues and started speaking in a language Blum didn't understand. But what she could see were their clear expressions of concern.

One of the men nodded and looked at Blum. "Who do you work for?"

"I told you. The FBI."

"I don't believe you."

"I work for no other *agency*." Blum feigned alarm when she said the last word.

The man looked at her triumphantly. "No other agency? Bull-shit." He leaned down so they were eye to eye. "Tell me who you're really working for. Don't lie to me."

Blum looked back at him stubbornly but said nothing else.

"All right. We will be back to talk to you. And then you will provide the answers we require about you and the man in uniform. Or you will die. Do you understand?"

Blum pursed her lips and looked down.

The men filed out and locked the door behind them.

It was only then that Blum looked up. Her subterfuge had bought them a little time, but that was all. She felt her spine grow soft once more as nearly all hope bled out of her.

Please, Agent Pine, please find us before it's too late.

CHAPTER

63

Pᴉɴᴇ ᴡᴀꜱ ꜱɪᴛᴛɪɴɢ ɪɴ ʜᴇʀ ʀᴇɴᴛᴀʟ ᴄᴀʀ. She had been speaking into the phone uninterrupted for nearly twenty minutes. Now she let out a long breath and waited. And waited…

Finally, Clint Dobbs, the head of the FBI branch in Arizona said, "Holy shit, Pine. You sure don't do anything by half measures."

"No, sir. Just doesn't seem to be my fate in life."

"Just so I get this straight, you're actually saying there is a blackmail operation that may reach into the highest levels of this government and then spreads out like a spider's web to God knows where? And the people being blackmailed are presumably doing things to help the blackmailers, using their positions of authority?"

"I don't think the facts can be explained any other way. And now Carol is missing along with John Puller's brother."

"I don't like the sound of that at all."

"Neither do I."

"You said you witnessed Gorman as the shooter?"

"Yes."

"I'll need an affidavit to that effect. That'll help me get the ball rolling."

"I'll get it to you ASAP."

"Nora Franklin? I've testified before committees she's on. I've socialized with her. I can't believe she would be involved in something like this."

"I'm sure, sir. But the fact is she's up to her eyeballs in this."

"But you have no proof of that."

"They got a four-star general yanked off this assignment at the Pentagon. Puller was stonewalled at every turn on a murder investigation involving a federal agent. He was nearly killed, and the grandson of Peter Driscoll *was* killed. And I've heard nothing in the news about it. And an agent friend of mine thinks NYPD is sitting on releasing Jeff Sands's ID as a favor to Driscoll."

"Are you suggesting that Senator Driscoll is involved in this, too?"

Pine said, "I don't know. I have no proof that he is, but if not, it's a big coincidence his grandson is involved."

"And this fancy apartment in New York?"

"Sir, I can think of no other reason to have camera equipment in bedrooms where sexual activity of a possibly criminal or professionally embarrassing nature is taking place. And Franklin's last political opponent quit the race weeks before the election for unspecified personal reasons, even though he was leading in the polls. Who does that, sir?"

"So you think he was blackmailed into getting out?" said Dobbs.

"I can't think of any other reason he would quit the race like that, just citing personal reasons."

"But you'd think the guy would have fought back if they tried to expose him."

"And what if they threatened his family?"

"So now we're getting into old mob techniques."

"Those techniques never go away because, unfortunately, they still work."

Dobbs said, "How many 'leaders' do you think they've compromised?"

"I'm not sure. Vincenzo said one night he saw people being taken into and out of the place for hours. He knew they were visiting that apartment because he knew the limo driver."

"Preying on the weaknesses of people," said Dobbs in a disgusted tone.

"I have no sympathy for people having sex with underage children," said Pine, thinking of Jewel Blake. "They deserve to have the book thrown at them. But for the others, affairs, drug use, all used for blackmail? That's different. That's screwing with people, destroying their lives. If they are using their influence to help, it's under duress. I think that must be quite a guilty burden to bear, knowing that you're selling out your own country to save yourself."

"I know we need to do something ASAP, Pine, but I also have to think about this. Find a strategy moving forward. We have to tread cautiously."

"I would be careful who you communicate with, sir. Otherwise, you might find yourself transferred to head up an RA so far in the wilderness they use tin cans strung with wire to talk."

"That thought *had* occurred to me. So, no leads on Carol?"

"Not yet. But someone is working on it, and I will move heaven and earth to get her back safe and sound."

"I know you will. Hang in there, Pine. I'll get back to you."

He clicked off, and for some reason Pine's hopes immediately plummeted.

I really can't count on anybody to help me because who the hell knows how far this goes?

She looked out the window at the darkened street, and her imagination raced to all sorts of terrible fates for Carol Blum and Robert Puller. She never should have brought Blum with her.

And if I hadn't screwed up Puller's arrest of Tony Vincenzo, Robert Puller wouldn't be involved in this, either.

She was convinced that wherever Blum was, so was Robert Puller.

Pine drove directly to the FBI's New York Field Office, filled out an affidavit, had it notarized, then scanned it to Dobbs in Arizona. She noticed that several agents passed by and looked at her intently.

Is something going on here I'm not aware of?

For a panicked second she had the most horrible thought imaginable: The Bureau had also been compromised and she had been sent here by a devious Dobbs just so she could be arrested on some trumped-up charge.

As she was pondering whether to make a run for it, a man in his fifties, tall and imposing, and dressed in a dark suit with a blue tie over a stiff white shirt, came up to her.

"Agent Pine?"

"Yes?" Something about the man seemed familiar. She tensed.

"I'm Warren Graham. I'm the SAC here."

That's why Pine thought she knew the man. Graham was the special agent in charge of the Bureau's New York Field Office; it and the Field Office in DC were the top two outposts in the Bureau's universe. He was higher in the pecking order than Clint Dobbs, by a lot.

"I'd like to talk to you. In private."

Pine was led to a small conference room, and Graham shut the door.

Pine's heart was banging so hard, she thought she saw her shirt move.

Graham perched on the edge of the table and said, "Clint Dobbs and I were bunkmates at Quantico. We've remained close friends over the years. He phoned me after you talked to him."

Pine put a hand against the wall to steady herself because she had no idea what was coming.

"We've been looking at some of the same things you have, Pine. In fact, I'll let you in on something. There are three other luxury apartments operating in the same manner in addition to the one that you learned of and informed Clint about."

"So you know what they're doing?"

"We believe so, yes. The Russians call it *kompromat*. The Saudis have another term for it, as do the Chinese."

"Are they all involved in this, sir?"

"Actually, we don't think it's foreign states behind this, Pine. We think it's a private group that is doing this for the oldest reason in the book: money."

"Did you know about Gorman and Franklin?"

"No, our attention had not turned to them as yet. We're getting search warrants and surveillance authorizations as we speak." He paused and looked chagrined. "I know Nora. I, uh, I have to say I'm surprised. I never would have suspected."

"I guess that's sort of the point, sir."

"You are exactly right about that, Pine. And it's another example of how in this game you are never too old to learn something new." His brow creased. "I understand that there are two possible hostages?"

"My assistant, Carol Blum, and Lieutenant Colonel Robert Puller with the Air Force."

"Gorman has them?"

"That's what we believe."

"We've done a quick and dirty on Gorman. Since he's head of Nora's security detail, he doesn't have the level of disclosures and vetting that ordinarily takes place for *staffers*."

"Which is why they set it up that way, I'm sure."

"Precisely. Am I to understand that the military is also on top of the search for Colonel Puller?"

"Yes, I believe they are. At least they're working on it."

She prayed that Puller had made progress on that from his hospital bed.

"Good. Well, Pine, you've done enough for now. You look dead on your feet. Go get some rest. You'll be no good to us if you're exhausted. It's going to be a very busy next few days." He paused. "And God help us if this thing turns out to be as deep as I think it is." He took out his business card and handed it to her. "My personal cell is on there."

Pine left and went back to her car. She wanted to do something, anything, but there was nothing else to do right now.

She drove back to Lineberry's condo and dropped into bed fully clothed. She pulled out the photo of her sister and stared at it for the longest time before she fell into a tortured sleep.

CHAPTER

64

PULLER LEANED BACK against his hospital pillow and stared at his phone. He had had to start hiding it from the nurses, who all wanted him to rest and sleep and —

Not do my damn job.

He had slept badly, despite the meds, and had been lying there for an hour desperately trying to come up with some way to turn the tables on this thing. He had made three calls. Not a single person had called him back, which was frustrating, but more worrying than frustrating.

His mind raced as he thought about who else might be out there who could help on this. If he could only find a person who had been affected by this, then he might —

Idiot.

He pecked in the number on his phone. It went to voice mail. He sighed. Not again. He left a detailed message and then let the phone drop next to him.

He eyed his vitals monitor. They all looked good. He remembered once back in Afghanistan opening his eyes and realizing he was in a field hospital after being wounded. The vitals monitor then had not looked nearly as encouraging. He hadn't known that one's blood pressure could go that low and the person still be alive.

He tried to move his injured shoulder just a bit and gritted his teeth. Even with the pain meds that was not a smart thing to do, he realized. And so he stopped and let his body relax. But when he looked at the phone he tensed once more.

Come on, come on, ring.

Five minutes went by, then ten. Ten became twenty.

He was starting to give up hope.

Then it buzzed. He grabbed it so fast with the hand on his good side that his injured side screamed in protest.

"Hello?" he said.

"Puller, it's Tom Pitts."

"Thank you for calling me back, sir. And I want to say how sorry I am for what happened to you. I was the one who called you in on this. I never imagined it would cost you your assignment at the Pentagon."

"No, Puller, *I'm* the one who needs to apologize. After we met at my office, I made some calls and follow-up inquiries. I thought I was actually making some progress. And then the next thing I knew I got rolled over by an Abrams tank. The Army is a funny mistress, Puller. And when you overlay the politics on top of it—and I'm not just talking about military politics, but on the suit-and-tie side across the Potomac—it gets complicated real fast. Now, I've gotten pretty adroit at reading those tea leaves and can usually see trouble coming from miles away. But not on this one. Seven A.M. I was having my first cup of coffee. Eight fifteen, I was ordered to pack my bags and head out to an assignment overseas. In the Netherlands, of all places."

"Is that where you are now?"

"I fly out the day after tomorrow."

"Well, again, I'm sorry I got you involved in this, sir."

"I'm not. It stinks to high heaven. And I don't intend to take this lying down, Puller. And while I know whoever did this has some major pull, I'm not without firepower when it comes to that."

"That's why I was calling, actually. I wanted to fill you in on developments."

"Where are you calling from?"

Puller hesitated but then decided to just say it. "A hospital bed."

"What?"

Puller told him about the shooting.

"And you think it's connected?"

"I know it is, sir."

"Tell me what you know."

In brief, organized sentences, Puller told Pitts about Nora Franklin and Adam Gorman. And Peter Driscoll's grandson Jeff Sands having been killed by the same bullet that had wounded Puller. He also filled in the general on the possible blackmail chamber operating in New York City. And he finished with his brother and an FBI employee gone missing.

"You think they've been captured by these people?"

"I can't think of another reason why they haven't answered their phones or called us back. I've called other people to help me out, but no one came back to me except you."

"They're circling the wagons, then," said Pitts. "I know many folks in the military who have confronted many an enemy on the battlefield and fought him tooth and nail, sustaining injuries and defeat, but fighting on until victory. And I've seen these very same people turn into cowards and run and hide at the first hint of a subpoena or a demotion or a call from a suit who doesn't deserve one ounce of respect. But perhaps unlike the others you called who never called back, I've got a dog in this hunt. I earned my four stars, and I earned my position at the Pentagon. And I don't take kindly to people screwing with me. If they think I'm going to take this lying down, they don't know shit about me. Even if you hadn't called, I was going public with this thing before I left the country. When someone hits me, I damn well hit back. Just harder."

"You sound just like my father."

"I'll take that as the highest compliment you could give me." Then Pitts's tone changed. It became more thoughtful. "Robert Puller, eh? A lieutenant colonel in the Air Force with the highest security clearances and a wealth of knowledge about our most precious military secrets."

"Yes sir."

"We need to get him back. Any idea where they might be located?"

"We're working on it, sir, I promise."

"Give me two hours, Puller. I still have some chits to call in. I think I can get it done. After that I just need a target."

"I was hoping you would say that. And can I ask a favor?"

"Yes. Anything."

"I know a certain FBI agent named Atlee Pine who would like to be involved."

"Can she carry her weight?"

"There will be no problem there, General."

As soon as he finished with Pitts he called Pine and filled her in on the particulars of what he was planning with General Pitts.

"Thanks for putting in a plug for me to be part of it," she said sleepily.

"You'd do the same for me."

She, in turn, filled him in on her conversation with Warren Graham.

"So we have the Bureau and hopefully the military coming at them from different flanks," said Puller.

"I think it's going to take all the firepower we can muster," said Pine. "Hey, don't military personnel carry RFID microchips in them, particularly an asset like your brother, so they can be tracked down easily?"

"They once thought about doing that, but it was too invasive and, more importantly for the military, too expensive. And there were the privacy concerns. And what do you do when they leave the military? Take it out? So, instead, the military issues GPS trackers that personnel turn in when they muster out."

"Okay, makes sense." Pine tried and failed to stifle a yawn.

"And I'm sorry for calling so late. I know I woke you."

"You're shaming me, Puller. You're in a hospital bed with a gunshot wound and you're still working, while my lazy butt is sleeping. Call me anytime you want."

Puller laid his phone aside and stared at the ceiling. He looked down at the lines covering him and sighed, feeling helpless for the second time in his life. The first time had been the situation with his father's dementia. He couldn't beat that on a battlefield. And now here he was helpless again.

Shit.

65

Pɪɴᴇ ᴀᴡᴏᴋᴇ ᴡɪᴛʜ ᴀ ᴊᴏʟᴛ late the following morning and jumped out of bed ready to hit the ground running, her heart racing and her nerves at their highest level. She tottered there for an instant before thinking, *What the hell are you doing? Calm down.*

She made some coffee and thought about the call from Puller the night before. It sounded like he had the assets to get this done, and now they just needed a location to strike. She checked her phone to see if by any miracle either Blum or Robert Puller had phoned or texted her while she had been asleep. They hadn't.

There *was* a text from Clint Dobbs acknowledging receipt of her scanned affidavit. He also added that the ball was rolling, that he had a strategy, and that the Bureau was fully mobilized on this. She was to follow up on any leads she had and relay any progress to both him and Graham.

She let out a long sigh. She had never liked Clint Dobbs all that much. But she did trust the man. He could not be bought, not by anyone.

She spooned some yogurt into her mouth and chomped down on a piece of toast. Then she showered, got dressed, and gunned up. She raced down to the garage, got into her car, and drove off.

Pine was sick of reacting to other people's moves.

It was time to take the fight to them.

She drove straight to Nora Franklin's office building and found a parking spot on the street. She knew she would need luck to help her at this juncture. If the woman had gone back to DC or to her office in upstate New York, Pine was screwed.

A half hour later the law enforcement gods answered the call.

A cab pulled up in front of the federal building and Nora Franklin got out and walked inside.

Pine immediately went to the same café where Blum had set up her surveillance.

A light rain had started to fall and the sky was darkening quickly.

She got a seat by the window and stayed there, sipping on a coffee and nibbling on a tuna sandwich. After three hours, one of the employees asked if she needed anything else. The clear implication was for her to leave, though the place was by no means full. Pine ordered another coffee and a bag of chips.

As Pine sat there she suddenly thought of something, maybe a way to get where they needed to go. She pulled out Warren Graham's card and called his cell. He answered on the second ring.

She told him where she was and what her plan was.

"That's risky, Pine, very risky. It could turn out disastrous."

"As disastrous as losing two of our finest, sir?"

He didn't answer for a long moment while Pine held her breath.

"Do it, Pine. And don't screw it up." He gave her a phone number to call when she accomplished her mission. Then he clicked off. Pine could feel the tension in the ether. If they blew this, she, Graham, and everyone associated with this investigation were history. The bad guys would win and America would be done.

At seven o'clock, with the rain ever increasing and the gloom of night falling, Nora Franklin finally came out of the building, a slim leather briefcase tapping against her leg. She must have called an Uber because a Prius pulled up in front of the building right as she came out. She got in and the Prius drove off.

Pine had already gone to her car and now followed her. The Prius drove to a restaurant in midtown Manhattan, and Franklin exited the car and walked into the place.

Pine made the driver of a town car move out of his parking spot by flashing her FBI badge. She pulled into the spot and waited.

Dobbs texted her twenty minutes later to tell her of the latest steps the Bureau had taken. She texted him back and told him what she was doing.

His next text was enlightening.

Dozens of search warrants about to be executed. Wiretaps already in place for Franklin et al. This thing is about to explode.

She texted back, *First time I've smiled in a long time, sir.*

Pine put her phone away, got out, and walked past the plate glass window of the restaurant. She couldn't see Franklin. She chanced walking in and looking around. There she was in the back, talking to a man Pine didn't recognize. Too bad. If it had been Gorman, Pine would have arrested him on the spot.

She went back out and got into her car.

At a little after nine Franklin came back out and hailed a cab. Pine followed.

They made their way south, down the West Side Highway, until the car turned left and navigated toward Greenwich Village, with its historic, high-dollar houses, oddly angled streets, and reputation as one of the most expensive zip codes in the area.

Old. Prestigious. And isolated, well, as much as it could be in New York City. Small-town feel. Locally owned restaurants. With fifty-dollar entrees and twenty-dollar cocktails.

The cab stopped in front of a four-story stone beauty with twin flickering gas lanterns bordering the blue painted front door with a brass knocker. It was attached to another stately home, though that house seemed to be vacant and undergoing renovation. Spend a fortune to buy an old house here and spend a second fortune making it livable, thought Pine.

Must be nice.

The old brick steps leading up to Franklin's house were bracketed by ornate wrought iron railings. The place looked old but had obviously been meticulously restored.

Pine wedged into a parking spot as the door on the cab opened and Franklin got out. The cab pulled away and Franklin headed up the steps. She never heard Pine until she was right behind her.

"Security team have the night off?" Pine said.

Franklin whirled around. Pine could see a small canister held in her hand.

"Pepper spray?" said Pine. "It's legal here so long as you buy it from an authorized source and fill out the necessary paperwork, which, being such a VIP, I'm sure you had a flunky do for you."

"Who the hell are you?" snapped Franklin, looking around as though hoping to see a passing police car.

Pine held out her badge and creds. "FBI Special Agent Atlee Pine. I need to speak with you."

Franklin's eyes had widened when she heard the name.

"Right," said Pine. "I was pretty sure you'd been kept in the loop on me. I suppose Gorman did the honors."

"If you want to meet with me, call my office and make an appointment. But I have to tell you it won't be happening anytime soon. I'm a very busy woman, Agent Pine."

"Oh, I know you are. Serving two or more masters instead of only one must really eat into your free time."

Franklin smiled politely. "I have no idea what that remark means, but it sounds like it's dangerously close to a slander action. Now, if you'll excuse me?"

Instead, Pine drew closer. "The problem for you is Gorman screwed up. He kidnapped people, one of whom works for the FBI. I know you have pull, but I doubt it's enough to overcome that one."

"I really have no idea what you are talking about."

"You won't deny that Gorman works for you?"

"Of course not. Adam has been with me a long time. He's the best in the business."

"Yes. But the business he's in is illegal. Blackmailing people in positions of power? Murder, kidnapping? That'll get you a long time in prison. Far longer than the time you've served in Congress."

For the first time Pine could see just the glimmer of panic in the woman's green eyes.

A group of young people with NYU sweatshirts trooped around

the corner. They had obviously been drinking and they hooted and waved stupidly at the pair.

Pine glanced at the front door and said, "Maybe this would be better conducted inside?"

Franklin glanced at the students. She said nothing but pulled out her key and unlocked the door, beckoning Pine to follow her in.

CHAPTER

66

"WHAT A LOVELY HOUSE," said Pine sarcastically as they entered the front room.

The floors were marble, the walls upholstered in what looked to be silk, and with the very finest wood trimmings done by an expert hand on the miter saw. The furnishings clearly coincided with the price tag of the real estate, and the paintings on the walls would not have seemed out of place in any of the myriad museums housed throughout the city.

"Thank you," said Franklin just as sarcastically.

A young woman dressed in a domestic's uniform entered the room and greeted the congresswoman.

"Ms. Franklin, do you need anything?"

"No, Lily, you can go up to your room. I won't require anything else tonight."

Lily glanced at Pine. "Would your friend like some refreshment? Carl is still in the kitchen."

"No, you can tell Carl that he can turn in for the night as well. I will let my 'friend' out later."

"Yes ma'am." Lily turned and hurried out, closing the door behind her.

"Let's go to my study," said Franklin curtly.

She led Pine down a long hall that, instead of marble, was floored in random-width walnut planks. She opened one of a set of double doors and motioned Pine inside.

She closed the door behind them and Pine eyed the book-lined room, the fire crackling and popping away in the hearth. There was a lovely wooden desk with leather trimmings and a set of antique writing instruments displayed on the surface that looked like they cost a mint. The carpet underneath Pine's feet was thick and forgiving. The whole atmosphere was of a great English country house dropped smack into lower Manhattan.

There was a bar set up against one wall. "Would you like a drink?" Franklin said.

"No, but help yourself. You may need one."

Franklin flinched for a moment but then poured out a snifter of brandy and swirled the liquid around in the glass.

She was dressed conservatively in a tailored dark blue dress suit. Franklin undid the bun in her hair and let the blond tresses flutter down to her shoulders. She sat down in a high-back chair and Pine sat across from her on a small settee.

Franklin took off her heels and rubbed her feet.

"You'd think by now women wouldn't have to wear these damn things."

"I think you're a woman in a position to wear what you want, unlike a lot of other women. But that's not what I came here to talk about."

"Okay, what *did* you come here to talk about, other than to make wild, unsubstantiated allegations?"

"Your net worth is really impressive. This house alone is worth what, five, ten mill easy? And you have another place in upstate New York, right?"

"And I have another place in the south of France. A charming villa." Franklin took a sip of the brandy and let it slide down her throat. The look she gave Pine was one of amusement, which Pine decided not to let go.

"For a woman who's been in Congress for the last dozen or so years at a fixed salary of a hundred seventy-five thousand and change, that's really quite an achievement."

"I was a lawyer before that."

"Right, but only for a few years. And not in any practice field that pays big bucks."

"I invested well."

"And your position in Congress allows you to write laws that concern companies that you're invested in, I know."

"That would be a conflict of interest."

"Of course it is, but it still happens. Because people in Congress write the laws in a way that allows them loopholes the size of the Grand Canyon. And the burden of proof on public corruption is so high that it's almost impossible to get a conviction, so prosecutors have just stopped trying."

"Thank you to the United States Supreme Court for that. But if you have a complaint, you can speak to my assistants."

"I think you probably have done the conflict-of-interest thing. But I doubt that's where the bulk of your fortune came from. Your official financial disclosures only have to give broad ranges. You don't have to disclose the value of your principal residence, and assets in certain trusts don't have to be valued and disclosed at all. I would assume that you take advantage of all of those loopholes."

"On the contrary, I take no steps to hide my wealth. You knew where I lived, or else you followed me here. I've had parties and fund-raisers here, and at my other residences. My personal financial history is transparent."

"Not even close. And members of Congress don't have to undergo security background checks. So there could be a lot in your background that we don't know."

"The media would have ferreted out any issues. And if you're questioning my patriotism, we take an oath of secrecy, and as a member of the Intel Committee I took a separate oath."

"Just words, nothing more."

"I'm an *elected* official. The voters have vouched for my integrity by casting their ballot for me. So that case is closed."

Pine shook her head. "That hardly does it in my book."

"Look, it's been a long day and I need to get to bed."

"Trust me, your days are going to get longer."

Franklin sat forward and snarled, "I'm getting tired of this back-and-forth bullshit. And just so you know, vague threats do not move me. Try it again and you'll be looking at a lawsuit for slander.

And a congressional investigation into how the FBI vets its agents. I doubt the FBI director likes his agents going rogue."

Pine sat forward, too. "Then let me make it a little less *vague*. All the penthouses are under surveillance. Any time now you're going to get served with search warrants along with God knows how many other high-ranking officials and CEOs and judges and cops and other traitors."

"Do you think I've been blackmailed, Agent Pine?"

"I don't recall mentioning anything about blackmail. I wonder why you would."

Franklin tensed but then relaxed and sipped her brandy. "I made an assumption based on what you just told me. I'm allowed that, right? People in high places? Traitors?"

"Do you really want to know why I'm here?"

"Certainly. Then maybe we can draw this meeting to a close."

"I can cut you a deal."

Franklin almost spilled her drink. "A deal? I'm a lawyer, Pine. I'm assuming you're not. So don't try to intimidate me. I eat people like you for lunch."

"You weren't a *criminal* lawyer, but I'll give you the benefit of the doubt. They killed Jeff Sands. They gunned down Tony Vincenzo on a beach in New Jersey. Lindsey Axilrod, or whatever her real name is, was going to stick him with some shit in a syringe before I *temporarily* rescued him."

"I know none of those people and you have no proof that I do."

"By tomorrow the proof will be there. Do you want to be ahead of the curve, or behind it and in a jail cell?"

"The FBI really needs to start hiring higher-caliber personnel. I will be delighted to subpoena you to appear before one of my committees. I will tear you to shreds. You'll lose your badge and what little dignity you might have left. You can spend the next fifty years in regret."

"Do I take that as a no?"

"This meeting is over," snapped Franklin. "Please leave, now. Or I'll call the police."

Pine rose. "Okay, then I'll give Gorman the deal instead. He'll probably claim you ordered the killings *and* the kidnapping of an FBI employee and an Air Force lieutenant colonel. SAC Graham doesn't care where the inside help comes from. He told me it's full throttle all the way."

Franklin paled just a bit and her voice changed. "Graham? You spoke to Warren Graham?"

"He *is* head of the New York Field Office. Who else would be heading up an operation the size and complexity of this one?"

"Operation?"

"Yes, it's official title is Operation Stars and Stripes." She looked down at the woman in all her smugness. "But it has an unofficial name, just for the amusement of us FBI types."

"And what, pray tell, is that?" asked Franklin, giving Pine a cocksure smile.

"Operation Kiss Your Ass Good-bye."

Pine let herself out of the mansion.

67

Pᴵɴᴇ ᴄʟɪᴍʙᴇᴅ ɪɴᴛᴏ ʜᴇʀ ᴄᴀʀ and sped off. But she merely drove around the corner and parked. She called the number she had been given by Warren Graham. A woman's voice immediately answered.

"Okay, Agent Pine, we have the wiretaps on her phones—hardline, cell, and a second cell—and all her email accounts."

"I put the fear of God in her. She should be calling out to Gorman now. Then we can trace the call."

"Roger that. I'll let you know as soon as she initiates contact."

"There are other people in that house. A maid and a cook. What if she uses their phones or email accounts?"

"We have a digital blanket wrap on that house, Agent Pine. Anything coming from there we can sweep up. The warrant was broad enough to cover that."

Pine clicked off and then called Puller. She told him what she had done.

"As soon as she makes the call, email, or text we can trace it. These days they don't have to be on the phone for half an hour. The Bureau can make the connection really fast."

"Where are you now?"

"Outside of Franklin's place in Greenwich Village."

"Give me the exact address so I can relay it to General Pitts."

She did so and added, "But the FBI will be keeping a short leash on her. She's not going anywhere."

"Belt and suspenders, Atlee."

He clicked off.

And Pine waited. And waited. Forty minutes went by. Then an hour.

She called the number again. The woman said, "Nothing, Agent Pine. She's made no call or email or text. We got one text coming out of there about twenty minutes ago. A Lily Walker. It apparently was sent to her boyfriend because it had some, well, it would be reasonable to call it sexting."

Pine's spirits plummeted. How could that be? After their meeting Pine was sure Franklin would try to contact Gorman to warn him. She might try to go see him, too, but that would be far riskier. She would know she would be followed. Had she figured out that her phones had been tapped? Did she have another email account or a burner phone they weren't aware of? If so, her plan was not going to work.

She noticed movement on the street and tensed. Someone had turned the corner from Franklin's residence and was walking toward her. When the person passed under the streetlamp, Pine saw that it was Lily, Franklin's maid. Was Franklin using her as a messenger somehow?

Going with her gut, Pine got out and quickly crossed the street. The rain had stopped but the air was chilly and the pavement and streets slick.

"Hey."

Lily pulled up, looking fearful at first, and then, recognizing Pine, she relaxed.

"Sorry, didn't mean to scare you."

"Oh, that's okay. What are you still doing around here?"

"I had some other business in the area. I thought you were hitting the sack."

Lily smiled. "I took a catnap. But I'm heading to meet my boyfriend. There's a club in SoHo we want to try."

Pine looked at her watch. "It's after midnight."

Lily smiled. "That's when things start really going."

"Ah, to be young again."

"And my room is pretty small and there's not much to do. But when Ms. Franklin finishes renovating the other house, she said

I'll have my own sitting room and access to an indoor *pool* and a home theater. That will be so cool."

"Other house?" said Pine.

"Yeah, the one next to hers. She bought that last year. She plans to combine it with the existing residence. I don't know why they haven't started construction yet. I thought it would have started a while ago. I'm kind of bummed."

"Lily, is there any connection between the two buildings now?"

"What? Oh yeah, that was the cool thing. Ms. Franklin told me. See, those two homes used to be owned by the same person, like nearly a hundred and fifty years ago. Then, at some point, they were separated and sold as two houses. Talk about minting money. But there's an old passageway between the two. It goes under both houses. Cellar to cellar. It's boarded up now, of course. But I've seen the door to it. Ms. Franklin showed me a while back."

Every muscle in Pine's body tensed. She pulled out her badge and creds. "I'm an FBI agent. And I need to get inside that house now."

"What?" Lily took an anxious step back.

"When was the last time you saw Adam Gorman?"

"Mr. Gorman?" She looked confused for a moment. "He…he came by last night."

"Do you know why?"

"No."

"How long did he stay?"

"I think about an hour."

"How did he come? By car? Did he walk?"

Lily didn't answer right away. She stood there looking pensive. "That was the funny thing."

"What?"

"I never heard a car pull up. I was actually looking out the front window. Then, when I turned and walked back down the hall, there he was with Ms. Franklin, going into the library."

"Could he have come in the back door?"

"No, they're all on a chime. I would have heard it."

Pine was barely listening. "You said there's a connecting passageway between the two houses?"

"Yes, there is. What is going on?"

"I don't have time to explain. Let's go."

As they rushed back down the street, Pine called the woman at the FBI surveillance center and told her what she had just found out.

"We'll get a team there as fast as we can, but if it's listed as a separate residence, we don't have a search warrant for that house, Agent Pine."

"Screw the search warrant. I'm going in."

She texted Puller and relayed the new information. Then they reached Franklin's house.

"Where is Franklin?" asked Pine.

"I thought she went to her room."

"I don't think so. Take me in the back way." Pine pulled her gun.

"You're scaring me," wailed Lily as she glanced at the weapon.

"After we get in there, I need you to take me to the passageway connecting the two houses."

"And then what?"

"And then I want you to get out of the house and go see your boyfriend. And don't come back here."

Lily led her into the back garden and down a set of steps. She unlocked the door and they went inside. Pine made Lily stop and she listened intently. Then she nodded.

Lily led her down a set of steep stairs that ended in a stone passage that smelled of mold and age. At the end of the passage was a door.

"It's open," said Lily, looking alarmed.

"Saves me the trouble," replied Pine. "Now go!"

Lily flew up the steps and out of sight. Pine pulled out her Beretta backup and started down the hall.

CHAPTER

68

THE MUSTY, FUGGY ODORS INCREASED as she moved down the passage. Pine glanced at the walls. They were a mixture of old stones and aged brick. The floor was stone as well. And the temperature had dropped about fifteen degrees. The illumination was a series of single light bulbs with a power line snaking between them.

She rounded a corner and found a partially open door facing her. She eased up to it, trying to move as silently as possible. So much for military quick-strike teams and an overpowering force from the FBI.

It's just me and my two guns until the cavalry gets here, if it ever does.

She slowly peered around the door and two things caught her eye.

A pair of women's shoes that she recognized as belonging to Blum.

And a military dress jacket with its myriad ribbons, no doubt belonging to Robert Puller, was draped over the arm of a wooden-backed spindle chair.

Pine had a sense of inward relief. If their things were here, it was a safe bet that they were, too.

She didn't want to open the door farther, afraid that it might make undue noise. Instead, she squeezed her body past it and entered the small room. There was a hallway running off to her right where the passage no doubt continued.

On a foldup table next to the chair were two empty pizza boxes and three open beers. Pine hoped whoever she was about to confront had been drinking. It might slow their senses long enough to let her prevail against what would undoubtedly be superior numbers.

She stopped to text her location and how she had gotten into the house to the FBI team and Puller. Thankfully, the text went through, even this far down and with stone walls and ceilings.

She continued on down the passage, listening intently for any sound that might give her some intel on who was down here and where they were. Ten more seconds passed, and she heard something that made her freeze.

The raised voice said, "So how the hell do we get out of this?"

It was Franklin's voice. It was tense, angry, and blunt.

The next voice was Gorman's. Pine recognized it from when Gorman was playing the role of police officer after gunning down Jerome Blake.

"Calm down, Nora, I have this covered."

"Bullshit. I told you that you never should have taken them."

"And what exactly did you want me to do? She was filming us in the hotel. She met with Robert Puller in an alley and they were discussing us. Did you want me to just let them walk away?"

"I am telling you that the FBI is about to come down on us like a ton of bricks."

"One agent, this Atlee Pine, put that notion into your head. I have feelers out everywhere and I've heard nothing of the kind."

"She's a good liar, that Atlee Pine," said a new voice.

Pine's fingers tightened around both guns.

It was Lindsey Axilrod.

Axilrod continued, "She knows a lot, too much, but she doesn't know about either of you. She just thinks this is about drugs."

"Now you're the one lying," snapped Franklin. "She told me about the penthouse. She's figured out its true purpose. How the hell did they find out about that?"

Axilrod groaned. "Shit, Tony. He must've found out."

"And she mentioned Warren Graham."

Gorman snapped, "She's full of crap. If Graham were onto us I would know, trust me."

"Well, we have to get rid of Puller and the woman," said Axilrod. "And we have to do it now. And then I'm going to find Pine and slit her throat."

The next moment Pine kicked the door open. One pistol was pointed at Gorman, the other at Axilrod.

"Well, here's your chance," said Pine.

They all three turned to the doorway. Franklin screamed as Gorman grabbed her and put her between himself and Pine. He held a knife blade against the woman's neck.

"Put down the gun or she's dead."

"That won't be happening," replied Pine. "So slit away."

Axilrod heaved a chair at Pine and she had to duck. A second later the trio fled out of sight and continued down the passage.

Two shots fired at her kept Pine from charging headlong after them.

She waited a few moments and then peered around the corner. She jumped back as another shot tore a chunk of the wall off. Some of the shrapnel cut her cheek.

She peered back around the corner, saw the hall was clear, and hustled down it. She launched sideways, rolled, and came up firing as another man, large and beefy, charged at her from another doorway. Three rounds from her Glock hit him in the chest, and he slumped against the wall and slowly slid down it, dead.

She kept going and started to sprint as she saw a doorway farther down the hall start to open. She left the floor, leaping forward, then landed a devastating kick against the door, slamming it backward and catching the man behind it flush in the face.

He screamed in pain and tried to lift his pistol.

He never got the chance because Pine crushed his hand between the door and doorjamb. He dropped the gun, fell to his knees, and caught a kick right under his chin, lifting him backward. The back of his head banged into the wall, and he slipped into unconsciousness.

Pine heard someone scream.

It was Blum.

Pine rushed into the room and around a corner. And stopped

dead, her chest heaving and both pistols held out in front of her. She had a myriad of targets.

And two hostages. Three, if she counted Franklin.

From above them, they heard the cacophonies of sirens.

As she faced off with Gorman and Axilrod, she also was looking at Robert Puller and Carol Blum. They were both bound and gagged. And Gorman was pointing one gun at Blum's head, and one at Pine, while Axilrod had her weapon pointed at Puller. Franklin was cowering on the floor in the corner.

"We seem to be at a standoff, Agent Pine," said Gorman calmly.

"I don't see a way out for you," said Pine, lifting her gaze to the ceiling for a moment. "The cavalry is almost here."

"Doesn't matter."

"I'm not sure what you expect to get out of this," said Pine.

"We have hostages. That gives us leverage. You want these people alive, there is a price to be paid."

"I would imagine that you know the FBI does not allow kidnappers to walk out with hostages."

"Then they're dead. Are you prepared for that?"

Pine forced herself not to look at either Blum or Puller.

"I won't be the one pulling the trigger on them. But if you do, I will pull the trigger on you."

Gorman shook his head and smiled. "Goes with the territory."

Pine said to Axilrod, "That go for you, too, Lindsey? Are you sure you can pull the trigger with that bum hand?"

The woman just stared back venomously at Pine and said nothing.

"You need to become more nuanced, Lindsey. Your poker face sucks."

"You're not walking out of here alive, Pine," snapped Axilrod.

"If I had a dollar for every time I've heard that." She glanced at Franklin, "Well, Congresswoman, where do you stand on all this? You ready to go down with the ship?"

Franklin fought back tears and whimpered, "I...I don't know what to do."

"Well, thanks for the help," said Pine derisively.

The sirens had stopped but now they heard feet thundering above them.

Pine slid her fingers right up to the triggers on both her guns.

"You're out of time, Gorman," she said.

"Good-bye, Pine," said Gorman. "You fought the good fight. And see what it got you?"

The shot hit him right in the middle of the forehead, and blood geysered into the air from the entry spot. He slumped to the floor dead.

Pine jumped to the left wondering where the hell the bullet that had just killed Adam Gorman had come from.

Axilrod had ducked down out of the way. Now she screamed and started to raise her gun to shoot Blum, but Pine hit her with a ferocious kick that leveled the woman and sent her gun spinning out of her hand.

When Axilrod tried to struggle to her feet, Pine laid her out with a crushing blow to the jaw that put the woman down for good.

Pine whirled around at the doorway where the kill shot on Gorman had come from.

The door swung slowly open.

And there stood a heavily bandaged and pale John Puller, his M11 dangling down next to his right side. In a flash, Pine realized that Puller had fired through the gap between the back edge of the door and the doorjamb.

"John?" said a bewildered Pine. "What in the hell?"

"Army strong, Atlee," he said quietly before collapsing to the floor.

CHAPTER

69

"THERE WILL BE *VERY* LIMITED public disclosure of this," said Warren Graham.

He was sitting in a conference room at the New York Field Office. Arrayed around him were Pine, the two Pullers, and Carol Blum.

"Why?" said Pine sharply.

Graham placed his hands palms down on the table as though he needed additional support for what he was about to say.

"It's complicated and multilayered, but I'll give you the Cliffs-Notes version." He paused, seemingly to marshal his thoughts. "We have dozens and dozens of open indictments. They range from politicians at the federal and state levels to Wall Street money types to CEOs to judges to bureaucrats to cops to intel agents, and even to some people who 'used' to work for the Bureau. There will be more indictments as this unfolds. We have also arrested twenty foreign suspects."

"So were other countries behind this?" asked Robert Puller.

"Doubtful. Our counterparts in other countries are now investigating similar operations going on there. Apparently, blackmail and pay-to-play ops do not stop at one country's borders."

When Pine started to say something, Graham lifted his hand. "Let me finish, Agent Pine. I will not downplay the seriousness of all of this. We all paid the price for their dereliction of duty. Now, some of them were innocent dupes, caught up in something that they never imagined would happen to them."

Pine could contain herself no longer. "But they had choices, sir.

They could have gone to the police. They could have come to us. They could have gone public."

Robert Puller added, "Or they could have resigned their positions and thus taken away the possibility that they could use their positions to hurt this country."

"They could have done all those things," agreed Graham. "But none of them, not a one that we know of, at least, chose to do so."

John Puller said, "But after having been blackmailed, why wouldn't they warn others about this scheme? I mean, if they knew colleagues were going to these places and would be filmed and then blackmailed?"

"I have personally questioned seven of them on that very point. Their answers were remarkably the same: They were ashamed and they couldn't bring themselves to tell anyone else their secret. And after they used their official positions to further their blackmailer's biddings, well, it became legally impossible for them to admit to anything without suffering the consequences. That is a blackmailer's stock in trade."

Robert Puller said, "So how bad was the damage?"

"Very bad," said Graham grimly. "It will take us years to unravel it all. But it does explain many decisions and acts by public officials and companies and other interests across a broad spectrum. They were serving another master, not the people of this country. The public servants violated their oath of office. The others committed serious felonies. This thing has apparently been going on for quite some time."

Robert Puller said, "But Gorman and the like were being paid by others to blackmail these people to take the action they did. What about those folks? They are definitely enemies of this country. There needs to be consequences."

"We're interviewing people and compiling those lists. More indictments will come, as I said. I can tell you preliminarily that other nation states, foreign and domestic companies, and other monied interests are on those lists. If they couldn't win by healthy competition, they apparently resorted to cheating by having folks in positions of power side with them for fear of their own sordid secrets coming out. Blackmailers usually just want money. Gorman and the others were playing a more sophisticated game. A court decision here, a law passed there, a merger okayed or not, a criminal prosecution dropped, a company making a decision to leave a market, the possibilities were endless."

"Why did they have the parties up there for Tony Vincenzo and the others?" asked Blum.

Graham said, "They were filming them, too, and many of them were doing drugs and other illegal activities and engaging in things that might be embarrassing if they were ever made public. They figured it was a way to keep them in line down the road. Stay the course or the film ends up with the cops."

"What about Peter Driscoll?" said Pine.

"Ironically, we could find no evidence that Driscoll was involved in this. But he's not entirely blame free, either. Turns out his grandson, Jeff Sands, tried repeatedly to meet with him to seek help for his drug addiction. Driscoll never did so, apparently afraid that conceding that he had a drug-dealing relative, even one who was trying to beat his addiction, would tarnish his own reputation."

"And Nora Franklin?" said Pine.

"One of the first recruits to the scheme. We've thoroughly interviewed her. That trip she and Gorman took overseas? It was to get her into the fold. She came back and immediately sought political office, backed by Gorman and his associates. And she won, and kept winning, gaining seats on powerful committees and relaying top secret information to Gorman, who, in turn, sold it to our enemies for top dollar. And she gained a fortune in the bargain."

"And the opponent in her last election?" said John Puller.

"Became a significant threat. Franklin had begun to ignore her constituents. A local and charismatic businessman who was running on a campaign of reform came out of nowhere and was leading her by double digits."

"How did they blackmail him?" asked Puller.

"They couldn't find a way to do that, so they took a different angle. He grew seriously ill and had to drop out of the race. The doctors couldn't identify what was wrong and he was still suffering. But knowing what we did, we had him tested for a variety of poisons. It was an industrial chemical that he was somehow exposed to. Now that they know, he can be treated. He'll never be cured, unfortunately. But it can be managed."

"Well, he's luckier than Jerome Blake or Agent McElroy," said Pine. "Jerome died because he knew about Jewel's having sex at that penthouse. They were afraid of who he might talk to. And while McElroy was the one to die, I think they were aiming at John and me. But regardless, they were always going to pin it on Jerome to get him out of the way and scare Jewel into never talking."

"I think you're right about that," said Graham.

"What about Lindsey Axilrod?" asked Pine.

"Her real name is Svetlana Semenov. She was an agent with the FSS, which is the successor to the KGB. She's been in this country for years after having her real identity thoroughly laundered through three different countries. She is a real IT expert, and that landed her the job at Fort Dix."

"But I thought you said foreign states were not involved in this," said Robert Puller.

"Semenov wasn't working for the FSS, at least not for the last ten years. We've had discussions with our counterparts over there. She went AWOL around that time. I think she eventually hooked up with Gorman and they decided to go the private route, with money as the objective."

"And what will happen to her?" asked Pine.

"That will largely be up to DOJ and the State Department. She could be a powerful chit."

"You are not thinking about a prisoner exchange or anything like that," said Pine sharply.

"If it were up to me, the woman would never see the light of day, but it's not up to me," retorted Graham. "Then again, sending her back to the Russians, after she screwed them over?" He smiled. "That might be the best thing we could do to punish her."

"And what will happen to Franklin?" asked Pine.

"Oh, she's going to prison. We're going to do a deal with her to avoid the need for a trial. The charges will remain sealed. She will never speak of it publicly. The basic rationale will be put down to financial misdeeds."

"So it will all be buried," said Pine. "I just don't get that, sir."

"I never said I was in agreement with it, Pine. And that decision came from several levels above me. The down-and-dirty explanation I was given was that if the public found out, they could never trust their leaders again."

"Well, they apparently *can't* trust their leaders, so isn't that the point?" interjected Robert Puller.

"Well, even with the breadth of this scheme, these folks only represent a small fraction of people in positions of power and influence."

Pine said, "You know some journalists are going to start digging into this and they're going to uncover the truth and people are going to win slews of Pulitzers off this."

"And part of me hopes that they do," replied Graham. "Freedom of the press is in the very *first* amendment, after all." He paused again and surveyed them. "But with that said, you will have to hold this in the strictest confidence all the way to the grave. I'm certain I can count on you for that."

It wasn't spoken as a question.

Then Graham said, "I was told to make that statement to you, and I did. What I wasn't told to say is what I'm going to say now. Each of you put your lives on the line for your country. If it were up to me, the public would know all about it and would be singing your praises, and you would be given all the awards and recognition that you undoubtedly deserve. That would be in an ideal world. We, unfortunately, do not live in that kind of a world. But I want you to know that certain people *do* know of your sacrifice and loyalty to this country, and they wanted me to extend their thanks and through them the heartfelt gratitude of a nation. And now I will stop making speeches, and all of you can go on with your lives. However, if there is anything that you need, all you have to do is call me." He glanced at Pine. "And my old friend, Clint Dobbs, is lucky to have you out there in Arizona. Tell him to be careful—other field offices might want to snatch you up, starting with this one."

"I'll be sure to tell him that, sir," said Pine. "Everyone needs a bargaining chip now and then."

They all filed out. The Puller brothers walked ahead of them and were in conversation.

Pine said to Blum. "I'm so sorry for all this, Carol. I know I keep apologizing, but I feel awful."

"Please don't, Agent Pine. Aside from being beaten and almost killed, it was very exciting. Put a spring in my step."

"You really are a national treasure, Carol Blum."

"Remember to put in a good word for me when it's time for salary review."

"Oh, I see quite a nice bump in your pay after this. And Dobbs may finally approve a new SUV for me. The one I drive now has two hundred and fifty thousand miles on it."

"Would you ever actually think of going to another field office?"

"No, but if I ever do, I'll check with you first."

"Well, I would hope you would give me a heads-up if you were leaving."

Pine gripped her by the shoulder. "You're missing my point. We're a package deal. If I go, you go, too. And if you won't go, I won't, either. Now, I need to talk to the Pullers."

They caught up with the brothers.

"How are you feeling, John?" she asked.

Puller was still bandaged up but looking far healthier and stronger. "Almost back to normal. I'll still need more rehab. Although I am persona non grata at a certain New York City hospital ever since I 'escaped' that night."

"And boy, am I glad you did," said his brother. "Your timing was spot-on, as usual."

The Pullers looked at Pine's grim features, and their joking manner quickly dissipated.

"What is it, Atlee?" said John Puller.

"I need some information on two Vietnam-era soldiers."

"You know their names?"

"One you already know. Ito Vincenzo. The other is a Leonard Atkins. He lives or he lived in Taliaferro County, Georgia. He apparently served with Ito Vincenzo. And Atkins apparently saved his life over there."

"And why is Atkins important?" asked Puller.

Pine held up the photo of Mercy. "Because that's who Ito gave my sister to."

CHAPTER

70

THE FLIGHT TO ATLANTA FROM NEW YORK was not even three hours. Yet to Pine it felt like three years. She sat next to Blum, alternating between staring out the window and looking at the old Polaroid. She had scrutinized it so many times, it surprised her when she saw a detail she hadn't observed before. The long hairs on Mercy's exposed legs. The tear in the shoulder of her dress. How her little finger was bent in at an awkward angle. What looked like a severe burn on her ankle.

And behind the three people and next to the mobile trailer, the snout and curved ears of a large hog. And behind that, ominously, a steel peg in the ground with a chain attached.

Surely for a dog, thought Pine. *Surely.*

Blum turned and saw what Pine was doing. She reached over and gripped her hand, surprising her boss for an instant before Pine smiled embarrassedly. "I guess it's sort of crazy to keep looking at this picture."

"It's not crazy, it's perfectly natural. I can't imagine what you must be feeling right now. But what you should keep in mind is how much progress you've made, Agent Pine. Look at where we're headed right now. A short time ago did you ever think this would be possible?"

Pine squeezed her hand. "You're right, Carol. And thanks for helping me keep this in perspective."

They landed and drove in a rental car straight to Jack Lineberry's house about an hour south of Atlanta.

He was sitting up in a chair in his bedroom at the palatial estate.

Looking out a window to the rear grounds, Pine saw where the cottage had been—the cottage that had been bombed while she had been inside it. It had been demolished, and a crew was now rebuilding it. They were finishing up pouring a new foundation. She saw stacks of boards lying nearby. She assumed those would be used to frame the house next.

She glanced at Lineberry, a tall, handsome man in his sixties, as he sat in a chair. He looked pale and still weak, but there was strength in the hug he had given her and his eyes were clear and focused.

When Pine showed him the photo, he at first shook his head, and then his chin dropped, and the man began to weep. This was so unexpected that Pine didn't know what to do. Blum put a comforting arm around his quaking shoulders.

Then it struck Pine.

Shit, you idiot, that's his daughter.

That truth had come so recently to Pine that it hadn't even occurred to her when she handed him the photo.

"I'm sorry, Jack," she said, kneeling down on the other side of him. "I just wasn't thinking clearly."

He waved her apology away and composed himself. He handed her back the photo. "Do you know where that was taken?"

"Taliaferro County. North and east of here. Ito Vincenzo could have made it there and back in one day. Which he did."

"And you're sure this is…Mercy?"

"I have other evidence which supports that conclusion."

"The Atkinses, Len, Wanda, and Becky?"

"Ito served in the Army with Leonard Atkins. I found out Atkins was severely wounded. He came back to the States, was discharged, and moved back to Georgia."

Lineberry looked puzzled. "But if he was of Ito's generation, he would be far older than would be typical for someone wanting a child Mercy's age. I'm presuming that Ito brought Mercy to them as…I don't want to say a gift, but you know what I mean."

"You're right. But during a battle with the North Vietnamese, Atkins saved Vincenzo's life. That's how he was wounded. The wound was in an area that made him…it caused Atkins to be unable to father children."

Lineberry's eyes narrowed. "Okay, I hope I'm wrong, but I see where this might be going."

"I believe Ito kidnapped Mercy and took her to the Atkinses to repay Leonard Atkins. There was a letter from Atkins to Ito that basically said that."

"Stealing a child to repay a debt? That is sick," said Lineberry.

"But it may also be the truth."

Blum said, "But why did he try to kill you? Why not just either take you both or do something less than attempted murder?"

Pine looked at the photo. "I've been giving that a lot of thought. From everything we've been able to learn about Ito, he was not a violent mobster type like his brother. But he *was* angry when he learned that Bruno thought he'd gotten screwed on a prison deal. And he blamed my mother. But I don't think he was some monster. I think he was caught between a rock and a hard place. And when it came to it, I think he just wanted to take one of us. That's why he did the nursery rhyme. Then he tried to knock me out so I couldn't raise the alarm. But he hit me way too hard. And I nearly died."

"But how could he have found your family in the first place?" barked an agitated Lineberry.

Pine leaned away from him. "We met up with your ex-fiancée."

"You talked to Linda? You didn't tell me that."

"I'm telling you now."

"What did she say?"

"What I thought she would."

He shook his head. "No, there is no way. I can't believe it."

"She *was* the leak. She admitted it. She had you followed, she searched your briefcase, she overheard conversations. She met with Bruno; she found out about him through a mob buddy of his. She was even going to rep him, but another attorney took over for some reason. She steamed open a letter of yours that laid out my parents' new identities and where they were going to live in Andersonville, and she made sure that Bruno got it.

And he told his brother a sob story and guilted an otherwise law-abiding man into coming down to Georgia and turning into the devil."

For a moment Pine thought Lineberry might faint or have a heart attack or lash out at her. There were so many emotions sweeping over his features, and his body tensed and untensed to such a degree that she grabbed his arm to make sure he didn't slide out of the chair.

He finally put a hand to his face and quietly started to weep again.

Pine looked at Blum, who shook her head and put a hand to her lips signaling Pine just to remain quiet.

A long minute passed before Lineberry finally straightened and wiped at his eyes. Blum gave him a hand towel from a table next to the chair, while Pine poured him out a glass of water from a pitcher on the table.

He wiped his face, drank the water, and sat back in the chair, looking about a decade older than he had two minutes before. He gripped Pine's hand.

"I am so sorry, Atlee. So sorry. This is all my fault."

"No, it's not, Jack. You trusted someone who abused that trust. But to be fair, I can understand her anger. You *did* leave her for my mother. You had two daughters with my mother."

Lineberry passed a hand over his forehead. "I loved Linda with all my heart. Right up until the moment I met your mother. Then, for me, there was no one else. I'm not proud of what I did, but I'm just telling you the truth. If I had controlled my feelings better…"

"My mother was obviously attracted to you."

Lineberry shook his head. "I was quite a bit older. I was in a position of influence over her. I was a professional who did something stunningly unprofessional. I never thought our relationship would result in pregnancy. I hated myself for having put her in that situation."

"Did Tim know?" asked Pine.

"Please, call him your father. He was more of one to you than I ever was."

"Okay, we sort of skirted around this issue before, but did my *dad* know that you were the father?"

"I never told him. And the timing of when he and your mother met was close enough that he had every reason to believe that he was the father. I don't believe your mother ever told him differently."

"But she loved him?"

Lineberry nodded. "She told me one night. He was her age. He was handsome and funny and just a good person. I could see why she loved him. At least now I can. But I was hurt—devastated, really."

"If that was the case, why did you break things off with Linda? Why did you go to Andersonville? Because it was your job?"

"No, because you were my flesh and blood." He finished his water and slowly put the glass down. "And despite what I told you earlier and how I reacted when you just now told me about Linda...I had suspected that the leak might well be coming from her. I knew she was smart and resourceful. I knew she might have found out about Amanda. It made me angry. And my suspicions caused me to care even less for her. And I needed to get away from her and take Amanda and her family with me, so I could watch over them. But I swear to you that I never knew Linda had found out about Andersonville."

Pine rose and looked down at him. "I believe you, Jack."

"Are you going to see the Atkinses?"

"We are. I have no idea if they're still there or not. It's been over two decades since that picture was taken. I called the police in Taliaferro, but I've heard nothing back."

"Do you have the address?" asked Lineberry.

"I have the letters that Atkins sent Ito. The envelopes had a return address on them. I did a Google map search. It's...remote."

"What will you do if they are still there? And...Mercy is with them?"

"I'll cross that bridge when I come to it. But if Mercy is there, and depending on what condition she's in, I will find a way to tell her the truth, and I will bring her home."

"Will you let me know what you find?"

"Of course I will."

"I hope that…that she's alive and well."

"From your lips to God's ears, Jack," said Pine before walking out.

CHAPTER

71

THEY PULLED ONTO A GRAVEL ROAD and continued down it until the gravel disappeared and the road turned to dirt. And then the dirt turned to wild grass and weeds, and then some young trees blocked their way.

"This doesn't seem promising," said Blum.

Pine added, "Looks like the forest is reclaiming its land."

They got out of the car and threaded their way through this maze, finally emerging into an open area. Next, they came upon a rusted mailbox perched on a rotted, leaning post. Pine looked inside, but it was empty. She examined the faded metal numbers someone had hammered onto the post.

"Matches the number address on the letters the Atkinses sent," said Pine.

They cleared a small bend in the path, and in front of them was the mobile home trailer that they had seen in the photo. It had not aged well. One part of the front wall had fallen off, exposing ratty, filthy insulation. The door was off its hinges, and a section of the roof had collapsed. A large cinder block provided the steps up to the door.

"Clearly no one has lived here in a while," noted Pine. She stepped up to the door and looked through the opening. "Shit!"

She jumped back and her feet hit dirt. She pulled her weapon but didn't fire.

"What is it?" asked an alarmed Blum.

"Snakes," said Pine as she slowly backed away. "Copperheads. A whole nest of them in there, all over the place." She holstered her gun. "Well, we're not going to search in there, not that we'd be able to find much."

"What did Atkins do after he came back from the war?" asked Blum as they walked back to the car.

"I couldn't find out much about him or his family. We need to check in with the local cops. They never did get back to me."

"I wonder why," said Blum.

"Let's go ask them."

They drove to the county seat in Crawfordville and entered the sheriff's office located there. They told the woman at the front desk who they were and what they wanted. She directed them to an office down the hall, where a uniformed man in his thirties sat behind a desk. He was short and wide, his hair was neatly parted on the side, and he was freshly shaved.

Pine again explained who they were and why they were there.

"Go ahead and grab a seat," said the man. "I'm Deputy Sheriff Tyler Wilcox, by the way. You say you contacted us?"

"I left a voice mail and sent an email."

"Huh. Never heard it or saw the email. But we got some glitches in our system."

"I hear you all are the biggest employer in the county," said Pine.

Wilcox chuckled. "We're one of the *only* employers in the county. I'm born and bred here. I love the place, but it's not for everybody. Probably why our population keeps going down."

He shuffled some papers on his desk and then leaned back in his chair. "So you want to find this fellow Leonard Atkins?"

"Yes. We went by his last known address, but it's obviously been abandoned for a very long time. Full of snakes now, in fact."

"Lotta places like that around here," noted Wilcox. "I don't know the name, Agent Pine. But I've only been with the sheriff's office for ten years. From what you're saying this goes back a lot further than that."

"Yes, it does. The photo I have is from 1999." She took it from her pocket and passed it over to him.

He looked it over before passing it back.

"Don't recognize them. So the husband and his wife, and, what, their daughter, Becky?"

"We think so, yes."

Wilcox adopted a cautious look. "Can I ask why the FBI is interested in them? I mean, is there anything I need to know from a local cop's perspective?"

"The FBI isn't interested in them. *I* am." She added, "It's a personal matter."

Wilcox glanced at Blum and then directed his gaze back at Pine. "Well, okay. Look, the man you might want to talk to is Dick Roberts. He was the sheriff way back. Retired now. But Dick knew pretty much everybody back then."

"Is he still around here?"

"Oh, yeah, I'll give you his address and then phone him to make sure he's okay with talking to you."

"Can you do that now?"

"I can see this 'personal' matter is important to you."

"It is. Very important."

He wrote an address on a piece of paper, slid it across to her, and then picked up the phone.

It rang twice and then Wilcox said, "Hey, Dick, it's Tyler Wilcox, how you doing? Right, good, good. Well, I ain't had a chance to do much fishing, and last time I went only thing I caught was the flu." Wilcox chuckled at his joke as Pine watched him impatiently.

"Look, I got an agent from the FBI here, an Atlee Pine and her associate. They want to talk to you about a family that used to live around here a long time ago. Yeah, a Leonard Atkins and his wife. And his daughter. Right, okay. That sounds good. Thanks, Dick."

Wilcox hung up and looked at Pine. "He'd be glad to see you. Lives about ten miles from here. Put that address in your GPS and you'll get there."

"Did he say anything else?" asked Pine.

"He said he knew Atkins, and he'll be glad to talk to you about it."

"Well, thank you very much for your help."

"Always glad to help fellow law enforcement."

They walked out and Blum said, "What do you think Roberts can tell us?"

"Hopefully, everything."

CHAPTER

72

THERE COULD NOT HAVE BEEN a greater contrast between the Atkinses' old homestead and Dick Roberts's place.

It was a neatly constructed log cabin with window boxes where fall flowers popped out in burgundy and gold. The grass was healthy and trimmed, and the flower beds were well laid out and meticulously weeded and pine mulched. A metal carport next to the cabin housed a new-looking cobalt blue Ford F150 pickup truck. Smoke was coming out of the stone chimney on this chilly day.

As they pulled up and got out they could hear a dog baying.

When they walked up the pea-gravel drive to the house, the front door opened and a large white-and-tan basset hound bounded out and continuing its baying.

A man appeared in the doorway.

"That's Rosie," he said. "She sounds all ferocious but give her a sec and she'll roll over to get her belly rubbed."

A moment later Rosie did just that. Pine knelt down and performed the rub while Rosie wagged her tail and smiled up at her.

"You folks come on in," said the man.

"You're Dick Roberts?" Pine rose and walked toward him as Blum and Rosie followed.

"In the flesh."

Roberts was in his early seventies, around Pine's height, lean and wiry with silver hair and a mustache of the same color that drooped around the edges of his mouth. He had on faded denim jeans, old leather boots, and a red flannel shirt with the sleeves rolled up to the elbows showing muscled forearms.

He had the eyes of a cop, thought Pine. Observant, suspicious, expectant.

They followed him into the house. The front room held a fireplace, which was glowing warmly and invitingly. On the wooden mantel were pictures of people, probably family and friends, Pine surmised. The furnishings were old, but they were well built and looked comfortable. A colorful rug covered part of the plank floor. A gun rack with an over-under shotgun and a deer rifle hung on one wall. There were some pictures and framed photos on the log walls. Everything appeared neat and clean and well organized to Pine's eye. She hoped his memory was just as clear.

"You folks want some java? Just made a fresh pot."

"Yes, please," said Blum, and Pine nodded.

He got their drinks, and they settled into chairs around the fire while Rosie plopped down next to Roberts's feet and promptly fell asleep. He gently stroked her head and said, "You can't train a basset hound. No better scent dog in the world, in my opinion. But that's why you can't train them. No manner of obedience lessons can stand against their natural scent instincts."

"Well, she's very cute," said Blum.

"We keep each other company," said Roberts, settling back with his coffee.

"Is it just you and Rosie here, then?" asked Blum.

He nodded, his eyes crinkling a bit in sadness. "My missus died two years ago. Out of the blue. Alive one night and dead in the morning."

"I'm very sorry," said Blum. "Sudden loss like that is impossible to make sense of."

"But you got to go on living," said Roberts. "And we had a lotta good years together. Just not as many as we thought we'd have. We raised us a passel of kids and they're all doing good. And they don't live that far away. Three in Atlanta, one in Macon, and one over in Tennessee."

"I'm sure having them close by is very comforting," said Blum. He nodded and then looked at Pine. "Len Atkins?"

"I understand that you know him?"

"That's right."

"Is he still alive?"

"That I don't know. He's long since moved from here."

Pine's spirits plummeted. "We went out to where he last lived. The trailer. Now it's just full of snakes."

"Didn't know that. But I haven't been over there in a long time."

She showed him the photo. He looked it over carefully and nodded. "Yeah, that's Len and Wanda for sure."

"And the girl?"

"Don't know her, at least I don't think I do. You can't see her face in the photo. But she's a big girl."

"The name says Becky. The picture is dated July 1999. You ever hear of a Becky?"

He shook his head, looking uncertain. "I'd have to think about that."

"When did the Atkinses move from here?"

"Shortly after their son died."

Pine and Blum exchanged a stunned look. Pine said, "But I understood that Atkins couldn't have children because of an injury he sustained in the Vietnam War."

"Well, that's right. He did get shot up over there, from what I remember. I lucked out, my lottery number was really high, but not old Len. He had to go over to those damn jungles and fight for who knows what."

"So his son?" prompted Pine.

"Len and Wanda had Joe *before* Len went to Vietnam. Hell, if I remember correctly, Len was only twenty or so. I guess he couldn't have any *more* kids after his injury."

"So when you went to visit Len and Wanda, was there anyone else living with them?"

"Not that I ever saw. I mean, their trailer was real small, I'm sure you saw that for yourselves. Barely room for them and Joey when he lived with them."

"Did they ever come into town or anything? Were they ever seen with someone who looks like the girl in the photo?" asked Blum.

"Len didn't really come into town. He was a rural postal carrier. Wanda did some sewing and cleaning for ladies and businesses here and there. But they kept to themselves. I knew Len, but I can't say I really *knew* him, if you understand me. I don't think anybody did. The war, I think, messed with him, like it did a lot of men."

"And his son, Joe?"

"He lived with them till he got married. And Joe was young. Maybe nineteen. Oh, that was back in the eighties, I guess. Then he had his own little place not too far from them. He worked as a security guard at one of the big manufacturing plants we used to have near here, when they actually made stuff in America. Then after that closed, he started selling security systems and gadgets like that for companies and such. Made a pretty good living from what I understand." His brow furrowed. "His wife was a strange one. Can't remember her name off the top of my head. She was into all sorts of crap: voodoo and I guess what you'd call holistic stuff. But she had a mean streak."

"How do you mean?"

"Got called out to their place one time—oh, this was over twenty years ago if it was a day. Somebody had reported screams and such. Well, that sick woman had tied down a damn dog and was *branding* the thing all over. Poor cuss. I cut it loose and it went tearing away barking its head off. Wrote her up for animal cruelty, but that was about all I could do." He snapped his fingers. "Desiree, that was her name, all right. Desiree Atkins. Anyway, I remember her looking at me with these eyes. Dead eyes, I call 'em. Nothing behind them. Chilled me to the bone—and I'm no scaredy-cat, I can tell you that. I figured it was because of her condition."

"Her condition?" said Pine.

Realization spread over Roberts's lean features. "Hey, maybe that's how you got mixed up."

"Mixed up?"

"See, it was *Desiree* that could never have kids. Something to do with a woman's issue. I know old Len and Wanda wanted themselves some grandbabies, but it wasn't to be."

Pine glanced at Blum again. It seemed both women were jumping ahead to an awful conclusion.

Pine said, "Mr. Roberts, could the girl in the photo, Becky, could she have been maybe adopted by Joe and Desiree? I mean, at first I thought she might have been Len and Wanda's daughter, but their ages would have been off to have a daughter that young. But Joe and Desiree would have been the right age, I'm thinking, if they were married in the eighties."

"Well, it could be. I mean, I never heard of them having no kid, but they didn't come into town, just like Len and Wanda didn't."

"But if they had a child, surely she would have gone to school," said Blum.

Roberts shook his head. "Lots of folks homeschool their kids. They did back then and they still do today."

"So you're saying if Becky did live with them that maybe no one else would know?"

"It's certainly possible. This is a big county land-wise, and there ain't that many people that live in it. You could go for miles without seeing another house. And with all the forests and such around here, the homes are tucked away, not easy to get to and not easy to see from any road." He eyed Pine with interest. "So where are you going with all this?"

"Apparently, in an unexpected direction. You mentioned that Joe died?"

"That's right?"

"How?"

"Well, he was murdered."

"What!" exclaimed Pine.

"If memory serves me correctly, this was sometime in the late spring of 2002. Fortunately, we don't have too many murders around here, and the ones we do have tend to stick with you."

"Were you the one to investigate it?" she asked.

"I did. Me and my senior deputy at the time."

"Can you share any details?"

"I'll do my best. And what I can't tell you, they'll have files of at the sheriff's office." He finished his coffee and settled back. "We got the call in the morning. Man's body was found near a road by a guy out walking his dogs. Head bashed in and a knife sticking out of his back. It was Joe. And it was obviously a murder, all right."

"And where was Desiree?"

"Damn good question. She vanished. Never did find her. Now, we couldn't prove she did it. But I'm as sure of that as I am of anything. Why else would she have disappeared like that?"

"Did you find any evidence? Prints on the knife, signs of a struggle, anything back at their house? Anything to show how he got to where he died?"

"No prints on the knife. No tire marks to show a vehicle having been there. He bled out where he was found. Ground was iron hard back then. You know our good old Georgia clay. Like concrete. We went to the house. Couldn't find Desiree. No signs of forced entry. No signs of a struggle. We checked the closet, and while there were some women's clothes in there she might have taken some and we wouldn't ever know it."

"Any vehicles missing?" asked Pine.

"Joe's pickup truck. It was found abandoned about ten miles from here. We checked it for prints. There were two sets in there: Joe's and Desiree's. Which was to be expected. Nobody else's."

"Were there any signs of a third person living with them?"

"So you're really thinking this Becky person might have been living with Joe and Desiree?"

"I think it's possible. She was in that photo with the Atkinses a few years before Joe died."

"So you think they had, what, adopted her or something?"

"It could be."

"But there'd be paperwork on that. I mean, there's a legal process to go through," pointed out Roberts.

"Not if you do it illegally," countered Pine.

Roberts stiffened. "What are you we talking about here? That they were just dodging the law some, or are you saying that this girl was maybe, what, held against her will?"

"I'll be candid with you, Mr. Roberts, because you've told us a lot we didn't know."

She proceeded to tell him about Ito Vincenzo and Len Atkins being soldiers together. The checks that she had seen payable to the Atkinses and the correspondence. And about a girl being abducted by Ito and possibly taken to the Atkinses. She didn't tell him that the girl was her twin sister.

He said slowly, "So let me just get this all straight. You thought this Ito character kidnapped this girl to give her to Atkins because Atkins saved his life in Nam. Only the child didn't end up going to Len, but to his son and Desiree?"

"That's right. Vincenzo might not have known that. All the info I found had the checks being made out to Len Atkins. Now, he might have given the money to his son, if Joe actually had the girl and was caring for her."

"And the FBI is involved because kidnapping is a federal crime?"

"Right," said Pine, with a quick glance at Blum.

"But this case is really old," pointed out Roberts.

"I'm working it as a cold case. The Bureau does that from time to time."

"Well, I wish I could be of more help."

"No, you've been a big help. One more question. Can I see where Joe and Desiree lived?"

"I suppose so. There's a family living there now, but I know them. I can go over there with you if you want."

"That would be great, if it's not too much trouble."

"I don't have anything else to do. Retirement sounds great till you realize there's not enough stuff to fill up your days. And it rankled me not being able to solve Joe's murder. It cut his parents up hard."

"Right. And they left town, but you don't know where they moved to?"

"No, we lost touch over the years."

"Well, if we need to, we should be able to track them down. Shall we go?"

Roberts swiped an Atlanta Falcons ball cap off the side table and stood. Peering down at Rosie, he said, "Okay, girl, no belly rubs from strangers. And hold the fort down."

73

ON THE DRIVE OVER IN PINE'S RENTAL, Roberts had phoned the couple who now lived in the house and explained what he wanted. They had readily agreed to the visit.

"They're Pat and Hazel Simmons," he explained. "They bought the place out of foreclosure. Got it for a song, I heard. This was obviously after Joe Atkins died and Desiree disappeared. Pat's a long-haul trucker. They've got two kids, both in high school."

"So you're friends with them?" asked Blum.

He nodded. "We go to the same gun range and church. And we both like to hunt and fish. And there just ain't that many people who live here. So most folks know each other. He's a good guy."

Later, they pulled up in front of a small house in the woods. Parked next to it was an enormous Kenworth sleeper cab tractor painted bright blue. Next to the truck was a small, red KIA crossover, and next to that a Dodge pickup with a dented front fender.

"The big one's Pat's ride. Nice. Like a little apartment inside. He's on the road a lot, but he's obviously home now."

"Must be pretty hard for his wife with two teens," noted Blum.

"Oh, Hazel keeps them in line. But they're both boys, so you're right, she has her hands full."

Pat Simmons answered the door and had them come into the small living room. It was neat and sparsely furnished. A seventy-inch Sony TV hung on the wall, and Pine saw a glass-fronted gun cabinet with different models of rifles and shotguns and two handguns inside.

Pat was short and chubby with longish brown hair, and he wore a Kenworth ballcap. His beard was scruffy and his eyes were a dull brown. Hazel Simmons came into the room wiping her hands on a towel. She had on black leggings with a long white T-shirt. She wore no shoes.

She asked them if they wanted something to drink, but they all declined.

Roberts introduced Pine and Blum and they sat down.

"So you're interested in the folks that used to live here," said Pat.

Pine nodded. "Joe and Desiree Atkins."

Pat looked at Roberts. "Yeah, I remember that. Guy got murdered, not in the house but out in the woods."

"Probably why we got the house so cheap," added Hazel. "And it's really not close to anything, grocery stores or hospitals. Both our boys were born in the bedroom. They came too quick to get to the hospital."

"That must have been tough," said Blum.

"I did it twice. Never do it again," said Hazel, laughing.

Pine said, "After you moved in, did you find anything the Atkinses might have left behind?"

Pat shook his head. "Place was pretty well cleared out. Bank took the furniture and sold it, I guess. Along with the personal effects. There were some pots and pans in the kitchen. Some old clothes that they probably overlooked."

"Do you still have the clothes?"

"No, they long since got donated or thrown in the trash."

"Did you ever see anything to indicate that *three* people might have lived here, including a child?"

The couple looked at each other. Pat shook his head. "I didn't. But I wasn't around much after we moved in. As you can tell from that big-ass truck outside, I drive for a living."

Pine looked at Hazel. "How about you?"

Hazel pursed her lips and rubbed her fingers together. "I can't think of anything that stuck out. And it was a long time ago. The place needed a lot of TLC. It's only got two bedrooms, so the boys have to double up. But the previous owners didn't do a lot to keep the place up, I can tell you that." She suddenly looked up at Pine. "You know, I do remember something. When we first moved in, there were these drawings on a wall in what's now the boys' bedroom."

Pine tensed. "What sort of drawings?"

"They were like you would see a kid do, you know, stick figures. I had forgotten all about them. I painted over them."

"Do you remember anything else about them?"

Hazel mulled over this. "Well, I do remember there were different scenes, I guess you'd call them. You know, the stick figures playing or sitting at a table." She smiled. "In one drawing they looked like they were drinking out of cups. And there were always two of them, stick figures, I mean. And they had, well, they had long hair, so I guess they were girls. I remember that because back then we didn't have kids and I always wanted a girl. Didn't turn out that way."

"Maybe they were having a tea party," said Pine quietly.

Hazel smiled again. "That could be, sure. I used to have tea parties with my sisters and friends when I was little."

"So maybe the little girl stayed in that bedroom?"

"It could be. By the time we got here, like Pat said, the furniture was gone. I guess you could check with the bank, but I suppose most of those folks are probably no longer there."

Pine looked out the window. "Are there any other buildings on the grounds?"

"Other buildings?" said Pat. "No, just the house. We don't even have a garage. I'm gonna put in a carport but haven't gotten around to it. This place wasn't a farm or anything, so there's no barn."

"There's the cave," said a voice.

They all looked up to see a tall, skinny teenage boy standing in the doorway. He had on baggy jeans, a Nike sweatshirt, and an Auburn ball cap. His long hair hung out from under it.

Hazel said, "This is our youngest son, Kyle. What cave are you talking about, son?"

"It's about a half mile from here. In the woods. It's cut into a little knoll." He eyed Pine. "Trey, that's my brother, and me found it when we were little. We used to play fort and keep some of our stuff there. You know, like a hideout. We would even sneak out and sleep in there."

Hazel said in a scolding tone, "Kyle James Simmons sleeping in a cave? That's not safe. It could have fallen in on you and your brother. Or a bear could have been in there."

"No bear could've gotten in there."

"Why?"

"Cause it had a really thick door with a lock on it. Me and Trey thought maybe it was an old mine or something. I mean, there was stuff in there."

Pine said quickly, "If it had a lock how did you get in?"

"The padlock was on the ground. It was all busted and rusted. But the door was shut. When we opened it, it smelled all musty and stuff."

"And you said there were things in it?"

"Oh yeah."

"Can you take us there?"

Kyle looked at his mom, who nodded and said, "Just be careful."

"I got a couple of flashlights," said Pat. "Can I come along, too?"

Pine was already out of the room and didn't answer.

Blum looked at him. "Absolutely."

74

KYLE LED THE WAY TO THE CAVE. It seemed to Pine like ten miles instead of a fraction of that. She could feel her heart racing. And she felt light-headed.

Calm the hell down, Atlee. It won't help Mercy if you drop dead from a stroke right now.

They had to pull at some vines and push through some bushes that had grown up on the path they were heading along.

Kyle explained, "We haven't come back here in a long time. Guess it kind of grew over."

Forcing their way through some more underbrush, they finally reached an old wooden door set into a small hill with ivy growing up all around it. There was an open and rusted padlock hanging from the clasp.

Kyle said, "When we found this place, the door was busted open. We fixed it up and got a new padlock."

Pat Simmons looked it over. "I can't believe this. All the time we've been here and we never knew about this." He eyed his son. "Why didn't you tell us?"

He shrugged. "It was me and Trey's special place, Pops. Then when we stopped using it, we just sort of forgot about it, I guess."

Pine impatiently pushed past them and thrust the door open. She turned on her light and entered. The others followed as Pat Simmons used one of his flashlights to help illuminate the way and handed one to Roberts, who did the same.

The space was small, maybe ten by ten. As Pine ran her light over the room, she saw many things. An old table, some rickety chairs. Boards on cement blocks for shelves. Some empty glass jars, a cracked baseball bat, a rotted sweatshirt, and some old tennis shoes. The floor was made up of sections of plywood that must have been laid right on the dirt, because they were dark with rot. There was the sickly sweet smell of old vegetation and exposed red clay. The walls were the rock and dirt of the hill.

Pine's light hit near the back of the room and she froze.

It was a small cot, though there were no covers on it and the exposed mattress was old and rotted. She turned to Kyle. "Did you and your brother bring the furniture out here, and the bed?"

"Nope, that was already here. And those makeshift shelves. We found old cans of food and some water bottles. We used them for target practice with our .22s."

Pine moved around the space, examining every inch.

She stopped and bent down near the bed.

Her light hit on a chain that was coiled up under the bed. One end had an open clasp that could be locked with a key. The other end of the chain had been sunk so deeply into the rock wall that Pine could not pull it free.

Blum came to stand next to her and eyed the chain.

"My God," she said quietly.

Kyle joined them. "Yeah, that was here, too. We thought maybe they kept a dog or some other animal in here."

Roberts came to stand on the other side of Pine and said quietly, "Or maybe the girl. Becky."

Pine didn't answer because her light had fallen on something else. It was hanging from a nail driven into the rock. She walked haltingly over to it.

Sally. It's been over thirty years since I've seen you.

Pine picked the doll up and gazed down at it. This was Mercy's doll. It was a twin of the one Pine had owned as a child. Her mother had been looking for it after Mercy had disappeared. At least someone who had known her parents in Andersonville, Georgia, had told her that; her mother had never mentioned it.

Pine looked down at the large, soft eyes of the doll, whose name was Sally. Pine had named her doll Skeeter, after the character in the *Muppet Babies* TV series. She had tried to get Mercy to name hers Scooter, because that had been the twin on the TV show. But Mercy wouldn't hear of it because Scooter was a *boy*.

Pine's features crinkled at the memory, but then she felt like sobbing.

Kyle said, "Yeah, that was kind of creepy. We thought about getting rid of it, but neither one of us wanted to touch it. It was pretty old and ratty."

Roberts said, "You think that belonged to the girl?"

Pine nodded but said nothing.

Pat Simmons, who had overheard this, exclaimed, "Wait a minute, are you saying those people kept a little girl out here? What, like chained up and shit?"

"That's exactly what we think happened here," said Blum, watching Pine closely.

Pine turned and looked at Roberts.

"I'll take you up on the offer to get the file on Joe Atkins's murder. And anything you have on Desiree Atkins."

"Okay. It won't be much, I'm afraid."

"It will be more than I have now. How big were Joe and Desiree?"

"Not big. Joe was about five seven, hundred and fifty pounds wet. Desiree was a petite thing, five feet, ninety pounds, maybe."

Pine nodded. "Okay, does the sheriff's office have a forensics tech?"

"Oh yeah."

"I'd like prints and DNA samples taken from here. We can take samples from Kyle and his brother for elimination purposes."

"Do you have samples of the girl's DNA?" said Roberts.

Pine thought, *Yes I do, because it's the same as mine.*

She nodded. "And any prints found here I'd like to match against Joe and Desiree, if you have those on file."

"We have Joe's for sure. I don't know about Desiree's."

"Okay."

They left the cave, with Pine reluctantly leaving Mercy's doll behind, because this was a crime scene now. But then she stopped and turned back to the door.

"You said Joe Atkins was in the security business?"

Roberts nodded. "Yeah. He'd put together alarm packages, whatever you needed. Most folks around here don't even lock their doors. But most of his clients were businesses. So he'd put in surveillance cameras and—" He broke off when Pine rushed back to the door and started ripping at the ivy that had grown up on the rock wall and around the door.

"Agent Pine?" said Blum.

Pine said, "Help me pull down this ivy."

They all joined her and in short order had ripped enough of it away to reveal a small, decrepit surveillance camera mounted onto the rock wall and pointed at the door, with a cable snaking down the face of the wall and into the ground.

"Damn," said Roberts. "He had this place under surveillance."

Pine eyed the cable. "And this was before everything went wireless. I think that cable may run all the way to the house."

"Well, let's find out," said Pat.

Pine sprinted back to the house and the others followed.

75

THEY REACHED THE HOUSE and searched the exterior all over for the other end of the cable.

Kyle spotted it behind an overgrown bush.

The others quickly joined him. Pine looked at the spot where the cable entered the house.

"What room is that?"

Kyle said, "That's me and Trey's bedroom."

"I wonder if Atkins used that as a home office when he was here?" said Blum. She added in a disgusted tone, "Since they only needed the one bedroom, apparently, once the girl got too big to keep in that room."

They rushed inside, and Kyle led the way to the bedroom. It looked like the bedroom of a typical teenager, meaning there was junk piled everywhere. And there was a giant flat-screen TV set on a table with Xbox controllers set in front of it.

"Where's your brother?" asked Pine.

"He works at a 7-Eleven."

She surveyed the room, eyeing the beds on either side.

There were two windows in the room, and one faced the rear yard.

"If I'm Atkins, I think I'd want to be constantly looking in the direction of that jail cell, because let's just call it what it is."

Roberts stepped forward. "Okay, desk about here," he said. "And if he was using cable back then, I bet he was also using a VCR with a videotape."

Blum said, "You would think that if whoever the bank used to clean out the house had found a tape they would have looked at it or turned it in."

"Maybe it was in a place they couldn't see," said Pine, staring at the floor. "That carpet. Was it here when you bought the house?"

Hazel Simmons had joined them and answered. "No. It was hardwood floors. Made the room too cold."

Pat added, "There's no concrete slab under the house. It's on raised footers with a crawlspace under it."

"Okay, if the desk was there then, we have two options." She glanced at the Simmonses. "Can we take the carpet up and look under it?"

Pat said, "Hell, yes, I'll help you."

They worked on both corners simultaneously.

Pat got his section up first and was examining the flooring.

Kyle reached down and started feeling around each of the boards. "Hey, one's loose here."

They rushed over, and with everyone helping, they soon worked free a section of the hardwood flooring. What was revealed set inside a wooden cubby was a Sony VCR.

Kyle reached down and pulled it out. "Wow, never actually held one of these before."

Blum said, "Look, the cable is still attached."

Pat pulled the cable free and said, "We can hook this up to the boys' TV over there. It has the connections in the back."

"I'll do it," offered Kyle.

He carried the VCR over to the table the TV was on and started working away. Within a minute he had it all connected. He turned the power on and hit the Eject button.

"Oh my God," said Blum. "A tape is still in there."

"It has to be the last one that he put in there before he was killed. Let's hope it's still good," said Pine.

"That cubby it was in looks well insulated," said Pat.

"We don't have the remote," said Kyle. "But looks like I can work it from the VCR."

He turned the TV on, rewound the tape to the beginning, and hit the Play button.

They all stood there and watched.

Pine felt herself getting light-headed and realized it was because she was holding her breath.

And then there was the door to the cave. Minutes went by and nothing happened. Then—

"That's Joe Atkins," said Roberts.

Joe Atkins, wearing jeans and a flannel shirt with a baseball cap on his head, appeared. He held a shotgun. Then next to him appeared a small woman with long, dark hair and a brooding expression. She was carrying a tray of what looked to be food.

"And that's Desiree," said Roberts.

Blum noted the date and time stamp that appeared at the bottom of the frame. "May thirty-first, 2002," she read.

Roberts said, "That's right. Joe's body was found the very next day."

Joe pounded on the door and called out, "Get away from the door, Becky. Food's here."

Joe waited and then unlocked the door. He stepped back, readied the gun, and nodded at his wife. She cautiously opened the door and placed the tray on the floor and used her foot to slide it in.

Then she slammed the door shut.

Joe got the padlock back on just before something hit the door with a tremendous blow; it made Joe and Desiree jump back. Joe fell on his ass and dropped the gun. From inside the cave they could hear peals of laughter.

Joe scrambled to his feet and picked up his shotgun. "You cut that shit out, Becky. You do that next time, Desiree gonna add another mark to your hide, you got that?"

The laughter died away.

"That's right, Rebecca," said Desiree in a subdued tone, as though she were on some sedative. "We don't want that, do we? Marks on your hide?"

There was no response from behind the door.

Pine thought she might be sick. Blum put an arm around her shoulders and whispered, "Agent Pine, I am so sorry."

Roberts looked at the pair curiously.

"Hey," said Kyle, whose gaze was still riveted on the TV screen. "Dude forgot to close the padlock."

Pine said, "You're right. Can you fast-forward this?"

"Yeah." He hit a button and the video leapt forward. Pine watched the frames like she had never watched anything else before.

"Stop," she said.

Kyle immediately hit the Play button, and the frame speed returned to normal.

The door had just been hit by another blow. And then another, even more powerful one.

"Why is she doing that?" asked Pat. "She must know the padlock's on there."

Pine said, "Stop the tape for a sec."

Kyle did so, and Pine looked at Pat Simmons. "She knows he didn't close the padlock."

"But how?" said Pat.

"Because she'd been in that hellhole for years, and she knew every sound. And she didn't hear *that* sound that night."

Blum said, "Do you think that's why she didn't jump out at them when the door opened? She waited until he was putting the lock back on, but before he actually locked it she hit the door to distract him?"

"I think that's exactly what she did," said Pine. And with that statement, she felt an immense sense of pride in both her sister's patience and her cunning. All those years a prisoner and she had remained vigilant, just waiting for an opportunity.

"Turn it back on, Kyle."

Kyle did so, and they watched as three more blows hit the door. Then the fourth one was the charm. The open padlock flew free of the clasp and the door swung open.

And there…there, just like that, was Mercy Pine, tall, lean, strong, filthy, dressed in rags and looking quite…

Pine had to admit it to herself.

She looks...not in her right mind. And who the hell could blame her?

Pine's hand shot out and hit the Pause button, freezing Mercy's image. She was staring right at the camera. Pine thought she must have known where it was located. She took in every atom of her twin's appearance, trying to wind it all back to when they were six and then carrying it forward once more to this...person.

Roberts said, "Is that the person you're looking for, Agent Pine?"

Pine didn't answer him right away. Her gaze kept searching, the eyes, the nose, the forehead; the body was of no help, it had changed too much. But then she leaned forward and gazed closely at something.

It was the freckle. On the nose. As a child Mercy had told her twin that God had done that because she had come out first and their mother needed a way to tell them apart.

Pine straightened and nodded. "Yes, it's her."

I never thought I would be able to say those words ever again.

Her head was filled with so many thoughts, some happy, some insanely sad, some that were threatening to tear her apart. In desperation, she hit the Play button.

Mercy came to life, looked around, and then dashed off to the right, heading toward the house and out of the camera's view.

The tape kept running, and they all jumped when they heard the shot. Then screams. Then another gunshot. Then more screams. They couldn't make out who was screaming, and they had no way to know who was shooting, although Pine assumed it might be Joe Atkins. Then things grew silent and the tape continued to run. But the only image on it was the busted door.

Pine finally reached over, turned off the VCR, ejected the tape, and picked it up.

Blum looked at her, lips trembling. "At least...at least she escaped."

Pine wouldn't look at any of them. She said, "Yeah." And then walked out.

As she headed back to their car, Pine slowed so Blum could

catch up to her. Roberts was on the front stoop thanking the Simmonses for all their help.

"That must have been terrible for you to see, Agent Pine."

"I've been waiting almost my whole life to see Mercy. And she's alive—at least she was in 2002."

"Yes, absolutely. That is a huge positive."

Pine stopped walking. "Roberts said that people reported hearing screams and he found Desiree branding a dog."

"Right," said Blum.

"But dogs don't scream, Carol."

"You...you mean...?"

"That's what Joe meant when he threatened Mercy—Desiree would make 'marks' on her hide again. They used the dog to cover that up when Roberts got there."

"Those evil, evil people."

"And Joe Atkins was murdered and Desiree Atkins vanished."

Blum stopped walking. "Wait a minute, what are you saying?"

"Seeing her in the photo and now in the video, Mercy is taller than me and weighed maybe a hundred and sixty pounds and none of it was fat. She looked lean and rock hard. The Atkinses were small. She was bigger than both of them."

"Agent Pine, you can't mean—"

"I mean, Carol, that it's possible that my sister escaped, they tried to stop her—we all heard the screams and gunshots—and...she killed them."

"But where is Desiree's body if she was killed?"

"Who knows? If she buried her, it could be anywhere. After all these years, there wouldn't be much left."

"But why bury Desiree and not Joe?"

"She might not have had the opportunity."

"That is all speculation."

"I agree. But if it's not that, then it's something equally improbable."

They started walking again.

Blum said, "Well, if she did kill them, she had every right. I mean, that was her home? A cave, for all those years? The abuse. The horror. I can't even imagine. I can't even contemplate—"

"Ariel Castro in Cleveland? Jaycee Dugard? Elizabeth Smart out in Utah? There have been lots of others. I just never thought my sister would be one of them."

"But why would they do that? They were given a child because they couldn't have one of their own. Why turn her into…into a prisoner?"

"Mercy was old enough to know who she was and where she belonged. She might have resisted. Tried to run away. They got scared that if she told the cops they could get in trouble. And Desiree 'Voodoo' Atkins, who brands helpless dogs, doesn't sound like your normal nurturing type. As the years went by and Mercy became an adult, they had to take more drastic measures, like that jail cell back there. And they knew if she ever got away, they were going to prison for a very long time."

"Do you think Leonard Atkins knew?"

"They were in a photo with her. They could see how she looked, the wounds on her, the fact that she wouldn't even look at the camera. Yeah, they knew, and they didn't do a damn thing about it. And when their son was killed and Desiree went missing? They probably thought Desiree killed Joe and vanished with Mercy. Or else, Mercy had killed them both and made a run for it. Either way, they wanted nothing to do with that. They ran away instead."

"Disgusting," said Blum. "Just disgusting. After what they did, they don't deserve to be called human beings."

They drove Roberts back to his house.

"I'll call the sheriff and tell him," said Roberts. "And I'll let him know you'll be by for the file."

"Thanks, Mr. Roberts."

"Agent Pine?"

"Yes?"

"This isn't just a cold case for you, is it?"

"Why do you say that?"

"I was a cop a long time. Still got the nose for it. I saw how you were looking at that doll, for one thing. Like you'd seen it before. And then with the video, well, it just seemed *personal* to you."

Pine sighed. "She's my sister, Mr. Roberts. She was kidnapped from her bed when we were little, and she's been missing for over thirty years now."

He nodded, his expression one of sorrow. "I thought I recognized your name. I remember the case 'cause we got a BOLO on her. Mercy Pine, right?"

"Yes."

"I'm sorry."

"Thank you."

"But it seems like you've learned a lot here."

"I have. Now I just have to find her."

"You know she might be—"

"I do, Mr. Roberts, maybe better than anyone. But I can't let it go. I have to know either way."

"I wish you luck then. I really do. Nobody deserves what we just saw, especially not a little girl."

"No," said Pine. "They don't."

76

THE COLDEST OF CASES.

Pine had the file on Joe Atkins's murder and the disappearance of his wife spread out on the bed in her motel room. The unofficial conclusion by the local cops was that Desiree had killed her husband and fled. They had no idea that another person was living with them, so that person was never a suspect.

Not just a suspect. My sister.

She had seen Mercy on the video, she was sure of that. But she now had another piece of evidence leaving no doubt. DNA could live a long time on certain surfaces, and there were many things in that cave that Pine had never touched that had come back as confirmed to be consistent with her DNA.

Not mine, of course, but Mercy's.

The file did not have much in it. The autopsy on Atkins showed that he had died from a knife wound that had severed his aorta. He had bled out. But he also had severe blunt force trauma to his head. The trauma had clearly been done before he died.

Beaten and then stabbed.

The chain in the cave broken. The door busted. Mercy escaped. Captured on that video for all time.

And...maybe during that escape she had exacted her revenge on her captors.

She knew where Joe Atkins was. Six feet under. But where was Desiree? Where had Leonard and Wanda Atkins gone? Were they still alive? Should she try to find them?

Deputy Sheriff Wilcox had listened patiently to Pine's speculation and information. He had provided her copies of the case file. He had looked at the video. He had even gone out to the cave to see it for himself. He had been intrigued by the possibility of another person present at the scene. He had been surprised that that person was Pine's twin. But he seemed to have no desire to pursue an investigation into the matter. And neither, he told Pine, did his boss, the sheriff.

Wilcox had said, "We're really not equipped to handle cold cases. And from what you said, seems to me that this Joe Atkins fella got what was coming to him."

Now she went outside, where it was starting to rain. She drove to the one restaurant in the area, went inside, and ordered a coffee.

The rain picked up and she gazed out the window as it poured down. She sipped her drink and saw in the rain nothing positive. Not one damn thing. On the one hand, she had made tremendous strides in tracking down what had happened to her sister. Mercy had been abducted by Ito Vincenzo and given to the Atkinses, and then Len Atkins had passed her off to Joe and Desiree Atkins. At some point—Pine didn't know exactly when—Mercy had gone from the room in the house to a locked cave.

As Pine sat there, her mind wandered deeper and deeper into terrifying thoughts. Instead of finding her sister alive and well, or at least being able to locate and identify her remains, she now had to contemplate the possibility that her sister had killed one and maybe two people and was out there somewhere, doing God knew what. Pine knew that after her years of brutalization at the hands of the Atkinses, there was little possibility that she would even be able to recognize her sister, either physically or emotionally.

She closed her eyes, and the image of her sister in that video returned to haunt her.

Pine had had her sister with her every day of her life for six-plus years. And then for thirty years, nothing. Until now. And she could not reconcile the woman on that video with the little girly-girl who loved her tea parties and stood up for her little sister whenever Pine had gotten in trouble.

I just want to find her. I want to help her. I want her to…have the life she should have had.

Her ringing phone was a grateful distraction. She didn't recognize the number, but she answered it anyway.

"Hello?"

"Hey, Agent Pine, this is Darren Castor from Trenton. You talked to me about when I worked for Ito Vincenzo."

"Yes, Mr. Castor, what can I do for you?"

"Well, you said to call you back if I remembered anything. And I do. See, I got my dates wrong."

Pine stiffened. "Excuse me? The dates wrong?"

"I told you that I started working for the auto body place in 2001."

"Yes."

"Well, I was wrong. I started working there in *2002*, not 2001. It was during the first week of June. Should have known it wasn't 2001. I mean, three months later 9/11 happened."

"You're sure?"

"Yep. I checked my pay stubs and some other records I'd kept around."

"You said the summer. Do you have a specific date? That would be really helpful."

"I do, as a matter of fact. The day he didn't show up was June first. I remember that because my wife's birthday is the second of June."

Birthday?

"Well, hope that helps," said Castor.

"What, oh yes, thank you very much, Mr. Castor. It was a big help."

She clicked off and stared down at the phone. A terrible thought, a truly bizarre piece of speculation, was making the rounds in her head like a bullet caroming around.

She called Blum. "We need to go see Jack Lineberry. Right now."

CHAPTER

77

Pᴉɴᴇ ᴅʀᴏᴠᴇ ꜰᴀsᴛ ᴀɴᴅ ᴍᴏsᴛʟʏ ɪɴ sɪʟᴇɴᴄᴇ. She had not explained to Blum why they needed to see Lineberry. She could not bring herself to even say out loud what she was thinking. If it turned out to be true, it would be horrendous.

Yet nothing will surprise me anymore.

She had called ahead and they were let in at the gate after identifying themselves. They drove up to the house and were surprised to be met by Lineberry at the front door. He was using a walker but ambling around pretty well.

"You've made progress," said Blum.

"I feel much better," said Lineberry. "I was just about to have some lunch if you'd like to join me."

Before Pine could say anything Blum said, "Well, I'm hungry."

They went to a glass-enclosed conservatory with views of the rear grounds where the construction crew was now framing the cottage. They were finishing the fourth wall and would probably start putting up the roof joists after that.

"I hope to never have another explosion at my house," said Lineberry as he also looked out at the crew working away.

Lunch was served by a maid in uniform and was delicious, though Pine hardly touched hers, something noted by both Blum and Lineberry. When Lineberry gave Blum a questioning glance, she shrugged.

They finished their lunch and made their way to the library, where they had coffee in front of a crackling fire. A light rain had started to fall and it was chilly outside; the warmth from the flames felt good.

"Have you found out any more information?" said Lineberry. "You were going to Taliaferro?"

Pine said, "We found out a lot, and none of it is good or pleasant to hear."

Lineberry looked stricken at her blunt words. Blum glanced at Pine in surprise.

"My God. Mercy, she's not—?"

"No, she's not dead. At least that we know."

"What then?"

"She was held prisoner by a family in Taliaferro. Not the Atkinses I mentioned to you, but his son and daughter-in-law."

Lineberry leaned forward and put down his cup of coffee. He looked pale and distraught.

"Did you say, 'held prisoner'?"

"Yes. In a locked cave that I wouldn't let a dog live in. It was filthy, terrible, appalling."

"Agent Pine," said Blum in a remonstrative tone. "Jack is still not well."

Pine didn't appear to hear her. "She was living like an animal, Jack. No one to help her. No one to save her. So she ended up saving herself."

"How…how do you mean?"

"I mean, she broke out of her chains, busted down the door of her prison, and tried to flee."

"*Tried* to flee?"

"This is obviously speculation on my part, but I think that as she was escaping, Joe Atkins caught up with her. Maybe he was going to try to bring her back. Maybe he was going to kill her."

Pine was squeezing the wooden arm of her chair so tightly that her knuckles were red and her limbs were shaking.

Blum observed this and said, "Agent Pine, are you all right?"

Again, Pine did not seem to hear her; she kept her gaze on Lineberry. "But Mercy turned the tables. She went after him. I can only imagine all the years of pent-up hatred she rightly had for him and what that couple had done to her. She beat him up, struck him so hard he had blunt force trauma to his head. She was big, taller than me, and she was strong. She would be a force to be reckoned with even if her strength hadn't been turbocharged by her emotions. Joe Atkins was a small man. She quickly overpowered him. Took his knife...and..."

Lineberry was leaning so far out of his chair that he was in danger of toppling out of it.

"And what?" he said in a hushed voice suffused with an underlying terror.

"I think she stabbed him in the back, severed his aorta, and killed him," finished Pine.

Lineberry fell back in his chair and started breathing heavily.

Blum grabbed a glass off the sideboard, poured out water from a pitcher, and hurriedly carried it over to Lineberry. He drank half of it down and handed it back to her, thanking her with a look, though his features were still full of horror.

Blum gave Pine an annoyed glance and sat back down.

Pine continued, "I have no idea what happened to the wife, Desiree. She has been described to us as weird, and she has been observed to be violent toward animals. I have no doubt she was cruel to a staggering degree with Mercy. She branded her, Jack. Like she was an animal."

"Oh my God!" bellowed Lineberry.

"Agent Pine!" exclaimed Blum.

"She might have killed Desiree, too, or the bitch saw the predicament she was in and just fled on her own. She would have gone to prison for her crimes against Mercy."

Lineberry covered his face with his hands and muttered, "My God. My God."

"Yes, my God," parroted Pine in a fierce voice.

Lineberry uncovered his face and stared at her, realization spreading across his features. "Is there something else? Something you haven't told me?"

"Yes, Jack, there is. A definite *something*."

There was a bite to the woman's words that made Blum glance sharply at her.

Pine said, "I got a call from a man who used to work for Ito Vincenzo. He had given me dates for when Vincenzo had gone missing. He went back and looked at some old pay stubs he'd kept and gave it some more thought, and it turns out he was off by about a year. Ito didn't disappear in 2001. He vanished in 2002. And Castor was able to give me the exact day that Ito didn't show up for work." She paused here and studied Lineberry, who stared dully back at her. But there was something in the eyes that heralded the man had a premonition about where this might be going.

"Turns out," continued Pine, "that Castor remembered because his wife's birthday is the day *after* Ito didn't show up at the store." She paused again. "June second."

Blum exclaimed, "But that's your birthday, too."

Pine kept her gaze on Lineberry. "That's right. And on June second, 2002, on my birthday, my father took his own life at his apartment in Virginia, not in Louisiana like my mother told me. And you were there, *conveniently*. And you identified the body for the police."

Lineberry started to gum his lips, like an elderly gent with no teeth might do.

Pine leaned forward in her chair so that her face was maybe a foot from his.

"I want the truth, Jack, and I want it now," she barked.

As though he were a snowman melting under a scorching sun, Lineberry collapsed against the upholstered chair and slumped down. He covered his face with his hands once more, but Pine pulled them away.

"Now, Jack."

Lineberry sat up straighter, glanced at Blum, and then stared directly at Pine.

"I didn't know the man who tried to kill your father that day was Ito Vincenzo, that I swear. And I still have no proof it was."

"Wait a minute," said Blum sharply. "What man who *tried* to kill him? I thought Tim Pine killed himself."

Pine said, "That's what I was always told. By my mother. And by *you*, Jack. And you lied to me. Just like she did."

"What are you saying, Agent Pine?" said Blum. "You can't mean—"

"I mean that Ito came to kill my father, and probably my mother, not knowing that they were separated. But my dad killed Ito instead. And Jack was there, not by coincidence, but by plan, and he identified my father as the dead man. And with a probable suicide and a positive ID by a close friend and later the man's ex-wife, there would be a limited investigation." Pine stopped speaking and seemed to marshal herself. "So now I know what happened to Ito. Now I want to know where my father is. Is he with my mother? She abandoned me while I was in college to go to him, right? He supposedly died on June second. I went back to college in July of that same year because I was competing in weightlifting. When I got back in August my mother was gone and all she left was a note saying basically nothing." She paused, struggling mightily to retain her composure. "Their divorce was a sham, wasn't it? They always planned on ending up together. And leaving *me*."

Pine had slowly stood, and her voice had risen along with her. "Isn't that the truth, *Jack*?"

Lineberry looked up at her with a helpless expression. He said, "The divorce *was* a sham. But they separated to keep you safe."

"Bullshit."

"It's not bullshit, Atlee. It's the truth."

"How would you know *anything* about the fucking truth?"

"I will tell you what you want to know, if you will just listen to me."

"Please, Agent Pine, it's for the best. You need information," added Blum.

Pine slowly resumed her seat and waited expectantly, but every one of her limbs was still quivering with anger.

"I didn't know where you and your family had gone when you all left Andersonville. We were frantic. We looked, but it was like you all had disappeared into a dark hole. And back then there wasn't the internet or smartphones where everybody was taking photos and video of everyone else. People really could vanish."

"And then?" said Pine.

"And then, many years later, I got a frantic call out of the blue from your father."

"How could he reach you?"

"I had given your parents a special number. It was one that I maintained all those years just in the hopes that...Anyway, he told me he was in Virginia and that a man had tried to kill him, only he had killed the man instead. A shotgun blast to the head."

"If he was living in an apartment building, how come no one there heard it?" said Pine.

"Because he wasn't living in an apartment building."

"So that was another time you lied to me?"

Lineberry hurried on. "I flew there right away. The man's face was missing. I didn't know who it was and Tim said he didn't, either."

"How could he not recognize Ito Vincenzo?" interjected Pine. "He had fought the guy in Andersonville?"

"Over a *decade* before, Atlee. And people do change. Anyway, Tim told me he didn't recognize him, and I certainly couldn't have with the damage to his face. We hatched a plan that would substitute Tim for Ito, if it really was him. That way the world would think Tim was dead."

"So Ito Vincenzo is buried in my father's grave. And my mother?" Pine added in a trembling voice.

Lineberry broke off eye contact. "She...understood what was at stake. She played along. That allowed your father, and her, to safely disappear."

"And then she joined him a couple months later," said Pine bitterly. "And left me by myself."

"They...thought it best. They thought you would be better off, I swear. She left you money to finish college and—"

Pine barked, "Where are they now?"

"I don't know."

"Jack!"

"I don't know," he said sharply. "That was by design. People kept tracking them down. There had to be a leak. At that point no one was above suspicion, not even me. It was thought best that no one knew where they were going. I haven't seen them since then. No contact at all. None."

"And I'm supposed to believe that, considering how often you've lied to me?"

"I can't make you trust me, Atlee. And I haven't earned that trust anyway. But I also didn't have to tell you what I just did."

"So why did you?"

"Because you deserved it. You've earned it. And I'm tired of not telling you what you need to know."

His words didn't mollify her, but she sat back and tapped her fingers on the wood of the chair. She stared off for so long that she had almost forgotten that Blum and Lineberry were still in the room.

"Why do they need to keep running and hiding?" asked Blum. "It's been, what, thirty years now. Is there anyone around who would still be after them, or even care?"

Lineberry shook his head. "I don't know, Carol. The Mafia has a long memory. But they've been on the run and off the grid for so long now it's probably all they know anymore."

"But they left me, as a sitting duck," pointed out Pine. "Ito took my sister and nearly killed me. So my parents run off and leave me to face the people coming after them?"

"I think they believed you were effectively off the radar by the time you were an adult," said Lineberry.

"Ito found us. Who's to say someone else couldn't?" she countered. "It wasn't like they had changed my name. I was still Atlee Pine. How many of those are there?"

"I don't have a good answer for that. I really don't."

"And you could have found me, if you had really wanted to. I have my own Wikipedia page someone set up when I was competing for the Olympics. I became an FBI agent. My name appeared in the news from time to time."

Lineberry wouldn't meet her eye. "I . . . I guess by then I had just stopped looking. And your father didn't tell me where you and your mother were when I went to help him."

"Sure he didn't. Ignorance is bliss, right, *Dad*?"

"What…what will you do now?" asked Lineberry, who was looking paler by the minute.

Before answering, Pine stood. She looked down at the fragile Lineberry.

"I came here to find my sister. I'm a lot closer than I was. And now I'm going to do all I can to bring her home, even if you won't."

"What are you saying? I want that, too. She's your sister, but she's also my daughter," said Lineberry.

"Oh really?" she snarled, her face contorted in fury. "You don't give a shit about either one of us."

"Atlee, of course I do," he said, stunned by her reaction. "How could you say that?"

Pine closed her eyes and when she reopened them she stared out the window at the cottage. Something seemed to occur to her, and she turned and stormed out.

"Where is she going?" said Lineberry.

Blum said nothing.

A minute later they both saw Pine on the rear grounds, marching resolutely toward the cottage.

T HE RAIN WAS STARTING TO FALL more heavily as Pine neared the cottage construction site. There were five men framing away, two on ladders and three on the ground.

She stopped in front of the cottage and called out, "All of you leave now."

The men glanced curiously at her but continued to work.

Pine pulled out her gun and her FBI shield and called out, "FBI, everybody leave. Now!"

Now the men all stopped what they were doing and looked at her, and then glanced at each other nervously.

Pine knew they probably thought she was unhinged.

And maybe I am.

A large man in a construction hat gingerly headed over to Pine. "Ma'am, we got a job—"

Pine pointed her gun at the sky and fired two shots. "Now!" she screamed.

Some men scrambled down ladders, others on the ground grabbed lunch coolers and coats, and they all hustled from the area, looking back at her with panicked gazes. Pine watched as they exited the rear gate, jumped into their trucks and cars, and sped off.

Pine lifted her pants leg and took out her Beretta backup gun. She laid both guns on a wooden table, slipped off her jacket, placed it on the table, and placed a waterproof tarp over them. As the rain started to pick up even more, she stepped inside the shell of the cottage and looked at the wooden framing.

She knew exactly why she was here.

He took something from me. The truth. My truth. And now I'm going to take something from him.

She spied a sledgehammer, picked it up, studied the configuration of the framing, and then lashed out and hit a king stud near the front doorway. The wood splintered. She hit it again and the double boards broke free. She next took out the crippled studs underneath a window adjacent to the doorway and smashed out the sill plate. When she broke out a stud next to that, a portion of the framed panel gave way. Pine next took out a whole row of studs. She kept striking away at the wood until the entire wall broke loose and fell outward, landing in the grass.

Pine wielded the hammer like a baseball bat as she attacked another section where the walls intersected. She swung away and splintered wood and ripped out nails that flew everywhere. The entire panel finally came crashing down, but with her last swing the hammer's wooden handle splintered and then broke in half.

The rain was pouring down now as the heavens completely opened up. Flipping her hair out of her eyes, Pine, her chest heaving with her exertions, approached the third section of wall, sized it up, and used a whip kick to crack a board on the lower section. Then she aimed higher and kicked one short board clear from the framing nails used to hold it in place. The metal of the nails looked like dead, gray worms stuck in the wood that remained.

She kicked at another board and then used an elbow strike on a sill plate to break it in half. A chop on another board took out a section of wall along with the window frame that it held. She tore out other parts of the framing using a series of kicks and hand and elbow strikes.

The wall panel, uncoupled from the one next to it, was swaying now, and Pine repeatedly kicked at it as the rain streamed down and the wind howled. Her breaths were coming in gasps now. She then pushed and pushed and tugged and kicked, and with a scream of intensity, she finally managed to topple the wall.

She turned to the last section standing and faced it like it was every nightmare she had ever endured, and she had more than most.

Before she attacked it, Pine turned around and stared up at the house where Lineberry and Blum were watching her.

Inside the room Lineberry moaned, "I have to stop her. She'll hurt herself."

Blum firmly clenched his arm.

"You will not stop her," she said sternly. "She's your daughter, Jack Lineberry. And she needs to do this. And you are going to stand here and watch while she does."

Every muscle Pine had was twitching uncontrollably, like she was an addict going through withdrawal. She could barely see for the rain, and she had to keep pushing her hair out of her face. In exasperation she looked around and spied a soaked cloth on the floor and used that to tie her hair back. She charged the last wall and slammed her shoulder into it. As the only wall remaining, it didn't have the support and thus the strength of the other three walls. But it also was not going down that easily.

For the next full minute Pine kicked and punched and pulled and tugged, but she was far weaker now, so exhausted that her strikes were feeble.

You are not going to beat me.

She sat on her haunches, eyeing the wall like it had been the cause of every tragedy in her entire life. Pine couldn't even catch her breath anymore, and her limbs were shaking so badly she couldn't kick or punch if she wanted to.

In desperation she looked around, and her gaze finally alighted on what she needed.

She staggered over and gripped the handles of the portable cement mixer. It was heavy-duty and set on a pair of rubber wheels. She hoisted it by the handles, pointed it directly at the wall and pushed off, slipping and sliding on the slickened floor, but gaining traction and speed as she went. The cement mixer hit the middle of the wall and drove right through it, taking Pine with it.

They both sprawled outside. Pine lay face-first on the ground and turned over in time to see the wall implode and tumble down.

Her mission complete, she rose up on all fours and vomited. Then she collapsed to the wet grass and lay there for a few moments. She rolled over, stared up at the dark sky, and let the rain cover her like dirt in a grave.

She slowly rose, sucking in deep breath after deep breath.

She picked up her guns and put them back in their holsters. She put her jacket back on over her soaked clothes. She walked away without once looking back at the main house.

She staggered out the rear gate and headed to the front. She spat out bits of vomit and rainwater as she walked. She pulled off the cloth tie around her hair, and it fell once more in her face. She knew she looked like a deranged, walking nightmare, and she didn't give a crap.

When she approached her rental car, she stopped and stared.

Blum was in the driver's seat with the engine running and watching her expectantly.

Pine started walking again and opened the passenger door. She gripped the top of the car roof and leaned forward into the opening, the crown of her head pointed at Blum, who just sat there and said nothing.

Her belly heaving, her lungs gasping, Pine held on to the car's metal roof like it was her last tether to earth. She took one last deep, shuddering breath, and her tensed body relaxed. She lifted her head and looked at Blum.

"Are you ready to go, Agent Pine?"

Pine stripped off her soaked jacket and hurled it into the back seat.

Without a word she climbed in, shut the door, and clicked her harness into place.

Blum put the car in gear. And they left that place behind.

And moved onward.

Which was the only place left for them to go.

ACKNOWLEDGMENTS

To Michelle, Atlee Pine rides again. Thanks for being my role model for her!

To Michael Pietsch, here's to three more years in partnership!

To Ben Sevier, Elizabeth Kulhanek, Jonathan Valuckas, Matthew Ballast, Beth deGuzman, Anthony Goff, Rena Kornbluh, Karen Kosztolnyik, Brian McLendon, Albert Tang, Andy Dodds, Ivy Cheng, Joseph Benincase, Andrew Duncan, Morgan Swift, Bob Castillo, Kristen Lemire, Briana Loewen, Mark Steven Long, Thomas Louie, Rachael Kelly, Kirsiah McNamara, Nita Basu, Lisa Cahn, Megan Fitzpatrick, Michele McGonigle, Alison Lazarus, Barry Broadhead, Martha Bucci, Rick Cobban, Ali Cutrone, Raylan Davis, Tracy Dowd, Jean Griffin, Elizabeth Blue Guess, Melanie Freedman, Linda Jamison, John Leary, John Lefler, Rachel Hairston, Suzanne Marx, Derek Meehan, Christopher Murphy, Donna Nopper, Rob Philpott, Barbara Slavin, Karen Torres, Rich Tullis, Mary Urban, Tracy Williams, Jeff Shay, Carla Stockalper, and everyone at Grand Central Publishing, for being the best of the best.

To Aaron and Arleen Priest, Lucy Childs, Lisa Erbach Vance, Frances Jalet-Miller, and Juliana Nador, for just getting better and better.

To John Richmond, best wishes as you begin a new chapter in life. You will be much missed!

To Mitch Hoffman, for hitting all the right targets on this one.

To Anthony Forbes Watson, Jeremy Trevathan, Trisha Jackson, Alex Saunders, Sara Lloyd, Claire Evans, Sarah Arratoon, Stuart

Dwyer, Jonathan Atkins, Christine Jones, Leanne Williams, Stacey Hamilton, Charlotte Williams, Rebecca Kellaway, and Neil Lang at Pan Macmillan, for being the most wonderful, fun, and nice people.

To Laura Sherlock, for being a rock star of PR.

To Praveen Naidoo and the stellar team at Pan Macmillan in Australia, for bringing *Walk the Wire* in at number one!

To Caspian Dennis and Sandy Violette, for being amazingly smart and the most delightful friends!

To the charity auction winners Lindsey Axilrod (Read Alliance), Linda Holden-Bryant (Soundview Preparatory School) and R. Jeffrey Sands (Mark Twain House & Museum), thanks for supporting such great causes, and I hope you all enjoy seeing your character names on the page getting into all sorts of trouble!

And to Kristen White and Michelle Butler, for really going above and beyond!

OUT NOW

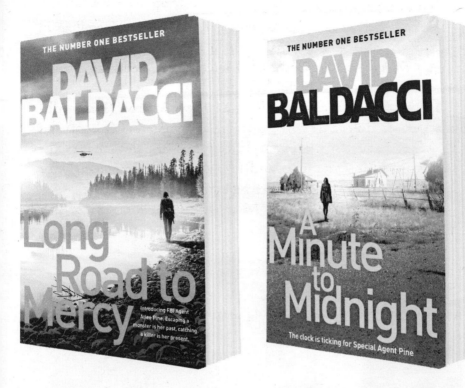

Return to where it all began in the first two explosive thrillers in David Baldacci's bestselling series featuring FBI Agent Atlee Pine, a tenacious investigator battling personal demons and determined to uncover the truth about the disappearance of her sister over thirty years ago . . .

OUT NOW

Remember my name . . .

Discover David Baldacci's bestselling series featuring the Memory Man, Amos Decker, a damaged but brilliant FBI Special Agent who possesses an extraordinary set of skills. His photographic memory means he forgets nothing and sees what others miss . . .

Once read, never forgotten.